# Drive ME Crazy

## JERÉ ANTHONY

Edited by Amy Lancaster

Cover Design by Bailey McGinn

ISBN 978-1-7368195-0-0

ISBN 978-1-7368195-1-7 (ebook)

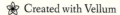 Created with Vellum

*To Stephen*
*My real-life romance hero.*

# CONTENT WARNING

While Drive Me Crazy is a laugh out loud romcom, it does touch on some heavier subject matter.

Here's a list of possible triggers:
- *Anxiety/Panic Attacks*
- *Grief/Loss of a Loved One*
- *Workplace Harassment*
- *Sexual Assault*

# ONE

Elliot

"Breathe in... one, two, three, four, and out... one, two, three, four. And in... one, two, three, four, and out... one, two, three, four. Use your ujjayi breath, seal your lips, closing off your throat, and exhale through your nose. Now take a deep breath in, hold it. Now try to breathe a little more... big exhale through your mouth. That's right. Let it all out. These next few moments are about you; this is your practice. Take this time to get in whatever position that makes you feel the most comfortable. You've earned this savasana."

I've earned this savasana all right. Between the last two weeks of bartending down at Scary Terry's and getting hit on by creepy men, I'd say I deserve this time to decompress. This week was Maggie's pick for girl squad exercise day, and she picked hot yoga.

Maggie is our yoga friend, while Gwen is the spin girl and I prefer my torture in the form of long-distance running—aka free exercise. The three of us met our freshmen year in college when

we were randomly assigned as roommates, along with Francesca whom we no longer speak of for various reasons but mostly it involves her love of eating peanut butter in the bathtub.

In case you're wondering, that's how you get ants.

Maggie and Gwen have been by my side through all the chaos of university and the trying years to follow. What started as a random roommate placement with two girls I'd have never met otherwise turned into the kind of friendship that lasts a lifetime. Unlike me, they both figured their shit out early on. Gwen's managed to spin her expertise of social media into a thriving PR business while Maggie's love of plants and yoga has her working on opening a mashup studio, unlike anything I've ever seen. And then there's me...the poster child for Murphy's Law.

I lie still on my mat with my palms up, fighting the urge to squirm and wiggle. The sheer focus of keeping myself still contradicts any benefits meditation may bring me, but I won't tell Maggie that. Worrying thoughts of eviction notices, overdue bills, and my ever-dwindling bank account only seem to compound further when I'm forced to stay quiet with only my thoughts as a soundtrack.

I'm pulled from my anxiety loop as the instructor's voice jolts me back into the present. I hear the dreaded, "Take your peace fingers and wrap them around your toes. This pose is called 'Happy Baby.' Push your spine into the ground for the full expression."

The Happy Baby pose is the bane of my existence. It's the most vulnerable position one can put themselves in with butthole and vagina on blast for all to see. I begrudgingly do as I'm told, though, pulling my feet into position. Unfortunately, once they're floating in the air above me, a gas bubble from the depths of my innards is jarred loose. My stomach announces its plans with a low but distinct gurgling sound. Gwen looks over at

me with fear in her eyes, no doubt recognizing the familiar call of gas gone rogue. Before I can untangle myself from the pose to save myself from a heap of embarrassment, my ass expels the loudest fart that is only enhanced by the sweat that has accumulated between my butt cheeks. The sound reverberates off the walls, echoing throughout the otherwise silent room.

Gwen's expression shifts from shock to amusement, and the instructor stands over us, at a loss for words. Then Gwen loses her shit, laughter erupting from her belly while she gasps for air.

"I'm so sorry. That was my foot... it slipped when I grabbed it." I try to demonstrate the movement but when I grab my foot again another fart escapes my clenched butt cheeks, and now my explanation has only made matters worse.

This, of course, only encourages Gwen's laughter. "That was not your foot, you nasty bitch!"

I decide to come clean since this space is sacred and I don't want any bad juju. "You're right, Gwenneth, it wasn't my foot. It was the damn chili with the discount meat I ate for dinner last night; are you happy?" I'm all but yelling now and everyone in the class has abandoned their Happy Baby poses to witness the show in the back of the room.

"Ladies, if you could please..." The instructor tries to compose herself but her normally neutral face is showing the slightest flush on her cheeks. "Please quiet down. The end of class is the most important seven minutes of our practice, where we collect our thoughts and take a load off from our busy minds."

"Looks like Elliot needs to take a load off..." Gwen doubles over cackling like a possessed hyena.

"Oh my God, I can't take you two anywhere!" Maggie stands up, rolling her yoga mat frantically. "Jesus, Elliot, what did you eat anyway?"

"I told you, it was the expired chili," I shamefully whisper.

Head down, I follow suit, gathering my yoga mat in silence, dragging my stank ass out of the studio followed closely by a giggling Gwen. The warm room temperature does me no favors masking the scent of death I leave behind in my wake.

---

"I'll have a large cup of coffee, please; plain black is fine."

I put in my order for my weekly coffee splurge and wait for the barista to hand over my treat. If I'm being totally honest, I can't afford this $2.50 coffee but it's awkward to go out with friends and not order something. Plus, I don't need Gwen and Maggie trying to give me a handout. It's embarrassing to be the poor friend in the group, and I don't want to be an inconvenience to them.

"I'm going to grab our table." Maggie waves and disappears into the quaint coffee shop. We've been coming to Heroes Coffee since college; it's a Saturday morning tradition. It has a real cozy-meets-modern feel to it, complete with a glass wall where you can see how they roast the beans.

Maggie's sitting by our favorite window at the front of the shop, with sunlight beaming around her head like a halo, illuminating the angel that she is. Her vibrant red hair is wild from the wind and the light dusting of freckles on her cheeks make me feel the comfort of a warm summer day. Gwen walks to her spot, pulling her metal chair loudly against the concrete floor, a stark contrast to Maggie's gentle vibration.

"Jeez, Gwen, could you make any more noise if you tried?" I ask her with a smile..

She doubles over in laughter. "Not sure, but we all know you can!"

"You're never going to let me live that down!" Tears fill my eyes and I wipe them away, today's events still fresh in my head.

Maggie's outraged expression, Gwen's hysterical laughter, and the instructor's shock all play back in my mind.

Maggie stares daggers as she takes a sip of her chai latte. "You two have no couth. I'm going to have to go back and apologize to Melanie. I'm a member of the studio, Elly. I can't just ghost everyone in the class like you two idiots!"

"I'm sorry, Maggie, you know I didn't do it on purpose!"

"Yeah, well, this one over here didn't exactly behave like an adult back there!" Maggie points toward Gwen and her face turns to shock.

Gwen clears her throat as she sets down her Americano carefully. "I'm sorry... but you can quote me on this: I will never not laugh at a public accidental fart, especially in hot yoga class." She wipes a stray tear from her cheek.

"Thank you so much for that sincere apology," Maggie says with a roll of her eyes.

Maggie may seem annoyed with us but we both know that she secretly loves all the excitement Gwen and I bring to her life. On her own, Maggie always chooses the safe bet, and Gwen and I bring the fun. We challenge her to loosen up and she's the voice of reason that keeps us all out of jail.

"So, I have some good news." I spin my coffee cup in my hands, waiting for their attention. "I finally got a call back to substitute teach at the high school!"

"Elly, that's wonderful! You're going to do great!" Maggie's encouragement feels like a warm weighted blanket, easing my anxiety.

"What does that have to do with marketing or branding? I've got a bad feeling about this." Gwen bites her bottom lip. "Are you sure you need to surround yourself with teenagers... and you know, be responsible for them?"

Maggie gasps. "Gwen! How can you say that?"

Gwen holds up her hands in surrender. "All I'm saying is...

well, we know Elliot's track record with these temp jobs. Plus, this isn't even close to her dream."

"I can't believe you are going there right now; we need to be supportive..." Maggie and Gwen seem to be having a second and wordless conversation with their eyes.

"I know, I know. Teaching doesn't seem like it'll put me on the path to my dream job, but you both know that right now I just need any job so I can stay in this city. Plus, who knows what could happen? Maybe the kids will think I'm awesome and I'll be their favorite cool teacher that they can talk to. Maybe I'll be able to prevent teenage pregnancy and stop mean girls before they ruin the lives of smart girls everywhere... maybe I'll—"

Gwen cuts me off. "Oh shit, she's been maladaptive daydreaming again."

"Here's the thing." Maggie interrupts. "Elly, you are going to go into that school and do the best job you can, and they'll call you next time they need a sub. You'll get real-world experience outside of Terry's, and I promise that you'll catch your big break soon."

I stir my coffee nervously. Even though it's just black and my stirrer is unnecessary, I always grab one so I have something to fiddle with.

"Thanks for your encouragement," I say. "I know you guys realize how tight things have been lately." I break eye contact because this vulnerability is too much. I don't want their pity, but honesty about my situation feels like a warm bath at the end of a long day. "I'm afraid if I don't get a steady gig soon, I may have to move back home."

My parents have been nagging me for the last three months about coming home to save some money while I figure out my life. They make valid points about building a sizable nest egg and saving money while I'm still young enough to get away with living at home. Since I can be a bartender anywhere, they don't understand why I need to live somewhere I can barely afford and struggle this much. I get their concern, so I'm breaking one of my core beliefs and giving myself a timeline. "If I don't have a full-time job by the end of the month, I'm going home."

Silence fills the air between us until Gwen speaks.

"Sis, I've got eyes and ears all over this city. Trust me, your big break is right around the corner. I can feel it." She places a gentle hand on my arm and all joking is gone.

"I hope you're right."

# TWO

Elliot

I tear through yet another eviction notice that's conveniently taped to my front door after my horrendous, failed attempt at a workday. Somehow I don't think the $35 I earned from a half day of substitute teaching is going to do much to help me with this one.

To say today was a total fail would be an understatement. First, I woke up late because my power went out during the night, so I had to frantically rush to get to the school on time. I almost collided with a speeding tractor trailer trying to turn left onto a four-lane highway, which goes against everything in me, and once I was there, my first gym class was full of prepubescent girls with curvy butts and hourglass figures that made my body look like a twelve-year-old boy in comparison. The girls took a game I wanted to play out of context and, needless to say, I may have contributed to a new choreographed TikTok dance that's already sweeping the nation.

All in all, I was vehemently asked to leave early and never apply to substitute teach again.

I rack my brain trying to figure out what I'm going to sell to afford this month's rent since Destiny's late on her half, and I don't have anything in savings as a backup. I glance down at my feet, thinking back to the weird foot fetish guy who randomly messaged me when I posted a picture of my new toe socks on Instagram. I can hear Gwen's voice in the background of my mind scolding me. *Don't even think about it; besides, your feet are kind of weird-looking and you've got that pre-bunion bulge and you can't even afford the pedicure to get started.* Invisible Gwen's right; I can't even afford the startup costs to get these puppies in shape.

I pull my phone out of my pocket and text Terry, asking if I can pick up extra shifts this weekend. I'll just work double shifts Friday and Saturday, and if I'm lucky and I can talk my way into closing. I'll have to wear my tight pants. I fucking *hate* the tight pants, but they are scientifically proven to bring in thirty percent higher tips. I may not have cute feet in my arsenal but there's no denying I have a great ass. When you're anxious and exercise is the only form of treatment you can afford, a great ass is a lucky by-product.

An incoming video call interrupts my pity party, and I know if I don't answer my parents' call, my mom will freak out and possibly show up at my apartment in the morning and that's the last thing I need right now. I do my best to push all the unpaid bills out of eyesight, swipe away the running mascara from under my eyes, and free my hair from the rat's nest encasement on top of my head. She's going to see right through me, but I don't have time to do anything else. I grab Destiny's abandoned dirty coffee cup from the coffee table and act as if I've just sat down for a leisurely cup of afternoon tea as I answer.

"Hey, Mom, Dad!" I say a little too enthusiastically.

"Elliot, goodness, are you sick? You look awful" My mom's voice pierces through the silence, reminding me that I can't sneak anything past her. My parents are sitting side by side on the living room sofa with their tablet propped on the coffee table. My mom is wearing an apron that's lightly dusted in flour, while Dad's in his bathrobe.

"Nope, not sick, you just caught me doing some chores around the apartment. Those baseboards aren't going to clean themselves!"

"Well, dear, you really should tend to your appearance. You know how I feel about looking put together; you never know when you'll meet your future husband," my mom scolds.

"Barbara, she looks fine. Besides, just knowing she's keeping a clean house would have any man interested enough to give her another chance to see how she cleans up!" He chuckles, clearly tickled with his pun.

This is exactly why I hate talking to my parents. The 1950s-style small-town simplemindedness somehow didn't fizzle out through my family's generations. They'd love nothing more than for me to move back home, marry a nice accountant, have some grandbabies, and stay home cleaning up after said family. Quite frankly, I'm not sure how two people can produce a child so vastly different from themselves. My whole life has been a battle, with me trying to hide my ambition and no one ever taking me seriously. Unlike many of my peers, I didn't move back home after I finished my degree, knowing that if I ever did, I'd never get another chance to break free.

My dad's voice brings me back into the moment. "Elly, how did that..." He snaps his fingers together, trying to remember my latest job attempt.

"The substitute teaching," my mom answers him, aggravated with his poor memory. "Really, Walter, she just told us about it a week ago. I don't know how you manage to remember your name sometimes." She rolls her eyes and leans forward toward the screen, waiting on my response.

This is it. I know I can't lie to them, but I've got to soften the delivery or my mother may have a heart attack.

"It's funny that you mention it..."

"Oh, dear Lord, Elly... nothing is funny. Please tell me nothing is funny!" My mom dramatically turns away, leaning into my dad's shoulder.

Dad leans forward. "Would you let her talk, Barbara!"

"Well, it just wasn't the best fit, that's all. I don't think I'm cut out to be an educator. Some of the girls took a game I suggested in a completely different direction. There was inappropriate dancing, but I handled it."

Dad's guffaw startles me. "Christ, Elliot! I could've told you it wasn't going to work out, with your track record and all!" He slaps his leg again, this time rustling the bathrobe free from his thigh, giving me a prime view of his hanging scrotum.

"*Ahhhh! Dad*! Your balls are out!" I cover my face with my hands, screaming. I don't think I'll ever be able to unsee my father's hanging ball sack; I'll never look at him the same way ever again.

"It's that damn chafing from my golf game; the boys needed to breathe!" he says as if the explanation suddenly makes things better. He scrambles to cover himself, knocking over his coffee cup while my mom jumps up frantically to grab a throw blanket while trying to contain the spill. "Oh, Walter, you've done it now. I don't know how I'm going to get the stain out of the sofa!" And just like that, the trauma of seeing my father's scrotum is forgotten when faced with the real issue of stain removal.

I chance a glance and see the scene has been remedied, the best it can anyway. I'll still probably need therapy to overcome the trauma but I'll add that to the list when I can afford it.

Now that Dad's got a blanket draped over his legs, leaving

no chance of another accidental exposure, my mom picks up as if nothing happened. "You know, I ran into Daniel yesterday at the Wal-Mart and he asked about you."

I pinch the bridge of my nose. "Mom, it's just Wal-Mart, not *the* Wal-Mart, and how many times do I have to ask you to not talk to my high school boyfriend?"

"Oh, Elly, he misses you and I'm not going to be so rude to not answer if he specifically asks about your life. You know what I think? I think he's still interested. I bet if you'd move back home and give it one more try, he may even take you back..."

"OK, well, I think my roommate's just walking in. What's that, Destiny? Of course, I can help you set up the tripod in your bedroom! I've got to go. I love you!" I slap the computer shut before they can add more insult to injury.

---

Two hours later, after I've cleaned every surface of the apartment—even tackling a strange dried substance on the kitchen counters that took a mixture of hot bleach water and an old toothbrush—my phone buzzes to life in my pocket.

GWEN
Happy hour after work tonight? 🍸

MAGGIE
It's a weeknight. Are you mad, woman?

GWEN
Not mad but we do have some celebrating to do! :balloon emoji:

MAGGIE
OMG! Did you get the promotion?

GWEN

Nope, but I did break up with David! Here's to my newfound single-ness 🫶

I can't tonight, rain check?

GWEN

Come on, girl, I'm buying!

In that case... I could use a stiff drink.

MAGGIE

How was your day? How did subbing go?

I can neither confirm nor deny that I had any involvement with mass gyrating adolescents.

GWEN

NO... please tell me you had nothing to do with it!

MAGGIE

What are you talking about?

GWEN

It's all over Twitter. Don't worry, Mags. I'll send you a link

MAGGIE

Uh-oh, there's a link?

GWEN

And a few videos... it was quite entertaining actually. Elliot, maybe you've got a budding career in porn screenwriting?

Eww!

Maggie, I'll catch you up at happy hour.

GWEN

Ok meet me at 6 at Terry's and I need all the deets

You know I always deliver my drink payments in the form of embarrassing stories

GWEN

Truth

Although I'm not exactly excited to be spending my night off at Terry's, he does give us discounts on our drinks, and since Gwen's paying I don't get a say in where we go. I throw on a black pencil skirt and a loose-fitting top and, since I had a really bad day, my black stilettos and bright lipstick for a confidence boost. Just because my life is falling apart doesn't mean I have to look like it.

Gwen is already sitting at the bartop nursing her drink when I walk in. Terry's is a quaint hole in the wall dive bar centrally located near all of our houses. We started coming here in college and the tradition just kind of stuck. I've been working here on and off since then; it's one of those places that just feels comfortable. The people are good, staff and patrons alike, except for the owner Terry, hence the name. I glance around and survey the staff. Thankfully Simon's on duty tonight. He's gorgeous, ex-military, and—best of all—quiet. At least one thing is going right today. I know Simon will bring us our drinks and leave us alone, unlike some of the newer bartenders that still need the reminder that I'm not interested in dating in this season of my life.

"Well, if it isn't my little train wreck of a bestie," Gwen greets me. "What are you having?"

I sit down at the stool next to hers. "I think I'm going to drown my sorrows tonight, so I hope you aren't in a hurry. After all, I don't have anywhere to be in the morning."

"Some of us are professionals. Sounds like you need a stiff

one. Simon, could you bring us each a gin and tonic with a twist of lime?"

"Gwen, you know I hate gin! Last time I had gin, it tasted like I was puking Christmas trees all night! Sorry, Simon, don't make that drink. Could you just bring me an old-fashioned?"

Gwen giggles. "Well, isn't that sophisticated of you?"

"I figure I can at least look like a grown-up since I hardly feel like one."

Simon slides my old-fashioned over to me and I take a slow sip, savoring the orange flavor on my lips. "Thanks, Simon, you're winning the favorite bartender award tonight."

Simon chuckles. "Elly, considering I'm the only bartender here tonight, I'm not sure how I feel about that compliment."

"Simon, you know we love you. Keep the drinks flowing tonight, OK? We've both had a rough go of it."

"I don't doubt that, there's never a dull moment between you three. Terry told me you'll be taking my Saturday morning shift; that helps me out. I've got a boy's trip planned and was going to have to leave later. Now I'll be able to head out Friday night."

Gwen and Maggie raise their eyebrows at this piece of information, and I change the subject, not wanting to get into it tonight. "Hey, Mags, is that a new purse? It's super cute!"

"Yes, thank you. I just got it, and look what else I've got!" She reaches in her bag and pulls out cucumber sandwiches and celery sticks. "I thought I'd bring a light snack since it's Tuesday and the two-for-one burger deal brings all the tourists out and about. We know how Gwen gets when she is hangry."

Leave it to Maggie to always come prepared. Now if we could only get her to come prepared with something a little less grandma-ish...

Gwen reaches over first and takes a cucumber sandwich

triangle and shoves the entire thing in her mouth. "It's duh-lish-us," she smacks with her mouth open.

I turn to Gwen, seeing her blatant lack of manners for what they are, a diversion tactic. "OK, Gwen, spill the beans... What was wrong with David? I thought we liked David?"

She rolls her eyes and takes another generous gulp of her gin. "Ugh, don't get me started about David and his complete lack of awareness."

Gwen's dating life has been through the wringer and it seems that poor, innocent David is her latest flop.

"Gwen, you can't keep finding things wrong with these guys. Surely by now you would have made a solid connection with someone. For crying out loud, at this point, it's a numbers game!" Maggie scolds.

"Well, actually, it didn't dawn on me what my issue with David was until I walked in on him screwing my assistant in my office."

"Oh, Gwen, I'm so sorry. That was so insensitive of me to assume..." Maggie trails off.

"What did you do?" I ask.

"I did the only logical thing I could think of. I grabbed my phone and started a live video and set it on the shelf beside the door. In their frantic efforts to separate themselves, there was plenty of face time on my live stream, and then I shared the video and now it looks like it's going viral. They are calling it 'The Hairy Humper.'"

"And just think, I was starting to feel sorry for you," Maggie says.

"Sweetie, don't feel sorry for me; I can handle my own. I just hope that hussy, Dana, likes getting coffee."

"You're not firing her?"

"Nah, we ladies have to look out for each other. I've already embarrassed her enough that if she doesn't quit on her own, then I may need to give her another chance for having bigger balls than I do."

"Gwen, please stop referencing your testicles in public!

"Enough about my testicles, Elly. I believe you have a story for us..."

So I tell them the entire thing... every grueling detail.

"I feel like we're going to need another drink. Simon, how about a round for my girls here."

# THREE

Elliot

"Elly, you didn't!" Gwen gasps, throwing her head back, almost causing her to fall backward off of her barstool.

I throw back my shot and wince as the burning liquid coats my throat. "Yes, I did. It was an honest mistake but—"

"I knew something would happen," Gwen says, cutting me off, "but this is even better than I could've imagined. Elliot's not cut out for the rigidity of school or anything with too many rules. Teaching is one of the most structured professions, not to mention her impulsive nature."

"What do you mean? Elliot is responsible, hardworking, and I've never seen someone as stubborn when they set their mind to something," Maggie retorts.

"Yeah, but she is clearly too accident-prone to work with anyone under the age of eighteen, so we need to consider that for our next idea."

Gwen and Maggie have clearly taken it upon themselves to adopt me as their fixer-upper project.

"I don't see why you can't give teaching another chance," Maggie says. "Maybe if you tried middle school?"

"Maggie, thanks for the offer but I don't think I'm cut out for it. The minute I walked in that gym, it's like they saw my biggest weakness and fed on me as prey."

"You're right, you're too nice and teenage bitches eat nice little innocents like you for dinner. I should have put a stop to it." Gwen chugs her drink and slams it down on the bar, signaling to Simon that she'd like another. Subtle. A composed Simon appears, switching her glasses before fading back into the crowd of randoms.

"You say that like she's a lost cause! Elliot's smart and energetic and that's not a bad thing. She's going to find her place, and when she does it's going to be the most obvious perfect fit, and we're all going to be shocked that we didn't see it sooner."

"Maggie, you are too precious for this world. You're right, this was a minor setback and I'm going to dust myself off and start my job search first thing tomorrow morning."

I bite into the cherry from my drink, savoring the juicy flavors before tying the stem in a knot with my tongue. "How's that for a sweet little innocent?"

I hand it to Gwen and she rolls her eyes.

"I see you, sis. Now we just need to find a real-life man for you to practice these skills on. But first, we drink!" Gwen grabs the three overflowing shots and hands them over to us. "Here's to new beginnings, good dick, and getting up when you get knocked down!"

"Cheers!" we yell in unison.

I take my shot and slam the glass down on the wooden bar counter, feeling empowered and ready to start over. Words cannot express my devotion to these girls. We've always been there for each other over the years. Through heartbreaks, college craziness, and acclimation into the real world after college. Between the three of us, we've seen it all.

"I need to pee!" I halfway yell to everyone sitting near me.

"OK, sis, you go take care of that; let me know if you need any help." Gwen giggles as she stuffs a martini olive in her mouth. When did she start with the martinis? That girl must have a stomach made of steel.

I leap up from my seat, causing my head to spin, and start on my journey to the bathroom stalls across the bar. My shoe choice for tonight was a little ambitious considering I knew I'd be getting tipsy or whatever level is past tipsy but before wasted. They should make a name for that kind of drunk. It's the perfect level of 'I don't give a shit' but "I'm also not going to flash you my boobs for some cheap plastic necklaces that I could buy for a nickel—you can take the girl out of Louisiana." My cheeks are warm and a smirk is plastered on my mouth. Despite my circumstances, I feel overwhelmingly happy and grateful right now.

As I step into the dark hallway approaching the women's bathroom, I hit a brick wall. My face smashes straight into the rock-hard chest of someone who smells of delicious man soap and something so masculine, I could write a fanfiction based on the smell alone. Without meaning to, I let out a guttural groan and look into the very angry eyes hovering before me. This giant man of marble has to be at least six four, and my five-three frame cowers underneath his glare. His dark features are breathtaking, with whiskey-brown eyes with gold flecks around the center, and short brown hair that casually sticks up a bit. His facial hair is just a little longer than a five-o'clock shadow, and has my belly doing cartwheels.

Yeah, it's definitely the facial hair, not my consumption of mixed alcohol.

"Watch where you're going. Dammit, if you got lipstick on my shirt..."

My eyes roll down his face, down his neck, and back to the place where my face made contact with his rather impressive chest. That's when I remember something I did right tonight.

"Ha! This new lipstick really does work. I have to say I was skeptical when it claimed to be transfer-free but look at that, your white shirt doesn't have a stain on it! It's a lip stain. Usually, I wear liquid lipstick but Gwen talked me into buying this stain last time we were at Sephora."

The angry marble man raises an eyebrow and studies me. "Are you always this happy when someone yells at you?"

Just as I open my mouth to answer him, the door to the bathroom swings open, making contact with my back with such force that I go flying forward. I bear down in my stilettos and slide, once again, straight at the angry man's chest. My face seems to slide across his shirt in slow motion, this time leaving an actual imprint of not only my lipstick but also my face.

I stare into my makeup imprint on his very expensive white tailored shirt. This time when I look up at him, his eyes have narrowed and I think I see actual steam coming out of his ears.

"Oops, I guess even the best lip stains still have their limits." I bite my lip and search for a way to apologize, but before I can get a word out he turns on his heel and heads straight to the door. I'm left to wonder where he was going and why it was such a big deal that I messed up his fancy shirt.

I collect myself and assess the havoc that's been wreaked over the last five minutes. My left shoe is broken, the heel snapped and sticking out at a ninety-degree angle. My shirt has completely come undone from my stylish French-tuck, and my pencil skirt is turned completely sideways. I look like a three-year-old who's learning to go potty by themselves.

"Great," I mutter under my breath and hobble into the women's bathroom.

Upon seeing my reflection, I am horrified. Am I the actual joker? What in the hell is this look? My mascara has migrated down my face, giving me black eyes that would make any raccoon jealous. I've got red lipstick smeared everywhere around my lips, but hardly any on my lips themselves. My skin is shiny and slick from the central heating; we have passed the dewy stage and have gone straight to 'honey, are you feeling OK?' clammy. I guess my perfect state of drunkenness has deceived me.

I wash my face with the hand soap, trying to make as little contact with the actual dispenser as necessary. Why do bathrooms have such disgusting soap dispensers? Sometimes I feel like my hands are dirtier after touching them. Working the floral, old-lady fragrant soap into a foam with the ice-cold water, I rinse, dab, and repeat. Then I look in the mirror and find my mostly clean face staring back at me. My big brown eyes are a little bloodshot, and my previously curled and teased dark-brown hair has gone completely limp. I study my features and think that it could definitely be worse before hobbling back to my friends to tell them my exciting story of how I just face-stamped the most gorgeous man I've ever seen.

When I make it back to the bar, I find Gwen and Maggie surrounded by a mass of people. There are screams of excitement and I see Gwen has a small remote in her hand. Maggie is standing right behind her saying something in her ear. "Gwenneth Jade, I thought I told you to never play bar poker again! You know the people riot against you every time you win!"

Gwen's retort is lost when she takes in my dilapidated state. "What the hell happened to you? You look like you just went swimming in the river."

"I washed my face in the bathroom sink," I say, my chin held high. Having confidence in the way you look is half the battle to being attractive. "I was tired of the lip stain; it doesn't work, by the way."

The two women before me stare daggers into my eyes and Gwen slowly drops the digital poker remote and says, "OK, fellas, I'm out; the game's all yours." Cheers and cries of joy surround us as the other bar patrons fight for their chance to win a million virtual dollars.

"I will never understand everyone's obsession with that game," I say. "It's not like you're actually winning money."

Gwen looks over at me. "You'd be surprised what a man will do to keep his pride intact, heaven forbid he lose digital poker to a woman!" She throws her head back and laughs, giving off her best evil villain cackle.

Maggie grabs her Mary Poppins purse, the cardigan she brought 'just in case there's a chill in the air,' and wraps her hand around my waist. "I don't know what happened to you, but you look like you could use someone to lean on."

"Mags, you are the sweetest." I rest my head on her shoulder as we wait outside, deciding our next move.

"Why don't y'all come back to my place and we can have a nightcap and a sleepover?" Gwen asks.

Considering that Gwen's place is in downtown Chicago, in a high-rise apartment with a cushy doorman and my alternative is my shitty apartment complete with a questionable roommate, I don't hesitate. "Yes, ma'am, let's do this thing!"

Gwen pulls out her phone and requests an Uber to carry our half-tipsy asses back across town.

"It looks like we have about ten minutes before the Uber is here. Elliot, why don't you share what happened?"

"All you need to know is that though this lip stain may stand up to one blow to the face, when you incorporate friction to the blow, it's a goner. I ran into a strapping young gentleman with the most beautiful eyes by the bathroom."

"Oh my God, did you get his number? Did you kiss?"

"Gwen, it's like you don't even know me at all. I ran into him—literally—as he was leaving. Not to mention I stamped my face on his clean, white shirt. Apparently, he was going somewhere and I ruined his night. All I know is that he was an angry man and was not happy to make my acquaintance under the circumstances anyway." I shrug because the story is kind of funny, even if the angry man was upset.

"Well, he can go suck on a giant dick!"

"Gwen!" Maggie scolds. "You can't yell dick out in the open for everyone to hear!"

"Dick, dick, dick, dickety, dick!"

"You are such a child." Maggie rolls her eyes, but we all know that she's amused. Deep down she loves my free spirit and Gwen's blunt nature.

"OK, the Uber is pulling up, let's get our asses in the car. I'm craving ice cream. Hello, Mr. Uber driver, do you think you could stop by Dairy Queen on the way to our destination?" Gwen opens the passenger door and has no qualms about sitting up front next to the complete stranger.

With the slam of the car doors, we're off to get our fill of Dairy Queen blizzards and to finish off a bottle of wine. I can't help but think how lucky I am for such amazing friends in my life. Now if I could just afford for this to be my reality rather than my best friend's treat, I'd be on the right track.

# FOUR

Benjamin

The buzz of my alarm startles me awake, and I rub the sleep from my swollen eyes. Fuck, my head hurts. Drinking half a bottle of whiskey in a dive bar on the south side of Chicago wasn't my brightest moment, but I had to numb the pain somehow. I glance over at the photo of the three of us wrapped up in our parkas at the Christmas parade downtown, and my heart sinks into my stomach.

"I'm so sorry, Sarah. Fuck, I miss you both." I kiss my fingertips and touch the photo before throwing off the blankets and heading to the shower to wash off the smell of bar smoke and poor choices.

I wince as the hot water hits my skin and I crank the temperature up higher as if I can wash away the memories from last night. A wave of nausea radiates through me and I steady myself on the tile in front of me while I let it pass. *Fuck, Benjamin, you're not twenty-one anymore, and you can't go out and get shit-faced on a worknight. You deserve every ounce of pain you suffer today because you did this to yourself.*

Last night I was trying to take my mind off the pain, and I stupidly thought that going out to a bar as far across town as I could get and hooking up with a nice piece of ass would distract me from the anniversary of their death. But all I managed was to do was drink too much whiskey and land a hookup with a blond bimbo who couldn't eat or drink anything before she took a picture of it for Instagram. I'll never understand this social media culture; sometimes it seems like we're living the real-life version of the movie *Idiocracy*. I had my driver take us back to her place and I was in and out within thirty minutes, not my best performance I'll admit. Overall, she was unmemorable, but I just needed a warm place to stick my dick to forget the pain.

Too bad I was an asshole to the brunette bombshell with the fuck-me red lips. There was something about her that drew me like a magnet. I followed her to the bathroom to get a closer look. I was hoping to work up the courage to ask her to come home with me but as soon as she opened her mouth and started talking, I knew she was too nice. I have no business hooking up with nice women. I may be a monster, but I'd never pull someone so pure-looking into my shitty existence even if it was just for one night. I did manage to snap a picture of her sitting at the bar with her friends and text it to my boys; they both agreed, so I know it wasn't just my whiskey glasses.

I grab my phone, pull up the picture, and move it to a secret folder. I'll definitely be visiting this one for a long time to come. I label the picture 'The hottest girl in the world' even though it's the only one in the album. Hey, maybe I can add to it one day. I know I'm a pathetic piece of shit but it's a picture of her sitting at the bar with her friends; it's not like a sicko Peeping Tom or some shit. I'll just have the photo for a visual when I need to pretend that I'm not a lonely pathetic widow. Yes, it's a good thing I yelled at her rather than put on the fake charm. She's better off.

The nightmares are really strong on significant days like their birthdays, our anniversary, and especially the anniversary of the accident. Last year I had to drink a whole bottle of wine and take an Ambien just so I didn't leave my house and do something stupid. Thank God for my boys, Jack and Sam, who didn't leave my side the entire night. This year, though, I thought I'd try a new approach. I've been testing out the waters on the dating apps and they've proven to be an excellent source of women looking for a no-strings-attached good time. We drink, fuck, and part ways.

Don't get me wrong, most of them are lackluster and have zero depth, not that I'm even attempting to get to know them. Hell, half the time I don't even tell them my last name. I use them and they use me. After the goods and services are exchanged, I leave, never to see them again, and that's exactly how I like to keep it. They can go back to their socially curated lives while I fall back into my pitiful existence.

I let the scalding water rinse the suds from my hair and step out of the shower just in time to purge the contents of my stomach. Yep, today's going even worse than I expected.

---

It's only Wednesday and I'm nursing a hangover from hell. I even had Wilson, my driver, stop to grab me a Gatorade and some aspirin at the convenience store on the way. I use my Gatorade as an ice pack and make my way into the building, collecting my mail from the front desk on the way up.

"Damn, Benjamin, you look like shit," Eliza, our receptionist, calls out just before I manage to turn the corner. She's in her early twenties and started working for me during her senior year of college. Now she's getting her masters and I don't know if I'm ready for her to move on with her life or not. Right now, I'm thinking the former.

"Yeah, um, I guess I had a late night. Not that it's any of your business." I shoot her a disgruntled glare and she brushes it off.

She folds her arms over her chest and gives me a look of sympathy that can only be rivaled by my mother's. "I wish you'd start taking better care of yourself. You deserve to be happy, Benjamin, no matter how much you disagree with me."

"Thanks, Eliza," I snap before she gets any ideas that I want to hear her lecture. "Could you order me some soup for lunch with a loaf of bread?"

"A loaf of bread? You must really be hurting." A grin splits across her face and I know she's enjoying seeing me in pain. "Sure thing, boss. I'll bring up Panera right after your eleven o'clock meeting with–" she glances at my schedule on the calendar–"Thad Powell."

My stomach drops and if I hadn't already vomited its entire contents this morning, I'd have gotten sick upon hearing his name. A million questions flow through my mind, and I'm suddenly too dizzy to think logically. Fuck, the whiskey was such a stupid decision. I could've numbed myself just as well with beer, still gotten laid, and now I wouldn't be feeling like I'm on the brink of death. How could that sleazebag show up here today of all days, and what could he possibly want now?

"Thanks for the heads-up, Eliza. Do me a favor and have CJ escort him up." I wink.

"Looks like I'll be eating my lunch at my desk today. Dinner and a show, I can't wait." She giggles before typing a reminder on her daily schedule.

"Get your grubby hands off me! *Ouch*! You're lucky I'm not pressing charges; I think I may have a bruise developing on my wrist."

I hear Thad's nasally voice before I look up to see CJ ushering him into my office. "Here you go, sir. This one's squirrely, didn't like my standard pat-down. His balls shriveled right up in my hand. He didn't do well in memorizing the fire escape plan either, mocked me the whole time, but I take my duties here seriously and I'll not have you die on my watch. Last month's smoke alarm mishap in the kitchen was just another reminder that we all need a crash course." CJ shoves Thad forward and he stumbles on the rug in front of my desk.

"You're right, CJ. Why don't you send out a company-wide memo reminding everyone of the procedures? Do you still have the illustrated sketch you did, and the recording of the jingle?"

She nods her head, puffing out her chest. "Of course I do."

"Send it out and offer a free PTO day to anyone who recites the jingle to you by Friday."

Her grin spans across her face before catching herself. She relaxes her expression and gives me a salute before turning to leave. All the while, Thad stands there in shock. My relationship with CJ is a special one, as eccentric as she may be. She was my first hire here, and she stepped up after I lost Sarah. I'll never be able to repay her kindness of taking over vital tasks and delegating what needed to be done for the entire month while I grieved. She started as my assistant, but we quickly learned that the real place she shines is in HR. She's head of all safety committees, and head of security by choice. She's kind of like a border collie, super smart and hardworking, but you've got to give her lots of jobs and responsibility or she may eat a wall. The fire safety jingle was something she developed last year and it's quite time-consuming to quiz every staff member on their memory of it, which is exactly what I need to keep her out of my hair while I nurse this god-awful hangover.

I glance back down at my spreadsheet. "Thaddeus, what brings you here on this fine day?"

I let the heavy words sink in and he winces slightly from my tone.

"Benjamin, you know I wouldn't be here today unless it was an absolute emergency." He takes a seat in the chair across from my desk and pulls out his briefcase. "As you know, I've been tremendously successful in my entrepreneurial efforts over the last five years, but my family still needs some help. We've... well, we're in a pickle and my father asked me to reach out to you about a partnership."

A frustrated sigh escapes me and I take another gulp of my Gatorade. If I can just make it through this conversation without spewing my breakfast all over this office. Thad Powell is my late wife's brother and the quintessential baby boy with a silver spoon in his mouth. Nothing has ever been his fault and his parents think he can do no wrong.

"As you know," he continues, "my parents had high hopes for Sarah helping with the family business. She was our numbers girl; they'd cultivated that gift in her through private school education, college courses, and special tutors. She was going to inherit the role of COO of my father's company—"

"Yet your parents cut her off when she showed up pregnant? Where are you going with this, Thad? It's too fucking early to play mind games and I'm well aware of how brilliant my wife was. What do you want from me, today of all the fucking days?" My last bit of patience finally snaps. This conversation is making my head pound and it's taking all my strength not to strangle this poor excuse for a man sitting in front of me like he's trying to taunt me.

"We need to partner with you; we need your skill set or the business will tank," he finally admits.

"Absolutely not. No. The answer is no. Now get the fuck out." I slap my laptop closed and stand to open the window. Fresh air, that's what I need right now, if I could just breathe in some fresh fall air.

"You see, Benjamin, I'm not really asking you. My father sent me as a courtesy. We've got every right to sue you for what happened. You've single-handedly taken one of my family's most prized commodities away from us. Essentially, you owe us this."

"Jesus Christ, Sarah was not a commodity. Do you even hear yourself?" I blurt, knowing my reaction will go in one ear and out the other. Sarah's family only treated her well when she could give them something, but as soon as her father learned that she was expecting and her boyfriend, the worthless piece of shit, didn't want a part of any of it, they cut her off. 'You're dead to me,' he had said, and I was the one who picked up the fucking pieces of her heart and held her together. Now they're trying to pull this bullshit on me, two fucking years after her death.

"I'll take that as your acceptance." Thad stands from his chair on wobbly legs and I can see the nerves he's trying to hide. Good. I hope I intimidate him. I have no intention of stopping for as long as this thing lasts.

"I'll have my assistant send over the paperwork this afternoon. Good day, Benjamin." Thad walks out of my office, taking the last bit of my pride with him.

---

I drag my tired ass through my building up to the tenth floor, tipping Carl, the doorman a little extra than usual because I at least hope to bring joy to someone else today. Sarah always believed in karma so it's the least I can do to honor her memory. I open my door to find Sam rummaging through the kitchen while Jack sits on my couch with a deep-dish Chicago-style pizza and Sports Center playing the highlights of this weekend's game.

"Dude, you look like shit!" Jack calls.

I don't even flinch. I know I look like shit; that's only a fraction of how horrible I feel both physically and emotionally. I'd like to say I'm annoyed that my guys just let themselves into my apartment without my permission, but the truth is it's nice to have the company. I won't be drinking any of the beer they brought, but they probably weren't planning on sharing that anyway.

"Benjamin, when was the last time you cleared this dump?" Sam calls. "It smells like musty old socks and rotten eggs in here!" He stands up from digging in the fridge, pinching his nose. "I'm calling my housekeeper first thing in the morning. Consider it an early Christmas gift."

"Thanks." I plop down on the sofa next to Jack and pull out the contract. I've read it over approximately twenty times since Thad sent it over.

"What's this?" Sam walks over, picking up the papers. "You're merging the company with..." He pauses, no doubt in shock, "...with Sarah's family's company? Benjamin, why would you ever want to do that? It's clear as day they're barely treading water."

I take the papers from him. "Yeah, well, they're blackmailing me into the merger. The good news is, it says after two years I'm free to get out, provided I leave and sign a non-compete agreement." I fall back into the couch, feeling pure defeat. My company was something I started straight out of college; it's all I've ever known and now I'm handing over years of hard work to a family that hates me.

"What do you mean, they're blackmailing you?" Sam questions. "They can't do that."

"They fucking can. Trust me, I've already been on the phone with my attorney. I was at fault in the accident. They can sue me for reckless driving and that's the last thing I need on my record. I could not only lose everything, I could go to jail. The Powells are a bunch of white-collar criminals; I wouldn't put anything past them."

"So what does this mean?" Jack says through the pizza he's chewing.

"It means that starting Monday of next week, the former company known as Williams Media will be known as POW! and I'll be co-CEO to Sarah's dipshit little brother."

"Damn, bro, and I didn't think today could get any worse for you." Jack shoves another piece of pizza in his mouth.

"Me either. I'll pay for that mistake for the rest of my life." I scribble my name on the contract and scan the document with my phone before emailing it over. My stomach feels like I've swallowed a rock, and just like that, the last thing I loved has been taken from me once again.

# FIVE

Benjamin

"Benjamin, Mr. Powell is ready to see you now." The voice of Jennifer, my assistant, cuts through my daydream of strangling Thad Powell.

I'm staring out over the expansive cityscape through our agency's new cushy sky-top building. It's been exactly two weeks since the merger went into effect and it's every bit of the nightmare I thought it'd be. Our agency is now under the name POW! and I'm no longer the only one in charge. Thad and I are co-CEOs. My focus is primarily on the financial strategy while he focuses on only God knows what.

Everything about this place makes me miserable. Our once-cheery staff have dwindled to the ones holding master's degrees. Thad laid off a great deal of our older employees, justifying himself because their salary was higher than the younger ones. Alas, my hands are tied and now my interest is purely selfish—I'm sticking it out for two years and I'm out. I was once an all-around caring guy. I started my company with the best intentions: to provide a fun work environment that people enjoyed coming to every day. But I'm not that man anymore.

"Thank you, Jennifer, I'll be right there." I exhale a sigh and head to the conference room where I will stroke Thad's ego in our monthly board meeting. Everything about this merger rubs me the wrong way. Our once small and intimate environment that allowed me to know each member of my staff personally is long gone. The place is crawling with entitled fucks with trust funds, some of whom don't even know how to properly send an email. I had to threaten Thad's ability to procreate just to keep Jennifer, CJ, and Eliza.

By the time I arrive at the board meeting, everyone is seated around the large white conference table, waiting for my arrival before they'll get started.

"Well, well, well, Benjamin, so nice of you to join us this afternoon." Thad's patronizing voice echoes throughout the stale walls of the empty room, save for the large table, chairs, and mounted TV.

I make a show of glancing down at my watch seeing that I'm indeed one minute early for this unnecessary meeting. "I'm terribly sorry to keep you waiting like this; heaven knows you wouldn't be able to get this started without me. Don't worry, I'm here now. Let me know if you have any questions about what the grown-ups are saying."

"Gentlemen, let's get down to business, shall we?" Thad's father, Thaddeus Sr.—yes, you heard that right, the name's so good they had to continue it for another generation—breaks through our argument. My former father-in-law is dressed in a navy jacket with white dress pants and black shiny shoes. He looks like he's stepped straight off a yacht to be here today. I knew Sarah came from money when I met her, but nothing could've prepared me for the old-money mindset of her family. The minute she did something to stain the family reputation, they cut her off—that is until she finished her degree anyway, baby in tow, and started her own analytics company. Sarah successfully freelanced her way out of debt, positioning herself as the expert in her respective industry. Once her little side hustle started getting attention, suddenly her family was back in our lives acting as if nothing happened. Sarah was quick to forgive them because theirs was the only love she'd ever known before meeting me. I, on the other hand, never got over my grudge.

"Our financial statements for the last quarter. Benjamin, I presume that you've brought yours." Thaddeus Sr. slaps the papers onto the table for me to compare. I suppose I should enjoy being the only one in the room who has any business sense when it comes to running a company, but I don't. The Powells have quite the résumé but they've also got a reputation for dirty deals. Of course, I don't know anything specific; before now I've always tried to keep my distance.

I ruffle through the financial statements in confusion. At first, it appears that they've made a profit, and I don't have a calculator in front of me to be certain, but things don't seem to be adding up. After further reading, I can only come to one conclusion. "I believe POW! will be bankrupt within six months if you continue to run your business the same way that you've been doing for the last several years."

"That can't be right." Thad snatches the papers from my hand. "We've done everything we've been advised to do... I've got the most qualified people in Chicago working for me—"

"With all due respect, sometimes the ones who seem more qualified on paper don't even know the basics about business," I gesture through the glass toward all his incompetent new hires.

"What do you suggest we do then?" Thaddeus Sr. asks.

"I think we need to expand into a new market. We need to train our new hires to do their jobs better. And for the love of

God, please don't hire anyone else. I'm going to make a copy of these records and examine them further to..." I pause, trying to sound casual. "...to make sure we're getting all the tax breaks we can. Sometimes filing can make all the difference when it comes to paying Uncle Sam."

On that note, I stand up to leave. "If you'll excuse me, gentlemen, it's lunchtime and I'm famished from analyzing all these shoddy financial statements."

---

I'm holed up in my office, trying to get as much work done as possible while also laying low from Thad, who seems to be having a temper tantrum because of my bad news. I threatened to have CJ lead her new fire-safety dance she's choreographed to go along with the jingle if he didn't shut up and leave me alone for the rest of the afternoon. I can't do much to boost morale around here, but this place is sucking the life out of everyone in it. I don't want everyone around me to suffer just because my life's a dumpster fire.

I've got a stack of papers printed out with different industry portfolios and I'm creating a risk analysis for each. This is the way I grew my company exponentially in just five years: hard work, studying the facts, and perfectly-timed action. Erick Baker sings along in the background, lulling me into a calmer headspace, and I've even broken out my favorite man candle that Jack gave me last Christmas. My phone buzzes, breaking me free from my trance.

JACK

Benji, tell me you're going to make it to shoot with us next week... we miss you

SAM

Yeah, Benjamin, we miss you. You can't hide behind those financial statements forever

Financial statements are the least of my worries right now. I'm trying to string this place back together piece by fucking piece. I think Thad's been up to some shady shit too, but I can't prove anything just yet. I need to do some more digging.

SAM

Come on, dude, you've flaked out on us for the last month

Even before your demotion

JACK

*eating popcorn GIF*

I've been busy. And it wasn't a demotion. I told you they're fucking blackmailing me!

JACK

Betcha wished you'd have taken me up on my offer. Adventure tourism is where it's at, man. You could've been my assistant, holding my camera for me, booking flights. Really, Benji, you could stand to feel the wind tickle your bare nipples on a mountain top. It changes a man.

SAM

Ew, Jack, now all I can think about is your nipple hair blowing in the wind. Hey, Benjamin, let's forget about Jack and start a new friend group.

You know that's very tempting...

JACK

Ok, that's enough of that. You know you need me to keep things fun around here and you know how important bro time is to me. You never make time for me anymore, Benji!

SAM

Yeah, Benji, why don't you make time for us?

You assholes know I hate that nickname...

JACK

He's avoiding the question. Sam, did you notice he is avoiding the question?

SAM

Benjamin, you should know better than to avoid us. We're persistent motherfuckers... we won't leave you alone until you agree to a bro date.

JACK

BRO DATE! BRO DATE! BRO DATE!

SAM

Benjamin, please don't make me beg. You know I'm not above it.

JACK

Hello? Benjamin? Dude, I think he's ignoring us.

SAM

Do you think he's lonely? Are you going to the dark place, Benjamin? You can tell us, that's what we're here for. Step back into the light...

JACK

Maybe his Vitamin D levels are low? Benjamin, have you been taking your multivitamins that I bought you? You know how important the sunshine vitamin is for combating seasonal depression.

For the love of God!!! I had to step out to solve a crisis and you two dingbats have trapped me in a group message that I can't escape.

JACK

*Clutches pearls* There's no escaping our friendship, Benjamin. I'm appalled that you'd even suggest it!

SAM

Yeah, that's what we're here for and I think we've done a damn good job of it. So just agree to the bro date and we'll leave you alone.

YES! I WOULD LOVE TO GO ON THE BRO DATE, THANK YOU FOR ASKING ME IN THE MOST UNANNOYING WAY THAT WAS NOT AT ALL ANNOYING.

JACK

See, now I feel like he's being sarcastic.

SAM

Next Wednesday, meet us at the basketball courts. 6 PM.

JACK

Don't you dare think about canceling on us... AGAIN

Fine. Now please leave me alone!

SAM

I'm starting to think that Benjamin needs to get laid. Just a hunch

JACK

You mean he needs to hunch!

Benjamin has left the chat room

JACK

Nice try, you can't get rid of us that easily!!!
BWA-HA-HA-HA

Once my phone finally stops buzzing, I try to finish the project that I started but I can't focus. Sam and Jack were by my side throughout college; they were there when I met Sarah, when we eloped, and ultimately when I lost her. Those two idiots have seen me at my highest point, feeling on top of the world in my personal and professional lives and at my lowest, the miserable widow who's lost the one last piece of himself. Frankly, I'm surprised they'd still want anything to do with me; it's not as though I'm a joy to be around these days.

I flip through my phone, find a picture of Sarah and Maddie, and my heart feels like it's going to explode in my chest. Sarah was so young when she had Maddie, and despite that the world was against her, she still proved everyone wrong. I'll never be a dad again, but being Maddie's stepfather was a title I wore with honor. I'd never have given her conditional love or made her work for it. Unlike Sarah's parents, I'd have loved her no matter what choices she made. I'd have supported her dreams, no matter how silly they may have seemed.

"Benjamin." Jennifer's sharp voice interrupts my thoughts. I look up to see her standing in front of my desk. "Mr. Powell is in his office and he says that he needs you to come see him immediately. It's an 'emergency,'" she adds with air quotes.

"Right. Tell him I'll be right there." After Jennifer leaves, I open up my calendar and type BRO DATE before sending an invite to Sam and Jack. Hopefully they'll trust I'm not going to flake out on them again. I shove my phone in my pocket and set off to handle yet another crisis involving Thad Powell.

# SIX

Elliot

Red and orange leaves fall around us, blanketing the streets and paths, and the scent of autumn surrounds me. The soft crunch of leaves under my feet has me feeling nostalgic for simpler days when I first moved to this beautiful city and experienced my first real Midwest fall, a stark contrast to the deathly sticky heat of Louisiana. As the leaves fall slowly to the ground, I'm reminded that the trees have to lose their old leaves to endure the winter and that new lush green leaves grow back every spring. Perhaps my life is simply going through a season of change as well. Hope warms the icy worry in my chest, and I blink back tears from the realization.

"Dear God, how much longer?" Gwen's voice breaks through my moment of peace, bringing me back down to earth from my daydream. I glance at my running watch, a gift from Gwen and Mags last year. "We've only gone a half mile."

"Ugh, this is the worst!" Gwen's not very keen on running and this Saturday was my girls' group exercise pick.

"You've just got to push the pain to the back of your mind, concentrate on your breathing and you'll get a second wind." I don't mention that her second wind likely won't come after only half a mile.

Maggie runs silently on my other side, distracted by the music playing through her earbuds.

I fumble in my fanny pack for my headphones. "Gwenny, if I put my headphones on, are you going to keep up?"

She gasps, struggling to breathe. "Of course I'm going to keep up. I may bitch and whine the entire time, but you know I'm not a quitter."

*Good, I need to work through some of these issues.* I put my headphones on and turn on my badass playlist full of songs about girl power, confidence, and some other raunchy stuff that gets me motivated. Since the weather is so perfect today, we decided to meet at Millennial Park downtown for our run. The paths weave through the vast outdoor area, giving us views of nature while surrounded by skyscrapers and modern art sculptures. This is my happy place; this is my favorite spot in the city to work through my troubles. There's not a single problem life has thrown at me that I haven't been able to figure out on a long run.

I settle into my pace, trying to stay with my girls but needing a little bit of a challenge. Macklemore's "Can't Hold Us" plays through my headphones and I take off, riding the wave of adrenaline. Forgotten are my financial strains and problems, forgotten is the Elliot of the past who was never good enough for her family, forgotten is the constant sting of mistakes I've made trying to find my ideal career. I'm stripped of every painful memory that haunts me; there is only this beautiful sunny day before me and the feel of my feet pounding the pavement with each stride.

I dig a little deeper, pushing through the pain in my thighs.

Cool air fills my lungs and I am reminded of the healing power that running has over me. Glancing down at my watch, I see that I've gone two miles. I grin, knowing I've got at least three more in me before Gwen proposes we stop for the day. She may hate running, but we're all addicted to the endorphins from our cardio workouts, and I know she won't say anything until a full hour's passed.

---

Approximately one hour later, the girls and I are nice and exhausted from our run, settled in at our favorite brunch spot. We sit at a table overlooking the outdoor area with a fountain and a beautiful view of Millennial Park. I exhale a sigh of relief and pull the menu up to my eyes. I don't know why I bother to look; I've never gotten anything besides the huevos rancheros, but since I'm on a stricter budget these days, I figure it wouldn't hurt to look for a more budget-friendly option. This is my last splurge for a while. After picking up the extra shifts at Terry's, I was able to barely scrape by covering both mine and Destiny's halves of the rent, but unless I find a real job soon, I won't be able to keep the bill collectors at bay for much longer.

Our server comes over and we place our orders, eggs Benedict with the bottomless mimosas for Gwen, Belgium waffle with extra powdered sugar and a chai tea for Maggie, and scrambled eggs, toast, and black coffee for me.

As soon as our server is out of earshot, Gwen turns on me. "Scrambled eggs and coffee?" She raises her perfectly sculpted eyebrow in question and lets out a judgmental, "Hmmm."

"Just trying to stay budget-friendly," I reply through gritted teeth. I know Gwen knows my financial situation and wants better for me. She calls me on my bullshit. When I'm having a severe moment of imposter syndrome, she's the one to slap me out of it, reminding me of how I killed it in college and how any company would be lucky to have me. This is her gentle, not-so-subtle reminder that I need to take action and stop letting life pass me by.

"I know, I know. I'm pathetic these days." I glance down at my hands which I'm wringing in my lap. Looks like the run wasn't quite long enough to take the edge off this anxiety.

"Sis, you know I love you—" she starts.

"But?" I interrupt her.

"But... you've got to do something with your life and picking up extra shifts at Terry's is *not* what I mean. I don't want to see you move back to your parents'. Let me help you figure something out."

"What's there to figure out, Gwen? I'm a screwup. I've never been able to hold down a job—besides bartending—for longer than six weeks. I don't think I'm cut out for a career. Maybe my parents were right all along?"

Maggie reaches for my hand under the table, giving me a soft, reassuring squeeze.

The waiter interrupts my pity party, laying down the elaborate dishes before us. I take a bite of my plain toast, trying not to compare my meal to my friends'. It seems this is the case in all areas of our lives now.

Gwen takes a sip from her mimosa. "You're *smart*, Elliot. Don't downplay your gifts like that. You just haven't found the right fit yet. You need a job that lets your creativity free, something with structure and freedom to dream."

"Gwenny, if I didn't know better, I'd say it sounds like you have an idea." Maggie's eyes light up in response and my heart does a little shuffle with hope.

"It's an idea that came to me in the shower last night, as most of my good ones do. Elliot, what's your strongest attribute?"

The question catches me off guard. "Umm, my spreadsheet skills?"

Gwen slaps her hand down on the table. "No, it's your persistence! I've seen you time and time again pick yourself back up after being fired and let go for a whole slew of reasons. I've never met someone overcome near-constant rejection, no offense, and consistently put themselves out there again and again the way that you do."

A light blush creeps up over my cheeks. I don't know whether to feel flattered by the compliment or ashamed that it's so blatantly obvious that I'm a screwup to everyone around me.

"So, here's what you're going to do. There's a party taking place here tonight at seven. One of my clients invited me and you're going to be my plus one. We'll drink some free booze; you'll be your awkwardly charming self, and I promise you'll make a connection that'll give you a lead. It's the way these things work. I hear millionaire, Thad Powell, will be here and he's going through a big merger with his agency. This could be the perfect opportunity to rub elbows with the right people. Trust me, sis, I've got a good feeling about this."

"I'll have to call in and see if someone can cover me at Terry's, but I can't think of anything else I've got to lose." I take a hesitant sip of my piping hot coffee and hope like hell that Gwen's plan works.

---

"That dress makes your legs look amazing!" Gwen stands behind me, observing her handiwork in her floor-length mirror. She lent me an emerald-green fitted sheath dress that hugs every curve. The neckline is modest but off the shoulder, and my dark-brown hair is pulled up dramatically on one side and cascading down my other shoulder in loose, flowing curls. My minimalistic makeup sets off my winged black eyeliner, and I've decided to tone down the lipstick tonight and instead wear a nude gloss to bring the attention up to my eyes.

"You're stunning and look highly professional. There's no way you won't demand the attention of everyone around you looking like this. Are you ready?" Gwen adjusts her black sequin number that's a fun Gwen-twist on the LBD. Her legs are covered more modestly than mine but the dress clings to her every curve with an exaggerated slit starting at the knee all the way up the back where her thighs meet. I'm thankful my stylish friend and I wear the same clothing size because there's no way I'd have anything that would blend in well for this fancy party. I grab my borrowed gold sequin clutch and my phone. "Let's go schmooze it up!"

The Uber driver drops us off at a club I've never been to before, probably because I don't have the kind of money to run in this type of circle. We step inside toward the huge suited gentleman holding a clipboard and Gwen finds our names quickly. I don't miss the way his stare trails the length of her whole body before letting us through. That's the thing about Gwen—she's a firecracker and she owns her confidence in a way I wish I was capable of. She throws him a courtesy wink before pulling me through the doorway into the ballroom that's been transformed into an expensive-looking lounge that looks more like Cinderella's ballroom. Lush velvet armchairs are paired together with leather couches in groups so people can sit and chat. The crystal chandeliers offer dim lighting to the otherwise dark space. It's half club, half gala and I'm impressed with the concept. There's a live jazz band playing background music toward the back of the room, giving everyone plenty of room to spread out and make connections.

"These things always start as business mingling, but don't you worry. By the end of the night, half the women will be smashed and you won't be able to see the dance floor. Let's grab some champagne; there's someone here I want you to meet."

We make our way to the bar. This is nothing like the bars I'm used to—nothing like Terry's at all. The bartender is clothed in a dress shirt and vest and is shaking a martini shaker when we approach. Gwen orders our drinks and he hurries himself to pour them; there's no wait time or fighting to be seen over anyone.

"Wow, that was fast; how much did you say these tickets cost?" My eyes widen as she leads me toward a table in the back.

"Don't worry about that, Elly; they were a gift. But to answer your question, about three grand apiece."

My jaw drops in response and I take a giant gulp of my champagne to cover up my shock. Yeah, I'm a fish out of water over here. The crisp bubbles slide down my throat and at that moment I can't think of anything I've ever had that tasted this amazing. It's like I'm drinking bottled up birthday wishes and sunshine.

Gwen pulls me toward a group standing around a tall table in the back of the room.

"Good evening, Miss Bennett, you're looking lovely as usual." The tall blond man pulls Gwen into an embrace. "Who is this stunning woman you've brought with you tonight?"

Gwen smiles a deep, confident smile and pushes me forward slightly, breaking me from my moment of panic. I reach for the gentleman's hand and he plants a gentle kiss on my knuckles—now that's a first. I feel as though I've stepped back in time with a greeting like that. A small blush creeps up my neck.

"This is my long-time best friend, Elliot James." Gwen pinches me on my side, reminding me to use my manners and speak when spoken to.

"It's a pleasure to meet you, Mr...."

"Powell. Thad Powell and trust me, Miss James, the

pleasure is all mine." His eyes drift from my face slowly down my body, lingering on my neckline a little longer than professionally acceptable. I know I look amazing tonight and I'm so desperate to make a work connection, I don't cower under his gaze. Instead, I hold my head up confidently, feeling a little too much like Julia Roberts in *Pretty Woman*, except this gentleman is closer to my age and I have no intentions of sleeping with him for money, although I'd could be swayed into starting a foot fetish Only Fans if only I had cuter feet. A girl's got to make rent, after all.

The conversation between the group flows from a mountain climbing trip they all took last summer and transitions into the recent merger between Mr. Powell's company and Williams Media. My ears perk up at the change of conversation, finally interested and hopeful.

"We're all very excited about merging the companies. I know my partner, Benjamin Williams, will be happy to have some help running things. He's a bit scatterbrained when it comes to leading a company and after losing my sister, I'm afraid he's been struggling to keep his head above water. We couldn't pass up the opportunity to join forces to take control of the market. It's all very exciting. Now remind me, Elliot, is it? What do you do?"

Gwen nudges me under the table, and I feel the heat rise in my chest as I try to keep my cool. This right here is my golden opportunity; this is the exact reason I came here tonight.

"I... um... well, actually, I'm in between jobs at the moment. I've taken on some temp jobs trying to decide which direction I want to focus on, but if I'm being honest, my dream is to start my own brand strategy agency one day." I bite my lip, feeling slightly embarrassed at this public admission of my dream. Growing up I quickly learned that you can't trust just anyone with emotions as fragile as your dreams, but I'm sitting here at rock bottom and I don't have anything to lose anymore.

Mr. Powell assesses me once more. "Interesting, branding, you say? Why branding?"

"Well, I love storytelling, and I think branding goes so much deeper into the why behind things. It's not just marketing but the essence of a business, everything from the language they use to the design to the collaborations. I did a branding project before I graduated and I fell in love. I just don't have any experience, because it seems like you need experience to get experience these days."

"Why don't you meet me for lunch Friday afternoon? We can grab a bite to eat at the little deli across from our new location." He hands me his business card with his contact information. "I think this could be the start of a beautiful relationship, Elliot. Now if you would excuse me, ladies, I need to go say my hellos before the alcohol consumption gets out of hand." He gives my hand a gentle squeeze and walks away, his colleagues following right behind.

"Oh. My. God. Gwen!" I screech, grabbing her in a tight embrace. "You were right!" I fight back tears of joy at this amazing news.

Gwen releases me and raises her glass. "Cheers to your next chapter!" She throws back the sip of champagne and we make our way back to the bar, the weight of the world suddenly lifted off my shoulders. I have a feeling this is going to be a really good night.

# SEVEN

Elliot

It's Friday morning and I've already gone for a six-mile run, cleaned the bathroom, showered, and am sitting across the street from the deli where I'm meeting Thad in thirty minutes. My mind is racing as I play back my every professional and educational accomplishment on repeat, trying to psych myself up. I try to calm my nerves with the breathing exercises that Maggie swears by; in hindsight, I probably shouldn't have had that fourth cup of coffee.

Since this interview is over lunch, it took me forever to figure out the perfect outfit for the occasion. I decided to go with a smart casual look and paired my pleated ankle cropped gray trousers with a form-fitting black turtleneck and my white platform sneakers. I look professional and fun, which I hope is the vibe he's looking for around the office.

I spent all of last night putting together work samples with everything from complex spreadsheets to writing samples. I even pulled some of my marketing projects from my classes in college and printed out letters of recommendation from my professors. I barely got any sleep, working through every possible outcome I could think of, and I think I've got a plan for all of them.

With ten minutes to spare, I make my way toward the deli and see Thad taking a seat by the window. I silently scold myself for not coming in even earlier, I wanted to be the first one here to show my punctuality, which is not my biggest strength naturally. I have to work really hard to be on time for things, sometimes leaving a full hour before I need to. Over the years I've learned to compensate for my shortcomings, but somehow I still find myself in the most awkward situations. I'm beginning to think someone has a voodoo doll with my face on it and they're using it as a pincushion.

I approach the table and extend my hand to greet him. "Hello, Mr. Powell, sorry I'm late. Well, I'm not exactly late, it's just that you were early and now I feel that I'm late because you got here before me."

A sly grin stretches across his face at my admission. "Elliot, I'm so glad you could make it. My last meeting ended early, so that's why I'm early. I hope you don't mind but I took the liberty of ordering us some salads for lunch." His smile meets his eyes, and my stomach takes the opportunity to gurgle her annoyance. After my run this morning and the limited groceries in the apartment, my body is furious with me and dying for some substance. Not that I don't love a good salad, but my thighs could stand a cheeseburger or two. I feel my loose dress pants shift around freely as I take a seat and it's a physical reminder of my financial situation. No matter where I go or what I do, I can't escape this body that's screaming at me to eat something. I just wish I could afford to feed her like she deserves.

"Salad is perfect, thank you," I lie.

He claps his hands together and braces his hands against the table. "Why don't you tell me a little bit more about yourself."

This is the question that kept me up all night long. The question that will inevitably be asked during every interview. It seems like such a straightforward get-to-know-you question, but I know that it's a loaded one. Luckily my anxiety has prepared me for every possible outcome from my response so I won't be caught off guard by his reaction. "I'm from a small town in Southern Louisiana, graduated high school at the top of my class, and put myself through college at the University of Illinois. I currently work at Terry's Bar downtown. In my spare time, I enjoy reading and exercising. I love branding and hope to one day start my own agency." *Shit, I didn't mean to give that much away; I don't want him to think I'm using him as a stepping stone or anything.* "But I know that's a pipe dream and will probably never come true, so I want to offer my skills and curiosity somewhere that actually exists so I can make an impact in real life." There, that's better, a clean-cut response, giving him all the important information he needs to know to show I'm qualified for a job at his company.

He grins smugly as our server places our food down in front of us, then spreads his napkin across his lap. "Well, aren't you prepared?" He takes a bite of his salad and a sip from his sparkling water. "You're competent and all of that sounds great, but I want to know more about you."

His response catches me off-guard. I just gave him my elevator pitch and I'm not so sure what other accomplishments he wants to know about. Luckily, he sees the wheels turning in my mind and asks a more direct question.

"Tell me about your family. Are your parents still married? Do you have any siblings?"

"Oh, well..." The seemingly innocent personal question doesn't feel the most professional but maybe they're looking for a certain personality type, so I oblige. "My parents are still married and they live in Southern Louisiana with all their siblings. I'm the first person in my family to move away. They're not exactly excited about it either. I...um.... I'm an only child; they've always been pretty protective."

He examines me, giving me a moment to cram as much salad in my mouth as possible. The gesture was sweet, but my appetite is raging. I would've loved a piece of bread and a little protein, maybe even a hot bowl of queso. I know women think that eating salad looks like the dainty thing to do in public, but let's be honest, I look more like a cow chewing on cud right now.

Thad notices my vigorous munching. "Hungry?"

Embarrassment courses through me. I knew I should've just dealt with the hunger pains that were radiating throughout my stomach. "I've been intermittent fasting!" I blurt, hoping he can't see through the lie. It was the only thing I could think of to cover up my financial struggles and why I can't afford food these days. I've been relying on leftovers at Terry's most nights and scraping by on my friends' handouts. The whole situation makes me sick to think about; all I've ever wanted was to be able to provide a life for myself, and lately, I've become a charity case.

"You're a runner, huh?" He dabs his mouth with his paper napkin, making me feel like a caveman in comparison.

"Oh yes, it's my therapy... er, not that I *need* therapy... well, that's not true. I most definitely need therapy; I just can't afford it right now..." *Shit, what is wrong with me? I guess I can kiss any chance of getting this job goodbye. Why can't we stick to the normal interview questions?*

His smile stretches across his face and meets his eyes. "You're pretty cute when you're flustered. I noticed your nicely toned legs at the gala; running would explain how you're able to maintain such impeccable muscle tone." He lifts his glass as if he's saluting me and takes a long gulp.

My mouth goes dry. This interview—if you can even call it that—feels a lot more like a first date than an actual interview.

Thad clearly notices my internal panic and his expression shifts. "I'm sorry if that sounded crass; our agency believes that excellence physically is synonymous with excellence mentally."

I breathe a sigh of relief, easing the built-up tension. "Oh, well, I can definitely agree with that. I think that long-distance running teaches you that you're able to push through the pain, and that skill can be transferred over in any other situation."

"Exactly." He smiles and sits back in his seat, covering his plate with his napkin, signaling for our server to take the plate away. I've still got half my food but now doesn't seem like a good time to finish eating. "You are a beautiful woman, Elliot. I've always thought turtlenecks were underrated, especially if you've got the curves to fill them out." He winks and before I have a chance to question his last little admission, Thad stands up, grabbing his coat. "Listen, I've got a call that I need to get to, but I have a good feeling about this; why don't you start first thing Monday morning?"

I choke on my water. "Start first thing this Monday?"

"Yes, since the recent merger, I no longer have an assistant. You seem like you'd do the trick nicely." He winks and then stands, pulling on his coat and scarf.

My belly flip-flops in excitement and I shudder with disgust, the juxtaposition of finally catching my big break but at what cost? There's something about Thad Powell that doesn't quite rub me the right way, but right now I'm desperate. I shove my intuition out of the way with both hands and let my survival instincts take the wheel.

I stand up and shake his hand vigorously, as the weight of

the world is lifted off my shoulders. "Oh my God, yes! Thank you so much for the opportunity!"

"Great, I'll have my HR department contact you with the paperwork." He dislodges his hand from my grip and shakes it out. "Goodbye, Miss James, I'll see you Monday morning."

"Yes. Right. Goodbye, Mr. Powell, and thank you so much for the opportunity; I promise I won't let you down!" I'm not sure where my confidence in making that statement came from since the only thing I've ever successfully done in a job is let everyone down, but it feels like something I should say right now.

Then he's gone and I'm left in this deli, the smell of cold cuts and cheese surrounding me. I make my way to the counter and order a Philly cheesesteak sandwich and a large side of French fries to celebrate my first real job as my stomach cries out in relief.

---

After I texted Gwen and Maggie my good news about landing the job, Gwen wanted to go shopping for a first day of work outfit. We've shopped all afternoon, taking stock of every thrift store within a thirty-mile radius. I've got two bags of steals. It feels like we're back in college trying to find the hidden fashion treasures throughout the city. Gwen and Maggie have graduated from the college budget lifestyle, both working in their dream jobs, and I'm just thankful they still enjoy the hunt as much as I do.

After the shopping spree, Gwen insisted that I get a manicure before my first day. I'm not sold on the almond acrylic tips, but Gwen was very convincing with her argument. "Almond nails are all the rage right now, and trust me, you want to show up on your first day looking polished and confident. Plus, if anyone tries to cross you, you can gouge their eyes out."

"Gwen, please don't give her any ideas. Elly, try not to gouge any eyes out on your first day," Maggie says with a smile.

"Yeah. Yeah. We all know I'll read anything on the teleprompter, so don't give me any ideas."

We grab a pizza and some Pinot Noir for a low-key celebration dinner and fashion show at my apartment. It may not be much, but Gwen and Maggie are good sports about it, especially since we never know what we'll encounter with my highly eccentric roommate.

I begin the ascent to the second floor, dodging the rotten wood on every other step. It's like a dance now that I've learned where all the problem spots are; I could do this in my sleep. I pull out the keys from my back pocket and jiggle them in the lock. There's a method for getting the door to unlock; you have to jiggle to the left and then slightly lift the key up in the lock to find that sweet spot. I hear the subtle click from the lock releasing and turn the doorknob and slowly push the door forward.

Have you ever seen a sight so grotesque that you wish you could go back in time and un-see it? Add the sight of my roommate, Destiny, and her boyfriend of the week dressed in full Renaissance costumes, except he isn't wearing any pants, and there is definitely no adult chaperone to protect her virtue. It's not that I am a total prude, but there is a lot of sweat on his face and we didn't exactly catch his good side, if you catch my drift. One could argue that a hanging nutsack isn't the shining star in a male's anatomy... Destiny and, let's just call him Zak the sack, are going to pound town on the kitchen table, and our eyes are violated by the low-hanging fruit swinging between Zak's legs. I am so enamored by this that I freeze in place; where does he keep his balls? Surely that can't be comfortable to stuff inside his pants...

"Eww!" Maggie is the first to shriek.

The one-way trip to pound town comes to a halt and Destiny dares to look at me like I am inconveniencing her.

"Umm... I'm home," I nervously say, not knowing the cordial thing to say when you walk in on your roommate boning.

"Ugh, get out! Give us a minute to finish!"

"We'll just be in my room!" I announce and walk with purpose straight to my room. The three of us rush through my bedroom door and collapse on my bed in hysterical laughter.

"I can't believe my eyes!" Maggie squeals.

"I've never seen a pair of kahunas that big!" Gwen says.

"OK, I can't talk about it anymore; someone just play some music. I can still hear the grunting."

Gwen puts on her pumped-up playlist and we dig into the pizza, eating it straight from the box.

"Elliot, I want to say this from the kindness of my heart, and I want you to know that I am in no way judging you... but why are you doing this to yourself? You know Mags and I would both take you in in a heartbeat."

I bite my lip in embarrassment. Gwen's not one to beat around the bush. "I told you things are tight right now, and I don't want to impose on you. I want to do this myself, and I can't afford even half the rent at either of your places. I'm not a charity case, OK?"

"That's fair enough." She raises the bottle of wine that she somehow managed to uncork that fast. "To new beginnings." We pass the bottle around, reveling in the pure randomness of the moment.

After we've finished off the wine and performed a full fashion show with every possible outfit combination in my closet, complete with notes and instructions from Gwen about what combos are absolute "fire," I walk the girls out.

Maggie gives me a giant hug. "Please tell us everything as soon as you get off tomorrow."

"I'm proud of you, sis." Gwen kisses me on the cheek, and I am so thankful to have such supportive friends, especially since that's not something I can expect from my parents. When I called to tell them about the job, my mom barely let me finish talking before she told me about her friend Sherry's new grandbaby.

"I love you both. I promise to text as soon as I leave from work tomorrow!" I close the door behind them and am careful to lock up. Destiny seems to have exhausted herself and is already in bed. I'd say from the short scene I witnessed, she ought to be tired.

I take a quick cold shower and snuggle into my bed, haunted by dreams of giant swinging ball sacks all night long.

# EIGHT

Elliot

The buzzing of my alarm clock jolts me awake. It's five a.m. Before I can think about what I'm doing, I leap from the bed and throw on my running gear. I'm determined to take this lucky break and make the most of it, and since my nerves kept me awake most of the night, I need to take the edge off with some running endorphins. Careful not to make too much noise and spook Destiny and her overnight guest—the last thing my eyes need is an anatomy lesson this early in the day—I grab my sneakers and tiptoe out the door.

The cool fall air has a bite this morning as the wind whips my ponytail into my face. I pull out my headphones and turn on my Boosie playlist. Maggie would have a fit if she heard just how loud my music blares in my eardrums, but I've got to get this energy out, and listening to angry rap music while my feet pound the pavement is the only cure.

After a solid ten miles are in the books, I'm feeling I'm like a champion, like I can conquer anything this day is going to throw at me. I take the stairs two at a time and make a beeline to the coffee pot to pour a generous cup of glorious black brew into my favorite hand-thrown coffee mug. I carry my overfilled steamy mug back to my bedroom to start my morning routine before I begin my beauty regimen. I pull out my journal and make a quick list of the top five things I'm grateful for.

1. *A good night's sleep*
2. *First day at my new job*
3. *Coffee is the perfect strength and temperature*
4. *Destiny and company weren't nude in the common area*
5. *Peanut butter pumpkin spice breakfast muffin I saved from brunch for a delicious breakfast*

After I make my list, I chug the rest of my coffee and head to the bathroom for a quick pick-me-up shower to start the day. I take my time getting ready and follow Gwen's direct orders and dress in the outfit she preselected. I stick to my old faithful orange-red lip stain and meticulously apply, blot, and touch up. Since this lip stain has passed the test of face smashing into a white shirt, I know there are limitations to its survival, but I don't plan on repeating those activities anytime soon. I grab my muffin and my keys and I'm out the door.

At least my car was on her best behavior this morning; she opened her doors and allowed her engine to crank on the first try. I take this as a good omen. My commute isn't too bad, with minimal left turns. Beyoncé sings about being drunk and in love and I'm so captivated by the emotion that I forget all about my pre-first day of work jitters.

By the time I've reached the building, the song ends and my favorite Cardi B song starts playing, giving me a second wave of adrenaline. I've been told my taste in music is eccentric, and I pride myself on knowing every single word to this song. I decide since I'm early anyway, I'll finish this track with the proper respect it deserves.

I find a spot in the back of the parking lot so I don't disturb anyone around me and let myself get lost in the song. Cardi gets me, and as I sing along, completely captivated by the beat, I fail to realize that another vehicle has joined me in the back of the parking lot, until I look up and make eye contact with a handsome man in a black truck. I have no idea how long he's been there, but from the size of his eyes, I imagine he just saw my last little number where I grabbed my boobs as I belted out the chorus.

Once I realize I've been spotted, I do the only thing I can think of; I reach down the side of my seat and pull the lever to throw it back so he can't see me. Sure, it's not the most mature solution to my problem but I'm afraid that I may die of embarrassment if I have to make eye contact with the beautiful man again. Hiding out like an ostrich with my head in the sand seems to be my only logical response.

After ten minutes pass, I slowly pull the seat back up into a sitting position and regain my composure.

I snake my neck around, checking to see if the coast is clear and shake out my nerves. If the worst thing that happens today is a handsome stranger catching me singing, then I'll call that a win. Steadying my gaze, I step out of my beat up vehicle and head towards my future. I breathe in the fresh, brisk air that smells like a new beginning.

POW! is a sight to behold. I knew the two companies merged and they moved into a new building, but I had no idea how posh of a space I'd be working in. The building is lined from floor-to-ceiling in glass walls that showcase the beautiful Chicago city views. As I reach to open the door, nothing happens. It appears that the door is locked. I look around and see people filing in everywhere. A woman wearing a white oversized man's shirt tucked in sloppily with khaki pants and Dr. Martens approaches me from behind. Her hair is cropped short and she's got a giant FBI-looking badge hung across her neck.

"Excuse me, miss, I don't believe you have access to this building."

"Oh, that's because it's my first day." I point toward the reception desk. "I just need to check in and I'm sure they'll be able to sort everything out."

She lifts her eyebrows, studying me. "Is that so? Your first day?"

"Yes, ma'am." I stutter nervously.

"What's your job, then, sweetie?" she says, her fake high-pitched voice oozing mockery. She leans in closer so that our noses almost touch.

"I'm Mr. Powell's new assistant. He hired me Friday at lunch. We went to a nice little deli just down the street, and he ordered me a salad even though I was starving and—"

"That's the most ridiculous thing I've ever heard. I knew it. 'If you can just get inside.' Marvin from the Safety Commission sent you, didn't he?"

"No... I..."

"Geez, you could at least *try* to look convincing." She eyes me. "I'll tell you this, sweet cheeks, the name's CJ Montgomery, and I'm the head of the safety committee in this building. Absolutely no one is permitted to enter without a badge. So little miss red lips, do you have a badge?" She dramatically holds her hand by her ear, waiting on my reply.

"No, because today's my first day and—"

"That's just what I thought. Go ahead and be on your way.

You can tell Marvin he can suck on a big one for trying to pull some fast shit on me."

I'm about to accept defeat and retreat with my tail between my legs but something stirs within me. Call it stupidity, call it desperation, but this job has the potential to change my shitty living situation and I'm not leaving here because of a misunderstanding with this mall cop wannabe.

I dig my heels into the ground. "I work here. I had an interview with Thad Powell last week and he hired me. I am not leaving here until you call him and ask him yourself!"

CJ's eyes widen and even I'm shocked by my boldness. She pulls her cell phone out of her pocket when the receptionist comes rushing toward us.

"Jesus, CJ. How many times have I told you not to interrogate the visitors? Let her through to the front desk before you break out your Rex Kwon Do moves on the poor girl." She turns to me. "I'm so sorry about CJ. She means well. I'm Eliza." She reaches out her hand to shake mine and then pulls me by the arm, removing me from the possible threat of the safety officer. "Let's just say she takes her committee roles a little too seriously sometimes."

CJ brushes off invisible dust from her shirt. "I will not apologize for taking your and everyone in this building's safety seriously. Let me ask you this, Elliot. Do you smoke?"

"Um. No, ma'am," I answer, unsure where this is going.

"Good, because there are approximately five hundred fires a year that occur from the ember of a cigarette. Fire safety is no joking matter! Now quickly, what are the first three things you do if you notice a fire in the workplace?"

"Um. Stop, drop, and roll?" I stutter.

"Wrong! That's only if you are actually on fire. In this office, I serve as fire marshal as well as chief safety officer and we take these things very seriously. The order of operations when you suspect a fire is–" she counts off on her fingers– "one: call me immediately; two: call 9-1-1; three: blow your emergency fire whistle that you will keep attached to your badge at all times! Understood?" she yells.

"Of course." Now I'm really scared because I'm pretty sure there's no way I'll ever be able to remember those rules if I were in an actual fire emergency.

"Don't worry, we'll go over procedure later. I've just added a choreographed dance to help you remember the motions and the jingle, of course." She turns and runs toward the stairwell in a full sprint.

"Yes," Eliza answers without my asking. "She's always like that. She doesn't believe elevators are safe, so she runs up the twenty stories to her office twice a day. Come on, I'll get you signed in. Are you here to visit someone?"

"No, actually, I work here... today's my first day."

"Gotcha. I just need to see some ID. And then I'll show you to your desk."

I dig through my purse and pull out my ID. Eliza takes it and types my information into the computer system and scans a copy and then pauses. "So you're Mr. Powell's new assistant?" She glances up with a concerned expression. "Well, welcome aboard. I've not been here in the new building very long, but I can say that working for Benjamin has been a wonderful experience."

She leads me to the elevator. "Right this way, Elliot."

I follow her in and just as the doors are about to close, a hand reaches through, causing them to open again. I could never trust my appendage with an elevator door. In college, we had an elevator that had a broken sensor and if you weren't quick enough, you'd get chopped.

A tall, handsome man walks in to greet us. "Good morning, Eliza. How's Mr. Fuzzybottoms?"

"Good morning, Benjamin. He's feeling much better, thank you. The vet said the nerf dart came out easily."

"Who's this? Are you here visiting someone?"

His whiskey eyes meet mine and I'm instantly taken aback. I've seen those eyes before, and this pleasant, handsome man feels so familiar. I see the realization on his face as he seems to have made the connection too, as I remember his eyes staring me down over his steering wheel in the parking lot and the feel of his impressive chest like stone under my smooshed face at the bar.

Benjamin furrows his brow.

"I'm Mr. Powell's new assistant, Elliot." I hold my hand out to shake his, but he doesn't reciprocate.

Instead, he pulls out his phone and angry types on his screen. All the warm fuzzies about this man that I just felt are gone and he's back to his grumpy stone-like version that I ran into at the bar. Eliza's eyes go wide at his sudden change in demeanor and mouths, "I'm so sorry." I shake my head like it's not a big deal, but I'm cringing internally at the uncomfortableness of it all.

"I fucking told him not to hire anyone else," he not-so-quietly mutters under his breath. Without giving me another glance, we ride up to the twentieth floor in silence.

---

"Mr. Powell, I have Miss James here to see you," Eliza says, breaking Thad from his trance. He's sitting at an enormous desk surrounded by stacks and stacks of paper. When he sees me in the doorway, he slaps his hands together. He runs his eyes up the length of my body, slowly taking in every inch of me. Even though I'm fully clothed and dressed modestly, I feel my skin warm at his glare as if I'm standing before him in my underwear.

"Elliot, it's so good to see you again." He stands to greet me and takes my coat, hanging it on the coatrack by the door. Placing his hand on the small of my back, he leads me toward a small glass desk in the corner of his office. "This is your new space. I'm sorry it's not much, but my office isn't big enough to accommodate a larger desk. You'll be working closely with me, so I thought sharing a space made the most sense. I hope you don't mind."

"Not at all." I force out a grin and once again push my intuition aside.

"Good, why don't you get settled. We have a meeting in about thirty minutes."

I take a seat at my desk and pull out my IT paperwork to begin setting up my laptop. My rumbling stomach reminds me that I forgot to eat my breakfast, so I pull the peanut butter pumpkin spice muffin out of my purse and inhale it while I have a free moment. As I'm stuffing my face, I see Benjamin talking to Thad in the hallway.

"Dammit, Thad, could you be any more obvious? I'll just be in my office looking for new revenue opportunities since you can't seem to control your urges." Our eyes make contact through the crack in the door and a rush of embarrassment courses through me.

*What did he mean by 'you can't seem to control your urges'?*

---

The conference room is full of powerful-looking men in silk ties, pocket squares, and matching vests. Why so many layers? Is there some kind of fashion formula to follow when you're rich? The head of each department sits around the long conference table and there's a giant screen for connecting to their computers. The screen alone probably costs more than my car. Thad and I take the last two seats at the head of the table.

"Thank you all for being here on time," Thad says.

I can't believe I'm sitting in a boardroom with the two leaders of this giant agency, surrounded by VPs and directors alike. I do my best to put on my most professional face, listening intently as each person reports to their respective departments. Benjamin is all business and doesn't seem the least bit fazed by Thad; he fires away questions about productivity, numbers, and performance projections for the next quarter.

A scrawny man with black-rimmed bifocals plugs into the screen. "We've been presented with the challenge of expanding our services and I've got the next big idea! Take a look at this." He passes around a stack of papers for everyone to examine for a product called Imposter Chicken. The papers make their way toward me and I take them from the man to my left. I see a breakdown of investment costs across different markets.

My fingers brush over the papers and I notice the residue from my peanut butter pumpkin spice muffin has adhered to the bottom of the page. I groan, thinking how disgusting that is. These fingernails may look nice, but they are a breeding ground for bacteria. Just then Thad snatches the papers out of my hand and licks his thumb to flip through the pages.

"Let's have a look then." He's flipping through the pages one minute and suddenly his breath hitches and his voice cracks. I pull my gaze up and see his face turning red. His eyes look like they're going to bulge out of their sockets, and he croaks out a gurgle. Gasping, he makes the sign for choking before falling backward in his chair.

The room is in chaos but all I can do is stare at him. People are screaming and running to get help; papers are flying in the air. I glance at Benjamin in shock, and he yells, "Did you eat peanut butter this morning? He's deathly allergic to peanuts!"

"No, I don't think I did." But then it dawns on me that my muffin had peanut butter in it. The residue under my fingernails must've gotten in his mouth when he licked his finger.

Thad is convulsing and gurgling on the ground, and just as I reach to see if he's wearing an EpiPen, I see Mrs. Montgomery running full speed like a linebacker, taking down anything and everything that crosses her path. She is on the complete opposite side of the office and is heading our way in a full-on sprint. The door bursts open and she screams, "Everyone stay calm! Everything is under control! I'm the fire marshal and I've trained for this the moment I learned that Thad had the peanut allergy!" She leaps from the doorway and slides across the table like a ninja, reaches into the holster attached to her thigh, and brings the EpiPen above her head.

"Stand back!" she commands.

I jump backward, colliding with Benjamin just as CJ stabs the needle into Thad's thigh.

"Thad, can you hear me?" she asks. "You are going into anaphylactic shock; I'm going to perform CPR now!"

She begins chest compressions and breathes deeply into Thad's mouth every thirty compressions. After a moment his body stops convulsing and he appears to regain consciousness.

Thad lifts his sweat-drenched head and looks right at me. "You did this to me!"

Luckily someone had the foresight to actually call 911 despite the impressive CPR skills from CJ. The paramedics arrive with the gurney and strap Thad in before carrying him out to the ambulance.

Of course, Mrs. Montgomery insists on riding with him

despite his protests. "Thad, I'm not taking no for an answer! You are under my watch until we reach the hospital!"

I watch as the crew carries him to the elevator, Mrs. Montgomery closely on their heels. My eyes well with tears, and I look up at Benjamin who's wearing a look of disgust.

"Thad really knows how to pick them. You may need to lose a few of the buttons on your top so he doesn't fire you as soon as he's out of the hospital, but that's how you got the job in the first place, isn't it?"

My body burns with shame and I feel as if I've been body-slammed into a bed of hot coals. Just when I thought I couldn't be more of a screwup, I send my boss into anaphylactic shock all because I was pretending to be something I'm not. I sag my head and walk out of the office in defeat.

# NINE

Benjamin

"Hand down, man down." Sam shoots over Jack's head, sinking the shot straight in the net.

"Oh, you got jokes? Well, how about this?" Jack dives for the rebound and attempts to hustle down the court for a layup, but trips over his shoelace and falls flat on his face, skidding another three feet. The screech of his body dragging across the gym floor pierces my ears; he's going to have a hell of a strawberry or two tomorrow.

I make my way over to the drama king and offer my hand to help him up. "Come on, Larry Bird, we've still got about ten minutes of playtime before they give the gym to the badminton club."

"I'm sorry, did you not see me wipe out there? I need to lie here and make sure there are no deeper injuries. The shock hasn't had time to wear off yet, and my adrenaline surge could be interfering with my pain tolerance." He assesses his ankles and wrists for any breaks or tears. Jack's sport is soccer, not basketball, hence the theatrics of falling and milking it for all it's worth.

He cuts his eyes toward Sam. "That was a foul, so once I recover from my spill, I'll be happy to take my free throws."

"Dude, I wasn't anywhere near you! You can thank your crazy chicken dribbling for this spill, not me!" Sam dribbles the ball between his feet, passing it back and forth, then spins it on his finger. I'm the basketball guy in the group, and though Sam is athletic enough to hold his own, he prefers his exercise in the form of rock climbing. He climbs competitively with his rock climbing gym and is ranked in the top ten in the nation.

"OK, children, you both begged me to play tonight so I suggest you—" I point to Jack— "get up and get back to it. The clock is ticking."

My threat worked; playing the guilt-trip card always works with these goofballs. Jack jumps up from his lying position and bolts toward me, trying to steal the ball I'm slowly dribbling. I see where he's going with this, so I fake him out like I'm passing to Sam. As he bolts to the side, I race to the hoop for a layup.

"Hey! You could've further injured my ankle!" Jack calls down the court. "What about my free throws anyway?"

———

"Dude, you can't just tell us the hot chick you ran into at the bar that night now works with you and not elaborate!" Jack takes a huge bite of his BLT, barely chewing what's in his mouth before continuing. "I mean, what's her job, have you hidden out in the supply closet and made out yet? I need details!"

"OK, details, let me think." I scratch my face, taking a full minute before I drop this bomb. "She's Thad's new assistant that I told him not to hire. She also ate some kind of peanut butter baked good before the meeting..."

Sam's eyes go wide. Once during my engagement with Sarah, Thad offered to throw me a bachelor party. I adamantly resisted because that's not my speed but always looking for an excuse to party, he planned a night at the strip club anyway. Jack was traveling so Sam was my only invite. Thad, on the other hand, showed up with his boys in tow, ready to party until one of the strippers allegedly went down on him in a backroom after eating a PB&J before her shift. Much like today, firemen and EMTs showed up to haul him off-site, only his dick took on most of the swelling since it didn't get in his mouth. He later sued them, and the club shut down because of it.

"What does that have to do with anything?" Jack chimes in.

Sam leans forward, biting his knuckle. "Please tell me he went into anaphylactic shock. Please, oh please."

"He went into anaphylactic shock. I'm talking body spasms, choking-almost-died allergic reaction. If CJ wouldn't have rushed in with her emergency EpiPen, I think he may have died... which would be tragic, but half of my problems would have been solved." I take a sip of my coffee, letting the hot liquid soothe me from within as I'm reminded of my unfortunate circumstances.

"Oh, CJ. Is it crazy that I actually miss her sometimes?" Sam grins. "Remember that time she caught that new hire smoking in the bathroom while he was taking a shit?" He doubles over laughing. "She thought there was a fire because she smelled smoke and rushed in with the fire extinguisher and coated his ass from head to toe."

Jack joins in. "Or the time we had someone come to clean the exterior windows to the building and she thought it was an active jumper situation. She had her megaphone and made us all go outside to discourage him from jumping while she climbed through the window to grab him."

Now we're all laughing about the crazy memories we made

when my company was in its early years and these two knuckleheads stood by my side and helped me build it to what it is today... or at least what it was before I was blackmailed into my current situation. Now I spend my workdays doing the grunt work and babysitting Thad, trying to counteract his spending habits.

"Yeah, as obnoxious as CJ can be, it wouldn't be the same without her. She even rode in the ambulance with him, trying to continue mouth-to-mouth up until the paramedic told her it was no longer necessary."

"Well, I think she deserves an award. You've got yourself a modern-day hero on your hands," Sam says before taking a gulp of his milkshake. "Ahhh, brain freeze!"

Jack places a gentle hand on Sam's shoulder as if to soothe him, then leans in to whisper, "That's what you get for laughing at me when I fell.."

Sam slaps Jack's hand away. "So what are you going to do about the hot girl? You're not going to fire her, are you?"

I sigh and lean my face into my hands. "I'd be lying if the thought hasn't crossed my mind. Sure, she's hot, but the way Thad's spending money like we're printing it is going to catch up to us real soon. She can't be old enough to have any real work experience, not to mention Thad doesn't do any work to need an assistant. If anything, I could use the help since Jennifer has to take time off for her husband's back surgery."

"Oooh, you should make her your assistant so you can say that you're fucking your assistant! That's some bucket list shit, man!"

"I'm not going to sleep with her." I send them both a warning glance. "Besides, I get my needs met; all I have to do is open an app and choose what flavor I want for the week. This girl's different, she's wholesome." My words drift as I envision her. There's something about Elliot James that drives me crazy with a mixture of anger and lust like pouring salt on an open wound. She's so awkward and funny; it's like the light she radiates aggravates my darkness, and I can't stand to be around her.

"We're not saying you should marry her, but if the attraction is there, why not have a little fun? Maybe she could even get you to smile or something crazy like that," Jack says as if it's not a huge moral issue to sleep with my employee.

"I said she's hot, but that doesn't mean I want to sleep with her. Thad has his reasons, which are probably her hot body and great tits."

Sam chimes in, placing his hand on my shoulder. "I hate to say this to you, brother, but Sarah's not coming back. You don't have to torture yourself."

"Actually, I kind of fucking do. Besides, the poor girl is better off meeting someone capable of treating her well, not a selfish asshole like me, even if it's just for a lay." My mind drifts back to Sarah. She was the light of my life, but her light was somehow different than Elliot's. Sarah was ambitious, driven to the point where I sometimes had to remind her of what was important. She had a chip on her shoulder to prove her family wrong; she'd be sick to know what they've done to get back at me. Wouldn't she?

I bury my face into my hands, more confused than ever. Fuck, why couldn't it have been me? Why couldn't I have died in the wreck?

"Sorry, dude, I don't mean to be insensitive." Sam's apology breaks me free from the familiar bargaining of my grief that I can't seem to shake.

Jack slaps me on the shoulder, offering me comfort. "We miss her too."

"The good news—" I change the subject so I don't break down in this diner— "is that after Thad's reaction, he has to stay home for the rest of the week to recover from the muscle spasms. The bad news is I'll have to give Elliot work to do and help train her on the project management systems, so she'll be able to keep Thad in line when he gets back."

Jack wiggles his eyebrows at me. "You're totally going to fuck her in the supply closet. I'm calling it now."

———

"Good morning, Benjamin!" Eliza's cheerful voice greets me as I enter the office. It's moments like these when I arrive before everyone else that I'm nostalgic about the good ol' days when the company was just a group of friends working our asses off to gain momentum.

"Good morning, Eliza." I take a cautious sip of coffee from my steaming travel mug as I head straight toward the elevator. I've decided to start my day an hour early to catch up on Thad's current projects and to find my bearings with the new assistant's responsibilities. After Thad's emergency departure, there wasn't much work for Elliot to do, and if I'm going to be employing someone, you better believe I'll find some work for her, even if it's just sorting emails. It dawns on me that I still have no idea of this woman's supposed skill set. And I'll need to find her application and résumé in the system, assuming Thad followed the proper hiring procedures.

The elevator pings, announcing its arrival on the twentieth floor. I step into the hallway and make my way straight to my office, still nursing my too-hot coffee. I come to an abrupt halt at the sight of the sexiest legs in printed black stockings. Elliot's bent over my desk, searching through papers, completely unaware that her ass is giving me the show of a lifetime.

"Can I help you with something?" My voice is breathless

from the surprising sight before me and comes out a little more accusing than I intended.

"Cheese and crackers!" The stack of papers she was holding go flying through the air. "Benjamin, oh my God, I'm so sorry!" The papers fall around her and we're both left awkwardly staring at one another. I don't feel like I should have to ask what she was doing meddling through my office, so I wait.

"I was just... I wanted to get a head start on the day and since Mr. Powell is out, um, sick, I thought if I could find the paper that we referenced in the meeting..." Her voice trails off.

I walk over to my desk and take a seat, trying to reorganize the mess of papers strewn across the top. "Yes, well, while I admire your enthusiasm, I'd appreciate it if you didn't rummage around my things while I'm not here. Honestly, I feel like this is pretty basic business practice. I don't know what bar Thad found you in, but this is the real world. This company is my life's work."

She stands slack-jawed in the doorway and I notice the dark circles under her eyes, and I wonder if she didn't get much sleep. She's probably still upset about yesterday's events. Her lips quiver as she tries to hold her resolve, and she discreetly rubs a stray tear with the back of her hand. Her moment of weakness pierces my hardened heart and I can't help myself.

"If you're looking for more work to do, I could use some help inputting the data from the Grouper account."

"Yes. I'd love to!" she says with newfound excitement as she rushes toward the door. "I promise, Benjamin, I won't let you down! Oh, and I'll never come in your office ever again unless I'm specifically invited!" She rushes down the hall toward her workstation, leaving me wondering where on earth Thad Powell found someone so refreshing.

# TEN

Elliot

"Good morning, Eliza." I hand her the piping hot coffee I brewed at home along with the gluten-free, nut-free, and egg-free muffin that I've been perfecting over the last several weeks. After Mr. Powell's near-death experience, I'm taking no chances. I was lucky to make it out with my job after almost killing my boss on my first day.

"Thank you, Elliot!" Eliza hesitantly takes the offering, placing the muffin to the side. "You are too sweet. You know you don't have to bring me coffee every morning."

"You have to be here an hour before everyone else, I feel like it's the least I can do." I wave goodbye, hoping she doesn't crack a tooth on my new muffin recipe, and head up to face the music. Mr. Powell's been a little distant since his return from his traumatic hospital stay. I can't say that I blame him, but it's made working from his office quite awkward. If Jennifer, Benjamin's assistant, wouldn't have taken pity on me, I don't know if I would've been able to show up after the incident.

Luckily, I've had plenty to work on between Jennifer showing me the ropes in preparation for her FMLA leave that goes into effect today. After learning the various client groups, I feel like I'm finally starting to find my footing. I've taken Benjamin's spreadsheet and fluffed it up a bit, mainly just because I was bored. But I think we can save some of the time spent running reports day in and day out. I've just got to find the right moment to bring it up.

"Elliot, just the woman I was looking for!" I startle at the sound of Mr. Powell's voice echoing through the hallway, spilling my piping hot coffee all over the front of my nicest white blouse.

I muffle the curse, baring my teeth into the knuckles on my free hand. "Mr. Powell, I'm so sorry, I didn't see you there. Here, let me find a towel." I turn toward the bathroom when I feel a gentle heat warming my back.

"Don't apologize when you did nothing wrong." The deep sound of Benjamin's voice turns my insides to liquid as his broad chest grazes my arm. How is it possible to go from complete and utter panic to aroused in five seconds? This man is the most intense person I've ever met. He never smiles, but there's something about him that calls to me. It's like an electric current between us whenever he's near, though, no doubt, it's only on my end.

"Oh, sorry, I just hate causing a scene." I try to brush him off but his glare stills me in place.

"You did it again." He doesn't move, standing like a mountain between me and the bathroom door. Having stare-downs outside bathrooms seems to be a growing trend between us.

"Sorry, I..." I stop myself, biting hard on my bottom lip. "I mean. I'm *not* sorry. I revoke that apology and the one before it. Now if you will excuse me, I'd like to wipe off the coffee before it ruins my shoes." I point to my chest at the saturated top, trying desperately to catch all the drips as they fall.

Benjamin's face blushes a deep red as he steps to the side. "I... um... I'm sorry."

The irony of his apology is not lost on me as I burst through the bathroom door to assess myself, checking for a rogue booger or some other embarrassing oversight. Suddenly his blush makes so much more sense, my button-up white oxford shirt is completely translucent from the spilled coffee, giving Benjamin the perfect view of my black lace bra, the one without any padding, nipples on full display. I think I just flashed my boss.

---

Neither Gwen nor Maggie could bring me a new shirt and it's not even lunchtime yet, so I'm stuck here, burning up, wearing my parka to conceal my bosoms. A thin sheen of sweat forms on my brow, and I wipe it away with the back of my sleeve. It seems the office is especially warm today.

A thick stack of papers falls on my desk, fanning me with a delicious gust of recycled air.

"I'll need you to input this data before the three o'clock meeting today." Mr. Powell peers down at me, looking disgusted by my sweaty, bedraggled appearance. "Are you sure you don't have another shirt you can change into? I'll expect you in the quarterly meeting to take notes. I'd hate for our partners to get a bad impression of the staff here at POW!.

"No, sir, but I'll button my jacket up the rest of the way once the meeting starts. Until then, do you think we could turn the heat down just a hair?"

He turns with a grunt and I take the dismissal as a no. I pick up the giant stack of papers and hope that if I skip lunch, I'll have this done by the afternoon meeting.

"Thank you all for coming to our second quarterly planning meeting." Thad takes a seat clear across the room, leaving me to squeeze in between someone who loves onions and another who's sweating so profusely he brought a hand towel to the meeting. Meanwhile, I've adjusted to my new warmer body temperature and have stopped sweating like I'm in spin class. If I'm being honest, I think Eliza took pity on me and adjusted the thermostat.

"Hey, pretty lady, why don't you take off your coat and stay awhile?" The man sitting next to Thad chuckles and I realize since I'm the only woman in the room, and also happen to be wearing a parka, he must be talking to me.

My eyes pan between the older man and Thad and the resemblance is striking; surely he is Thad's father, but why would he care about this quarterly meeting? "I've had a bit of a chill all morning, and I'm comfortable bundled up. Don't mind me." I shuffle the papers nervously and pull out my laptop, ready to take notes on behalf of Mr. Powell.

Benjamin's down-to-business voice booms over the boardroom. "Why don't we get to work, considering these meetings tend to get off track and I've got somewhere to be at five thirty."

My eyes go wide at his slip of personal information. Benjamin never converses with the staff and it's the first time I've heard him speak about anything regarding his personal life. It's probably a date. He's got a date with a beautiful, leggy supermodel.

Thad playfully punches Benjamin's shoulder. "Got yourself a hot date tonight, Benji?"

"No, Thad, not that it's any of your business, but I would

like to get back to the topic on hand. Carl, do you have any updates for D87?"

The abrupt change in conversation startles Carl. As he shuffles papers around, I see a bead of sweat slide down his forehead.

"Yes, sir, if you remember the product we talked about at the last meeting. The one where, er, Mr. Powell—"

"Almost died from anaphylactic shock," Thad interrupts. "Yes, I believe we all remember that day. Please continue." He throws himself back in his chair, crossing his arms over his chest.

"The Imposter Chicken Bar has the potential to be the next craze in vegan food culture, and we've just closed the deal with product development." Carl points the clicker to the big screen hanging on the wall, bringing up a poorly-executed bar chart of customer demographics. "If you look here, there's been a steady increase in vegan diets in millennials, and the trend is projected to increase by five percent in the next year. We've partnered with the development team to create a protein bar that looks, tastes, and smells like chicken."

Carl grabs the large cardboard box from the corner of the room and begins passing out Imposter Chicken Bars to everyone in the room.

Thad catches his bar but pushes it toward his father rather than opening it. "I think I've had my fill of dubious foods from coworkers during meetings."

A warm flush spreads over my face and brings my body temperature higher. I know I deserve the dig but it will be nice when I'm not known for being the new hire that almost killed her boss on her first day. My internal body temperature is steadily rising and I wipe the sweat from my brow before I start to look like Carl sweating through this presentation.

Benjamin notices my not-so-subtle sweat-swipe and slaps his hand down on the table. "For the love of God, please take off the fucking parka. I'm getting hot just looking at you and no one cares if you have a coffee stain on your shirt!"

I flinch at his sharp tone but oblige since, yes, I am burning up and my shirt is no longer see-through since the coffee dried. I figure I've already experienced my worst-case scenario in this room, so I don't have anything else to lose.

"Now that I don't have to witness Elliot have a heat stroke, Carl, would you please continue."

Carl proceeds to give us details about the product, its ingredients, and the estimated launch date six weeks away.

"We expect great success with this product. I believe that if we can target our ideal demographic, we'll change the game in the health food industry." Carl stills his trembling hands and takes a seat, seemingly relieved to have the presentation behind him.

"How do we expect to find our ideal market? Carl, don't you think you should've covered that in your presentation?" Thad says in a patronizing tone.

"We've had a little trouble on the marketing side of things. As you know, we had a lot of layoffs in the marketing department since the merger. Unfortunately, our team hasn't had the bandwidth to begin developing the campaign," Carl mutters.

So that's why he's been so nervous during this presentation. He knew Thad was going to grill him about not being able to deliver the whole picture. Immediately the wheels in my head start spinning, thinking of all the ways we could make this work.

"It's all right, Carl, we've got a team of experts in this room; I'm sure we can come up with a decent marketing plan to get the ball rolling." Benjamin's voice is gentle like I've only witnessed when he's talking to his old staff.

"What if we run a TV spot on the Food Network?" a man in the back corner suggests.

"We could approach the big health food chains directly," another man adds. "I've got a contact at Whole Foods. I could make a few calls,"

Before I know what I'm doing, I pipe in with an idea. "What about using Instagram influencers to build up the hype? You could spread the word with influencers to build product awareness before you approach the big health food stores?" I say it like it's a question, but the reality is that I've done extensive research in the influencer industry, and I think this product is just niche enough that it might take off.

I see the shock register on Thad's face. Whether it's from what I said or that I dared to speak up in a meeting, I don't know. Maybe it's a little bit of both. "That's an idea." He pauses. "Why don't we let the professionals come up with the ideas and you can just stick to the note-taking."

His words slap me in the chest, bringing back the familiar pang of guilt for sharing. It was stupid to say anything; what was I thinking of speaking in a meeting when I've been here for all of five minutes in comparison to all these Ivy League-educated middle-aged men?

"Elliot, I'd like to hear more about your idea." Benjamin surprises me with his genuinely excited-sounding tone.

"Well, studies show that millennials aren't influenced by traditional advertising like our parents were. We've evolved. Word-of-mouth advertising is still the best route to make a sale. Customers are more dependent than ever on testimonials and reviews." I pause, unsure if they all think this background information has any relevance to the topic at hand. "Working with influencers who serve your ideal customers is the fast-track way to getting those reviews and getting the product in people's hands."

You could hear a pin drop in this room as the group stares at me slack-jawed, some clearly flummoxed by what I've just said, some looking bored, but mostly they seem…impressed.

"Elliot, I'd like you to do some research on these *influencers* and give me a marketing plan with a six-week trajectory." Benjamin leans forward, pinning me with his intense stare that makes me feel like he can read my mind. "I'll expect the marketing plan on my desk by the end of the day Friday. If you manage to pull this off, I may just find room in the budget to keep you on staff." He pushes away from the table and gathers his things. "Now if you'll excuse me, gentlemen, I've got somewhere to be."

Everyone begins to file out after him, and I'm left sitting like a stunned idiot. I can't decide if I've been offered a promotion or just had my job threatened if I can't deliver. I guess it's a little bit of both.

I bite my cheek to stifle a scream and wipe the wild tears that fall from my eyes. I have the most delicious sensation of fear and excitement at war in my gut, giving me that all-too-familiar feeling of my back against the wall, and I love it. This can mean only one thing; it's time to get scrappy.

I pull out my phone and send an SOS to the girls.

> My place tonight. I've got a work opportunity and I need to collab.

GWEN

> Do you have wine or should I bring some?

MAGGIE

> I'll grab the Chinese food

GWEN

> Then it's a white wine party

> NOT a party! This is a work brainstorming session

GWEN

I do my best brainstorming after 2 glasses of wine...

MAGGIE

I'll bring the charcoal pills

That's not necessary. I'll see you tonight

GWEN

Can't wait

# ELEVEN

Benjamin

"Benjamin! Benjamin!" The nasal voice pierces my ears through my phone's intercom.

"What is it, Thad? I told you I need to be left alone if you want me to have this contract completed by noon." Thad's neediness has come to an all-time high over the last few weeks. It's apparent that he has no idea what he's doing, and since I've banned him from spending any more of our corporate dollars on galas or business trips, he's going stir-crazy trying to play CEO.

"I need you to help me with this spreadsheet; the formula you showed me last week isn't working. I think my Excel is broken."

I roll my eyes and get up from behind my desk, moving the stacks of paperwork I have yet to even crack open. It seems like my entire day consists of trying to keep this business above water, while simultaneously babysitting a toddler who's incapable of taking care of himself.

I barge into his office, with no qualms of knocking and am

surprised to find Elliot standing on his desk trying to, what seems like, dust the air vent with an extra-long Swiffer. There is no hiding the fact that Thad is enjoying himself as he sits just below her with the perfect view underneath her dress.

"What's going on here? Why do you have Elliot dusting your air vent?"

He startles at my question and shrugs. "I've had a tickle in my throat all week and when I looked up and noticed how dirty the vent was, I asked Elliot if she could clean it for me. You know I'm allergic to dust mites, and well, after the whole peanut butter debacle, Elliot didn't want to wait to get rid of the dust. Benjamin, I think we've got ourselves a potential employee of the month on our hands." He gives me a disgusting wink as if I'm his perverted co-boss teammate or something.

"Elliot, get down from the fucking desk before you break your neck and we have a workman's comp claim to deal with. This office would implode if I wasn't here to keep you both from trying to kill each other, or yourselves." I throw Elliot my best look of disgust, hopefully discouraging her from putting her safety at risk again for something as dumb as Thad's made-up dust mite allergy.

"Benjamin, I would never sue the company for anything like that. I just wanted to make sure Thad was safe and he didn't want to get any closer to the dust than was necessary. You know, because of the allergy." She rubs her hands down the length of her dress and I can see the discomfort written all over her face.

"Why don't you get back to work and I'll call maintenance to clean the vents while you and Mr. Powell are away for lunch?" My softer tone seems to relax her, and she takes a seat at her tiny desk behind her puny laptop—we've got to get her a better setup if she's going to continue working here. I make a mental note to talk to CJ about getting Elliot a real workstation set up, something outside of Thad's office.

I step around his desk to get a closer look at his triple monitor setup. "Now, what was so urgent that you needed me to leave the Henely contract?"

"See here, when I click on this cell, it's not pulling the data in this column like it is in this one."

"Are you using absolute reference? The formula won't work if you drag it down like that unless you use absolute reference." I take his mouse from his hand and remedy his issue with a few strokes of the keyboard.

"That's what I tried to tell him last week."

Elliot's retort surprises me and her as well because she starts backtracking. "I mean, I probably didn't explain it correctly, and Thad didn't understand what I said. I mean, you know what. I'm not even sure that's what it was. I was probably confused." She freezes in her seat, and our eyes meet. I stare her down, waiting for the next piece of the puzzle to fall into place. *Come on, surprise me again.*

"I'm sorry. I really shouldn't be eavesdropping. I'll stop talking now." She grabs for her headphones that are slightly too large for her head and attempts to zone back out into her email.

"What the hell is going on with you, Thad? You can't have some tiny woman standing on your desk to clean the air vents. Don't think I'm not onto you; I know what you're doing." I say the last part in a whisper, hoping she can't hear over whatever she's listening to on those ridiculous-looking headphones.

Thad's devilish grin crinkles the skin around his eyes. "I don't know what you're talking about, Benjamin. I assure you I have zero ulterior motives with Elliot." He rubs his carefully-manscaped beard as if he's deciding if what he's about to say is a good idea. "I'm growing rather fond of having Elliot around here; I hope we can find it in the budget to keep her on staff full-time. She's kept up with my appointments better than any assistant ever has before, though I have to say, those legs are doing terrible things to my self-control." He brings his voice to a whisper and leans in closer. "Today the red thong pushed me over the edge...if you know what I mean." He backs up and gives me a wink. "Look at that, Benjamin, I don't know what I'd do without you around here to fix my computer glitches. Now if you'd excuse me, I'd like to speak with Elliot about my calendar."

He gestures toward the door and I take the hint, backing up ever so slowly.

"Why don't you close the door on your way out." I hear his request but decide to ignore it. I'm not going to have any part in the exploitation of his assistant.

---

I've been staring at this report for the last ten minutes but I can't get the image of Thad staring up Elliot's dress, out of my head. My conscience is eating away at me and there's a pull in my gut telling me to do something about it, to intervene. I reflexively tighten the muscles in my hand, itching to punch something. Thad's face would be the ideal target right about now, but I can't do that. I can't let this inner protectiveness get the better of me. For all I know, the girl's playing up the innocent assistant bit, doing whatever it takes to keep her job. Hell, anyone with a heartbeat can see Thad for what he is—his tactics are transparent. She's probably eating up the attention. For all I know they've got something going on behind closed doors, and who the fuck am I to get involved? The thought of Elliot and Thad being involved sends a rush of anger through the base of my stomach, causing a visceral reaction in my body. Before I know it, adrenaline is coursing through my veins and I'm out of my seat, throwing on my coat. There's only one way for me to process this level of anger. If I don't handle it right this second, I may find myself doing something I regret.

I peek my head back into Thad's office. "Elliot, cancel my four o'clock with Greg. Something's come up that needs my immediate attention." I don't wait on her cheery response before I rush toward the elevator, practically jogging, and bump into Ricky from accounting, knocking the stack of papers he just copied onto the floor. Ricky is a middle-aged balding guy with a short-sleeve button-up and a pocket protector. Normally I don't mind the guy, but right now he's holding me up when I'm desperate for an escape.

"Whoa! Where's the fire?" Ricky chuckles, adjusting his collection of pens in his pocket protector.

"Sorry, I'm just in a rush." I bend down to help him with the papers when I hear the heavy thud of feet rushing toward me. *Please no, please no, not right now.*

"Did someone say fire?" CJ leaps through the air, landing in a crouching position before roll-diving toward the closest fire extinguisher.

Fuck.

She brings her whistle up to her mouth and blows until her face turns red from the strain. My ears are ringing, and the shriek reverberates around my brain as the sharp sting of a headache pierces my temple. For a moment I think she's about to spray me down but instead, she hits play on the speaker she's conveniently carrying on her belt and begins singing and dancing to the fire safely jingle.

Fuck me. I stand up, following the motions, and force out the song to the tune of the "Twinkle Twinkle Little Star" Eventually everyone on the floor joins in and CJ's chest swells with apparent pride.

"Good job, everyone!" She claps. "Next week I'll send you the second verse. Don't worry, you'll pick it up easily. And remember, don't use words like 'fire' so flippantly!" She scolds Ricky and he blushes crimson. He's going to have a hell of a time making this up to all the staff on this floor and he knows it.

"Thank you, CJ. I feel safe knowing you're watching over all of us so well." I clap her on the shoulder and rush to the elevator before, God forbid, someone mentions another form of natural disaster.

---

*Swish.* It's just me and the basket; at this moment nothing else matters. Just ten more. I won't let myself leave this gym until I've sunk thirty shots. I've had a love of this game since I was a kid, but after losing Sarah, basketball has become my main coping mechanism. I'm alone in this run-down city rec, trying like hell to clear my mind from the racing thoughts that have plagued me for the last few weeks. Those big brown eyes, those pouty red lips, that tight ass, and a smile that could bring any man down to his knees.

A lump forms in my throat and as I take my next shot, I miss my footing and the ball bounces off the side of the backboard. *Shit. Get it together, Williams, you're no better than that worthless son of a bitch for jonesing after your employee.* She's a grown woman anyway. I don't know where this incessant feeling to protect her is coming from. I pound the ball into the wooden gym floor, a little harder than necessary as if brute force will shake the thoughts out of my head.

I fix my grip and set my eyes on the goal. I picture the ball going in effortlessly, then I take my shot. Just as I envisioned, the ball obeys my practiced movements and glides right through the hoop, bouncing in place before rolling back toward my feet. Now if I could handle all my life problems like that, things would be completely different right now.

I quiet my mind and push everything to the back, focusing on my next eighteen shots. This is the only form of therapy I need right now.

After I've finished my ritual, I carefully take a seat on the dilapidated bleachers to pack up my gear. My mind finally still from the intense drills, I can finally start to formulate a solution to my unsettling problem. It's going to take some convincing toward Thad, but I think I can spin this into the perfect little pet project that'll have Elliot out of sight and out of mind, which is all I can ask for, isn't it?

# TWELVE

Elliot

Ever since last week's quarterly meeting, I've spent every waking minute researching and putting together the best marketing plan of my life for the Imposter Chicken. I've read every book on influencer marketing I could get my hands on at the library, researched countless Instagram personalities, and cross-referenced sales data based on campaign length, season, and niche.

Gwen and Maggie have been the best support system, researching and sending me contact information for every potential influencer that crosses their paths. Gwen was even able to get me a call with a fashion influencer in Miami. She agreed to chat with me about the business and gave me advice for best practices in building my plan.

In a last-ditch effort to tweak my proposal, yet again, I've invited the girls over for pizza and beer. Since my bank account is mostly in the black these days, it's a small splurge I felt I owed them for all the long hours of pep talks, outfit recommendations, and panic attack cool-downs. This job means so much to me, and I know that my life with this company is literally on the line. If I don't nail this proposal, I'll be packing up my miniature desk with a one-way ticket straight to Louisiana, where I'll be the twenty-six-year-old living in my childhood bedroom. I can see it now: my parents will be thrilled, my ex delighted to have another shot to win me back, everyone in our small town rooting for the second-chance romance from the town's high school sweethearts that didn't make it after college.

"I'm telling you, Elliot, you're ready. I've looked it over five times and it's not missing any details. Trust me, sis, they're going to be impressed." Gwen's voice breaks me from my mini panic attack just thinking of what failure could mean. She takes a giant bite of her pepperoni and jalapeño pizza, and drips honey down her face.

She rolls her eyes back in her head as the pizza touches her tongue. "Oh. My. God. It's soooo good."

Maggie shudders. "Eww, Gwen. I totally just heard your sex voice when you said that!"

"Mags, you know what the sweet and the spicy do to me." Gwen wiggles her eyebrows.

"I don't want to talk about foods that act as your personal flavor of aphrodisiacs!" Maggie sends my only throw pillow flying across the sparse living room.

"Hey, take your annoyance out on each other with your own stuff!" I rub my hand over the pillow in a caress. "Some of us have to take care of the few luxuries we have!"

"Oh my God, Elliot, can you be any more dramatic? You bought that pillow at a garage sale during freshman year for twenty-five cents." Gwen rolls her eyes. "It's probably covered in syphilis-encrusted semen."

Maggie throws the pizza crust back into the empty pizza

box. "OK, now I'm done; thanks for looking after my figure, Gwenny!"

"Anytime." Gwen reaches into the pizza box to retrieve Maggie's mostly eaten crust. She pours a heap of honey on it and shoves it in her mouth. "OK, girlies, my loins are tingling, so if you'll excuse me–"

Maggie and I cover our ears before Gwen can say anything else. "It's OK, Gwen, you don't have to finish–"

"Don't worry about that, I always do." Gwen winks and I feel a warm blush cover my neck. I can only hope to be so confident in my sexuality one day.

"Well, I think we've gotten enough accomplished here tonight. Why don't we just part ways and catch up tomorrow?" I giggle.

Maggie jumps up from her spot on the carpet and heads straight for the door. "Good luck tomorrow, Elliot; let me know how it goes down!" She turns to Gwen. "As for you...please spare me the details. My fragile innocence can't handle any more stories from your boudoir."

Gwen hugs me and takes the opportunity to squeeze my ass; it's her way of showing her affection. "All I'm saying is, you're obviously doing it all wrong if you're both this embarrassed to talk about your sex lives."

"Obviously," Maggie and I say in unison. "Let me figure out the job, so I can afford this shitty apartment, and then I'll figure out the right way to do the sex."

"Ugh... Elliot, you don't 'do the sex.'" She uses air quotes around my words. "You *have* sex, and I'm here for you if you have any questions. I know it's only a matter of time before you're in a compromising position with Benjamin, after all." She bats her eyes.

"Gwen, you've got to stop huffing your permanent markers. No way in hell is that going to happen. The man, as stunning as he is, is a giant asshole and he hates me. He's doing everything in his power to get rid of me. This marketing project is obviously nothing more than a ploy to see if I can handle the pressure."

"Then I guess he's going to be shocked when he finds out who he's dealing with." She loops her arm through Maggie's, leading her away and leaving me feeling all kinds of unease. Great, just what I need. I was nervous enough about the prospect of losing my job tomorrow; now I'm thinking about having relations with my boss.

I spend the next day at work trying to muster the courage to present my proposal to Benjamin. I've seen him several times, even attended a meeting next to him, and he hasn't mentioned the project once. I'm starting to think he's forgotten all about it.

I look down at the time and see it's four forty-five. I've wasted this entire workday, and now I've only got fifteen minutes until Benjamin leaves the office and I miss the deadline. I give myself a quick pep talk and march my nervous ass straight to his office.

The door's slightly cracked, so rather than knocking, I swing it open absentmindedly. Benjamin is standing behind his desk in nothing but a pair of workout shorts—the tight compression shorts one usually wears under their real shorts. In the brief moment before his half nakedness registers to either of us, I'm gifted with the glory of his incredibly chiseled body.

Sculpted muscle stretches across the length of his torso that looks like it belongs to a Greek god. His smooth, tan skin begs to be touched, and I suddenly have the strangest impulse to run my hands through the dusting of dark chest hair that covers his impressive pecs.

He gasps, covering himself before I can steal another glance at the magnificent body that has my mouth suddenly dry with desire. "What the fuck are you doing, barging in my office without knocking?"

I open my mouth to speak but have to swallow a few times to regain control of my tongue. "Benjamin, I'm so sorry. I... I ... didn't mean to interrupt you." My cheeks burn with embarrassment, but I know it's now or never. I toss the marketing proposal down on his desk. I know I'm already at risk of losing my job, and this is my Hail Mary attempt to save my ass.

"I just wanted to give you this. It's the marketing plan you asked me to work up last week for the Imposter Chicken Bars."

His glare threatens me to run for the hills but rather than cowering, I stand my ground. It seems as if he's sizing me up, but then I realize his look is more shock than annoyance. He makes a move to pick up the packet and flips through the pages.

"I didn't think you'd do it," he admits.

"Well, I need this job." I cross my arms over my chest in defiance, not exactly sure why I feel the need to be defensive right now considering I just barged into his office while he was half naked, not the other way around.

"I see." Benjamin drops the papers down on the desk and turns his back to me. "Well, why don't you leave me to it then. I was going to meet some friends for a workout, but it looks like you've given me a business opportunity instead. It would've been nice to have this earlier. Lucky for you they're an understanding lot." He glances over his shoulder as I stand frozen in place. "Shut the door on your way out, would you?"

Somehow my feet move toward the door and leave him to decide my fate. Hopefully I've done a good enough job. Otherwise, I can kiss this dream of mine goodbye for good.

I'm eating lunch in the downstairs cafe, reading the latest romance novel, when a large shadow looms over me and darkens my phone's screen. I look up to find Benjamin staring over me, fidgeting with his cuff links.

Before I can ask him if there's something he needs, he takes the seat across from me and gets right to it. "Elliot, I looked over your marketing plan and I think you're really onto something here. I hope you don't mind, but I've taken the liberty to make a few adjustments to your budget and have extended a few of the contract lengths. If you're available, I'd like to send you out into the field on the next flight to Atlanta."

My jaw falls open and my eyes widen. "Are you freaking serious right now? Oh my God, I can't believe this is happening! I'm not sure I understand; why do I need to fly to Atlanta?"

"We're going to need someone to be there in person to present the contracts, especially since this is something so new to our agency. I thought you'd be happy for the opportunity to travel since this whole thing is your baby, but of course, if you're not interested, we could probably get someone from the marketing department to go."

"No, I can do it!" I blurt. "I mean, I'd love to go and represent POW!." I nervously take a giant gulp of water, which goes down the wrong pipe. I cough it back up through my parted fingers. *Smooth move, ex-lax; could you be any more awkward right now?*

"Uh...you OK over there?" He gives me a concerned look but makes no move to help me. I guess I know where we stand if I needed the Heimlich maneuver.

I wave my hand for him to continue. "Yes. Fine. Just swallowed wrong."

"Well, as I said, we'll get you on the first flight to Atlanta in the morning. I'll have Eliza send you a list of things you'll need for the trip and your itinerary for the next few weeks." He pins me with a glare. "Elliot, this is a monumental opportunity for our agency. I expect you to behave professionally. Please don't make me regret taking a chance here." His eyes soften and I see a glimpse of the real Benjamin. Or at least who I hope the real Benjamin is.

"Next few weeks? What do you mean by *next few weeks?*"

"You're the one who put the proposal together. You selected multiple influencers all over the country. We've contacted them and are coordinating the meetings as close together as we can, but you'll have to fly to the different cities." He pauses. "Was this not something you anticipated?"

His question instantly puts me on defense. "Oh, of course, I just didn't realize that I'd be the one flying all over the countryside..."

Benjamin raises an eyebrow, taking in the thin sheen of sweat that's forming on my brow. "Is that going to be a problem for you? I assumed you'd be excited about the opportunity."

"Of course I'm excited!" I hesitate, knowing I need to give him a little context here. "It's just that I've never flown before." I bite my lip nervously. "I kind of have anxiety but it's not a big deal. I can handle it. You can count on me." I put on a brave face and puff my chest out to show I'm tough.

Benjamin studies me and I'm not sure he's buying it. "Right. Well, I suppose there's a first time for everything." He starts to stand and I reach forward, squeezing his hand that's still resting on the table between us.

"Wait. Benjamin. I want you to know I can do this. I won't let you down." He stares at our connected hands, and a jolt of electricity forms at our connection. He pulls his hand away and at that moment I know that it wasn't one-sided.

"Very well. I'll contact Eliza to send you your travel information." He hastily stands and adjusts his tie. "Enjoy the rest of your meal, Elliot." And in the blink of an eye, he's gone.

I pull out my phone to text the girls.

> You're never going to believe what just happened!

MAGGIE

OMG, please tell me they loved it.

GWEN

You finally boned the boss???

> UGH, Gwen, no. They're sending me to Atlanta first thing tomorrow to be the one who negotiates the contracts with the influencers! I think I'm going to puke, I'm so nervous!

GWEN

Well, I suppose there's still time.

MAGGIE

But, Elly, you're deathly afraid of airplanes.

> Yes, that's true, but this is a once-in-a-lifetime opportunity. Gwen, I think I'm going to need to borrow some of your big girl panties.

GWEN

G-string or thong?

> Whatever you can spare.

# THIRTEEN

Elliot

I arrive at the airport three hours early, even though Eliza's directions said two hours would be just fine. Since this is my first time flying, I'm taking no chances. I'm going to prove to Benjamin and Thad that I'm cut out for this work. I give my foot a stomp and raise my fist to emphasize my internal monologue. An older woman with an enormous sun hat stands in front of me and turns around wearing a scowl.

"We've been in line just like you. There's no reason to get all in a tizzy about it!" she snaps.

"That's not what I... I'm sorry. That wasn't directed toward you; I was just pumping myself up for my flight."

"Maybe you should hold in those urges until you get out of the airport. Flying is stressful enough for a woman of my years."

"I'm so sorry." I reach out my hand to introduce myself. "I'm Elliot, and this is my first time flying." She stares at my hand and doesn't take it, so I awkwardly keep it extended just in case she changes her mind. "Sometimes when I'm nervous I talk to myself. Well, it's not like I hear voices, but I do hear my own voice in my head. Did you know there's a small percentage of people who have no inner monologue?" I let out a nervous laugh. "Suffice it to say, that's not me."

The woman's eyes grow large and she turns around ever so slowly. She leans forward and whisper-yells to the older gentlemen she's with, "Bruce! There's a lunatic behind us, I need you to put some pep in your step as soon as they call us to the desk."

"I can take the next guest," a woman announces, and the pair take off as fast as turtles racing through peanut butter to put some space between us. The older woman even glances over her shoulder to check if I've followed them. I give her a kind wave and stare down at my feet so I don't accidentally offend anyone else before I even make it to the airplane.

---

"Excuse me, pardon me, I'm sorry." I make my way through the air carrier, doing my best to bob and weave through the overcrowded vessel. I feel the panic start to rise in my chest and force myself to take a deep inhale, breathing in the heavily scented elderly man's aftershave. Yeah...it's not exactly the cleansing breath I was going for. Luckily for me, claustrophobia is only number four on my list of anxiety-inducing triggers.

I glance down at the boarding pass in my trembling hands. Seat 24A. I look up, searching the few empty seats that remain. Obviously, with such late notice, I was in the last boarding group possible. Everyone seemed so angry waiting to get on the plane that I just kept letting them get in front of me. I mean, sheesh, we're all going to the same place. I'm the last one in this line to find my seat and I quickly realize the overhead compartments are all full... Huh, I guess that's why everyone's in such a rush to board first.

I clench my carry-on bag, pulling it closer to my chest so I don't bump into the sea of elbows sticking out into the aisle when I finally make it to my row. I'm surprised to find a sweaty man wearing a wool vest and a bow tie sitting in my seat. Talk about a poor wardrobe choice. I glance down at the boarding pass to double-check and look over my shoulder, triple-checking the row numbers in case I've accidentally passed mine, but I am, in fact, in the right place.

I clear my throat. "Umm... excuse me, sir, I believe you're in my seat." I show him my boarding pass. "See, it says right here, Elliot James, seat 24A." I point to the small print just to be sure he's following me, the man doesn't flinch.

He places a hot hand over mine and gently squeezes. "Listen, babydoll, I'm accustomed to flying first class and I had a last-minute schedule change. This may have been your seat, but trust me when I say you don't want me climbing over you to get to the bathroom this entire flight." He gestures toward his takeout bag. "IBS... if you know what I'm saying." Then he winks, as if what he just revealed would somehow evoke anything other than pure repulsion.

"Very well." I grit my teeth, swallowing the nerves that have resurfaced after learning that I'll be sitting next to the window seat in the flying death trap. When I lift my gaze to climb over the Mr. Dursley look-alike, I meet the all too familiar whiskey-brown eyes that belong to none other than my boss, Benjamin Williams.

"Excuse me, miss, I need you to hurry and take a seat. We're running slightly behind schedule," the flight attendant says from behind me.

"Oh, yes, of course." I heave my bag up and throw myself in front of the two men as I sidestep toward my seat. Since there's no more room in the overhead compartment, it looks like I'll be sitting with my suitcase in my lap for the next four hours.

I adjust myself so I can see Benjamin over my bag. "Benjamin, what are you doing here? Are you visiting Atlanta as well?"

He glances up from his iPad as if I've just interrupted him. "I started thinking about how important this project is for our company, and I can't let just anyone go and represent us—no offense. I had Eliza book my ticket this morning. I'll be accompanying you to make sure things are handled properly." His face looks agitated that he's even having to explain himself. He brings the iPad back up and continues looking over the presentation he was working on before I sat down.

The shock from seeing him on my flight melts away at the realization that he's here because he doesn't trust that I can handle it. Just when I think I'm being taken seriously and take one step forward, my anxiety rears its ugly head sending me flying back two more steps.

A putrid aroma snaps me out of my pity party, and I look over and discover Mr. Dursley chowing down on his fast-food fish tacos like it's his last meal. Fish juice and mayonnaise drip down his forearm and rather than using a napkin, he sops up his leaking juices with a piece of toast and grunts as he shoves the whole piece into his mouth in a single bite.

"Please make sure your seats are in their upright position and your seat belts are securely fastened. You should turn off all electronic devices at this time as we start our ascent," the flight attendant's voice booms over the speakers. I have to push down the bile that's rising in my throat between the nervousness and the stench of takeout fish tacos. Seriously, who eats fish on an airplane?

The airplane begins its ascent and all I can envision is us charging full speed into another airplane. I clench my suitcase, still sitting in my lap, with a white-knuckle grip, and smash my face into the rough material. *This is all basic flying stuff here, everything's going to be fine.* My soothing thoughts are interrupted when I notice the man in front of me on his cell phone.

"Yes. We're taking off now... should be just a few more minutes," he whispers into his device.

Panic rises in my chest when I notice he's still on the phone. Why is this man still on the phone? The flight attendant just told us to turn off all electronic devices and he's still carrying on a conversation. I glance around at the people sitting near him, hoping to find his family sitting nearby. I'm not sure why that would be a comfort, but I feel like the chances of someone blowing up a plane are significantly less if their wife and kids are sitting with them. I see nothing.

"Oh shit. This is it." I throw my hands over my head and do my best to gasp for air.

Benjamin's concerned voice surprises me. "What is it? Elliot, what are you doing?" He grabs at my hands to pull them down, but I push him away.

"We're in the air... you got it." the man says into the cell phone.

"Oh my God," I mutter and the convulsions start. First, my hands start trembling, and then the sensation flows up through my arms and the rest of my body. I realize at this moment that my body is not actually convulsing; I'm just experiencing slight tremors from the overload of adrenaline. When I was younger I literally thought I was a superhero when I started having my episodes; my body felt like it was radiating so much energy that I could shoot lightning through my hands.

"What're you talking about?" Benjamin's voice breaks through my panic attack and I forgot I even said anything out loud.

"He has a phone. He's on the phone. Why won't he hang up the phone?" I point toward the man sitting in the row in front of us.

Benjamin's eyes go wide in question as I throw my head between my knees. The tremors are building and it takes everything in me not to leap out of my seat and throw myself into Benjamin's muscular arms. I bet he could easily squeeze me into a cocoon with those biceps...

The recent documentary about the civilian that saved a whole movie theater of people comes to my mind, and I realize what I have to do. If it's my life that needs to be sacrificed at this moment to save this plane full of people, then so be it. Without another thought I stand up in my seat and leap toward the man on the cell phone, hoping if I can interrupt the call, maybe the flight attendants will be able to stop whatever kind of bomb is set below the cabin.

*One, two, three,* I count in my head and leap.

"Elliot!" I hear Benjamin's cry as I'm falling over the seat in front of me, but it's too late. I've made my choice, and I choose to die saving hundreds of innocent people.

My face collides with the seat and skids down as gravity takes its toll on my airborne falling body. My hip is jolted against a sharp mass, probably his shoulder, before my body crashes down in the space between the back of the seat and the man's knees. The cell phone drops to the ground, hitting me in the face.

"What the fuck!" he yells.

I grab the phone and bring it to my ear; there's no time I've got to stop this before they detonate the bomb. "Listen, I don't know who you are... but this is over. We've got the Feds involved. They'll be here in thirty seconds."

A woman's voice comes across the line accompanied by a crying baby. "Hello... hello... Johnny? What's going on?"

I'm startled by her voice. "Um, excuse me? Hello?"

"What is going on? Where's my husband, is he OK?" Her cry pierces my ear through the phone. "Johnny..." Her voice trails off as the man snatches the phone from my grasp.

"What the fuck are you doing?" He yanks me by the elbow, bringing me up to eye level. I glance toward the aisle and see Benjamin moving toward him.

"Don't put your hands on her like that!" Benjamin lunges forward, restraining the man in an arm-bar. "Don't fucking touch her!"

The old lady sitting in the window seat next to him shrieks, and begins slapping the men with her purse. "Help! Help!" she screams over our muffled cries.

After what seems like two hours, finally, a flight attendant makes her way over to our kerfuffle. "What is going on here? Ma'am, are you all right?"

"Is she all right? The crazy bitch leaped over her seat and attacked me! She needs to be arrested!" he screams.

Benjamin doesn't let loose on his hold on the man. "Elliot, are you OK? Did he hurt you?"

I look up from my confined position on the ground, putting my face straight in the scary man's package. "Yes. I...I...I'm OK," I mumble. "But we've got to save the people!"

"What people?" the man manages to shout. "What are you talking about? Let me go. Jesus, I've done nothing wrong here!" Benjamin loosens his grip, letting him explain.

"What the hell is going on?" the flight attendant, who's now joined by her coworker, shouts.

"There's a bomb on the plane!" I yell as I scamper to my feet, accidentally stomping the scary man's toes in the process.

"Ouch. Shit. Will you move already?" he cries.

"Hold on," the flight attendant screams over our scuffle.

"How do you know there's a bomb?" She holds her hands out like a teacher breaking up a fight in junior high.

I grab the cell phone and hold it above my head. "I heard him! He was on his phone and you came around and said, 'please turn off any electronic devices' and he didn't! I heard him giving his partner step by step details about the plane's status!" I realize as I'm talking about the phone call, the person on the other end of the receiver is still on the line. I hold the phone out toward the flight attendant. "See? Here's the proof!"

She hesitantly takes the phone from me. "Hello?" she says through the receiver and the woman on the other end goes off into a frantic rant. I hear bits and pieces of "my husband," "the baby's coming," and "please tell me he's on his way home." The flight attendant pulls the phone away from her ear and pins me with a stare.

"Excuse me, ma'am and sir... if you could just follow me, we've got special seating in the back until the plane can make an emergency landing. Please do not cause a scene or I will be forced to use whatever means necessary to restrain you." She gestures for us to go ahead of her. She turns back toward the scary man. "The only reason you're not included here is because it sounds like you've got a wife in labor who's panicking awaiting your return, so I suggest you take a seat and for God's sake, turn off the phone!"

He doesn't hesitate and whispers into the phone's receiver, "Baby, I'll see you soon. It's going to be fine," before taking a seat.

"Right this way, you two."

My limbs obey, one foot in front of the other as we're led to the naughty seats directly in front of the cabin bathrooms.

"Benjamin, I'm so sorry!" I stutter. "I've got anxiety and he just...he wouldn't hang up the phone. I guess I assumed the worst."

"Don't speak. Don't say anything." He holds up his hand and his stern glare keeps me from visibly reacting. I swallow the apology and don't say another word until our flight makes its emergency landing in Northwest Arkansas.

And that was how I ended up on the *No Fly List* after only thirty minutes of my first time flying.

# FOURTEEN

Benjamin

I'm fuming. I'm on an airplane sitting next to the bathrooms with a crazy woman wearing fucking handcuffs. I tried to explain the circumstances, even going so far as to convince the flight attendants that Elliot was mentally ill and off her meds, but they're still taking all precautions necessary, and we're making an emergency landing.

"Right this way, you two." The air marshal guides us off the airplane toward the security office. My handcuffs were applied a little tighter than necessary thanks to the mall cop security officer, who appears to be taking his role a little too seriously. His guiding hands somehow found their way to Elliot's lower back.

"Oh, look, Benjamin, he's got a weapon on his belt. Officer, have you ever had to use that thing?" Her eyes go wide as she gestures toward the gun, which is conveniently located right next to his package.

If I didn't know this woman in front of me from having

worked with her over the last several weeks, I'd assume she was flirting her way out of trouble... But since I do know her, I see this is Elliot's regular disposition; she's truly just that in awe of the world around her. It's easily my biggest pet peeve and my favorite part of her personality. Unfortunately for this airport security guard, Elliot's flirtatious comments will fall flat as soon as he lets us go.

The cop lifts the gun from his holster and flexes as he poses. "Yeah, we've had a couple of drug busts that have gotten pretty intense. You can never take these things too seriously when it comes to public safety."

He begins to remove Elliot's handcuffs and I see the slightest caress across her bare wrists as he releases her. "Sorry, I had to do that back there. It's standard procedure." He lingers and a rush of heat flows through me. I can't hold back my aggravation a minute longer.

"Hey, Prince Charming. Why don't you wipe the drool off your face and get me out of these things?"

The security officer scowls. "Ah, it looks we've got a tough guy on our hands." He dangles the handcuff key. "I guess you ain't so tough with your hands tied behind your back, now are you, buddy?" He puts the key in his pocket. "I think I'll let you stay like that for a little while longer while I fill out this incident report."

Elliot makes her way over to me and places a gentle hand on my shoulder. "Benjamin, I think you should watch your tone." The officer glances over her shoulder. "He's a police officer, after all."

Her innocence does something to my insides and my balls clench in response to her touch. "Don't fucking touch me! This is all your fault." Elliot startles at my reaction and before I know it, mall cop is back in my face.

"Just for that, buddy, your ass is going on the No Fly List."

He scratches his signature on the clipboard and hands it to Elliot.

"I'm not your fucking buddy, so don't call me that."

Elliot's hand slaps over my mouth. "What he means to say is, we're really sorry. This whole thing was a misunderstanding. I've got Generalized Anxiety and Panic Disorder and I freaked out back there. Please don't do this; we've got this business trip all over the country and we don't have time—"

"Sorry, sweetie. It's done." He slaps the clipboard down and finally releases me from the handcuffs. "Maybe next time, you can sweet-talk your boyfriend here into not mouthing off to the only person with the power to get him back on an airplane."

I snatch the clipboard from his hands and sign, not caring if Elliot is behind me.

---

"You can't be serious." I slam my fist on the cold, hard countertop of the car rental facility.

"I'm sorry, Mr. Williams, with such late notice this is all I can do."

Martha, the very nice, albeit a bit matronly, salesperson dangles the key in front of me, inviting me to take the last car off the lot. It's not her fault the only vehicle she's got left in stock is a 2008 Ford Focus. I'm not saying I'm better than driving this everyday average car but it's been a long time. Thoughts of Sarah and Maddie rush through my mind, and suddenly my stomach feels like it's risen to my throat. I try one last time, pulling out the big guns as I turn to Martha and plead.

"Please, Martha, you're telling me there's nothing you can do here? You don't have a drop off location with rotating inventory anywhere?" I inhale and wait for her response with bated breath.

Martha sees the concern in my eyes. What started as pure rage from being placed on a No Fly List by no fault of my own has landed me in a testy predicament. "I'm sorry. If there was anything I could do..." I hold up my hand to save her the trouble of apologizing. It's not Martha's fault I've got an emotionally unstable employee who freaked out on a man trying to get home to his wife in labor. No, this isn't Martha's fault and it sure as fuck isn't my fault either. This is Thad Powell's fault for hiring the woman who's decked out from head to toe in a gray sweatsuit—we're talking gray slouchy pants with a gray oversized hoodie that she's wearing on her head—with no impulse control and an imagination that runs too wildly.

I glance behind me to check if maybe Elliot's somehow wandered off and has decided she no longer wants to work in corporate America. Perhaps the circus is hiring new acts for their anxious woman who freaks out over nothing performance, but there she is standing behind me, ramrod straight, wearing sunglasses inside the building.

"You look ridiculous, you know that, right?" I gesture toward her gray-on-gray ensemble. "What's with the sweatsuit, and why are you wearing your sunglasses inside?" I glance around us, indicating the concrete walls.

"Oh this?" She pulls at the oversized gray hoodie. "I just wanted to be comfortable, you know on the flight? I wasn't sure if the plane would be cold and I am pretty cold-natured; the only sweatsuit I had on hand was from my senior year track uniform..." Her voice trails off. "Benjamin, I'm really sorry about what happened back there; my mom warned me that flying was probably a bad idea but I didn't listen."

I hold up my hand to stop her. "I'm not going to tell you it's fine, but we're here now and we've still got a job to do." I glance at my watch. "What time is the first meeting tomorrow?"

"Ten a.m. I can see if she can reschedule; here, let me just find her contact information." She fumbles through her oversized purse, pulling out a neck pillow, ear muffs, and a blanket scarf.

"That won't be necessary. Atlanta's only a thirteen-hour drive and it's noon. If we leave right now, we'll still get a decent amount of sleep." I turn on my heel, making my way toward our Ford Focus. I hope it at least has heated seats. My abrupt departure must surprise Elliot, and she begins chasing after me.

"Wait, Benjamin, does that mean...does that mean the job is still on?"

I don't miss a beat, scanning the parking lot for the description of the 2008 red Ford Focus. "Of course the job is still on. I've got a lot riding on this opportunity, and we've already invested. We're at least going to see how this first meeting goes and see if you can deliver on this idea."

A faint gasp escapes her lips at the realization. She squares her shoulders. "Benjamin, I promise I won't let you down."

"Yeah, well, I think I've heard that before," I snap.

I study her stern expression, her emotions masked in pure determination for the first time since she walked into POW!. With a nod of my head, I peel my stare from her exquisite features and click the alarm button on the rental's clicker. A beat-up red Ford Focus chimes its response and I know at that moment that this adventure is only beginning.

With a rusty squeal, I pry the driver's door open and glance up at Elliot. "Well, what are you waiting for?" Her grin expands and she bites her lip as if to muffle her excitement.

"I know you don't know this about me, but I just love road trips!" She does a little dance in her seat.

"Well... that makes one of us." I shift the car into reverse, departing toward Atlanta. *Just 13 hours to go*, I remind myself.

After what feels like three hours, I've discovered that Elliot has a bit of a superpower; not only does she seem to know every song that's played on the radio, but she seems to have a choreographed dance to go with each one.

I feel my eyelid starting to twitch, which only happens when I'm severely sleep-deprived or highly irritated. Since both are true, I try to ignore it to the best of my ability. *Just think happy thoughts, Benjamin, playing basketball with the guys, Maui in the spring, the smell of freshly baked bread on a warm summer day...*

Elliot belts out the choppy lyrics, singing about walking five-hundred miles and doing her best to impersonate a British accent. I turn the radio off without saying a word, and she doesn't get the hint. She just keeps singing the chorus.

*Dear God, please don't let her finish it.* My silent plea goes unheard.

"*Da da da da!*"

"*Enough!*" I grip a handful of hair and drag my hand down my face in frustration. "I can't take it anymore!" Elliot startles in her seat as though my sudden outburst is out of nowhere as if she hasn't annoyed me down to my last nerve and is now swinging on it like Miley Cyrus on a damn wrecking ball.

Even my analogies are music-related now.

"Oh, you're not one for karaoke. I understand. My friend Gwen also hates karaoke. She has noise-canceling headphones that she packs when we have to ride in the car together any longer than thirty minutes." She pulls her feet up to the seat and hugs her legs in almost a childlike manner. Instantly, I feel guilty at the sight of her innocence. This woman is always smiling, even when I've just lost it on her. It's fucking maddening.

She tucks a strand of hair behind her ear and takes a giant sip of her blue raspberry slushie that she insisted she needed because it was a "road-trip tradition" and would be bad luck if she didn't have it. Seeing as we could stand to stay away from bad luck, I obliged. I think the blue food dye may be going to her head. Or maybe she's always this obnoxious.

"How about we play a game?" she squeals.

"I don't like games." I stare at the road between my hands, firmly gripping the steering wheel as if my sheer determination will somehow make this drive go by faster.

"Ok, Mr. Grumpy-Head, but if I can't listen to music and I can't play a game, this drive is going to be really boring..." Her head perks up at her idea and then she sneezes into her elbow. "Sorry, I don't know what's up with this sudden allergy attack." She wipes her eyes with the sleeve of her shirt, "I really wish I had some Benadryl or something. I feel like I'm losing my edge. Hey I know, how about you let me drive and we take shifts?"

"Absolutely not," I say. There's no way, I'm going to allow this woman, who I've mentally diagnosed with ADHD, get behind the wheel of our rental car... clunker or not. Suddenly, a brilliant idea pops into my head, "Hey, Elliot, you've really been sucking down that slushie over there, do you think you need a bathroom break?"

"Oh yes! I've had to pee for the last hour but I was too scared you'd be mad... since we've only been driving for an hour and a half." She gives me a sideways grin as if she's waiting on my negative reaction.

"Not at all. My legs are getting pretty stiff anyway, I'll stop at the next gas station I see."

Ten minutes later, I pull into a Chevron, and Elliot bolts from the car heading straight to the bathroom. I refill her slushie, as I promised, and grab a box of children's Benadryl, hoping she takes the bait.

"There you are!" She takes the slushie from me and I hold

up the box of allergy medication. Did you say you needed this?" I ask nonchalantly.

"Oh my God, yes! Thank you for reminding me. I don't want to be a sneezing mess when we get there." She swats at her pockets, realizing she left her wallet in the car.

"Don't worry about it, I've got this." I try to suppress the spark of hope that's flaring in my chest. Could I possibly be looking at some quiet time on this joy ride? One can only hope.

———

The snores coming from this woman could frighten a bear. Elliot's sprawled out in the passenger seat like a starfish, a stream of drool spilling from her parted lips. I take in the sight before me and I can't help but think this must be how parents feel looking at their sleeping toddlers. Though she is wild and unruly, causing me immense aggravation when she's awake, as she sleeps she looks so angelic. Her features are striking and I know that if the circumstances were different, there's no way in hell I'd let this woman out of my sight before asking her out.

A snort escapes her throat and I'm torn from my moment of insanity. Jesus, Benjamin, get a grip, this woman is unhinged... she literally threw herself at a random stranger on an airplane getting you both placed on the DO NOT FLY list... not to mention she's your mother-fucking EMPLOYEE. I shake my head as if the motion will rid the thoughts from my brain.

The silence is like a warm blanket for my chaotic mind, calming, and luxurious. I'm so thankful for her pollen allergies at a time like this, especially considering her energy was only compounding, I'd say that a well-timed nap was just what we both needed.

I reach across the console to move a strand of hair out of her face. Her warm, soft flesh is a stark comparison to my callused hands. I savor the moment our skin connects. As if she can read my mind and knows my grinch heart is growing from her presence, she snuggles into my hand and grips me like I'm her teddy bear. Even though I know this is wrong, it's crossing more line than just one, I don't move my arm, I let her hold me and I let the loneliness that plagues me fade away.

*Yeah, Benjamin, you've really done it now, catching feelings for someone who's completely off-limits who you'll never deserve, even on your best day... this work trip can't get any worse.*

# FIFTEEN

Benjamin

"Elliot... wake up. We're here..." I try to project my voice to wake her from her deep slumber, but she doesn't stir. "Elliot... we're here. You need to wake up. You can sleep when you get to your room." Still nothing.

This time I slap and jiggle her thigh, trying my best to make as little physical contact as possible. I feel bad enough that I drugged my employee so I could have a little peace and quiet, but to be honest, I regret nothing. Those precious three hours when all I heard was the sound of the highway and muffled snores of the sleeping beauty next to me were exactly what I needed. I was able to process the turns this business venture is taking and plan accordingly so we can still meet our deadlines and land the deals, just as we planned. Hell, I was even able to book our hotel stay for the night and get us a new rental car for the next leg of the trip. There's no way I'd have been that productive had the mouth of the south—a nickname I've decided fits rather nicely after discussing our favorite colors, holidays, and whether or not we'd survive a zombie apocalypse —been awake and talking to me.

Giving her Children's Benadryl did provide me with a few hours of much-needed solace but once she awoke, her battery was completely recharged, so the annoying banter returned tenfold. Lucky me. It seems that her energy must come in bursts, because when she finally passed out from sheer boredom, she's been sleeping like the dead. I even checked her pulse again a few times because the silence was so jarring.

I'm exhausted from the long drive and I don't have time to sit here and patiently wake Princess Aurora, so I do what any red-blooded male would do: I pick her up and carry her ass inside. I do my best to grab the luggage while balancing the delicate woman in my arms. When we finally make it inside, she stirs and snuggles closer into my chest. For a brief moment, the warm embrace sends a jolt of heat through my body, a heat that can only be described as bad...very, very bad.

I secure our room keys—thankful there were two rooms available—and tuck her into bed and set an alarm for seven a.m. I have no idea how long it'll take her to get ready in the morning, but I don't intend on being late. I leave through the adjoining door, but not before turning around and stealing one last glance. She looks so peaceful like this, and my heart is doing weird things in my chest at the sight of her. *You've been here before, Benjamin, and I don't need to remind you that it didn't end well.* I close the door and welcome another sleepless night where I'm haunted of the past, desperate for the reprieve that morning always brings.

---

I'm jolted awake by the strangest combination of music and screaming. Still confused and sleep drunk, I reach to hit my alarm to make this god-awful noise stop but nothing happens. After two more attempts to turn off the alarm, I realize that the sound isn't coming from my phone at all. I sit up on my elbows and glance at the clock on my side table; it reads five thirty... as in two hours before I'm supposed to be awake.

I had planned on sleeping in a little, not needing much time to get ready for the day. Driving thirteen hours yesterday has my body feeling like I've just run a marathon. I'm wide awake now and I know there's no hope of going back to sleep. I figure I may as well hit the gym and take advantage of this early start. Maybe I can work some of this stiffness out of my back.

I head to the bathroom to get ready when I realize where the sound is coming from; it's getting louder the closer I get to the wall Elliot and I are sharing. As I approach to investigate further, I hear her clear as day. There is some kind of rap music playing in the background but instead of lyrics all I hear is her chanting. *You're a bad bitch! You've got this! Screw Benjamin! Prove them all wrong! You are smart! Everyone loves being around you!*

I knew this girl was a piece of work, but screaming mantras at what I can only assume is her reflection in the mirror is beyond what I could've imagined. Obviously, Elliot is feeling insecure, hence her "screw Benjamin" line, and I can't help but be shocked by that. She seems like she's got it all together, or at least isn't bothered by her constant screwups. I throw on my workout clothes and head downstairs to the gym. Thanks to Elliot, I've got plenty of time for a decent workout.

I walk into the small hotel gym and see a squat rack, some dumbbells, two treadmills, and a rowing machine. It's not the best setup, but it'll do. I claim a treadmill and start my warm-up. Exercise is my therapy, and I find that it helps me deal with my stress when I don't numb my thoughts with music. I sink into my nine minutes per mile pace and set the treadmill for three miles. I'm a mile in when I see Elliot enter. She hasn't seen me yet and walks over to the weight area. She's wearing headphones and does a couple of yoga stretches to warm up. I'm having an internal war, trying to resist looking at her. She's wearing high-waisted red leggings that leave nothing to the imagination and a hot-pink sports bra. I'm instantly annoyed that she would be so careless to walk out in public with no shirt. Gym or not, there are perverts out there and I can't imagine anyone turning a blind eye to this bombshell looking like that.

I all but wipe the drool from my chin and silently scold myself for noticing her in that way. She starts adding weights to the bar: 25...50...75...90...125... This I need to see. I only thought I was staring earlier, but this woman has completely captivated my attention and I have to see what she's about to do. She's facing the mirror in front of her, giving me a prime view of her ass as she squats down to lift the weights. Her first lift is a little wobbly but by the time she does the first set, she is executing her squats perfectly. She drops the weights from her standing position and adds more on. This time her form is off; her knees aren't lined up underneath her shoulders. I see the miss in her step as she raises the bar. Before I realize what I'm doing, I've leaped from the treadmill, catching the bar before she is crushed beneath the ambitiously heavy weights.

Red-hot rage flows through my entire body. I toss the weights to the side and steady her, grabbing firmly onto her hips. "What the hell were you thinking? Elliot, you could have seriously hurt yourself trying to squat that much weight! If I hadn't been here, do you know what could've happened?"

I see the shock register on her face. "I... uh...I didn't realize you were in here."

I realize the anger directed toward her is irrational, but I can't help myself. "What do you weigh, like a buck twenty? You have no business trying to lift that much weight!"

Elliot bites her lip as if she's holding back an emotional response. Her eyes narrow and just when I think she's about to grow a pair and let me have it—much like I probably deserve—she turns and moves to her next exercise.

"I'm sorry."

Her quiet words pierce my hardened heart and just like that, I feel like a giant asshole.

"No, Elliot, you shouldn't be apologizing to me. It's just, I didn't sleep well and my fuse is pretty short." But my heartfelt attempt at an apology falls on deaf ears when I look up and notice she hasn't heard me.

Elliot's headphones swallow her small head, and the music is so loud even I can hear it. She makes a beeline straight to the treadmill right next to me and begins setting her pace. I'm shocked she didn't high-tail it back to her room to cry. She glances toward my machine and adjusts so her pace is just a little bit faster. There's no way.... She's not really going to race me after I just chastised her like that? There's only one way to find out.

I up my speed just a little and wait to see if she responds... sure enough, Elliot makes another adjustment, so I do the same.

Ten minutes have passed and gone is my goal of an easy three-mile run. I'm sprinting with all that I have to give while focusing on taking complete breaths so I can maintain this pace. Sweat drips from my brow and I've shed my shirt to cool down. Elliot and I have been going at it for the last mile and she doesn't show any sign of slowing down. This girl is next-level; she must train regularly to be able to keep this pace and maintain regular breathing. Her face is set with pure determination, and I can't help but be distracted by the way her body bounces with every stride—not that her sports bra is doing much to keep my impure thoughts at bay. I glance down at my treadmill and see we've gone five miles at this stupid competition, and I realize I don't have much more in me. This is where I accept defeat.

I stop my machine and wipe the sweat from my face. "Fine, you won this one," I acknowledge to the universe. She punches her fist in the air and does a victory dance on her treadmill. "Just so you know, I could've gone for another hour, but I'm really glad you stopped because I barely have time to shower now."

I hold the door open for her and we make our way back up to our rooms, not saying another word as I just watch the gentle sway of her tight, round ass taunting me. The score looms between us: Elliot 1, Benjamin 0.

# SIXTEEN

Elliot

After the gym escapade, I barely have time to shower and get dressed before our first appointment with Rose Allen, the first influencer on the scouting list. I decide, for time's sake, to let my hair air dry. Maybe I can stick my head out of the car window on the drive. I'm still freaked out about the way Benjamin flipped his lid back there, but I think we both feel better after that intense run. What Benjamin doesn't realize about me is I have to fight for my mental health. My anxiety is through the roof, and it's either a strict workout regime or another medication that makes me feel like a zombie. After much trial and error, my doctor and I have found the perfect cocktail of meds and exercise that have—until recently, at least —kept the panic attacks at bay, and my anxiety to a manageable level. I've added strength training to my running schedule to prevent injury, and my attempt to add on more weight to the bar may have been jumping the gun. I was just feeling so threatened by Benjamin and the way he treated me yesterday, I wanted to push myself to the point of exhaustion so I could let it go.

By the time I make it downstairs, there are only a few muffins left from the continental breakfast. I make a to-go cup of coffee and grab a blueberry muffin for the road, and we get into our Ford Focus and start the driving leg of the trip. We're meeting Rose at a coffee shop in the heart of Atlanta, and I'm preparing the interview questions while Benjamin shuffles us through rush hour traffic.

Since we aren't familiar with the Atlanta area, we asked Rose to pick a meeting place that would best represent her personal brand. I go over the fact sheet with Benjamin. "Rose Allen, twenty-four, Atlanta native. She has 300 thousand Instagram followers, considers herself to be a lifestyle influencer. Top three passions: Coco her Pomeranian, fashion, and healthy food." On paper, Rose seems like the perfect fit for our product, the Imposter Chicken Bar.

Benjamin and I pull up to the coffee shop to find an Instagrammer's dream. There's a giant mural painted on the outside wall that says *I love myself* complete with a line of people waiting to have their picture taken in the front of it. At the very back, we see Rose with Coco in a backpack, patiently waiting her turn for a photo op. "Oh, I see Rose." I point. "Why don't you go inside and grab us a table while I tell her we're here." Benjamin sighs and carries his computer bag inside the shop, and I make my way over to speak with the talent. Rose is one of those people that you just can't help but stare at. She's slightly taller than average, model thin with full cheekbones, fake overly-plump lips, and long dark hair extensions. Her hair is slicked back into a tight high ponytail, pulling the skin around her eyes to a slant. It looks painful.

She's wearing what seems to be a bra and high-waisted pants that give her a wedgie in the back and a full-on camel toe in the front... even though it's practically freezing outside. "Miss Rose Allen, hi, I'm Elliot James. My CEO, Benjamin, and I just arrived." I make a gesture pointing toward Benjamin. "Are you ready to—"

"Oh, thank God! I thought I was going to have to snap a selfie in front of this mural and really the whole point is to get a full-body shot, I mean, why would I wear a crop top otherwise?" *So that's what she's calling it, a 'crop top.'*

"Oh... you want me—" I look around for anyone else who could potentially step up as photographer— "to take your photo?"

"Of course, now get your cute little booty over here and wait with me!"

I put on my best professional face and take one for the team; I know Benjamin is going to want to strangle me for making him wait, but I'm just trying to make the client happy. We wait in the freezing line for approximately thirty minutes and I've heard all about Rose, her ex-fiancé who cheated on her in Vegas, how she stopped eating meat last year, and all about how she only washes her hair once a month. I can honestly say after standing close to her for so long, I could've guessed that. I realize what I thought was hair product keeping her hair slicked down is actually just her greasy unwashed hair. I have to turn my head away from her and take large gulps of air in between talking so I don't suffocate. It's dramatic, but I'm here to do a job and I'm not leaving until it's done.

We finally make it to the front of the line and she grabs Coco and strikes a *Charlie's Angels* style pose with the dog on her back. This woman has zero shame; next, she leans back against the mural like she's being ravished by a lover and has me stand just above her head to take the photo of her looking up longingly into the camera. We take a few more shots before she's satisfied with her mural haul. "You know, you're pretty good behind a camera." The compliment soaks into my bruised ego like a salve and I feel myself growing a little more confident, even if I do feel a bit violated.

Benjamin is waiting with an empty cup of coffee by the only TV, watching Sports Center. I don't want to know what he had to do to gain access to the remote, but I wouldn't put anything past him when he wants his way.

We order our drinks: me a plain Americano with an extra shot of espresso—Lord knows I need it now—and Rose a frozen cinnamon dolce latte with oat milk, sugar-free syrup, only half the espresso, and extra whip cream. We're sitting across from each other at the table and I can barely see her head because the damn milkshake is taking over all of our airspace. Yeah, I called her drink a milkshake because it is an abomination against coffee. Maybe my patience is running just a little thin with this girl.

"Rose, let's get to business, shall we?" I open my laptop, as does Benjamin, and begin reading off the list of questions. She's able to provide me with somewhat intelligent responses and neither Benjamin nor I can hide the shock on our faces. "I see here that you have 300 thousand followers; can you tell us how you would pitch our Imposter Chicken Bar to your fans?" Benjamin pulls the bar from his bag and slides it across the table. She looks at the bar like she's scared of it and finally says, "Oh, you want me to eat it right now? I'm using all my daily calories for this coffee..."

I take a sip of my steaming cup of coffee and swallow back my annoyance, and my palms start to sweat against the warm mug. I see Benjamin's eyebrow lift as he glances between us as if he wants to see if I have what it takes to take back the control. If we can't get a real reaction from her eating the chicken bar, there's no way the agency is going to sign a check for her for ten grand to do a campaign.

*You can do this, Elliot; what would Gwen say?* Before I can talk myself out of it the words are already leaving my mouth. "Rose, I'm only going to say this once, so listen carefully. You've completely wasted our time for the last hour with your selfie shenanigans and we are offering you a lot of money to do this campaign. If you can't even taste the product, please tell me now so that I can find someone else who would be happy to earn ten fucking grand to eat a piece of fake chicken and tell random strangers on the internet about it."

Benjamin nods his head slightly. I see a small smirk form on his lips for just a moment before he takes a sip from his coffee washing it away.

She picks up the chicken bar from the table and takes the tiniest bite possible. "It... it tastes like chicken." She takes another bite... "Oh my God, I forgot how much I love chicken. It's been so long! Do you have any more of these things?"

"Don't worry, that can be arranged." I pull out the contract, and Benjamin leads us through the signing and expectations from both parties. We negotiate that in exchange for an additional post, we'll throw in a box of Imposter Chicken Bars free.

She waves me goodbye but decides to go in for a hug with Benjamin. He stands there awkwardly, refusing to hug her back and we make our departure from our first transaction. Though the whole ordeal was highly stressful, I feel confident in my selection and I think Benjamin does too. I'm not going to hold my breath waiting on him to tell me that though. I grab my seat belt and click it in place, getting settled for the next leg when Benjamin asks, "Why did she smell like she hasn't bathed in a year?"

It's been twenty-nine years since the last time I heard another person's voice. I am in a vessel of isolation and this is how I die... Surely at least a decade had gone by? I nestle into the passenger seat, slowly losing my mind... or maybe I already lost it. There is no music, there is no conversation, and there is certainly no joy in this vehicle. I believe Benjamin sucks the joy from those around him to use as a life source—it's the only logical explanation why he could be so content and unwavering in his silence. Finally, something in me snaps. I can't take the silence... It's maddening!

"I don't care how much you hate me; we are human beings and we're made to survive in communities!"

Benjamin looks at me, and I can see him mentally watching the replay of what just happened to understand why I'm suddenly screaming at him. He lifts an eyebrow and turns back to face the road. Stupid safe driver.

"What was that?"

Oops, I guess I said it out loud. "Benjamin, I'm going crazy over here; can we play a game or talk or something?"

"No."

"I'm afraid I'm at risk of developing a split personality for survival purposes. I'm going to have to entertain myself somehow. What if the personality is a *bad* one?"

"Elliot, I'm afraid it may be too late for that." I can see he's fighting a slight smirk and this only encourages me. If I could win Benjamin over and we could become real friends, acquaintances even, it would make my heart so happy. It would make coming to work so much better. I can see it now, us walking in in the morning, wishing each other 'good morning.' We could eat lunch together in the cafeteria and talk about our favorite Netflix series. I could help him with his girlfriend problems—I take that idea back. I don't want to think about

Benjamin and his girlfriend; my gut starts to churn, and sadness overwhelms me. *Be gone, strange feeling! I do not allow it!*

Now he's turned to look at me, complete bewilderment on his face. Yeah, I definitely said that out loud.

"Here's the deal, we can either talk for a few minutes to ease my troubled soul or I can turn on some of my favorite old school R&B and belt it out at the top of my lungs... The choice is yours, Benji."

"Do *not* call me that! And I choose none of the above."

"Please, Benjamin, I'm going to die of boredom! I'm losing my social skills as we speak. I can*not* go on like this!" Am I being dramatic? Yes. Is it working? The verdict is still out, but you can't fault me for lack of trying.

"Three questions," he says. "You can ask me three questions, and I have the right to veto a question at any time."

I tap my finger to my lip. "Hmm, so if you veto the question, do I get to replace it with another question? Also, are you going to ask me any questions? What if I don't want to answer your questions?"

"I guess you can replace the question with another one, but just know I'm only answering three, and *no*, I don't care to ask you any questions."

"Well, that just feels rude. How are we supposed to get to know each other if the conversation doesn't go both ways?"

"Do you want to play? Those are my conditions. Take it or leave it."

I agree to his terms, knowing I'm pushing my luck with him. Now to think of the best conversation-starting questions.... They can't be yes or no, and anything that has a story attached may make him talk longer.

"Where did you go to school?"

"Penn State. Next."

Dammit, it wasn't a yes or no question but it may as well have been; I've got to step up my game.

My playful banter falls away when the next question pops into my head. I want to be brave again so I just go for it. "Are you grumpy toward everyone, or did I do something wrong?"

He exhales a long steady breath and tightens his grip on the steering wheel.

"I'm sorry," I say quickly, "that was out of line. It's none of my business and of course you probably hate me. God knows I've given you plenty of reasons."

Benjamin's stern eyes soften and he shakes his head. "No, I haven't always been this way. Believe it or not, there was once a time where I had everything I could've wanted; I was the happiest I've ever been. Then one day I lost it all, so no, Elliot, it's not your fault. Sometimes your joy shines so bright that it reminds me of all of my darkness. It's frustrating and sometimes I guess I get a little jealous."

I blink several times, and my heart skips a few beats. I don't know if I'm more shocked that he opened up to me or at his response. A nervous laugh bubbles out of me before I continue to pry. "That's ridiculous. How in the world could you ever be jealous of me? I'm a walking disaster." I laugh again at the absurdity.

Benjamin tugs on a strand of my hair. It's a playful, teasing gesture and I'm not sure what to do with that; Benjamin is anything but playful. "Elliot, you're not a disaster. You're actually kind of remarkable. Sure, you're impulsive and awkward but I think you have so much potential locked up in that brain of yours. Something just tells me you're afraid to show it. What are you so afraid of?"

Sweat begins to accumulate in weird places, like the bottom of my feet and the inside of my elbows, and my mouth goes bone-dry. I frantically search for some kind of words to say to recover, to make this conversation less... heavy.

"Ah, ah, ah, no, you don't. You said you weren't going to ask me any questions, remember?" I wave my finger at him, hoping he'll read the room. I see his face shift, his jaw tighten, and his shoulders tense.

I tap my lip playfully. "Hmm, let's see, how about...how do you and Thad know each other, and what made you decide to merge your companies?"

He grips the steering wheel tightly and reaches over to switch on the radio. "I'm done playing this game. Why don't you catch up on some sleep so I don't have to carry you inside when we get there."

And just like that, the tiny glimmer of the real Benjamin crawls back into his cave and I'm left with his cyborg copy. It seems we've covered both of our touchy issues in just a matter of seconds. Even though it's completely hypocritical of me, I can't help but wonder what he's hiding.

# SEVENTEEN

Benjamin

I pull up the calendar information and plug the address into the GPS and relax when I see our ETA. Timing road trips can be tricky, and I'm always nervous when I'm on a timeline and matters like roadwork and traffic are out of my control. It doesn't help that I've got the grown-up equivalent of a twelve-year-old riding with me. Between fighting with her over the radio station, turning the music down so that I can retain my hearing, and stopping for all the pee breaks, it's a miracle we've made it on time at all. Things got heavy with Elliot earlier and I can't seem to get the moment out of my head. Why did I go there, asking her such a personal question when there's no chance in hell I'd ever open up to her in the same way?

I take in the beautiful topography of this state that I love so much, the rolling hills and subtle mountains. The touch of city flair. Their combined effect brings to mind both country living and nightlife, and I am reminded of Sarah. She always wanted to settle down in Nashville. It seems that I can't escape her anymore. The memories flood back with every new experience I share with Elliot, and I'm starting to think maybe something is wrong with me. It's been two fucking years; the pain had dulled somewhat. Fuck, I was handling it the best I could anyway, but ever since I've been trapped together with Elliot on this stupid road trip, I feel like my grief is magnified. Every time she laughs at something or crinkles her nose up in that cute way, it's like I'm being stabbed in the heart.

The last thing I need to be doing right now is dwelling on the past and thinking about Sarah...or Maddie. *No, Benjamin, you are here now with your employee and this is work, not pleasure.* Albeit she's a beautiful woman, with gorgeously toned legs. After seeing her in the gym this morning, I can attest that her tight body is very much earned and not from starvation. I steal a glance and take in the bulky sweats and oversized sweater she's donned for the drive. Who would've known that this woman was hiding the perfect body under her obnoxious, baggy sweats, and why am I just now noticing it? I have no right to notice it. I shake the unwelcome thought away and bring my attention back to the task on hand.

"You get a chill or something?" Elliot asks as she applies a thick coat of mascara to her already black eyelashes. Really, why do women jump through so many hoops to make themselves up? It seems like a lot of work and maybe I'm only speaking for myself here, but most guys don't care about all that makeup anyway. She turns toward me, waving her hand in front of my face. "Hello? Earth to Benjamin."

"Huh, I'm sorry. I was focusing on the road," I lie. "Did you say something?"

"I asked you if we were making good time? Do you think I need to practice my pitch again?" She takes a sip of water with shaking hands.

I can see Elliot's nerves are getting the best of her, so while I want to say 'for the love of God, no, please don't make me hear your pitch again for the fourth time,' this is my company on the line, and I appreciate her taking things seriously.

"Yeah, let's hear it," I say. "Once again from the top."

---

I've got my back to the vehicle where Elliot is currently transforming herself from cozy traveler to business professional. I glance at my phone. Jesus, she's been in there for twenty minutes now; if we don't hurry we'll merely be on time, which by my standards is unacceptable.

I knock on the window. "Hurry up in there, will ya? We're going to be late!" The edginess that I've tried to tamp down is pushing through, and I inwardly scold myself for showing my frustration. If I know anything about Elliot, it's that she doesn't handle stress well. The last thing I need is for her to choke in this meeting because I worked her nerves. "Do you need any... help?" I add, hoping to soften the blow of my last message.

She flings the door open, her hair falling in a mess around her face, and jumps out in a rush. "I'm so sorry! I was trying to get the wrinkles out of this stupid dress." She pulls at the neck of her fitted sheath dress that looks a bit too close to a little black dress to keep me focused on the task at hand. I glance down and take in her toned legs, and I swear right there, a little bit of drool falls from my mouth. I feel like a twelve-year-old boy as I adjust myself and do everything I can to push the thought away. What is going on with me lately? She's just a silly, gorgeous woman. I've had my share of them and they're all the same in the end.

Except that Elliot is wildly different from anyone I've ever met.

"And then my eyeliner was crooked. Gwen filled me with way too much confidence when she gave me that winged eyeliner tutorial, so I had to remove it all and start over." She looks down at her phone. "Oh Benjamin, we need to go!"

Before I can catch up to the conversation I obviously spaced out for, Elliot takes off toward the building in nothing short of a sprint. The cool wind whips my tie into my face and when I pull it down, is that...no...that can't be right.

I wipe my eyes and bite back a chuckle. I don't know whether to laugh or to be incredibly scared about this woman who's taking charge on this account. Elliot's all but jogging in the parking lot decked out in an LBD, black pumps...and her dress tucked into her underwear. At this point she's too far ahead of me to tell her; I'm not exactly going to scream across the parking lot. So I do what any red-blooded male would do in this situation. I take in the round, firm ass that's presented itself to me in broad daylight. A warm rush of blood shoots to my cock and I realize I may be enjoying my view a little too much, considering I'm about to have to step into my CEO role in just a few minutes.

Elliot looks so ridiculous, running through the parking lot decked out in a fancy dress and shoes. Her youthful energy brings a smile to my face, and her beautiful innocence is a breath of fresh air. It's such a change from other women who seem to only be interested in superficial things like money or fame. Elliot is her own rare breed.

As she approaches the building, two men come into sight. Shit, I've got to catch up to her and fix her fashion faux pas, because as much as I've enjoyed my full moon view of the full cheeky panties, I'll be damned if I let some other jackholes see her like this. I take off into a sprint to catch up to her, lungs burning for air, and grab her just in time to block her backside from the men.

"Benjamin, what are you doing?" She gasps at my sudden embrace. I don't know what comes over me, maybe it's all the blood that's rushing to my cock, but I lean down and whisper, "Hang on just a sec, you've got a little..." And I pull her dress from her panties with a quick flick of my wrist.

A gasp escapes her lips and her cheeks burn red in embarrassment. "Oh. My. God. I'm the biggest klutz." Closing her eyes, she takes a deep breath and places her hands firmly on my chest to push me back, though just slightly. "I assure you, I'm going to overthink this for many years to come, but right now, I've got a client waiting on me. So can we just pretend you didn't just see my ass and this isn't awkward at all?" Her voice turns up at the end.

"Sure thing, sweet cheeks." As soon as it leaves my mouth, I mentally kick myself in the balls for being so inappropriate. Shit, I've been hanging out with Jack too much. I glance at my watch, bringing her focus back to the task at hand. "Ah, shit, we've got to get in there." I gesture for her to lead the way, shoving my hands in my pockets and replaying my latest basketball highlights in my head in a desperate attempt to calm the raging hard-on growing in my pants.

Bros' Gym lives up to its name. Walls lined with '90s Playboy posters and *Baywatch* babes, a crusty used-to-be velvet sofa furnishing the waiting room, and nothing short of a Hooters waitress greets us from the front desk. Jesus Christ, Thad's poor business dealings are still haunting me, and I'm 2,500 miles away.

I glance over and see Elliot nervously wiping the sweat from her hands onto her skirt. "Relax." I give her shoulder a slight squeeze. "You've got this."

She gives me a curt nod as she chews her lower lip, stands up a little straighter, and marches through the conference room to seal the deal. *That's my girl.* The moment the thought enters my mind, a hollow sensation fills my gut and I try to shake it away. *No, you asshole, she's not your girl. You're a damaged piece of shit and she deserves so much more.*

Chase Knight—or @ChasintheDream as he is more commonly known—and his real-life bro/business partner sit in their tank tops and boat shoes, waiting for Elliot's pitch. Overall, I'd say Chase is good-looking in a pretty boy, trust-fund kind of way.

"Thank you so much for allowing us to come to speak with you today. I realize this was relatively short notice, but I think you'll find that our product will be a great fit for your current clientele." Elliot begins her presentation, hitting all her talking points with ease. I sit in the back of the room and am dumbfounded by her natural talent. If I didn't know better, I'd say this girl—this woman had given multimillion-dollar presentations for the last several years. Elliot is a natural.

"We believe that the Imposter Chicken Bar will be the new staple for fitness gurus and bodybuilders, and don't you worry." She gestures to Chase's allergy bracelet. "It's completely nut-free.

"Thad Powell, our CEO, is also highly allergic to peanuts so trust me when I tell you it's completely safe!" She laughs a little nervously and continues. "I've put together a social media campaign here. As you can see on page ten of our presentation deck, I've laid out the potential profits from direct sales forecast over the next six months."

"Well, well, well... looks like this sweet little thing has done her homework." Chase nudges his brother, who appears to be more of the silent partner in the relationship. "Do you have a boyfriend, babydoll?"

Elliot's mouth drops open and she begins to recoil into

herself. "Mr. Knight, if you'd like to look over these projections, our team has taken the liberty to analyze your next—"

He furrows his brow in mock concern. "Relax, darlin', there's no need to be so serious."

"Mr. Knight, I'm sure you can appreciate that we're on a bit of a time crunch and want to respect your time as well. I think if we could all bring our attention back to the terms of the agreement—"

"All right, all right. I get it." He throws his hands up in defense and fake whispers to his brother, "It looks like someone wore her big girl panties to the meeting today." He waggles his eyebrows toward Elliot in what I can only assume is an attempt at flirtation. "Let me guess, you're more of a bikini girl. Am I right?"

"That's enough, Mr. Knight." I slap my laptop closed and stand up with such force that my chair smacks the tile beneath with an echoed *thwack*. Elliot's eyes go wide like a deer in headlights and she stands frozen at the front of the conference table, seemingly afraid to move. She didn't get the hint from my not-so-subtle thanks but no thanks grand gesture, so I gently steer her from the room.

"POW! will not be doing business with a bunch of misogynistic assholes. You can all go fuck yourselves."

I usher a confused Elliot from the building, silently fuming with rage. Rage toward the pigheaded assholes who think it's OK to treat women like pieces of meat, and rage toward Elliot for allowing anyone to treat her that way. Jesus Christ, had I not been there, how long would it have gone on? Would she just have stood back and taken the crude remarks and not stood up for herself? Shit, how has this woman made it this long walking the streets of Chicago with virtually no backbone in her body?

We reach the rental and I swing her door open with such force that she jumps back.

"Benjamin, what is going on? That was our top client for this proposal. Without Bros' Gym on board, we'll never reach our sales goal. Thad's going to send me packing. Before I left for this trip, he said, 'Elliot, this whole proposal is one hundred percent your responsibility; if it doesn't work out, this is on you.' And now you just told the CEO of the company to go fuck himself." She turns back. "We've got to go back and apologize; maybe if I go in alone and tell them you're bipolar or something, he'll hear me out."

I grab her wrist, a little harder than I mean to, and shove her into the passenger seat. "You will absolutely not go back in there and apologize. This is my company and I will not do business with the likes of those assholes. Jesus, Elliot, how have you survived this long?" I slam her door and she glares at me with confusion and fear.

"Put your goddamn seat belt on and please for the love of God, don't say anything. I've got to think this through." I put the car in drive and program the GPS on my phone to bring us to our next destination. The silence is deafening, and it takes all my concentration to focus on the road and not turn back to beat the living shit out of Chase Knight and his whole team.

# EIGHTEEN

Benjamin

*Two years earlier...*

"Sarah, have you seen my keys?" Shit, I'm going to be late if I don't leave in two minutes; traffic is always terrible on Thursdays. I ruffle through the pile of dirty laundry next to the hamper in our room. I don't remember moving my keys and I'm disciplined about hanging them on the key ring. I don't want to blame Sarah, but I know she's the culprit here.

She leans out of the bathroom to answer me, hair wet and in the middle of applying her makeup. "Are they not hanging on the hook? You always put them on the hook."

"Babe, I've checked the hook; that's why I'm asking you if you've seen them. Did you take the car yesterday?" I'm trying to hold back the aggravation building in my chest. I hate being late.

"I had to bring Maddie to her doctor's appointment, and then we went by the office to grab some paperwork."

"Shit." I rush to the front door and open it where I find the keys stuck in the lock. "Sarah, you've got to be more careful when you and Maddie are home alone." I pull the keys from the lock as she approaches.

"I'm sorry, Benjamin, my mind was racing when I came in. I turned on the TV for Maddie and had a heap of paperwork to go through. Clearly, I'd lose my head if it wasn't attached." She wraps the towel around her wet hair and pulls me into a hug. Her skin is clammy and cold, and I can feel her heart racing against my chest.

"Babe, you've got to start taking better care of yourself. You're running yourself ragged trying to take on all of those accounts. I can practically feel the adrenaline flowing off of you." I pull her into my chest again, not caring that I'm now officially going to be late.

"Benjamin, I told you if I can just land this new account with the Ferringtons, then my parents will see how valuable I am and put me back on staff. Then I'll be able to relax and enjoy the slower pace of life. I promise all of this hard work is going to pay off, you'll see."

"Benji, will you watch cartoons with me?" Maddie calls from the couch.

"No, sweetie, Benji is going to be late for work. I don't have time to watch cartoons with you, but I promise you when I get home we'll have a *Scooby-Doo* marathon. I'll even make popcorn."

"And hot chocolate?" she asks.

"Of course." I laugh. "Everyone knows you can't have popcorn without hot chocolate; they go together like orange juice and toothpaste."

"Eww, Benji, I do not like to drink orange juice after I brush my teeth. You're weird." Maddie turns back around on the couch and plops herself back down.

"She looks like she's feeling better; why don't you take her to the park today? She just learned how to go all the way across the monkey bars last weekend and it's—"

"Benjamin, could you please stop telling me what I should do?" Sarah snaps. "I don't have time to bring her to the park today. Don't guilt me for working."

"Sarah, you know that's not what I was doing. All I'm saying is you work too much, and a day at the park in the fresh air may do you some good." I shrug on my coat and open the door. "Please, could you just consider reading a book or taking a bath...anything that isn't work for even a few minutes today?"

She rolls her eyes and huffs out a sigh. "OK, I'll take a bath... only because I need to shave my legs anyway!"

"I'll take it." I give her a soft kiss goodbye. "I'll pick up dinner on my way home tonight. I love you."

"Love you too," she calls before heading back into her office in our bedroom.

I can't wait for her to close that deal; I can't wait to get my wife back.

# NINETEEN

Elliot

I wring my hands in my lap and steal a worried glance over my shoulder at the angry, silent man who's seemed to overtake Benjamin's body. I play back the memory for the umpteenth time and for the life of me, I can't figure out what happened, why he just snapped. I haven't felt this much like a scorned child since I accidentally broke my great-grandma's antique china during a pretend tea party when I was ten. My mother was so angry I thought her head was going to burst.

The thought that Benjamin may be mentally unstable crosses my mind. Oh shit, what if he's one of those serial killers who's been posing as a CEO, and he's driving me to a cabin in the woods to slowly peel back my skin and pluck out my toenails one by one?

I begin sweating, and I slap my hand to my forehead. To think I just willingly got in the vehicle with an angry man. What is the statistic? The first twenty-four hours are the most important for a victim to be rescued? I try to calm my breathing and realize my phone—my lifeline—is in my purse in the back seat. Since I don't want to make any sudden movements, I slowly recline my seat. Maybe he won't notice.

The roaring silence does me no favors as I try to slowly lean the seat back; the buzzing vibration might as well be a jackhammer. Benjamin's eyes find mine from the side of his face and I yawn dramatically. I even add in a big stretch just to really sell it.

"Well, I don't know about you, but I'm beat." Despite the midday sun beaming straight into my eyes, I do my best to look the part. I lean my seat back as far as it can go and wriggle my arms above my head. My purse has fallen on the floor behind Benjamin's seat, so while it would be easy to simply bend to grab it, that would be way too obvious. I squirm up in my seat until my feet are barely touching the ground.

"Elliot, what are you doing?"

"Oh, I'm just getting comfortable. You know, going to take a little snoozeroo for the next..." I glance at his GPS and wonder how dumb he must be to program our destination where I can see. "Fourteen hours." At least I'll be able to tell the police where he's headed.

My fingers brush the smooth surface of my fake leather bag and I lock my grip on the strap. My freedom is so, so close if I could just reach my phone....

Suddenly my body jolts forward in my seat. Benjamin must've seen my escape attempt and slammed on the brakes to interrupt. Thinking fast, I grab my purse strap and hurl it like a helicopter propellor over my head, channeling my inner junior high shot put thrower. "Hiyaaaa, motherfucker!"

The cheap faux leather of my purse crashes into Benjamin's face with a sharp *thwack*. I guess Gwen's idea of carrying all my makeup with me in case I needed a touch-up was a life-saving decision. Benjamin's hands leave the wheel and cover his left eye. "What the fuuuuuck!" He swerves off the highway and brings the car to a slow stop. "Jesus Christ, Elliot, what is going on?"

I pull my pocket-sized mace from my purse and hold it out in front of me like Percy Jackson yielding his special pen/sword. "I'm going to get out of the car now, Benjamin. Do not follow me or I'll shoot...er, I'll spray you in the eyes!" I hold up the mace to show him I'm not afraid to use it. "I will not be a helpless murdered woman. I'm calling an Uber and there's nothing you can do to stop me!"

"Hold on, hold on.... Hold the fuck on! What exactly do you think is going on here?" Hands raised above his head, I'm sure we're creating quite the spectacle for the oncoming traffic.

"Do you think I'm an idiot? I know what you're doing; that charade back there didn't fool me one bit!" I shake my mace and hold it out across my body, as if to get as far away from the spray as possible. "You're going to bring me across the country and chop me up into little pieces and pull out my toenails, but I won't go without a fight!"

I notice the cut above Benjamin's eye when blood starts pouring down his face. Oh God, there's so much blood. Why is there so much blood? He attempts to wipe the stream flowing down his temple with his shirt sleeve, but there's no help. The wound is pulsing, shooting forward, and I feel the bile rise in my throat and the sky turns white. I press the trigger before I go down and the world goes black.

---

A bright, offensive light burns directly into my retinas and I'm suddenly aware of the stinging cold ground beneath me. For a moment my body stiffens in panic; have I just been abducted? I blink away the beams of light strobing beneath my eyelids and am met with a hooded being hovering above me. Oh shit, it's even worse than I thought; am I in an alien spaceship right now? I knew my *Unsolved Mysteries* addiction would prepare me for this.

I attempt to scurry backward, not knowing if I'm hovering millions of miles away from Earth in outer space... "Please. I. Come. In. Peace." I slowly articulate each word on the off-chance the aliens speak English.

"Would you just stop! I'm trying to check to make sure you haven't given yourself a concussion!" Benjamin's words are like a bucket of cold water over my body, snapping me out of my alternate universe. I study him and realize what I thought was a scary cloak is actually my scarf tied around a large gash above his eye. Suddenly the happenings of the last—however long I've been passed out on the side of the highway—rush back to me.

"There. You need to lie still. How many fingers am I holding up?" His large palm cradles my neck ever so gently. A strange tingle builds in my belly, traveling lower and lower as he continues to hold me. I must've hit my head harder than I thought. I blink away the blur in my eyes and Benjamin's shape comes into focus. Swollen eyes stare down at me beneath the gash that trickles a stream of blood down the side of his face.

"Benjamin, what's wrong with your face? You look like you've been in a fight!" I reach up and gently push the scarf away so I can see more of his swollen features.

He rubs at the trickling blood with the back of his arm. "That would be your doing. You sprayed me just before you collapsed..." His voice hardens at the memory and I don't know whether he's angry or amused.

"I did? Oh my God, Benjamin, I'm so sorry! I thought you were going to kidnap me. Sometimes my anxiety has a mind of its own." I cover my face in my hands, wishing I could disappear. I don't know if I could manage to make things any worse if I tried. He's probably going to fire me for...well, there are so many things I can't even sum them up. What if he presses charges? I'm not built for jail; I'd never survive it.

Benjamin seems to see the wheels spinning out of control and places his heavy hand on my shoulder. "Relax, Elliot, I'm not going to fire you."

I exhale a sigh of relief.

"But I am going to need you to do me a favor." He tightens the scarf around his wound and hesitates. "Do you think you could drive the rest of the way? I can't see with these—" he points to his swollen eyelids— "well, at least until the swelling goes down."

"Of course!" My voice comes out a little too excited. I steady myself and pull up to a shaky stand, offering Benjamin my hand to show him just how capable I am. This is my chance to redeem myself, Minnesota, here we come!

---

We've been driving in silence for about eight hours. Benjamin's leaned his seat back and lost his battle to sleep. Even though I need to pee again, I'm holding out as long as possible. I know I can be an annoying travel companion, believe me, I've heard it all my life. I really am doing my best to control my talking and be on my very best behavior. I've even refrained from turning the volume on the radio up so I can jam out to this amazing '90s radio station so that Benjamin can catch up on some sleep.

A light dusting of snow begins to fall, and I tighten my grip on the steering wheel. I turn down the music to make sure I can see the road and so I can give every ounce of my attention to the winding country road before me. Benjamin stirs in the seat next to me. We pass the WELCOME TO IOWA sign and I breathe a sigh of relief. Benjamin has entrusted me to drive us a distance that I've never driven before. Of course, I wasn't going to tell *him* that. He doesn't need to know that I failed my driving test three times and had to hire a driving tutor when I was a senior in high school; he doesn't need to know that I usually take public transportation when it's snowing because even though I live in Chicago, I've never developed the particular skillset nor had I ever intended on doing so. I inhale a sharp breath and focus on my breathing to calm myself. I have to admit, it feels pretty amazing tackling such a huge obstacle.

I hear the faint beginnings of "Shoop" by Salt-N-Pepa coursing over the static station, and I can't help myself. Little by little, I slowly turn up the volume. I glance over at Benjamin, who still appears to be sleeping, before I break out the moves from the choreographed dance I performed solo at my seventh grade talent show. By the end of the song, I'm singing all the lyrics and have lost all anxiety about driving in the snow. I don't even register when it starts to snow harder; I just turn up the speed on the windshield wipers like I've been driving in the snow for years. I catch Benjamin staring at me out of the corner of my eye and am reminded where I am and who I'm with.

"Oh, I'm sorry! I didn't mean to wake you. I just really love this song." I reach to turn the volume down, but his hand meets mine and stills me. His large warm, calloused hand touches me for the second time today, and for the second time, a wave of electricity shoots through my body.

He doesn't immediately move his hand, "Don't. I mean, you're the driver, so the rules state that you get to control the radio." I give him a questioning glance and he shrugs. "I don't make the rules."

A warm blush crawls up my cheeks and I continue belting out the next song. Benjamin's smile reaches his eyes, and my stomach does a little backflip into my throat.

"Can I ask you a question?" Benjamin's voice cuts through the air like a knife. I've felt the tension growing thicker ever since he woke up, and I'd be lying if I said the little game of badminton in my tummy has eased up.

"Shoot."

He hesitates just for a moment. "Why would you ever let someone treat you like that?"

I blink back the confusion, trying to recall the interaction from our last stop when we had to refuel. "What do you mean? The lady was perfectly polite. I mean it's not as though I was expecting five-star treatment at the Kum and Go—I really hate that name."

"Elliot. Cut the shit," he snaps. The happy-go-lucky, relaxed Benjamin has been replaced with the scary-robot Benjamin from before. Dang, I was enjoying the new version.

For a moment my mind starts to wonder if he's bipolar... but the thought is once again interrupted by his piercing voice. "Chase Knight. The owner of the Bros' Gym. He sexually harassed you back there, I just keep replaying it over and over in my head and.... Fuck, Elliot, if I hadn't been there, would you have done anything? Would you have stood up for yourself at all? How have you survived this long?" He reaches into his perfectly unkempt hair and grabs a fistful.

"Oh, that. Benjamin, I assure you that's nothing. Believe me, I've seen and heard a lot worse. The most important thing is to keep your head cool and redirect the conversation. You're overthinking it." I chuckle at his overprotectiveness. It's a strange thing, having someone freak out on your behalf. Other than Gwen and Maggie, no one's ever made the effort before. Surely he's witnessed a woman being sexually victimized in the workplace...

"No, Elliot, that's not OK!" he says, annoyed.

"Well, if I had five dollars for every time I saw a woman being sexualized at work or even experienced it myself, I'd be a very rich woman," I say, unable to keep my sadness from seeping into my tone.

He leans up in the seat and turns to face me. "Elliot, why would you ever let anyone treat you that way? I wanted to rip that guy's face off but the way you...you just took it. I—never mind. You know what? It's not my business anyway."

I barely let him finish his thought before I counter. "I am so tired of everyone telling me how to let people treat me!" I can tell I've caught him off guard with my sudden spurt of anger, so I keep going to drive the point home. "Benjamin, no one cares how I'm treated, not even my parents. It's always been this way. You think you can spew out some blanket statements like 'stand up for what you believe in and things will work out.' Well, I am here to tell you that's the biggest load of bullshit I've ever heard!"

He meets my eyes and very calmly says, "Elliot, people will treat you how you allow them to treat you. Yeah, maybe it's a reflection on their poor character, but who's the common denominator in this scenario?"

If I could leap from my seat and pummel this man who just burned me with the harshest truth I've ever been the recipient of, I would. Instead, I glare at him and stick out my tongue. Real mature, Elliot. Just as I turn my head back to the very slippery, very icy road, I see the glowing irises of a gigantic elk standing directly in our path.

# TWENTY

Elliot

*OK, Elliot, remember driver's ed. What did we learn about stopping on the ice?* "Pump the brakes!" Benjamin yells, answering my question, making me wonder if I asked it out loud again. Immediately I heed his command and start pumping. The car fishtails, but it seems to be working. We're playing an incredibly dangerous game of chicken with this elk, who apparently has no fear of death. Benjamin's got a death grip on the 'oh shit handle' and I'm swerving all over the road, hoping and praying the elk moves out of the way but no such luck.

"You turn me on!" I yell, wanting Benjamin to know how I feel since these are clearly my last moments, but I don't stop there. "I think you're hot even though you're mean to me, and I'm sorry you're going to die at my hands!"

We ram into the immovable force and the car spins wildly. My airbag goes off, knocking the breath out of me, and the seat belt constricts, holding me in place. By the time the car stops spinning, I realize we've rolled into the ditch and I'm still alive.

Luckily, the car didn't flip or hit a tree. I do a quick assessment. I can move my arms and my legs, my neck doesn't hurt, and my fingers and toes are all wiggling. I turn to Benjamin who's looking at me with a mix of what appears to be pure shock and rage. Surely he didn't hear my confession; adrenaline was flowing like jungle juice at a frat party. But the look on his face tells me everything I need to know—he heard me and he's pissed.

Despite the dramatic showdown and crash with the fearless elk, our car has only suffered minor damage, and said fearless elk pranced off with a shit-eating grin on his face. OK, so maybe I didn't see his face, but clearly, he accomplished his goal and won the game that I had no interest in playing. Benjamin unbuckles his seat belt and stumbles through the knee-high snow to assess the damage. I don't know anything about engines —or cars for that matter, but I can identify a flat tire when I see one, and well, we've got two flats. I'm no mathematician, but I don't think our single donut emergency tire is going to help us out.

I stumble over to help Benjamin and hold my phone like a flashlight over the engine. He mumbles something about the radiator and then notices the flats. "Shit" is all he says at that realization.

I attempt to crank the car and the engine doesn't even turn over. "So do we call Triple A or something?" I throw out this possible solution, even though I know our cells don't have any reception here.

"Yeah, I suppose the Triple A fairies will come rescue us. Maybe you can bat your eyes and a nice trucker will stop to save us."

After the conversation we were having before the crash, his words are like salt in a wound.

"I'm sorry, just trying to come up with a solution. I'm sorry to annoy you with my terrible ideas. Have fun wallowing in self-pity; I'm going to find help." There's no other option, though. We can't stay here in these freezing temps, and it's not like we can run the car for heat while we figure out a plan. I remember seeing a sign for a restaurant about a mile back. I grab my coat out of my bag and change my shoes to rain boots and start walking toward the sign.

He crosses his arms over his chest. "What the hell do you think you're doing?"

"Finding help."

"So you're just going to walk then? You'll get hypothermia within the hour!" he yells after me, but I'm not stopping. I've screwed everything up and I know it's all my fault. I'm angry at him, but I'm even more upset with myself. Of all the guys to have a crush on, I've got to have the hots for the one man who hates me more than anyone in the world and just so happens to be my boss. *You really know how to pick 'em, Elliot.*

Benjamin follows behind me, keeping just enough distance so we don't feel uncomfortable talking, but staying close enough that his energy is negatively affecting my own. He's like my own personal cloud of sadness looming over me with every step I take.

"You know, you don't have to follow me. I can take care of myself," I call over my shoulder. If he thinks I need him to take care of me, he can think again. I'm a resourceful, strong woman, dammit.

"The hell you can," he mutters.

That's it, the chains on the last of my resolve have officially snapped. I think back on all the mistakes and trouble I've caused since I took this job and realize I can't do much more to land myself right in CJ's office as soon as this journey from hell is over.

I don't know what's come over me, but a sudden rage floods

through me and all I see is red. For once in my life I am so tired of being a screwup. The plastered-on fake happiness is gone, and I just want to fight. I spin on my heel and dive toward him, channeling my inner linebacker. Benjamin lets out an oof as my shoulder makes contact with his diaphragm, and we both fly backward into a soft mound of freshly fallen snow. The snow collapses from our weight, and we're surrounded by the freezing powder. I sit up and push myself away from him, frantic to put as much distance between us as possible.

My left boot has flown off somewhere behind me, and my frigid foot reminds me that we're lying in ice-cold snow in subfreezing temperatures. Now that I'm lying on top of his rock-hard body, I almost forget the reason for our entanglement, enjoying the human contact that I haven't experienced in, I don't know...five years, but who's counting?

Benjamin sits up and rubs the snow out of his hair. He leans back on his elbows, throws his head back, and lets out an unruly belly laugh that echoes off the trees. I study him for a moment, turning my head to the side. Maybe he's concussed? I've never seen him laugh like this...ever. He's really cute when he laughs; I could get used to the sound of it. Suddenly, though, the warmth in my chest toward him is extinguished when I realize he's laughing at me. Once again, ridiculous Elliot is the butt of the joke.

I force my chin up. "I'm so happy to see you're not all cyborg and you do have a fraction of a sense of humor. Now excuse me while I find my boot, then I'll just be on my way."

"You should have seen your face when you charged at me!" He cackles again and I can't resist getting in one more hit. I slap him with my gloved hands frantically, looking more like a puppy trying to do the doggy paddle upstream, which only eggs him on more. He tries to block my slaps, bringing his arms up to cover his still slightly swollen face, but I just keep at it. He grabs me with both hands and forces my arms to my sides to hold me still. My teeth chatter with my exposed foot in the snow.

"You are the strangest woman I've ever met. I'm sorry, OK. If I let you go, are you going to keep hitting me? Or do you think you can control yourself?"

I nod my head, unable to speak because of the violent chattering of my jaw, accepting defeat from the woman-to-man combat that I initiated.

He releases my arms and I reach up and slap the hat off his head before I start my recon mission to find my boot.

"Ouch!"

I must have caught him off guard, and I do a mental victory dance because at least I got a reaction.

"I thought we had a truce!"

I'm hopping on one foot, trying to minimize the amount of contact my bare foot makes with the snow. My rain boots are bright red so I should be able to find the missing one pretty easily in all this white. Benjamin and I spot the boot at the same time, and he bolts to get to it before I can. I must've hit him with force for it to fly into the tree line thirty feet away. He reaches the boot and carries it back toward me, holding it high above my head. "I'll give you this, but you have to promise not to try to tackle me again."

"I don't make promises that I can't keep, Benjamin."

The bastard dares to laugh, actually laugh. It's the most beautiful, bellowing noise, and it sends tingles all the way up my spine. It's the kind of feeling I could spend a lifetime chasing

"I was wrong about you, Elliot."

He's still holding my boot and I'm standing there shivering. "What's that supposed to mean?"

"Here I thought you were some skittish kitten, but you're more like a rabid raccoon." He's laughing again, but his expression shifts as he notices my violent shivering. "Oh shit, you're freezing." He reaches down to slip the boot on my naked foot. "Elliot, where are your socks?"

"Oh, uh, my feet were sweating in the car, so I took them off. I wasn't planning on making a journey through the snow to find help tonight."

"Come on." He scoops me up and slides me over to his back. "You'll never warm up if your only barrier is your boot. Why didn't you say something earlier?"

"Benjamin, I'm not about to let you give me a piggy-back ride, I'm a grown woman for Christ's sake."

"I didn't recall asking you. You can either shut up and hold on, or I'll throw you over my shoulder caveman-style. Your choice."

I tighten my grip around his neck, causing him to cough and gasp for air.

"Watch it. I take my chivalry seriously!"

"Are you kidding right now? You are the least chivalrous man I've ever met!"

"Said the woman who I am literally carrying to safety..."

"I didn't ask for this; you insisted!"

"Because I'm a gentleman...at least when I want to be."

Benjamin carries me for the mile trek to the little restaurant like I weigh nothing, and I try to ignore the gigantic butterflies that seem to have migrated into my abdomen in the matter of minutes. This is bad. Really bad.

# TWENTY-ONE

Benjamin

Elliot's strong legs are holding tight around my waist, and her body is pressed flush against my back. What started as a playful gesture to help a cold woman in the snow now has my mind some kind of fucked up and thinking things I have no business thinking. I shake my head, trying to dislodge the thought. I need to stop while I'm ahead; no good can come of it. I try my best to ignore the buzzing electricity I feel from her body pressed into my back. *Come on, Williams, get it together.*

I see the inn in the distance. It's a quaint little place in the middle of nowhere, and thank fuck it's open because we're both on the verge of hypothermia. We get to the front door and I wait until I've stepped across the threshold before I put Elliot down.

The inn has an older mom-and-pop-style diner with a bar on the bottom floor. The lights are dim and there's only a handful of patrons here. I'm starving and realize we haven't stopped to eat anything since breakfast. I make my way over to the bar and have a seat.

"What are you doing?" Elliot asks with panic in her voice.

"I'm cold, hungry, and it's been a hell of a day so I'm going to have a drink." I pat the barstool next to me, suggesting she take a seat as well.

She reluctantly slides onto the barstool and brings the large menu up to her face. "What are we going to do about the car? Don't we need to call someone, like a tow truck or something?"

The bartender, wearing a shirt with the name *Gus* on the pocket, rounds the corner and answers before I can say anything. "You won't be getting in touch with any tow trucks tonight, not in this storm. Can I get you something to drink?"

"Hi, Gus. I'll have a Makers neat, make it a double, and a cheeseburger, please," I say, handing my menu back to him.

He looks at Elliot expectantly. "I don't know if alcohol is the best choice, Benjamin. We still have to figure out how to get to Minneapolis tonight."

"Minneapolis? Good luck with that, darlin'. I hate to break it to ya, but you aren't going to Minneapolis tonight, not in this weather. Have you seen the news?" He points to a TV in the back of the bar. "They're reporting three feet of snow over the next forty-eight hours. It's the biggest blizzard this town has seen in twenty years. You may as well get settled and wait it out like everyone else."

Panic rises in her face, and she looks like she's about to cry. "But we've still got to get to Minneapolis to meet the next influencer in the lineup. It's going to look unprofessional if we cancel. What is Thad going to say?"

"I'd like to remind you that Thad Powell is not my boss; I can do whatever the fuck I please." I let my harsh words sink in before I continue. "I've been pepper-sprayed by a woman who thought I was trying to abduct her even though we've been working together for the last six months, rammed into an elk, and had to trudge through a blizzard with said woman on my back to find shelter. Thad can go fuck himself if he has a problem with it." The bartender slides over my drink and I take a swig of my whiskey, letting the warm liquid comfort me.

She stomps her foot and crosses her arms over her chest. "I have an overactive imagination, coupled with anxiety, and this has been a lot for me to overcome in a very short time. I will not apologize for my self-defense!" Her sharp voice cracks.

My jaw tightens in annoyance, but not toward her. I can see her fist clamped tight by her side, still slightly trembling from the cold. She's right, I can't imagine how she must be feeling with all this change, but does she believe I'm the one she should be afraid of? After what I saw today, I'm disgusted and outraged at what could've happened if I wasn't there.

*Let it go, Williams. She's not yours to protect.*

"Listen, Elliot, it's been a hell of a day. Why don't you take a seat, have a drink, and we'll figure everything out in the morning?" I see her clenched jaw soften as she accepts defeat, plopping down on the stool next to me. "Good. Now, what'll you have to drink? It's on me tonight."

"I guess I could stand to take the edge off a bit, but I feel like I should be the one buying you the drink for having to put up with me. Sorry about everything today." She winces as she grazes my swollen eyelid with her fingertips. "Does it hurt?"

"It feels about how you'd expect, which isn't great, but I've had worse."

She chuckles. "You've had worse? What've you been *stabbed* or something?"

"Not exactly, but the wound feels pretty fucking close." I take a long sip of my whiskey, ending the conversation just as the bartender approaches with Elliot's drink.

"Looks like it's your lucky night. We've got one room left in the inn, and it's yours if you want it. You two lovebirds will be all set in our honeymoon suite upstairs." He pulls the last hanging keys from the keyring behind the register and dangles it in front of us.

Elliot's cheeks burn red with embarrassment. "He is *not* my boyfriend. He's my *boss!* Do you not have two rooms available? Surely there has to be something. What will HR say if they hear we're sharing a room?" I'm reminded of her confession right before we hit the elk, making the air thick between us with tension.

"Sorry, honey, I didn't mean to assume." He stares between the two of us, probably trying to understand what kind of boss-employee relationship we have going on, considering I barged in here with Elliot's thighs wrapped around my waist. "The honeymoon suite is the only room available, and you're lucky the couple who previously booked it canceled at the last minute, something about finding the groom with the mother of the bride on the morning of the wedding." He slaps the bar top. "Anyway, that couple's misfortune is your good luck tonight. I assume you still need somewhere to sleep...unless you want to head back to my place?" He winks.

I take the keys from him, stopping him before I do something I'll regret. "We'll take it." I lean over to Elliot. "Don't worry. I'll sleep on the couch."

She nods and looks down at her shaking hands. Her sudden nervousness makes me feel as though I'm doing something wrong, even taking advantage of her. I make a mental note to keep my distance and pull out my phone to update the guys, knowing I'm going to have to push this trip out another week. Jack's never going to let me hear the end of missing out on boys' night.

> Ran into an elk, crashed our car, and stuck in a snowstorm. I'm not going to make boys' night. Sorry, Jack, looks like you're going to have to go see Brad Pitt all by yourself.

JACK

What? Dude, you can't be serious! I've been saving my quarters all week. We were going to beat the high score on Pac-Man!

SAM

Damn, are you OK?

Thanks for your concern, Sam, and yes, I'm OK. Just going to have to crash here tonight. For the record, I wasn't the one who crashed. Elliot was driving because my eyes were still swollen from the mace.

JACK

What? Who sprayed you with mace? Did it hurt? I've always wanted to say that I've been sprayed with mace.

SAM

I'm sure that can be arranged. In fact, I'd love to help you out with that.

So you're all alone, stranded in a snowstorm with your hot assistant? How convenient...

JACK

Totally boning in a closet. I called it. Let me ask you this, brother, does she wax, or is it all-natural?

Benjamin?

Benny?

SAM

Leave him alone. Hopefully he's going to finally make a move on his woman.

You're being ignored. I'm putting my phone away now.

JACK

OK, lover boy, stay safe 😄

Fuck off

JACK

One of us has to

I shove my phone in my front pocket and scold myself for giving away too much information. I'm never going to hear the end of it. Out of the corner of my eye, I see Elliot accepting her second drink.

"Moscow mule? I would have pegged you for a white wine kind of girl." Her once-rigid posture has loosened, and she's pulled her hair up in a messy ball on the very top of her head. She's sitting cross-legged on her barstool. She's the perfect mix of curious and sexy. I'm surprised by my feelings, but I'd be lying if I said that Elliot's confession before our crash hasn't been playing on repeat in the back of my mind ever since, not that I have any plans of acting on it.

"Things aren't always what they seem at first sight, Benjamin." She stirs her drink with her tiny cocktail straw, and my balls clench into my groin when I see her pouty lips take it between them. Elliot is oblivious to her hotness. There's no way this woman is remotely aware of how men respond to her. It's the most endearing, yet frustrating thing.

"Besides, only Woo-Girls drink white wine, and Gwen would never allow it."

"Woo-Girls?"

"Yeah, you know, Woo-Girls are the ones at the sorority parties that don't know how to hold their liquor. They get drunk and scream 'Woo' all night."

I know the exact girl that Elliot is describing, but I play dumb, shaking my head, wanting her to keep talking. This girl is so animated when she speaks; I have to battle my lips from grinning like an idiot. There's something about her happiness that seems to spill over onto anyone around her. It's like she's a joy glitter bomb and once you're around her, there's no escaping the feeling, no matter how miserable you are determined to be.

"You can't be serious; you've never seen a Woo-Girl? Benjamin, they drink too much alcohol and they dance like this." She hops off the barstool and begins swaying to the music, moving only her shoulders, and it's the cutest fucking thing I've ever seen. "Woo-Hoo." She throws her hands above her head signifying the song's come to an end, and my face loses its battle. A huge grin breaks through my last bit of resolve.

"So you're telling me, Miss Overactive Imagination is trash-talking sorority girls who can't hold their liquor?" I raise my eyebrow in question. Clearly the alcohol has warmed us both up a bit, and just for the night, I want to pretend that I'm the happy guy, the one who's fun and playful, not the wounded windower who's angry at everyone, most especially himself.

Elliot's hand flies up to her heart as if I've wounded her. "Benjamin, are you challenging me right now? Because it sounds like you don't think I can hold my liquor."

I take a long slow sip of my whiskey. "I'd be willing to make a wager."

"I'm listening. What do you want?"

---

Elliot slams the shot glass down on the bar top, causing a sharp ring in my ears. Her hair has fallen out of her topknot, framing her face in loose waves, and her knit cardigan slips down her shoulder. She's giving me sex eyes, only I know they're not really sex eyes. Having spent the last two hours drinking with Elliot, I've realized this woman has no idea how sexy she is. She's a flirty little minx, and any outsider would think she's putting out major hookup vibes, but I know that's just who she is. Elliot's bubbly personality is infectious; her laugh is larger than life, and when she smiles, it looks like her face could crack open from joy.

I inhale a long steady breath, grounding myself in reality. I'm such an idiot. Drinking whiskey alone in a bar with a beautiful woman, my assistant at that—the very one that I've sworn I'd never touch. What in God's name did I think would happen? I already know that I'm going to need some alone time in the bathroom tonight so I can ease this throbbing between my legs.

As soon as I made the bet, I regretted it. I thought she'd brush me off. I thought she'd say she was tired and head up to bed for the night, but that's not what happened...not even close. As soon as I bet Elliot that I could outdrink her and the winner takes the bed tonight, her eyes lit up in a way I've never seen. For the record, I may be an asshole most of the time, but there's no way I'd make her sleep on the floor. And then...she hustled me. Of course, we're using percentages to determine the winner. I'm not a complete monster. I know I outweigh her by at least one hundred pounds, and I don't need her alcohol poisoning on my conscience on top of everything else.

"I love it when you smile. Benjamin, you don't smile enough. You have the most amazing smile. Why are you always so grumpy?" Her words slur slightly, and she makes a cute little pouty face like she simply can't help herself. I can see that our game is quickly coming to an end.

I slide a glass of water toward her and wait for her to drink half of it, gesturing for her to keep going before I speak. "It's not that I'm grumpy—" She rolls her eyes. "OK, maybe I can be a little...tense. I've just got a lot to keep up with. The weight of the company rests solely on my shoulders and I'm constantly trying to keep Thad from fucking it up."

I realize I've said too much; I really shouldn't be talking about work, especially to Thad's assistant.

She studies me for a moment. "But Thad's your partner; why would you choose a partner you can't trust?" She takes a sip of her Moscow mule and waits in uncomfortable silence for me to speak.

I scratch the back of my head, trying to figure out how to be honest without giving everything away. "Well, things aren't always what they seem. Business relationships can be complicated, and I kind of owed Thad a debt. I mostly agreed to the merger to help him out." I scratch the back of my head again, trying to say as little as possible but not wanting to lie to her either. "I care about this company; hell, I started it with nothing to my name, with only my two best friends beside me. It's important to me. The people are important to me."

Elliot places her small warm hand on my shoulder and gently squeezes. "I don't know if I ever thanked you for keeping me on after Thad hired me; I know you weren't happy with his decision. I just want you to know how grateful I am for the opportunity." She opens her arms wide and looks up at the ceiling as if this run-down inn in middle-of-nowhere Minnesota is the exact place she wants to be.

This beautiful woman is so carefree and happy to be given the tiniest grain of respect when she was the one to earn it. Thad hired her as a piece of ass to ogle, and she's right. I thought she'd show up, sleep with him, then the fun would be gone and he'd fire her. The fact that she came in on the first day and almost killed him was nice enough, but the brilliance she's brought to her role is something I've never seen before. The way she embarrasses herself, then grits her teeth and tries harder and harder each day, it's not something that can be taught. That can only come from character. I make a mental note to meet with HR as soon as we're back to work out a promotion for her. I know for certain Thad's not paying her half of what she's worth, and she's far beyond an assistant.

"I know, and you've earned it." I leave it at that and throw back the whiskey left in my glass. Elliot follows suit. Even though it's five degrees outside, my internal temperature seems to be on the rise. I push my shirt sleeves up to my elbows and assess our damage. From the looks of it, with Elliot's two Moscow mules and one shot of tequila to my five whiskeys, it appears that we've got ourselves a tie. My head is starting to spin as the alcohol does its work.

"I have to say, sweetheart, I'm impressed you've been able to hold your weight. It looks like we've got a tie on our hands." I push away from the bar and grab my jacket.

"Oh no, you don't. Did you start something you can't finish, Benjamin Williams? I'm no quitter. What's the tiebreaker?" She crosses her arms over her chest, drawing my eyes right to her perky tits. I shouldn't look. I know I should avert my eyes, but right now the whiskey is in charge and he's like the little devil sitting on my shoulder whispering, 'go ahead, feast your eyes, buddy, because this is the only opportunity you're going to get.' I do as I'm told and scan her body slowly from head to toe; I don't even care that she notices. Good God, this woman is a sight to behold. I shake my head because it's a damn shame I can't touch her.

"Ahem." She brings her hand up to cover her mouth in a fake cough, breaking the heavy silence between us. "I said, what's the tiebreaker?"

# TWENTY-TWO

Elliot

"Here's how you do it. The rules are simple." He pulls out a deck of cards, laying them in a pile in the middle of the table. "Black or red?"

"Did you seriously pack a deck of cards in your suitcase just in case you got me drunk and needed a tiebreaker?" I wink, hoping he didn't notice my admission.

"Ha, ha, ha. Our friend Gus behind the bar helped me with the cards. Now, do you want to end this or not?"

"Yeah. Of course, but I need to pee. I'll be right back."

I can see Benjamin has severely underestimated my alcohol tolerance, and to be honest, I think my mouth is writing checks that my liver can't cash. Gwen says I'm a rowdy drunk, and she always knows the minute I've had too much, but I'm hoping that my confident facade is fooling Benjamin. I don't want him to think of me as a fragile, innocent girl. By the way he practically undressed me with his eyes earlier, I know he at least takes me a little seriously. Not that I want to hook up with my boss. I'd never actually make a move...unless he initiated it. Oh shit, I can feel the tequila's effects starting to impair my judgment.

I get up and swiftly make a beeline to the disgusting glorified gas station restroom and pull out my phone.

Quick, I need help! This is an emergency. SOS.

MAGGIE

OMG. I'm calling 911 right now, where are you?

Sorry. No, it's not like that. I'm fine. DO NOT CALL 911.

GWEN

What's up, sis? I'm at a work dinner, make it quick.

MAGGIE

Type BANANA if you need help.

I'm really fine, Mags... but I've kind of gotten myself in a bit of a pickle. I'm in this run-down inn in the middle of nowhere. We're snowed in for the night.

GWEN

Yes, honey, now you're speaking my language.

MAGGIE

Elly, are you OK? Remember the code word?

I mean, we did crash into a very large elk that had it out for me... but that's not what I need help with. I'm really drunck. Like Halloween 2017, Cat Woman drunck.

GWEN

Oh shit. She spelled drunk with a C. This is bad. What's the problem exactly?

MAGGIE

Remember the code! Just call me and say it.
Do you need me to call your mom?

DO NOT CALL MY MOTHER!

MAGGIE

Sheesh, I'm just trying to help.

I just need to know what I don't need to do.
Benjamin's drunck too.

GWEN

OK, here's what you're NOT going to do:

1. Don't practice your accents, they're not
funny

2. Don't eat cabbage, you know how gassy
you get

3. Please for the love of God, don't dance...

That's all I've got. Have fun, sweetie!

MAGGIE

She forgot to tell you to wear protection!
However, I advise against making a move on
your boss. Call me and say the code word if
you need me!

OK, I got to go. I don't want him thinking I'm
pooping in here. Bye, I love you both!

MAGGIE

Gwen, you've sent her out there with a head
full of ideas. I hope you're happy with yourself.

GWEN

Our little Cat Woman is growing up so fast.

I shove the phone in my pocket and make my way back to the bar as Benjamin lines up our final round.

He slides my beer in front of me. "Are you ready for this?"

"I was born ready." I take the mug and sit up a little taller, trying like hell to act sober.

Benjamin explains the rules of the game. We each draw two cards from our deck. We take turns flipping one card over at a time, and whoever's color is chosen has to drink. Once the game is over, the player with the most cards of their color has to chug another pint.

I decide on black and Benjamin turns over the first card in his deck, a black 2. I take a drink.

My turn to draw. A black queen. "Shit, I shouldn't have to drink if I drew my own color, right?"

"Rules are rules, baby. Drink up."

I do as I'm told and the word 'baby' ricochets around in my pounding chest like a pinball. I could get used to that.

Benjamin draws another black card. "This game is rigged!" I slam my hand on the counter and then shake it because, damn, I don't know my own strength sometimes.

"It's not rigged."

I draw my card. Red. Finally.

He takes a huge gulp of his beer and grins at me like the Cheshire cat. "See?"

---

Thirty minutes later, we've completed the game, and I have to say, losing doesn't look good on me. I just finished chugging my pint and I feel like I'm visiting Willy Wonka's chocolate factory. The walls are spinning around me. I'm not overly wasted in an 'I'm going to spend tomorrow in the bathroom' way, but more like an 'I don't really care about the choices I make' kind of way.

A group of bikers walks in and takes over a table in the back as "Pour Some Sugar on Me" starts playing through the jukebox. I hop up on the bar top and grab a glass of water. "Woo!" I throw my hands in the air and belt it out at the top of my lungs. Just before I can pour the glass of water on my chest and show off my moves, Benjamin's strong arms grab me at the waist and toss me over his shoulder.

"I thought you said you weren't a 'Woo-Girl?'" He laughs. "I think you've had enough excitement for one night. Come on, sweetheart, let's get you to bed." He grabs the key from Gus, who throws me a little wink. I do my best to not throw up in my mouth.

"But, Benjamin, that was my song!" I let my hands fall to the muscular curvature of his back, exploring the glorious ridges with only my fingertips. Jesus, this man is brawn and brains; does it get any better than this?

He carries me up the winding staircase, taking the steps two by two. I don't know if I could even walk up a flight of stairs in my condition, let alone carry someone on my shoulder. "Benjamin, as nice as this is, I think I should walk on my own. I'm a big girl. I can do it."

He chuckles and flips me over swiftly like a rag doll and places me down on my feet, hands lingering on my hips.

"All right, sweetheart, this I gotta see." He gestures for me to go ahead of him, so I take the opportunity to prove just how not drunk I am. I take a couple of steps and realize that the room is spinning more and more, and I scold myself for being such a lightweight tonight. I can hear Gwen's voice saying, "Really Elliot, what have we been preparing for during all those drunken girls' nights?"

"I'm sorry, Gwen!" I confess out loud.

Benjamin looks around. "Who are you talking to? Who's Gwen?"

At this point, I think the safest option is to crawl the rest of the way. I see a sign for the honeymoon suite pointing down the long hallway. I lower my body, cautious as ever, and proceed to crawl. It's the drunken-Elliot signature move, but one can never be too safe.

Benjamin lets out a loud cackle behind me. "What do you think you're doing, crazy woman?"

"What does it look like I'm doing?" I point my finger at a ninety-degree angle in the direction of the room. "I'm trying to get my drunk ass to that room."

Benjamin grabs my hand and angles my finger in the correct direction. "You mean that room?"

"Of course, that's what I meant!" I say, and from Benjamin's expression it may have come out more loudly than I intended. "It's just that my allergies are bothering me, and my equilibrium is thrown off. It's probably because of the snow!"

My bullshit doesn't faze Benjamin, and rather than walking at a turtle's pace behind me down the long hallway, he bends down and scoops me in his arms. Now, this is something I could get used to. I take advantage of our proximity and study his strong jaw, the way his pecs are so defined under his flannel shirt, and the bulge of his biceps that are wrapped around my back. I cannot keep my curiosity at bay and once again grope him, this time squeezing his bicep. "Mmm" is all I can manage. I am drunk on vodka and pure lust and, unfortunately for my pride, the alcohol is masking all my inhibitions. "Nice body," I gasp. My breath coming in uneven spurts, this physical contact is too much. My legs clench to ease the throbbing between my legs. How can a simple touch cause this much of a reaction? I feel like parts of my body are waking up for the first time. I'm feeling sensations that I've never felt. Warm heat is swirling beneath my belly button and slowly migrating down... down...down.

Benjamin places me on the ground in front of our door, completely interrupting the one-way trek to pleasure-town that I was happily riding in his arms, which goes to show just how sexually neglected my vagina is. I think she's probably grown over with cobwebs at this point.

"After you, madam," he says dramatically, throwing the door open to reveal a dated country cabin, complete with taxidermied animal heads glaring at us from each wall and a cozy fireplace in the corner.

I stand there, transfixed by the gloomy room of death before me. Ducks, deer, elk, bobcats, and a really big fish are just some of the animal bodies that cover every inch of dark wood paneling that lines the walls. There's one queen-size bed in the modestly sized room with a multicolored crochet blanket lying at the foot. It's a scene straight out of my grandma's house. I don't know if I've ever shared a room with this many formerly living creatures, but I don't have time to overreact and give them the proper response they deserve, because Benjamin walks in beside me, and I hear the catch in his breathing.

Benjamin clears his throat. "I...um...I know I technically won the bet, but you can sleep in the bed tonight. I'll be fine on the floor." He gestures to the small nook in the corner of the room. This honeymoon suite sure leaves a lot to be desired. I'd say it looks more like a fishing cabin but with the added class of a floor-to-ceiling mirror wall across from the bed.

The realization that we've walked here and all our luggage is in the abandoned car almost a mile away hits me. I look down and assess my outfit. Boyfriend jeans that are still damp from the snow, a white Henley top, and what Gwen calls a grandma cardigan.

"I think I need a moment to freshen up." I practically throw myself across the three-foot length of the room where I come face-to-face with my makeup-smeared face. My memory flashes back to the first moment I unknowingly crashed into Benjamin Williams in that bar just six months ago. How things have changed in just a few short months and yet here I am, still looking like Uncle Fester with faded lipstick.

I do my best to freshen up, brushing my teeth with my finger and the complimentary toothpaste, and splashing water over my tired face. Gwen would be proud of my self-care routine; even when I'm shit-faced drunk I still did what I could. Fifty-year-old Elliot is going to thank me for that.

I find Benjamin stirring a fire in our tiny shared room. I'm still wearing all my clothes because it's not like I've got an alternate option.

"Oh shit, you scared me." He jumps with the fire poker in his hand. He's made a pallet from the crochet blanket and taken one of the two pillows from the bed. "I hope you don't mind; I'm building a fire since we don't have another blanket."

"Oh, that's perfect, thank you. I love fires; they remind me of visiting my grandparents in New England when I was little. We'd drive two days just to see a glimpse of snow for the holidays."

"You're cute, Elliot, but you're smart too. I hope you know that, but I have a feeling you don't see yourself the way others do." I'm surprised when he makes a grab for my hand and places a feather-like kiss on my fingers. We're standing face-to-face and I can feel the heat of his body, and it warms me from the inside out. I've never felt so relaxed, so confident, so utterly alive than when I'm close to Benjamin.

"I've never been told that I was smart." I laugh. "But I'm glad you think so."

"Well, what have you been told then? That you're gorgeous? Kind? Pure sunshine?" He smirks and tucks a strand of hair behind my ear and I shudder at the contact, suddenly nervous that he may kiss me.

I bite my lip in embarrassment and admit, "Mostly I was told that I'm too much of all of those things. I've kind of had a hard time finding my thing, as you can probably imagine. Sometimes my anxiety takes over and has a mind of its own." I look down and around the room, trying to distract myself from Benjamin's tense stare.

His eyebrows crinkle in the middle like he's confused; it's mostly a face I see him make when talking to Thad. Pressing the worry line with my thumb, I say, "Don't do that or you'll get angry wrinkles. You don't want angry wrinkles; you want the happy kind." I smile big, showing him my crow's feet.

"Sometimes you're dealt a shitty hand and you get angry wrinkles, but thanks to you, I think I'm starting to get some happy ones too."

"Aww, Benjamin, that's the nicest thing you've ever said to me. I think we should toast to your new outlook on life!" I pull away from his embrace to search for something to take my mind off this sexually tense moment, and he pulls me back against him, angling my head up to look at him.

"You know what I think?" he whispers into the side of my neck.

"What do you think?" I say in a throaty whisper.

"I think you need to get some sleep. Come on." He scoops me up and lays me in the bed, tucking the blankets underneath my legs so I'm nice and secure. "Good night." He slides his fingertip gently over my bottom lip, hesitates for just a moment, and turns to his blanket pallet by the fire. I blink my heavy eyelids, fighting sleep, but in the end, it overtakes me.

---

*"Noooo! Sarah, I'm sorry!"*

My eyes fly open and it takes me a solid minute to realize

where I am. Who's screaming? Then I remember that Benjamin is in the room with me. Suddenly all the memories of last night come crashing back. I'm instantly embarrassed and ashamed, but I can't think about that right now because the sounds coming from the floor are scaring the shit out of me. For a moment I think someone is in the room attacking Benjamin, but I see his closed lids from the dim light of the burned-out fire.

"*Help! Someone, help! Do something!*" His arms are reaching for something to grab on to, and his feet are kicking like he's running. Before I can think better of it, I climb off the bed and rush to him.

"Benjamin, wake up." I rub his clenched jaw with the palm of my hand, but he doesn't wake. "Benjamin, you're dreaming, wake up." This time I lean closer and shake his shoulders. His body stops thrashing and he reaches up and pulls me down to him, wrapping his arms tightly around me so I'm tucked against his chest. His warm, muscular body gives me a feeling of safety that I've never experienced. I struggle to get free, but he doesn't loosen his grip, so I settle and fall back asleep.

# TWENTY-THREE

Elliot

The bright morning sun casts a gentle glow in the suite, and I struggle to take a deep breath. A heavy force is weighing on my chest, pinning me in place. I'm wrapped in a warm, tight cocoon and for the life of me, I can't recall a time when I've been more comfortable than I am in this moment.

I inch my heavy, sleep-encrusted eyelids open to see where the light is coming from. It's a decision I immediately regret as the piercing rays stab my eyeballs. A wave of nausea hits, and I struggle to remove myself from my entanglement that is none other than Benjamin Williams' gloriously corded limbs wrapped around me. There's no time to overthink the fact that I've just woken up in a heap on the floor with my boss. If I want to salvage my last bit of pride, I've got to scoot across this room so I can toss my cookies before he wakes up to see.

I try to slide out from under him but it's no use; panic isn't the only thing rising in my throat, so I muster up all my strength to throw his heavy leg off my body. He wakes with a grunt and I see the realization of what happened in his eyes just before I vomit.

I've only seen *The Exorcist* once, but the evil that just spewed from my body can only be rivaled by that infamous scene, without the head-spinning, of course.

"Oh my God, I'm so sorry!" I wipe a stray tear as a second wave hits me. This time Benjamin grabs me by the waist and hurries me into the bathroom just in time.

I silently sob between each painful heave; what have I done? Not only did I wake up asleep next to my boss, but I actually puked in front of him. My body convulses, releasing the rest of the contents of my stomach and I declare to never drink alcohol again.

I'm shocked when I feel Benjamin behind me; he rubs a gentle hand up my back before pulling my hair into a braid.

"Oh, sweetie, I'm so sorry." His calm, gentle tone shocks me as he rubs his hand up and down the length of my back. He drapes a cold, wet washcloth over the nape of my neck, and settles down behind me. "I shouldn't have encouraged you last night, Elliot. I'm so sorry."

I grab the washcloth and wipe the remainder of drool and puke from my mouth before turning toward him in astonishment. I need a moment before I can speak. "Benjamin? Why are you being so nice to me right now?" That's all I can muster. The muscles in my back and chest are starting to throb from the strain and I feel weak.

"Because I'm a decent human being," he says, "and because the drinking game was my idea. You'd be perfectly fine if it wasn't for that last round."

He pushes a strand of vomit-soaked hair out of my face. "Please forgive me, sweet girl."

Before I can say, 'of course I forgive you,' or question what he's done with the grumpy Benjamin, another wave hits.

Benjamin stays by my side the whole time, gently caressing me and rubbing my head in between my waves of nausea, only leaving to call downstairs for some ginger ale and crackers. I don't know what I did to deserve such kindness, but I know I'll be forever grateful for his tender touches. Ever since moving out on my own, I've missed having someone to care for me when I'm sick. Benjamin's presence gives me the comforting feeling of home, and rather than fight him off, I give in and accept the help.

"Here, sweetie, you need to get something in your stomach to stop the dry heaving." He comes back into the bathroom with the precious liquid, and I gladly take it with shaking hands. Once I've successfully kept down half a glass, he gives me a couple of crackers. We lie on the bathroom floor, my head in his lap, and even though I should be hating myself for the decisions I made in the heat of the moment last night, I don't. I just enjoy the uncertainty of the moment, soaking it up while I can.

"Looks like the worst is over. Why don't we get you cleaned up so you can get some rest?" Benjamin pulls me up to stand, and my legs shake beneath me. I lean heavily on him and he steadies me, strong arms wrapped tightly around my waist.

"Benjamin, you don't have to help me. I can manage on my own." I reach to pull back the shower curtain, showing him I'm capable of washing myself, but I stumble as I step over the side of the tub.

Benjamin's face goes stern. Crossing his arms over his chest, he shakes his head. "Absolutely not. I promise I won't look, but I'm not leaving you in here to fall and crack your head on the side of the bathtub. By the looks of this place, you'd develop ring worm or something. I'll just stand here behind the shower curtain until you're done."

He helps me climb into the shower, and hands me the complimentary shampoo and bar of soap. He even pulls out a toothbrush that he's preloaded with toothpaste and passes it to me. "Here, I'll just be right outside the curtain if you need anything."

The lukewarm water runs down my scalp, and goosebumps cover my body. I wash away the remnants of last night's poor choices and let the events of the past two hours sink in. Benjamin has only briefly left my side and has doted on me from the moment I puked on him. It doesn't make sense. I keep waiting for the other shoe to drop, for him to tell me I'm fired and that I need to find my own way back to Chicago. I finish washing with the thin bar of floral-scented soap and grab for the towel. I wrap myself, making sure all the important bits are completely covered before stepping out. Just as he said, Benjamin is sitting on the toilet, waiting for me.

"Do you feel better?" he asks with a genuinely concerned look on his face.

"Yeah, I think I got all the chunks out." I bite my lip. "I'm so sorry about that."

"Stop apologizing. I mean it." He stands and pulls out his button-up flannel from the night before. It's the only article of clothing that isn't covered in my bodily fluids since he took it off before he went to sleep. "I, um... I hope you don't mind—" He scratches a spot behind his head—"but I took your clothes downstairs to the laundry facility. Sharon at the front desk is going to bring them up when they're done."

I accept the shirt and slide my arms through the sleeves, then I button the buttons over my towel. My hands are still a little shaky from the lack of food in my system, so Benjamin takes over. Once the shirt is buttoned properly, I pull the towel down underneath. Although I'm technically completely covered, I can't help but feel exposed in front of this practical stranger who's just seen me at quite possibly the most embarrassing moment of my life...though there's been so many it's hard to choose.

"I think you need to get some rest." He leads me over to the bed, and I do as I'm told and climb in. The rock-hard mattress feels more like a plush cloud as I curl up and let sleep take me.

---

I blink several times, allowing my eyes to come into focus. My throat feels like I've swallowed a cotton ball, and my back aches. The room glows in streaks of golden light, and I have no idea how long I've been asleep.

"Good morning, how are you feeling?" Benjamin comes to my side with a glass of water. Without acknowledging him, I reach for the glass, and drink half of its contents before I attempt to speak.

"Better." I look around for a clock or my phone, but I don't see anything other than dead animals staring back at me. "What time is it?"

Benjamin pulls his phone from his pocket to check. "Seven p.m. on the dot. You slept the day away, sleeping beauty." My cheeks flush, and then I remember how I spent my morning. They flush a deeper red but this time, from pure humiliation rather than flattery.

I feel a cold gush of air on my bare legs, and I'm suddenly reminded of my lack of clothing. I look down and see that I'm wearing only Benjamin's flannel shirt from the day before and my granny panties... the good ones with holes in the most inconvenient of places. I pull the blankets up to my eyes, wishing I could just die here and now and be done with it.

"Have I done the proper amount of groveling to keep my job?" I feign amusement because that's all I can hope for at this point.

"Elliot, I've told you already; if anyone should be sorry, it's me." His large warm hand covers mine, pulling the blanket back down so he can see my face. "How unprofessional of me to challenge my employee to a drinking match, especially when I'm twice your weight. I hope you'll forgive me." His gentle hand cups my chin and I melt into the springy mattress that's growing more uncomfortable by the minute.

"We're supposed to be meeting Damian tomorrow. Benjamin, we've got to go." I jump up frantically and rush to the window to see a winter wonderland. Snow falls in big flurries and there's not a track in sight. I feel Benjamin's heat at my back before he speaks.

"Sweetheart, we're not going anywhere in this storm. If we're lucky the snow will stop falling tonight and we'll be able to make it out in the morning." He pushes the curtain out of the way, giving me a better view. The trees stretch as far as I can see, all coated in a thick dusting of snow that makes their branches bend from the weight. I've never seen so much snow in my life. I'm torn between giddy excitement and dread in my stomach for what this could mean for our relationship with the client.

"The deal..." is all I can muster. "I'm such a screwup." My lips quiver and I try to hold back the tears, but the events of everything over the last twenty-four hours hit me like a ton of bricks, and I can't stop the tears flowing down my cheeks.

"Oh, no...no, no, no, sweet girl." Benjamin wipes a rogue tear from my cheek. "I've already handled everything while you were sleeping. I talked to Damian's agent and he's aware of our situation. This isn't anything to be upset about." He brings me closer and wraps his arms around my body, pulling me into his strong warmth. "Shhhh, shhh, everything is going to be fine."

"Bu...but...have...y...you...told...Th...Thad..." I stutter over broken sobs. I don't know where this sudden wave of emotion is coming from. Maybe it's a delayed response to the wreck or the events back in Nashville or even my embarrassment from last night. If I could slap myself for looking so weak, I would. It seems like every past failure has bubbled up to the surface, like I'm a shaken-up soda can that's finally been popped open.

"Thad's well-aware, and, quite frankly, I don't give a fuck what Thad thinks." He pulls my chin ever so gently so he can look me in the eyes. "You let me worry about Thad. What do you say we order some sub-par room service and enjoy a quiet night in?"

My stomach chooses this exact moment to make her presence known with a guttural moan of agony—such a dramatic bitch. Benjamin's eyebrows perk up. "I'll take that as a yes."

Before I can object, he's on the phone ordering an array of food from the du jour menu.

"So, let me get this straight. You, the anxiety queen who's scared of flying, were arrested for skinny-dipping in college?" Benjamin clenches his side in laughter. We've eaten a spread of really bad diner food, and now we're lying on our sides, giggling like teenagers.

"No, I wasn't actually arrested. They just made us wait in the back of the cop car to scare us while they called our parents." I snicker at the memory. The whole thing was Gwen's idea; she had this stupid list of things she wanted to do before we graduated, and going skinny-dipping was last on the list. It was a month before graduation and Maggie and I didn't have the heart to keep her from checking every box, so we went along with it. How were we supposed to know we were trespassing on private property? In all honesty, I don't regret it; that was probably the most action anyone in that retirement community had seen in twenty years."

Benjamin sips his soda and listens to my retelling in clear astonishment. "A before-graduation to-do list, that sounds incredibly dangerous for someone like you." His eyes flare in amusement, showing off his smile lines. I reach up and graze my fingertips over the faint indents, remembering our conversation from last night. I'm not sure if I'm the one hallucinating, but Benjamin seems like a different person, ever since we hit that elk.

Or maybe it was the mace.

"Oh, come on, I can't be the only one who had a wild hair in college. I'm sure you got in your share of trouble." I poke him playfully. "Mr. Uptight, surely you've done something to break the rules." I ignore the kaleidoscope of butterflies that explode in my belly at the innocent contact.

A pregnant pause passes and I think maybe I've overstepped, but then his playful expression returns.

"Hey," he mocks me like I've wounded him. "There's no reason to be violent. My friends and I pulled the biggest prank on our RA freshmen year."

He tells me about the time his RA found an empty bottle of tequila in his room and they convinced him that they were making hand sanitizer because of a particularly bad flu season on campus.

"It was so convincing that the dean of the business department asked us if he could have some as well, then we had to scramble to find a recipe to actually make hand sanitizer. That was my first product; it taught me how to sell and how to pivot to what the market needs." He laughs at the memory, and I try to picture a teenage Benjamin spewing fake bullshit to get himself out of trouble.

I chuckle. "So I guess you're not so perfect after all."

"You think I'm perfect, do you, sweetheart?" He nudges me playfully, bringing back the lightness of the conversation.

Tingles work their way from my toes and warmth spreads through every cell in my body. I know we're at a crossroads here, toeing an invisible line that shouldn't be crossed, but I don't know how much longer I can pretend. For so long, I've felt like Benjamin was hiding behind something, and I finally feel like I'm getting a glimpse of the real him.

"I always thought you hated me," I confess. "Grumpy or not, though, I think you're pretty awesome."

"Yeah?" He leans in closer and I can feel his energy in the space between us. My nipples harden under his thin flannel shirt and I warm from the inside out. I know I should push away, create some kind of barrier between us, but every fiber in my being is screaming at me to stay the course, to see what he'll do next. My curiosity cries to come out and play.

"Benjamin." I sigh.

He brushes my hair away from my face, not retreating from the tension that's building like wildfire between us. "Yes?"

"What is this? What's happening right now?"

He leans closer and I feel his warm breath tickle my neck. "I've wanted you from the moment I saw you in that bar, and no matter how much I've tried to fight the urge away, I can't. You're like a drug to me, Elliot. You make me forget the pain, and I'm tired of fighting your sunshine." He lifts my chin to meet his eyes, and then his lips crash down on mine.

Our kiss is ravenous, messy and full of desire. It's desperate and panicked, and I almost forget to breathe because this feeling is all that matters. I can feel Benjamin's vulnerability as his trembling hands grip my hips, pulling me closer to him like he's afraid I may disappear. I wrap my legs around his waist to deepen our connection, and feel his rock-hard erection press against me. A whimper escapes my lips.

He breaks away from my lips to plant hurried kisses down the side of my neck. I feel a sharp inhale as he breathes in my scent.

"Fuck, you smell so good." He pulls my hair back gently and licks his way down to my collarbone like I'm his personal ice cream cone. There's no going back now. I melt into him and I am putty in his hands.

"Benjamin," I gasp in between kisses. "I want you."

# TWENTY-FOUR

Benjamin

"Fuck, Elliot, you have no idea how sexy you are." I slide my hand under the hem of her shirt, feeling her soft velvet skin under my touch, while a million alarms go off in my mind telling me this is a bad idea, it's too soon. I push the thoughts away and bury my face into her neck, sucking and nibbling my way down her collarbone.

"You've really thought of this before?" she says in a breathless gasp.

"It's all I can think about when you're around." I kiss back up her neck, reacquainting my lips with hers. I pull her into my lap and her smooth naked legs wrap around my waist. Behind my lips I bite back a low growl. So. Fucking. Sexy. I pull back from the kiss and push away from her, creating space between us before I get too carried away. I know she's been through a lot on this trip and I don't want to rush this; she deserves more than that. Besides, I don't have a condom and I won't trust myself to keep things above the clothes when I'm this turned on.

"Baby, we can't. I can't."

She misunderstands my pleading. "You can't?" Her eyebrows shoot up to her forehead as she gazes down slowly toward my cock.

"No, I definitely *can*, but this is going too fast. We should slow down." I move a stray strand of hair from her lips, silently pleading that she will argue and reveal a secret condom in her panties or something. It's been so long since I've had this kind of connection with someone. Yeah, I've had casual sex since Sarah, but that's just a mutual exchange of pleasure. This promises to be so much more.

She bites her lip and looks up at me. "I'm a big girl, Benjamin, I can handle it."

"Believe me, I'd love to find out." I kiss her on the forehead. "But I respect you too much to have unprotected sex with you tonight."

"That's the nicest thing a man's ever said to me..." Her voice drifts off and I can tell she's disappointed, which does nothing to convince my cock to stand down. Shit, I've got to think of something to distract myself before my body revolts against my mind and takes actions into its own hands.

I glance around the dated room, desperate for a subject change, and my eye catches on a checkerboard on the mantle. "How about we play a game?"

Her eyes light up and I know I've said the right thing. This beautiful, playful woman cannot resist a game; this is going to get interesting.

"I love games." Her eyes light up in excitement and I move us over to sit on the edge of the bed. I am keenly aware that everything's going to change after this moment.

Elliot sits across from me cross-legged, waiting on my next move. I lean in close and whisper, "Truth or dare?"

My girl is beaming with a giant grin, eyes sparkling full of wonder. She taps her finger to her lip. "Hmm... let's start with truth."

"Good, that's what I hoped you'd say." I adjust my position to mimic hers. "Elliot, is it true that you're a virgin?" I realize I'm coming out guns blazing with this question but before this goes anywhere else, I've got to know.

She glances around the room as though she's afraid someone may overhear. "Eh...no, it's not true."

Good, I think, but where I know I should feel relieved, instead I have the strangest lump of jealousy. I have no right to feel jealous, especially considering my past. "So this game is a little different, when you answer the question, you have to give a brief explanation... for clarity." Now that is total bullshit I just made up on the spot, but the burning curiosity isn't letting me move on just yet.

"Oh, well." She's obviously nervous to elaborate. "While I am technically not a virgin, I've only been with one person. We dated for like six years in high school and the beginning of college."

Before I can think, I ask, "That's a long time. What happened?"

"I guess everything changed when I went away to college. We tried to do the long-distance thing, but all he wanted was to stay in the little town we're both from and settle down. I wanted to chase my dreams and thrive in the city...and while I'm not exactly thriving right now, things are starting to look up for me." She shrugs. "Though my parents would be thrilled if they didn't."

I want to know more. Fuck, I want to know everything about her, but I realize that's not exactly fair. I'll take these small bits of her life and swallow them up whole.

A mischievous grin spreads across her face. "Enough about that. Truth or dare, Benjamin?"

"Dare." I lick my lips in anticipation. I said I wouldn't sleep with her tonight, but I'd be lying if I wasn't hoping for a little action.

She rubs her palms together. "I dare you...to...run outside underneath our window and make a snow angel...shirtless."

I'm dumbfounded by this dare. I thought she would dare me to kiss her, to undress...anything else. But I never shy away from a dare.

I stand up abruptly and remove my shirt, savoring the look of surprise on her face for just a moment before bolting out the door. I take off down the stairs, through the door like a madman, and around the building to find our window. Elliot is hanging out, waving and cheering me on. I complete the dare in the god-awful freezing snow and rush back up to meet her. She's sitting on the bed laughing hysterically when I open the door, and she knows she's in trouble when she sees my face. I lunge toward her, wrapping her in my cold embrace, and tickle her wildly. "You're going to pay for that!"

"Benjamin, you're freezing!"

I slide my palm slowly up her side. Her warm skin is a stark contrast, our body temperatures blending to make a cool connection. All playfulness is gone, and the moment is heavy with need and desire. I lean forward to where our lips are just barely separated. "Truth or dare?"

"Dare," she says in a breathless whisper.

"I dare you... to give me a striptease." I lean back against the headboard, sliding my hands behind my head. "Revenge is so, so sweet."

She surprises me, grabs her phone from the side table, and with a look of determination selects her song. Ginuwine's "Pony" starts playing loudly through the speakers, and she stands in front of the bed. Her hips sway to the music and I'm instantly hard again. Who knew this sweet, innocent woman was hiding all this sexy? She turns backward, giving me a prime view of her ass, which is rolling in motions that seem unnatural. Then she lifts the hem of my shirt, sliding it slowly up her body, exposing her tight little waist. She lets the fabric fall, and the shirt swallows her, hanging back down to her knees. She folds her body forward and twerks, her glorious round ass shaking in every direction, and my mouth goes dry in disbelief.

My cock is screaming to be set free, and I do my best to ease my discomfort, making the best adjustment I can given the circumstances. "Shit, Elliot, I don't know if I can take much more of this." I've got a death grip on the bedspread, holding on for dear life until this ride is over.

She looks over her shoulder in a sultry gaze and begins unbuttoning my shirt, ever so slowly, giving me just a glimpse of the cleavage she's hiding underneath. My jaw has completely unhinged from itself as I take it all in. Elliot wearing my shirt and a holey pair of underwear is a sight to behold, and I pity the man who never gets to experience it. I make a mental note to buy this woman some new panties she's worthy of just as soon as we get back home. I don't think I could sculpt this ass better if I were Michelangelo himself. Tight, round, and smooth.... Her hours spent in the gym are definitely noticeable.

"Fuck." I let out a pent-up breath, letting her know what she's doing to me, which only encourages her. I'm praying for this sweet torture to end and never stop at the same time.

She makes her way over to the bed and straddles my lap, giving me an up-close personal view. Sitting down on my cock and shifting slightly, she reaches up and grabs the strap of her bra and brings one side down, revealing a smooth, bare shoulder. She repeats this motion on the other side, her tits barely covered by the thin, lacy fabric, giving me the best view of her cleavage. My hands burn to touch her, but I lay still, letting her finish her performance. The right side of her bra gives way and slides down, revealing a small pink nipple that begs for my mouth around it. My vision blurs...I believe all my blood has rushed to my cock which is now record-breakingly hard. She slides her hands up her tight abdomen and runs her fingers over the exposed nipple while simultaneously grinding her clit against my erection.

A pained moan escapes my lips and I grab her hips to steady the sweet rhythm she's created. If I die here in this moment from pure sexual torture, it would be the best way to go. When she reaches down to pull the panties down her hips, my hands rush to stop her. The song ends and she looks at me wide-eyed. "Elliot, if you take those off, I won't be able to stop myself and I don't think we need to go that far tonight. Now button up this fucking shirt before I jizz all over myself."

She grins up at me as I lend a helping hand, letting my hand brush her soft, supple skin. Little does she know that I'm trying my best to think about my grandma and basketball so I don't accidentally blow a load in my pants. "Where in the world did you learn how to do that?"

"My friend, Gwen, made us take pole dancing classes after one of her breakups. I think we went to that class twice a week for six months until she got it out of her system. As much as I hate to admit it, they were really fun, and pole dancing does wonderful things for your abs."

I can't argue with that. So the little minx knew what she was doing to me the whole time. Here I thought I was going to get a goofy striptease, but in true Elliot fashion, she always surprises me. I'm still taking deep calming breaths when she leans over, and says, "Truth or dare, Benji?"

I wince at the nickname and she notices.

"Well, I don't know if I can compete with that performance, so, truth."

"Is it true that you hated me when I first started working at

195

POW!?" She looks down at her fidgeting hands. "You know, before the mace or car crash?"

I tilt my head to the side, studying her, searching for the right words to say without giving anything away that I'm not ready to reveal.

"I guess I'm just wondering if you hit your head or something, you know, when I crashed into the elk? Maybe you have a concussion and you're not being yourself right now. I keep thinking you're going to snap out of it and go back to the grumpy Benjamin from before."

"I didn't hate you. No one could ever hate you." I sigh. "Elliot, you make me feel things that I don't always want to feel yet...maybe ever. You walked into my life wearing the biggest smile I've ever seen, and it was a constant reminder of how miserable I've been. Not only did I want you desperately, but I was also jealous of your happiness and carefree life..." I trail off before I say too much. "For the record, you deserve so much more than me; I hope you know that."

"I do not have a carefree life. Hello, I'm the anxiety queen and I screwed up every opportunity I've ever been given. I honestly have no idea who let me become an adult." She laughs nervously and pulls the sleeves of my shirt over her hands and crosses her legs on the bed.

"Can I show you something and you not think I'm a creep?"

She winks. "I guess I'll be the judge of that. Let's see it."

I grab my phone from the side table and scroll through my photos, finding my secret album and the picture I took the first time I ever saw her. I hand her my phone. "I took this photo the first time I ever saw you in that bar. Elliot, I don't think you see yourself the way everyone else sees you." I take the phone and zoom in on her. Her head is thrown back and she's laughing with her friends like she's the happiest woman in the world. "You light up every room you're in. Your personality is magnetic, and you have a way of making people feel comfortable. That's why you're so good at this job. Clients feel your authenticity and what you see to be a flaw, everyone else sees as your greatest strength."

Silent tears stream down her face and I see I've struck a nerve. "Baby, don't cry. Come here." I pull her into my lap and wrap my arms around her small frame. "One of these days I hope you will see yourself the way everyone else sees you. I don't ever want you to change a thing. Do you hear me?" I gently press my lips against hers, kissing away her tears.

"Benjamin, will you hold me tonight?" Her soft voice melts my heart and a twinge of guilt pricks at me for not opening up myself. I know it's selfish, but I just want to forget about the past and savor this moment. Because I know good and well as soon as she finds out my dark past, I'll never get this back.

"There's nothing I'd rather do." I tuck her into me and pull the blankets over us. "We've got a big day tomorrow. We should get some sleep." She nuzzles against me and we both drift off quickly, and for the first time in two years, I don't have a single nightmare.

# TWENTY-FIVE

Elliot

Waking up in Benjamin's arms is heavenly. He's still got me tightly cradled against his chest; in fact, I don't think I moved all night. I slowly lift my gaze to see if he's still sleeping and meet those whiskey eyes staring back down at me.

"Good morning, gorgeous. I didn't want to wake you just yet. How'd you sleep?"

I reach my hands over my head, taking a long, deep stretch. "Amazing. How about you?"

He plants a kiss on my neck. "I don't think I've ever slept so well. I guess I'm going to have to keep you around, sweetheart." He slides his hand up my exposed abdomen and gives my hip a tight squeeze. "Jesus Christ, woman, if you want to get anything done today, I'm going to need you to cover yourself up."

My skin pebbles at his touch, and my body heats in response. I spin around in his arms, bringing my face to lie on his chest, and dance my fingers across his pecs.

"Mmm," is all I can get out before he flips me over and pins my hands above my head. Benjamin leans down and takes a tiny bite from my neck, working his nibbles down my collarbone. "You are so fucking sweet; I'm tempted to keep you here all day."

I narrow my eyes. "And then when I'm homeless because I'd inevitably be fired for missing the biggest deal of this whole project, I'm sure you'd find me irresistible then."

I try to sit up but Benjamin's strong arms only pin me down tighter. "Hey, don't you worry like that, you hear me? You've done an amazing job on this project, and I'd never let anything happen to you. Besides, you've still brought a whole new division of marketing to our agency." He winks. "You're a good bet, Elliot James."

My heart flutters in my chest at his kind words. *He thinks I'm a good bet? My whole life I've never been anything but a screwup.* "Are you sure you don't have a concussion?" I pretend to eye him with suspicion.

"I mean it, Elliot, you've got a serious knack for this stuff. You've already taught me so much. You don't give yourself enough credit for how amazing you are." His piercing stare seems to shoot straight through me, and I feel like Benjamin is the only other person, besides my girls, to truly see me for who I am. "Elliot, look at me."

I blink back the tears that threaten to fall, not wanting to show Benjamin my insecurity. I want him to look at me and see a strong, capable leader, not some naive crybaby. He cups my face, forcing me to look in his eyes.

"Elliot, you are so smart and you don't even realize it. I don't know who hurt you, but I promise if I ever find the bastard, I'm going to give him a piece of my mind. Now come on." He pulls me up, curling me into his lap. "We've got a big day ahead of us, and if I have to see you looking sexy as fuck in my shirt, we're never going to make it in time."

Thankfully, Benjamin rescheduled the next influencer meeting yesterday while I was sleeping off my hangover. I feel so pathetic that he had to do my job, but he's assured me that I'd have done the same for him, and it's true. I would've in a heartbeat. He even bought us train tickets to go back home, since we're still on the No Fly List. I'd be lying if I said I wasn't giddy with excitement over my very first train ride, but I try to keep my enthusiasm at bay.

The storm passed last night, and although there's more snow than I've ever seen in my life, the roads have been cleared and Benjamin has assured me that it's safe. A tow truck has been arranged to pick up the rental, and he's even arranged for a driver to bring us the next leg of the trip so we can work on our presentation.

"We've got a big day ahead of us. Are you ready to meet Damian Johnson?" Benjamin's voice brings me back to the moment. He squeezes my hand that I didn't realize he was holding and we climb into the back of the town car.

"This is the fanciest I've ever felt in my life! Benjamin, don't you think this is a little over the top for a meeting? How much does this cost?" My eyes look like they're about to pop out of my head as I take in the luxury car before me, complete with a suited driver.

"Sweetheart, let me worry about that. You just sit here." He buckles the seat belt over my body and plops my computer down in my lap. "There, all set."

"I guess this is a bad time to tell you I have a tendency to get carsick?"

---

I spend most of the commute making little changes to my proposal, tweaking things so they're as perfect as they can be.

Damian Johnson is a beauty influencer with 1.5 million followers. Since this guy is the big leagues, I want this presentation to be as buttoned-up as possible. It's easy for everyone to assume that influencers are dumb millennials with their phones permanently attached to their hands, but if you actually study the industry, marketing dollars spent on influencers yield tremendously more than traditional advertising.

Since we had such good luck with the first influencer in a public place, we decide to meet Damian at a local coffee and sandwich shop. The cold fresh air stings my skin and I pull my beanie down lower to cover as much of my face as possible. Benjamin sees me struggling to walk through the frigid windy parking lot and pulls me into his warm embrace, shielding me from the piercing wind.

Damian is already sitting down at a back table when we arrive, reading a newspaper—where did he even find a printed newspaper? Dressed in dark jeans, a crisp white button-down shirt, and a long wool coat, this man has some serious style. He looks like he just stepped out of a *Vogue* catalog. He's got a subtle made-up face with the most amazing eyebrows and contoured cheekbones. His skin is dark chocolate and flawless, and it's easy to see why he's such a successful beauty influencer. If there's any chance I could look a fraction as good as he does with makeup, I'd buy anything he told me to.

Benjamin approaches first and introduces us.

"Thank you so much for contacting me! I am always looking for ways to diversify my brand portfolio."

I set up my laptop and show him the marketing plan we've come up with. Since Damian's following is so tremendous, we've decided to pour most of the advertising budget into his campaign. Even though his followers are primarily interested in makeup and skin care, his vegan lifestyle is a huge part of his brand.

"We believe that if you post heavily around this content schedule, we'll be able to capture new customers and keep them. We'd ask you to post on your stories at least twice a week in a fun, organic way and follow up with a few sponsored posts. We'd also love for you to do some giveaways, and we've worked out a takeover feature with another vegan influencer so you would both benefit from sharing followers. Do you have any questions?"

He leans back in silence, contemplating the terms. "You know what, honey? I've never seen such a polished, well-thought-out proposal. You've really done your homework here. Are you sure you're not an influencer on the side? How do you know so much about the business?"

My first instinct is to brush it off, but the memory of Benjamin's healing words are still so fresh that they give me courage. "Thank you for saying that. I've seen influencers become successful and was curious about the process, so I started looking into how it all works. I guess once something interests me, I can't leave it alone until I've learned everything I can."

Benjamin jumps in. "Elliot's taken the lead for this whole endeavor, and it's been amazing to see all the details she's put into every single proposal." He meets my eyes, and I can feel his admiration warm me from head to toe.

"Mm-hmm..." Damian points between the two of us. "And what exactly is going on here? Girl, you know I'm going to sign that paper and agree to whatever you ask me to do, so spill the tea." He leans back in his chair and takes a sip of his chai latte.

"I...um...I...." My mouth opens and closes, making zero coherent sounds. I glance at Benjamin who doesn't seem to be the least bit fazed by our relationship being called out by a client.

"Here, just give me the damn paper." He grabs the paper

out of my hand and scans the pages, signing on each highlighted line, then pushes it back to me. "There, the deal's done. Now you don't have to worry about being unprofessional. I live for this fairy-tale shit." He gestures for me to keep talking.

Benjamin takes the bait and reaches over to hold my hand under the table. "I was living my pitiful existence of a life, and one day this bright-eyed, red-lipstick-wearing minx of a woman showed up at my office and turned my world upside down. Then she almost killed my business partner, which only made me crazier about her." He squeezes my hand.

"I love you in red lipstick. I'd pick one with a subtle blue undertone; it'll make the brightness of your skin pop," he says. "Sorry, I'm easily distracted by makeup talk. Please continue."

"Well, Elliot here is like no one I've ever met, and the more I get to know her, the crazier I am for her."

"Well, isn't that the cutest fucking thing I've ever seen. You two are perfect for each other. I read energy, you know. I knew from the minute you both sat down that there was something brewing under the surface...but I have to warn you, keeping secrets is never a good way to start a relationship." He raises his eyebrows, pinning both of us in a stare.

My mind begins to spiral with worry. Benjamin thinks he knows me so well, but he's a hot, successful, self-made millionaire. I can't imagine what he'd think if he knew the truth, that I'm barely getting by thanks to my rando-roommate I found on Craigslist, and every month I'm on the brink of eviction. There's no way we belong together, not in any universe. He's older, smarter, more successful, and unlike me, he's got his shit together. Damian sees it too, and now he's practically warning Benjamin to steer clear before I do some damage that can't be reversed.

Shame rushes up to my cheeks and I shoot up from my seat,

cutting Damian off before he decides to divulge any more private information with his freak-show talents.

"I think we're done here for today. Damian, thank you so much for your time." I reach out and shake his hand with my nervous energy. "I'll make sure to have those chicken bars shipped out first thing in the morning. Please feel free to reach out if you need anything else from us."

Benjamin's focus seems to be on his feet, like maybe something Damian said hit close to him as well? Or maybe he's realized it too, that we've crossed the line of appropriate workplace behavior and now he's either going to have to deal with the awkwardness of it all every day in the office or let me go so he won't have the reminder. My breathing quickens at the thought of losing him, so I shove my trembling hands in my pockets and plaster on a fake smile to hide my fears.

"Oh, sweetie, I'm so sorry. Sometimes I forget how much my little gift freaks people the hell out." He pulls me into a hug and whispers in my ear, "Call me if you need anything. I mean it." He plants a kiss on each of my cheeks.

Benjamin gives him a proper handshake and farewell, and I hightail it out of the quaint coffee shop where my past suddenly looms over me like a thick cloud of smoke. Panic prickles down to my fingertips. *Shit, shit, shit. Come on, Elliot, keep it together. You cannot do this here. You are OK. Everything's fine.* I get to the car a full minute before Benjamin, and swing the door open, jump inside, and throw my head down between my knees. The tears start falling and my body is convulsing, not just from the cold. There is no hiding my feelings now.

"Elliot, baby, are you OK? Oh shit, you're having a panic attack!" He answers his own question. Instead of staring at me like a lunatic like my parents used to do, he scoops me up and brings me to sit on his lap. Without me having to tell him, he reaches around my arms and squeezes me into his chest. "Just breathe. That's it, in and out. Just focus on your breath. You're OK."

A sob escapes me as a hot flash works its way from my head to my feet, followed by cold chills. This all-too-familiar feeling is torture, like I'm trapped inside my own body with nowhere to escape; all I want is to claw my skin off and curl into a ball.

"This is just a physical reaction; you're going to be just fine. This feeling will pass." He rubs his hands up and down my back, giving me another sensation to focus on besides the panic writhing under my skin. I try to think about his touch, his tight embrace, the light smell of his cologne, the feel of his five-o'clock shadow rubbing against my tear-covered cheek.

I don't know how much time passes before I feel the last of the panic release into his strong, loving arms. I've never in my life had someone walk me through a panic attack to that degree of care. The only logical explanation is that Benjamin must also suffer from panic attacks himself—either that or he's loved someone who did. My mind flashes to his nightmare two nights ago; maybe something horrible happened to him?

He brings my face up to look into my eyes and brushes the matted, wet hair from my cheek. "There you are, is it letting up? Are you feeling a little better?"

I answer with a nod and he pulls me back into his chest and squeezes me tightly. "Baby, you scared the shit out of me just now. Does this have anything to do with what Damian said back there?"

I'm so exhausted, I just nod and put my head back down on his strong, protective shoulder, grateful I'm finally not alone.

# TWENTY-SIX

Benjamin

We're on a train heading back to Chicago. The last week has stirred up a whirlwind of emotions.

Elliot's passed out with her head resting on my shoulder, and this time I had nothing to do with it. She's going to be so mad at me for letting her sleep through her first train ride, but I can't help myself. The dark circles forming under her eyes that are only growing deeper by the day. I know this has been stressful, and fuck, I wish I could make it better for her, but she won't let me in.

Damian freaked the hell out of me when he said we shouldn't start a relationship harboring secrets. Is that what this is, a relationship?

I never thought I'd see the day when I felt whole enough to move on from Sarah, but watching Elliot bloom into the person she's meant to be before my eyes, it's like falling in love all over again...but no, that can't be right, can it?

I push the thought from my mind, instead focusing on the

task at hand, the *job* at hand. I make a mental checklist of all the proposals we've seen over the last two weeks, making sure I didn't miss a single task before taking the weekend as a well-needed break.

Jesus, I can't wait to get back to normal, to sleep in my own bed. I look down at the beauty currently drooling on my shoulder, and I can't help but wonder what this all means for us. I sure as hell can't walk back into the office and allow Thad to ogle her in a pencil skirt again. Hell, I don't even know if I can let her leave my side tonight; I've gotten so comfortable having her close.

We haven't gone any further than kissing, but I'd be lying if I said I didn't want to get her alone again and see where things go once she's not stressed about closing a deal. Elliot's dedication to this job is unwavering; she checks and double-checks the numbers before every meeting, and is constantly researching market trends. She's told me about the courses she takes in her free time to learn the game and who the major players are. When she's not working, she's out running— literally. It's like the girl can't sit still, and her restlessness is only getting worse. I'm hoping that once we're back into a normal routine, her anxiety will settle.

I grip my handrest, angry at the thought of her thinking anything but good thoughts about herself. She's got such a beautiful, trusting soul; I just hope we both can walk away from this in one piece.

---

"Wake up, sweetheart. We're home." I reach across and lightly rub up and down her arm. She doesn't move, only proving how little sleep she's gotten lately. I make another attempt and this time her sleepy eyes blink open.

She rubs the sleep from her eyes and stretches in her cramped window seat. "Are we home?"

"Yeah, you slept through the entire ride."

Her sleepy eyes well up. "You mean I missed it? My very first train ride? How could you let me sleep through my first train ride, Benjamin?" She crosses her arms like a stubborn child.

I push her wavy, drool-encrusted hair away from her face. "Yes, sweetheart, I let you sleep because you were exhausted and you needed it. Now, let's get off this stinky train and grab some pizza. What do you say, takeout at my place? I'll only misbehave if you want me to." I wag my eyebrows and she playfully pushes me away.

"OK, Casanova, only because I haven't given my roommate adequate warning, and who knows what I'd walk into after being gone for two weeks. Plus, I'm starving and I'm growing more and more curious about you by the minute. I need to see you in your natural habitat."

"You've never mentioned having a roommate." I feel like I'm playing catch-up, learning the ins and outs of Elliot's life. It's only now that I realize just how much I don't know about this beautiful woman in front of me.

"I never mentioned her because there's nothing to talk about. She brings guys home almost every night, and thanks to her sexual endeavors, I now know way more about furries, BDSM, and role-playing than I ever wanted to." She rolls her eyes and at first, I think she's joking but realize she's telling the truth.

"Have you told her that you don't feel comfortable with so many guys coming around your apartment?"

"Not in so many words, but yes, she knows how I feel about them."

"So make her move out..."

"It's not that easy, Benjamin. She pays half the rent, and I can't afford to live there on my own. Honestly, I'm lucky to have her paying half the bills. I can't make her move out; it took me two months to even find a roommate willing to live in such modest accommodations as it is."

"What do you mean by 'modest accommodations'?"

"Oh, nothing. It's just that not everyone wants to live like I do. It's fine, I've got a plan and I'm working to find something better. Seriously, Benjamin, it's not a big deal. I'm not oblivious enough to think everyone can afford a nice two-bedroom apartment in their twenties."

I let her believe that I'm convinced, but the subject is far from over. I'm going to have to see this apartment of hers...really soon.

---

The driver drops us off in front of my building. I live in the heart of downtown Chicago in a sky-rise apartment. Elliot's surprise isn't lost on me when I open the door and lead her into the lobby. I usher her through the revolving doors of the building. The elevator brings us up to my private floor.

My apartment is sparsely decorated; I am a man after all. The mid-century modern decor was Sarah's idea, and I couldn't get rid of it as much as it pains me to have a constant reminder around me every day. The walls are painted a soft white and decorated with art that's moved me—and nothing else. I've got a brown leather sofa and a navy-blue love seat in the living room, facing a modest 55-inch flat-screen TV. The open floor plan looks into the kitchen and dining room. I lead Elliot to the guest room and put her suitcase in the closet, not wanting to pressure her. We slept together in the inn outside of Madison, but I don't want to presume that the offer still stands when two beds are available to us.

"Here's the guest room, make yourself at home. There's a bathroom attached, so you'll have your own space to get ready in the morning." Her eyes go wide as she takes in the luxurious room before her. A white down comforter covers the bed that's piled with all the throw pillows a girl could want. The Persian rug beneath our feet creates a warm contrast to the white walls and bedding, making the room feel cozy rather than sterile.

We finish the tour in my bedroom, which is similarly decorated to the guest room. I've also got a fluffy white down comforter and the wall behind my headboard is painted a dark forest green. Elliot makes her way over to the dresser and picks up a picture frame—one that I look at every single day. It's a picture of the three of us at Disney World. Maddie's arms are wrapped around my leg, beaming from just getting a makeover in Cinderella's Castle. Sarah's tucked into my body, and I've got my arms around them both. That day was one of the happiest days of my life. I wait for her response to finding the picture. I've done my best to get rid of most of Sarah and Maddie's things but there are sprinkles of our life together scattered throughout the apartment. I've moved places since the accident, knowing good and well there's no way I could have the reminder of our home gnawing at me day in and day out.

"Who's this?"

"That's, um...my sister and her daughter." The lie rolls off my tongue before I have time to think of a better response. I know I should've told her by now, but I can see the exhaustion in the dark circles around her eyes, and I know this whole trip combined with seeing my house and family is a lot to take in all at once. Having become quite familiar with Elliot's panic attacks, I don't want to stir up any unnecessary worry in her right now. I know I'm an asshole, and I'm going to work up the courage to tell her about my past, but I'm not ready yet.

She eyes me and glances back down at the picture frame in her hand. "Your sister is really pretty, and your niece is absolutely precious—just look at those cheeks." She places the picture back in its place and my throat burns as I hold back tears that threaten to fall.

I clench my jaw and nod in agreement. "Yeah, they're pretty amazing."

I lead her into the kitchen and get her a slice of pizza that she barely touches, and then I banish her to bed, the guest bed where she's all alone and safe from my wandering hands.

After I tuck her in tightly, get her a glass of water for her bedside table, and lock up, I make my way back to my bedroom and head straight to the shower. A wave of guilt slaps me in the face, and even though I've slept with plenty of women since Sarah died, this feels more like cheating than any of those one-night stands ever did.

I brace my hands on the tile and lose it. I let out all my repressed anger and cry for the first time since their funerals. *Fuck, what am I doing?*

# TWENTY-SEVEN

Benjamin

*Two years earlier...*

"How could you embarrass me like that in front of my client? Benjamin, I was so close to closing; are you trying to sabotage my career?" Sarah's high-pitched voice pierces my eardrums and I flinch.

"Sarah, how is reminding you that Maddie's dance recital was the same night as the party sabotaging you? Are you serious right now? Your daughter's first dance recital is next week; she's been practicing for this moment for the last six months. It's all she's talked about. You can't miss it for a dinner party," I snap. Normally I don't stand up to Sarah, but lately, her mood swings have been getting more extreme, and I draw the line when it comes to our daughter.

"There you go again, mom-shaming me. Maddie is five, Benjamin. She thinks the world revolves around her. Of course, she'd be upset but it's good for her to learn that life goes on when the world doesn't stop for you. Hell, I wish I'd have learned that lesson earlier; it would've saved me some heartache!" Sarah spits her retort like venom and, for the first time, I'm disgusted with her.

Where did my beautiful, caring, kind wife go? Ever since her father reached out to her a few months ago, reminding her of all the opportunities she was missing out on within their family business, it seems that all of her time and energy has gone into proving him wrong. From sunup to sundown, all she does is work. She forgets to eat to the point where she's lost an alarming amount of weight, and she hardly ever sleeps. I'm actually growing worried about Maddie in her care; I'm scared Sarah's going to zone out, focused on a project, and poor Maddie will be left alone to fend for herself.

I'm struggling to keep my new business afloat. We're growing fast but that comes with a ton of pressure. I've got employees now that depend on me to bring in the work that keeps the wheels turning. The last thing I need is to have to worry about Sarah being an irresponsible mother. I know she's trying to reach a certain level and I'm so proud of all she's overcome, but I can't help but wonder if it will ever be enough. Will I ever get my Sarah back, the one I fell in love with?

# TWENTY-EIGHT

Elliot

The smell of cinnamon and coffee wafts into my room, and my stomach rumbles loudly to protest that I'm still lying in bed. The bright sun pours into the room, lighting up the white walls and furniture. I've got the most beautiful view of the gardens from my window and can see the hustle and bustle of the city coming alive. It's Sunday, and I'm so grateful for the day of rest ahead of me. I've got a lot to do to get things in order for the coming workweek, including going back to my apartment and sanitizing the shit out of the common areas...no pun intended.

My phone is charging on the bedside table and since I have no memory of plugging it in, it means that Benjamin must've set it all up. I was so exhausted last night; I'm surprised I remember anything. I've got two missed calls from Maggie and about thirty texts from our girl group thread, all wondering if I'm alive, if I've made it home, and telling me to let them know I'm OK as soon as I wake up. I see the last message is from me.

> Elliot is safe. She's exhausted and I've taken her to my place for the night. Will have her call first thing in the AM. - Benjamin

My first thought is how sweet it was for him to let them know I'm OK... quickly followed by the panic that he could've scrolled up just a little and seen the step-by-step instructions for inserting a penis into a vagina, complete with pictures and video sent by Gwen just the day before.

I send a quick message.

> Just woke up. I'm alive and well. Nothing sexual happened but thanks for the instructional video...

MAGGIE

> I'm happy you're back! I've missed you so much. Let's grab lunch or dinner tonight. Just let me know!

GWEN

> I'm beginning to wonder about you, Elliot. You do still like the penis, right? You didn't switch teams without telling me, did you?

I choose to ignore this last response and give Maggie's message a thumbs-up. I send a quick text to Destiny, letting her know I'll be home in the next few hours and please move any sexual activities into her room.

The cinnamon smell has now blended with the delicious smell of bacon and coffee. I'm up and heading toward the kitchen before I realize I'm only wearing a t-shirt and panties.

Benjamin's back is to me as he stands near the stove, cooking French toast and bacon. I make a beeline to the coffee pot, pouring the nectar of the gods into the mug he must've set out for me. He hears me approach and turns around.

"Good morning, beauti—" Eyes wide, he lets his gaze drop to my bare legs and works his way up my body ever so slowly as if he's memorizing this moment. "Dear God, woman, you've got to give me some warning before you stumble in here half dressed like this." He motions to my entire body, and I see his physical response tenting the front of his sweatpants. I turn to leave with my coffee to go retrieve my pants, and I hear a guttural moan muffled by his hand. "Are you trying to kill me?"

I run to my bedroom to grab my pants, grinning. I assume his reaction was to the sight of my ass in these cheeky panties that leave nothing to the imagination.

Once I'm clothed and decent, even putting on a bra for good measure, I make my way back into the kitchen for breakfast. I can't quite pin down when the last time I ate a full meal was, so I'm grateful to pile a plate high with bacon and French toast.

"I'm glad to see your appetite is coming back. I was hoping my famous French toast would do the trick." Benjamin studies me over his steaming coffee cup, hip pressed against the countertop. I don't look up as he speaks, too busy shoveling this delicious breakfast down my throat.

"This is the best meal I've ever had in my life," I mumble through the giant bite I've just taken.

Benjamin smiles with his eyes. "I'm glad you like it. It's my family's recipe actually, passed down for three generations." He grabs my coffee cup and pours me a refill. "So what do you have planned today?"

I pause my grotesque shoveling, considering my answer. Benjamin and I have spent the last two weeks completely inseparable; going back to my apartment is going to feel so lonely. "Well, I was thinking of going for a run, and then I need to head back to my apartment so I can get a head start on the sanitation process. That will likely eat up the rest of my day, and I'm meeting Gwen and Maggie for drinks at Terry's tonight."

"Why do you think cleaning the apartment will take so long? Doesn't your roommate know how to pick up after herself?"

This actually makes me laugh out loud. "The last time I was out of town for the weekend, I came home to discover dried whipped cream all over every horizontal surface in the kitchen. It took me two days to get all the sticky residue off enough to get rid of the ants."

"What the hell was she doing with whipped cream?"

"I believe there was some type of party involving whipped cream bikinis....I can only imagine it resulted in multiple happy endings..."

Benjamin's face is horrified. "Elliot, you cannot live with someone who doesn't respect your boundaries and treats your property that way! Does she ever ask you before she pulls something like that?"

Shit. Now he's going into overprotective mode. I've got to clear this up because I don't need another person nagging me about my living situation. It's bad enough that Maggie and Gwen never let me hear the end of it; I don't need Benjamin riding me about it too. Unless these friends of mine want to pitch in and start paying my rent, they can keep their opinions to themselves. Not to mention, Benjamin's idea of a safe living situation and mine are vastly different. "Not exactly, but as I said, she pays half the rent so I can't exactly tell her how she uses the common space...especially if I'm not there."

He grabs his keys from the entryway table. "Get your stuff. I'm not letting you go back there alone."

I know there's no use in arguing so I go into the guest room and gather up my stuff. Luckily, I didn't really have time to unpack last night so it doesn't take long and we're out the door.

Benjamin leads me to his car that's parked in the building's covered parking garage and of course, it's a Tesla. "Really?" I ask as I pull open the crazy hinged door. "How did I not know you were so freaking loaded?"

"You didn't ask." His playful retort makes me laugh. "Get in the damn car, Elliot."

I do as he says and can't help the rush of excitement that fills me when he tells me what to do.

"What's your address?"

I take his phone out of his hand and plug the address into his GPS app.

"I don't think I've ever been on that side of town before..."

*Well, aren't you in for a surprise.*

---

Benjamin pulls up to the apartment, making circles around and around. "What are you doing?" I finally ask.

"I'm looking for your parking spot... Where is it?"

Part of me wants to laugh at the suggestion that he thinks I have my own parking spot but the bigger part of me is embarrassed that I don't. It's not something I've thought of as an option, and seeing Benjamin's lifestyle is showing me just how different our lives really are. "I don't have one," I say through the knot in my throat. "You'll have to make the block and parallel park on a side street." I gesture for him to turn down the adjacent one-way street.

When he finally finds a spot, I see the nervousness on his face. "Don't worry, if someone sideswipes you, at least you can afford to have it fixed. Cruella over there...." I point to my run-down car that's parked under an oak tree—that probably won't crank since it hasn't been started since we've been gone. "She's had her share of sideswipes, door dings, you name it, but the old girl doesn't complain too much."

I see the revulsion on Benjamin's face, but he shakes it off and keeps his comments to himself. I lead the half-mile walk back to the apartments, weaving in and out of cars, climbing broken sidewalks. We approach my run-down building and I look up at it, feeling embarrassed for the first time.

"Well, this is it, watch your step; this staircase has seen better days."

Benjamin follows me up the staircase to the second story, dragging my suitcase behind him. As we approach my apartment, I feel the treble vibrating through the building. Shit. I already know before I open the door that there's going to be a sight to behold. Turning around to Benjamin before he reaches for the door handle, I place my hands on his chest, trying to physically move him away from the door.

"You know what? I forgot I wanted to run today! Why don't we go right now?"

He looks at me questioningly. "Elliot, if we start running through this neighborhood, someone is either going to think we're in trouble or that we stole something. Besides, we're outside your door, let's just bring your stuff inside first."

"I really don't think that's a good idea."

He reaches around me and pushes the door open, ever so slowly. "Hello," he calls out. "Anybody home?"

They were home all right. Destiny and company have converted our living room into a Jell-O-filled wrestling ring and it seems that my roommate is the star of the show. Wearing nothing but a thong string bikini, she and another voluptuous woman were trying to push the each other out of the inflatable pool.

"Where did you get all that Jell-O?" I ask no one in particular.

Benjamin turns to me. "That's what you want to know right now? Where they got the Jell-O?"

"Well, yeah. I've never seen that much Jell-O in my life. In fact, if I were to buy the entire shelf of it at the grocery store, I don't think it'd be enough...and it looks like it's all the same cherry flavor..."

Destiny notices us gaping in the doorway. "Hey, Freddy, turn down the music; my roommate's here." She turns to face me. Her boob's halfway exposed, but she doesn't seem to mind. "Elliot, I didn't realize you'd be home so soon. I joined a wrestling league; isn't this great? It's amazing cardio, and the Jell-O is so much fun." She picks up a big scoop and lets it run down her face.

"I texted you this morning telling you I was coming home today. You could have mentioned you were having practice or whatever this is."

Tattooed muscle guys line the perimeter of the kiddie pool, staring at the show before them. The skinhead, the bulkiest of the group, nods toward me.

"Now that's a hot piece of ass. Why don't you take off your shirt and hop in here and show these girls what you've got? Or is your little boy toy there going to say you can't play with us?"

As soon as the words leave his mouth, Benjamin pulls me to the side. "Elliot, I don't want to go to jail, and if we spend another minute in this shit-hole apartment, that's most likely what's going to happen." He grabs my arm to pull me outside, but I jerk away from him. Defensiveness bubbles out of me and even though I know he means well, I can't help but feel like he's just insulted me.

A fresh wave of confidence ignites within me. Lifting my shirt from the hem, I pull it over my head dramatically and stare back at him. Wearing only my thin white lace bralette, I approach the kiddie pool. I strike my Wonder Woman power pose and stare him down.

"This is who I am Benjamin. If that's not good enough for you, then there's the door!" I leap headfirst into the kiddie pool. "I'm a Jell-O girl. Maybe you'd be more suited with someone who prefers tapioca pudding!"

I lunge toward Destiny, pulling her down into the Jell-O. Now seems as good a time as any to take out my frustration with this bitch for filling my living room with sugary goo. I can't even think about the ant infestation that I'm sure I'll be battling for the next month.

"*Scorpion Deathlock, bitch!*" I grab her feet, causing her to fall backward in the Jell-O. The men spectating scream my name as I dig Destiny's fake titties into this inflatable pool. I twist her legs around mine and I lean back, forcing a very painful backbend. She tries to scream, but her cries are muffled by the Jell-O. To my surprise, Benjamin doesn't leave. He's standing in the corner with his arms crossed over his chest, laughing hysterically at me...which only pisses me off more. I let Destiny up for air so she doesn't suffocate in Jell-O and hit her with a half-nelson. She's a pathetic fighter. For being six inches taller than me, you'd think she'd have a little bit more arm strength.

"Now, I'm only going to say this once, so you better listen up! You and your friends here are going to clean this up, and then they're going to help you get your shit, and you're going to move the fuck out of my apartment! *Do you understand?*"

"Yes, yes, I understand, now let me go! Dammit, Elliot, I'm going to have a bruise now! Where did you get that Hulk upper body strength from anyway?" She stands up and rights her bikini top. Her beefcake boyfriend helps pull her out of the pool, and everyone cheers me on. The raucous crowd slaps my back, causing Jell-O particles to fly everywhere.

"You know, I didn't mean to insult you...Jell-O queen." Benjamin approaches me hesitantly, glancing around at the dilapidated ceiling and walls, and wipes a loose chunk from my cheek. "Your apartment is great, and I think you are incredibly brave for living here."

"You can't just walk into my life and assume things, Benjamin. I've worked really hard for everything, and I'm proud of where I am. Maybe I'm not living in a penthouse in downtown Chicago; maybe I don't drive a Tesla, but I—"

He cuts me off. "Elliot, I'm sorry I judged your living situation. For what it's worth, I'm proud of you too. I can see that you've accomplished so much already, and the best part is still to come."

"You don't think you're better than me? You don't want tapioca pudding instead of cherry Jell-O?"

He grabs my hand, taking my entire finger in his mouth, and slowly licks away the Jell-O before leaning toward me with an intense look in his eyes. "I fucking love cherry Jell-O."

My knees go weak and I see the little birds and stars twirling around my head in cartoons.

"I'm taking the couch since I found it! Have fun sitting on the floor from now on!" Destiny yells from behind me.

Benjamin leans down, touching his forehead to mine. "You found your couch? Where?"

"It was barely used, just sitting there by the dumpster!" Destiny screams. "I already called it, so don't even think about fighting me!"

A smile breaks across my face. "Destiny, the couch is all yours." I grab Benjamin by the hand and lead him out the door.

# TWENTY-NINE

Elliot

Benjamin had to cover his car seat in trash bags for me to ride back to his apartment with him. I still can't believe I had the balls to kick Destiny out—finally—and I even got to slap her around a little bit and take out some of my pent-up frustration. I've been waiting for a moment like that for a really long time. I still don't know how I'm going to make ends meet without her half of the bills, but I'll figure something out. What I'll miss in rent money, I'll probably save in cleaning supplies anyway.

The gelatin is starting to harden, pulling my skin taut. It feels like my entire body is covered in one of those peel-off face masks. I can't complain—at least they chose cherry Jell-O, my favorite—but I don't think this bra is ever going to be white again. I don't know what happened back there, but something in me just snapped. I knew Benjamin was trying to protect me. It's a strange feeling; no one's ever made me feel that way before. After I saw his apartment and his car, and I fully realized his financial security, it intimidated the hell out of me. Why would someone so wealthy want anything to do with someone like me, someone just barely making ends meet? I don't want a handout from Benjamin. I don't want him to swoop in like Prince Charming and save the day. I want to build a career that I can be proud of. I want to be self-sufficient, and I don't want to have to thank anyone but myself and all my hard work when I finally reach my goals. Success will taste so much sweeter when I do it by myself, and I can't wait to take that first taste.

---

"I'm going to have to think of some creative explanation for why my girlfriend is covered head to toe in cherry Jell-O." Benjamin throws the car in park and makes his way around to open my door for me. I want to believe it's because he's a gentleman and has impeccable manners, but more than likely he just doesn't want me to touch his car any more than I have to.

"Did you just call me your girlfriend, Benjamin Williams?" I poke him playfully in the chest and he throws his arm around me, shielding me from the cold, obviously not caring that he's now covered in this sticky mess too.

He pauses his step, and a look of uncertainty washes over his face before he pulls me into him. "I think I did. Is that OK with you?"

My heart flips in my chest, and I'm at a loss for words. I've gotten us kicked off of an airplane, sprayed him with mace, and wrecked our rental car hitting an elk. He just witnessed me challenge my roommate to a Jell-O wrestling match in my living room, for God's sake. And he *still* somehow is interested in me. I think back to the picture on his phone, the photo of the night he first met me. I want to be that girl, the one he saw and was so captivated by that he had to take a picture. I want to believe in myself, that I can be both my quirky authentic self and a professional. Somehow Benjamin brings out all of my best traits at the same time, like he's a megaphone amplifying my voice. How did I get so lucky to meet such an amazing man, someone so opposite of me who balances me in a way I've never experienced?

Benjamin pulls me behind a large potted plant. "Wait here while I distract Alfred. I don't need the doorman making any assumptions, though I'd love to hear what they may be."

I crouch lower and watch him approach the elderly gentleman. "Hello, Mr. Williams. It's a fine Sunday afternoon, wouldn't you say?"

"It certainly is, Alfred. Do you think you could call a car detailing service to come by today for me? We were bringing some Jell-O salad to a friend's, and I hit a bump and you wouldn't believe the mess it made."

"Sure thing, Mr. Williams."

Benjamin hands him the keys to his car and turns back toward me with a wink. "Come on, let's get you in the elevator before you give old Alfie a heart attack."

Once the elevator doors close, Benjamin is on me. His arms wrapping tightly around my waist, bringing our mouths together. Benjamin plants hurried kisses along my neck, licking and sucking before making his way back up to my lips. He takes my full bottom lip in his mouth with a forceful suck and bites down hard. The contrast between the gentle caress of his tongue and his sharp bite causes my insides to flip, sending pure energy straight to my vagina.

"I fucking love cherry Jell-O." He pulls me closer, pushing his thigh between my legs, giving my aching clit the sweet friction it craves.

My hands are thirsty for his body and in the short time it takes the elevator to reach his floor, I've already removed his shirt, savoring every speed bump his abs have to offer. The doors open and Benjamin pulls me backward, never breaking contact with my lips. We crash into a wall, knocking down a picture frame, Benjamin's back taking most of the blow. He breaks away just long enough to place the picture back, then grabs my hand, leading me through his doorway. The door slams with a loud clang behind us like a gong before a fight.

"Elliot, if you don't want this... please tell me now."

He slides his fingers through my hair, gripping and pulling my head back gently, licking the sweet spot just below my earlobe. He bites me again, this time a little harder, and I yelp.

"Sorry, you just taste so good," he says. "I'm doing everything in my power not to eat you right here in this kitchen."

The most impure images run through my head of Benjamin laying me out on his cold, hard granite countertop, feasting on my body in broad daylight. I've never done this kind of thing before, and up until I made out with him at the inn, I didn't know my body was capable of feeling so alive. Yeah, I've had sex, but at the time it seemed obligatory to just lie there until it was over. I didn't know it could be different.

Benjamin cuts off my train of thought, grabbing my ass to pull me closer. "Elliot, I need you to say something. Tell me what you want."

I jump into his arms and wrap my legs around his waist, bringing my new favorite body part into contact with his massive erection. I meet his lips for a long slow kiss as I run my fingers through his thick hair. My tongue gently circles his as our bodies press harder against each other.

"I want to take a shower," I say, "with you."

His eyes grow dark with lust, like a shark catching the scent of blood in the water. "Yes, ma'am."

He carries me through the apartment, through his bedroom,

and into the master bathroom. With care, Benjamin places me down on the warm heated tile before turning on the shower. He turns back to face me and must see the nervousness on my face. Brushing my hair back, he leans in and plants a sweet kiss on my lips.

"You know you don't have to do this, right? You're in control and I want you to know that we can stop anytime you say. Got it?"

I nod. "I didn't think a guy could stop...you know, once he started—" I break off, looking down at my feet.

Benjamin's lust-filled eyes turn to rage. "Elliot, please tell me that isn't what he told you...." The muscles around his neck start to flex and tighten under my palms. I want to be honest with Benjamin, but I don't want to ruin this moment between us. The truth is, I've never felt the sensations I feel when I'm with Benjamin, and I can't help this needy feeling building within me.

"Well, yeah, I mean...I've only been with one guy before so that's all I know."

He leans down. "Then it sounds like you were with the wrong guy." His hand slides up my hip, then grazes over the side of my breast. I suck in a sharp, cold breath at the contact. Very gently he pulls my bra strap down, peppering my exposed shoulder in soft, gentle kisses. Steam from the hot shower surrounds us, softening the brightly lit bathroom and giving me a little boost of confidence. Benjamin repeats the motion on the other side and before I know it, the bra has completely fallen around my waist. He takes in my exposed breasts, gently reaching to circle my nipple with his thumb. I feel a pinch and the sensation shoots bolts of electricity straight down to my vagina. Eyes wide in wonder, Benjamin takes the encouragement.

"I'm going to have so much fun with you." He pulls my bra

free from my waist and shoves his pants down, revealing the largest erect penis I've ever had the privilege of seeing.

"What do you plan on doing with that thing?" I belt out before I realize what I've said.

I catch him off guard and a sexy laugh escapes his throat. Leaning down, he takes my earlobe between his teeth and gives it a small nibble. "Don't worry, I'll show you."

He slowly removes my pants, dropping my Jell-O-encrusted jeans on the floor with a harsh *thwack*, leaving me standing before this god-like man in only my panties. "These things are sure to kill me." He pops the side of my G-string against my hip. The look in Benjamin's eyes right now resembles a wolf staring down his prey; his hungry needy eyes roam my entire body and I feel his stare settle on my breasts.

"Shit." He rubs his large palm in the small space between my breasts up toward my throat. "I am one lucky bastard."

This gives me the last bit of encouragement I need, and I push my panties down around my ankles and step toward him, taking his hand and leading him into the shower.

"Holy shit, Elliot, I didn't peg you for a waxer..."

Before I have time to snap back a sassy remark about my grooming habits not having anything to do with having sex, he reaches between my legs and strokes me ever so gently with the softest feather-like touch. My body melts against him, experiencing a euphoria I've never felt before. Yeah, I've been touched, but it was always aggressive and fleeting. Benjamin, however, takes his time. He slides his hands over me like they're trying to devour me as if they can't touch me everywhere enough. For the first time in my life, I'm savored like a fine wine rather than shot-gunned like a cheap beer.

He takes the liquid soap in his hand and begins washing me. Starting around my neck and slowly making his way down my body, avoiding touching me where I crave it most, as my need for relief builds. The soft, warm bubbles soothe my anxiousness, though, and I become lost in this moment.

I reach around and grab the soap and begin my exploration. I've been dying to touch Benjamin's body since I first laid eyes on him. Like me, Benjamin is clearly obsessed with exercise, and I can see and feel the hours of torture he puts in at the gym day in and day out. His body deserves a shrine; ripped cords of muscle wrap around these arms that encase me against him. I feel so small and so protected wrapped up against him like this.

He lowers his face, planting a soft kiss on my lips. I rise up on my tiptoes, deepening our kiss. Desire gushes through my body, my hands gripping his thick head of hair, and I lick and suck.

Benjamin turns off the water streaming down on us and has me wrapped in a fluffy towel in two seconds. He then wraps a second towel around my hair before scooping me up and carrying me to his bed. He sets me on the very edge with my feet draped over the side, and lowers his body in front of me.

"I've been dying to do this ever since you gave me that striptease back at the inn." He kisses my closed thighs and every nerve in my body stands on edge. He reaches behind me and pulls my towel away so there's no barrier between us. Taking my foot in his hand, he gently rubs up the length of my leg and I can't help but giggle when he plants the most gentle peck on the bottom.

"Hmm... so you're ticklish?"

"Mm-hmm..." I bite my lip, anticipating his next move.

He grabs my arms and holds them above my head, "Do you trust me?" I nod and he's hovering over me, sliding my body up the bed where my hands are touching the headboard. He wraps my hands around the cold metal of the intricate design. "Don't let go, got it?"

My completely naked body is sprawled out on Benjamin's

bed and he wants me to keep my hands above my head so he can do God knows what to me? I panic for a moment, but realize that I do trust him, completely. I have no idea where this is going to lead but my heart is pounding so hard in my chest I'm afraid I may actually die before I find out.

"Yes, sir." I play into his demand, and bite my lip. Benjamin's eyes go black and I see that my response was definitely the right answer.

He gently rubs his hands down my collarbone, between my breasts, and lightly circles my breasts, not touching them. "Your tits are an unexpected surprise, Elliot. I seriously don't know how I've been able to keep my hands to myself all this time. You've tortured me from the moment I laid eyes on you in that bar; you know that, don't you?"

I simply nod because all words have left me. Every ounce of focus I have is being used to keep myself from levitating off this bed from pleasure and he hasn't even touched me yet.

He slides his hands down further, gripping my hips tightly. "These fucking hips of yours drive me wild." His fingers roam gently down to the crease in my thigh, careful not to touch me just yet.

A soft moan escapes my lips and I reach for his hand to urge him to my desired destination to give me some relief from this built-up sexual torture.

"Ah, ah, ah. I said to keep your hands just right here." He places them back where they were. "Now, you're not going to need me to tie you up, are you?"

I shake my head no and keep my focus on his soft touch, willing my hands to stay above my head. Usually, I don't like being told what to do, but I can't explain the excitement that Benjamin's orders cause me. It's magnifying every touch, every sensation.

"Good girl. Now I'm going to kiss you and you're going to stay just like this, understand?"

Yes, I think. I can stay still while he kisses me. My heart pounds in my ears, and just when I think he's going to move back up toward me and kiss me on the mouth, he lowers his head down and plants the gentlest kiss right on my pussy.

"Oh my God," I cry out. "Benjamin, what are you doing?"

I'm careful not to let go of the headboard, and my worried self-consciousness is lost as he slowly licks me. Chills cover my body and hot liquid heat rises to the surface. Benjamin keeps a steady rhythm and I feel a sensation building in my center.

"Your pussy tastes like the best fucking candy I've ever had, Elliot. I could eat you for dessert every night." He lowers his face to me again, and this time his hands work with his tongue. He inserts a finger, never breaking his mouth's contact. "You're so fucking tight." And then another finger. His fingers start pulsing upwards and his arm jerks up, giving him the best angle to hit the most sensitive spot inside me.

My vision goes black; breathing is now the only thing I'm able to control as my arms, legs, and vagina have stopped listening to me. I've got Benjamin's head squeezed between my legs and my hands are pulling his thick, wet hair, trying to brace myself for the imminent orgasm that is so close to exploding within me.

"That's it, baby, come for me. Come on my face right here."

Once the words leave his mouth, he sucks my clit so hard that I lose all control. He jerks his arm faster, hitting that spot again and again and again. My orgasm starts in my toes and works its way up my body so violently that I wonder if I'll ever walk again. The glorious heat washes over me and through me, and when the fog in my mind has settled, I open my eyes to see the most gorgeous man staring back at me with the biggest grin I've ever seen on his face.

"Oh my God, Benjamin, that was...that was...."

"Fucking magic," he answers for me.

He crawls up the length of my body and pulls me into his chest, wrapping me in a solid embrace. I feel like I'm floating on a cloud above my body, like an out-of-body experience. His wide grin lights up the room, and I lie there in his arms, speechless.

"If this is what an orgasm feels like," I say, "I don't know if I'll ever leave this bed."

He pulls me away slightly so he can look in my eyes. "Are you serious? That was your first orgasm? I thought you said you dated a guy for like six years?"

"Well...I...let's just say he wasn't as generous as you." I look up at his strong jaw and nervously wait for his reaction.

"Shit, I would've taken it a little easier on you if I'd have known that. You must be exhausted right about now."

A big yawn escapes me just as he finishes his thought.

He pulls me in tightly into his chest. "You just rest right here, OK?" He plants a kiss on my head and squeezes me close.

"But...what about you?" I let my eyes drift down to his painfully erect penis.

"Hey, don't worry about me. It's not the first time you'll have given me blue balls. We've got plenty of time. You just get some rest."

And just like that, I drift off into a delicious, post-orgasmic slumber, and I'm ruined for any man who thinks he can hold a candle to Benjamin Williams.

# THIRTY

Benjamin

Elliot's lying against me with her signature drool spilling out all over my bare chest, collecting in a puddle that periodically overflows and spills down my side, and I chuckle, trying to keep quiet so that I don't wake her. This crazy, beautiful woman has me mesmerized and she doesn't even realize it. What was intended to be a short nap turned into a full-on naked sleepover. Elliot hasn't stirred once since she passed out yesterday. Being mindful of her modesty and knowing she'd likely feel uncomfortable, I attempted to clothe her the best that I could, meaning she's still naked but wearing my oversized t-shirt. I threw on some boxer briefs and climbed back in bed before falling into a restful sleep.

I wake before my alarm, which I'd set early to allow Elliot plenty of time to get ready for the day. Closing my eyes, I take in her scent, the feel of her delicate body lying against me. The thought shakes me to my core, but I can't seem to deny it: I'm crazy about this woman and I don't know what happens from here. I've got to tell her. Fuck, I should've told her about my past before I crossed that physical line, but the way she looked up at me yesterday with those big brown doe eyes, practically begging me to touch her, I couldn't think straight. *Tonight. I'm going to tell her tonight.*

I think back on the short time we've known each other and how my feelings toward her have changed so much from that first night in the bar—hell, since the first time she walked into my office. How when I'm around her my nightmares seem to disappear, how she has a way of filling a void in my heart that I didn't think could ever be filled again. I feel like such an asshole. I just hope when she finds out the truth, she won't walk away. I don't know if I could take losing the love of my life a second time.

I lean down and brush a stray hair from her eyes before planting a chaste kiss on her forehead. "Elliot, baby, it's time to wake up." I gently rub her temple, waiting on the imminent panic from her realization that she's just spent the night at my place, on a worknight.

She bolts upright, giving me no warning to move out of the way, and headbutts me right in the nose.

"Shit!" I feel the warm trickle of blood instantly combined with the sharp stab of pain, and my eyes see stars.

"What day is it? Ouch! Oh, Benjamin, I'm so sorry!" She jumps up from the bed, grabbing the discarded towel from the night before, and I momentarily forget all about the pain of my nose and the blood that's now dripping down my face. Elliot's t-shirt—or my t-shirt, I should say, has ridden up her bare ass and she's leaned over me to help clean up the mess.

"Benjamin, I'm so sorry! I'm such a spaz. Are you OK? Does it hurt really bad? Do you think it's broken?"

Instead of answering her, I slide my hands around her waist, bringing her down on my lap. Right now, with Elliot's mostly naked body straddling me, the last thing in the world I'm thinking about is my wounded nose. The realization settles on her, and I see a change in expression. Her round eyes somehow grow even bigger, and she parts those soft, full lips, breathing out her desire. Her nipples harden under the thin white cotton of my t-shirt, and I'd be willing to bet if I reached down to touch her, she'd already be soaking wet.

Watching Elliot become aroused right before my eyes is the fucking sexiest thing I've ever seen. I wait for a brief moment, allowing her the opportunity to make the next move. She's had an eventful last twenty-four hours, and I don't want to push her over the edge.

She dabs the last bit of blood that's trickled down my lip before leaning in and planting a slow, needy kiss on my lips. Unable to hold back any longer, I deepen the kiss, pulling her head back closer to mine. She gasps for air before returning to meet my lips again. My cock hardens beneath the weight of her naked body over mine, and she slowly grinds her wet pussy against me, driving me past the point of no return.

"Elliot," I manage to gasp. "We have work today—" She interrupts me with more needy kisses, brushing my tongue with hers and doing that little swirl thing that drives me nuts. A moment passes and I try again. "Baby, I'm so fucking turned on. Are you sure you want to do this...right now?"

Rather than answering me, she reaches down under my boxer briefs and pulls my cock free, stroking me until I see stars. "Shit, woman, I guess you have some tricks up your sleeve too."

She bites her lip in response and throws her head back, allowing me full access to her throat and cleavage that's peeking from the dropped shoulder of my shirt. It's a sexy sight to behold but it's not good enough.

"Lift your arms for me."

She does as she's told, and I slowly pull the hem of the shirt up over her body, leaving her perfectly naked in my lap. To my surprise she doesn't shy away; she sits up taller and keeps working my cock in her small, but extremely capable hand. I take her small pert nipple in my mouth and savor the taste of her skin. With another firm stroke, I almost lose control and blow my load right there.

"Fuck, baby, you better stop or I'm going to be done for."

I lay her back down on the bed to revisit the new friend I made last night. I've eaten pussy plenty of times in my life, but Elliot's pussy is on a different level. She tastes like heaven and is so fucking responsive—just watching her could give me an orgasm. I kiss her gently with a long slow lick, working my tongue around her clit ever so gently. When she starts squirming beneath me, panting for air, I know I've got her close. She parts her legs more, giving me free rein to have my way with her. I give her clit one more long suck, and she's writhing against my face just like she did the night before.

Once her convulsing has stopped, I can't help the giant grin that finds its way to my face. "You are the most amazing woman."

I climb up her body, kissing her on the mouth, allowing her to taste herself on my tongue. At this point, the ball—or balls I should say—are in Elliot's court. I don't want to pressure her to do anything else, and from what she shared with me about her ex-boyfriend, it seems that she's deserving of as many orgasms as she wants and I'm happy to oblige.

To my surprise she wraps her legs around my waist, and I see in her eyes this little morning rendezvous is far from over.

"I want you, Benjamin." She reaches down to stroke my needy cock again, and I jump at her touch. I'm so turned on right now that I doubt I'll make a great first impression, but the pent-up desire from all of our almost-encounters is really starting to get to me. A man can only handle so much on his own, and the events of last night are weighing heavily on me.

"Oh, Elliot, I want that too. I don't know how long this is going to last but I promise I'll make it up to you." In a quick motion I reach into my side table to get a condom, roll it on, and press my head against her eager entrance. I see a slight worry in her brow. "Everything OK? Are you sure?"

She exhales. "Yeah, I'm sure...just nervous. You're pretty well-endowed and I've only been—"

I stop her before she can say anything else. "Let's not talk about that right now." The very last thing I want to think about right now is some other guy's dick inside my girl. I push inside her ever so slowly, stopping every few strokes to let her body adjust to my size. "Holy shit, you're tight," I gasp into her neck. I'm holding my body above hers, shaking and trying to keep from spilling everywhere before I've even really started, while keeping my weight from crushing her tiny frame.

"Oh my God...this is so...different." She rubs her hands up and down the tightened muscles in my back and I take it that she's comfortable.

I begin to move slowly at first, watching her face intently for any signs of distress. She wiggles her hips beneath me, aiding my motion. I keep my thrusts slow and even, focusing on that spot that most guys totally miss. I see in her expression once I've hit it as her face tightens in pleasure. I reach my hand around on the bed, looking for a cushion, and I make contact with a cool, crisp pillow. I shove it under her hips and she lets out a gasp. Yep, works like a fucking charm every time.

"Wha...what was that?" she gasps.

Her responsiveness is so sexy; it's taking every bit of restraint I have to keep this fucking pace, but it's not time yet. I reach up and grab her breast in my hand and squeeze it, rubbing her nipple between my fingers.

"Oh, Benjamin...it feels so good. I'm so close. I don't know if I can come again."

Her plea for help is all the encouragement I need. This beautiful girl hasn't had her needs met, and she obviously doesn't realize what her body is capable of. I'm no quitter, and I pride myself on my satisfaction record in the female orgasm department. It's time to turn it up a notch and blow her mind.

I reach between her legs and rub her clit as I thrust a little bit harder and a little deeper. I use my free hand to brace myself off her body so I don't accidentally crush her, making me extremely grateful for all those hours spent shredding my muscles in the gym. I'm working up a sweat from the intense movement combined with holding back my orgasm until she comes again.

"Yes! Yes! Yes!" She screams, her head thrown back, gasping for air. I increase my speed, and her tits bounce from the motion. I burn this image in my mind, and I know I'll be revisiting it quite often for my replay reel.

"Fuck, Elliot, your pussy is so tight. Are you ready to come for me yet?"

She moans in response. I grab her legs and throw one over my shoulder, giving me a new angle, and I thrust upward, hitting her G-spot. My girl loses it, and I follow suit.

"Oh shit. Shit. Shit. Shit. Dear God and all that is holy, holy fucking shit, Benjamin Williams."

Her body goes limp beneath me like a rag doll, spasming in bursts sporadically.

I lean down and kiss her deeply and lay my head down on her chest. I can hear her heart beat violently, and I know mine is going at the same rate. We're a sweaty, tangled mess. I reach up and brush her matted hair from her forehead. "You drive me crazy; you know that, don't you?"

She just bites her lip in response. "Benjamin.... Do you

think we can do that again? Well, we've got to get to work first."
She jumps up from the bed on wobbly legs, laughing as she tries
to make it to the bathroom without bumping into anything.

"Are you coming?" she yells from the bathroom.

"I'd follow you anywhere," I whisper under my breath.

# THIRTY-ONE

Benjamin

*Two years earlier...*

I walk into the house and shed my raincoat, trying my best to stay quiet. It's five in the morning and I'm just getting in from a long night at the office. We had a bit of an emergency to handle, and since Sarah's been so stressed out lately, I came home at three to check in on Maddie. After I put her to bed, I headed back in to the office.

I kick off my shoes and am grabbing a bottle of water from the fridge when I notice a note on the counter. It's folded in half and kissed with Sarah's unmistakable lips in my favorite red lipstick. I grab the note and open it, letting my eyes graze over the words. My heart shatters into a million pieces.

No, this can't be right; this is some practical joke she's playing on me. Surely she wouldn't tell me something like this in a fucking letter left on the countertop. I rush to the bedroom and throw open the door, hoping and praying that I find her lying there asleep, but the bed's empty. Sarah's dresser drawers are all open and disheveled like she packed up and left in a hurry.

No. No. No. I rush to Maddie's room and see much of the same thing. Her bed's unmade like she was woken from her sleep. I see her favorite stuffed animal, Bunny, still lying in her bed like she's waiting on her girl's return. Anger rises in my chest at the thought of Maddie being snatched up out of her bed and hauled off. She doesn't even have her Bunny to make her feel safe. How could Sarah forget Bunny?

Sarah hasn't been herself lately and the letter explains it all, but I still can't wrap my head around it. How could I not have seen the signs?

I find a coffee cup sitting on the kitchen countertop and pick it up to inspect it; the cup is still warm so they can't have left that long ago. I grab my keys and slip on my shoes and fly out the door. If she's going to her parents' house, then at least I'll head in that direction; maybe she stopped to fill up with gas on the way and I can beat her there.

Rain beats down on the windshield and my wipers fight to keep up. The thought of the two of them out in this weather driving makes me sick with worry. I pause at the red light and dial her number again, praying she picks up and talks to me. If I could just get her to talk, we could work this out.

The light flashes green and there's a small break in the rain. I pass through the light and see the faint glimmer of taillights just ahead. *Please, please, please.*

A white sticker of a ballerina catches my eyes and I recognize Sarah's car just ahead.

We're on a small two-way road and I honk the horn and wave my hand out of the window to get her attention. As we approach another light, I see it turn yellow and I dial her number again. "Fuck, Sarah, just talk to me!" I'm getting ready to get out and run to her when I see that she doesn't stop at the light. Sarah hits the gas just as a semitruck crashes into the side, sending the car spinning into the trees.

My heart sinks to my stomach as I launch myself out of the car and run toward them in a full sprint. I know then and there that I will never be the same.

# THIRTY-TWO

Benjamin

Elliot and I decided it'd be best if Wilson drops us off separately, so as not to draw any unwanted attention to this new thing between us. We drop Elliot off at the front, and I wait ten minutes before making my way into the building.

"Good morning, Mr. Williams!" Eliza's excited voice echoes through the lounge. "How was your trip? You look great. We've all missed having you around so much." She laughs a little nervously and I realize what she's saying without saying. "Just don't leave again anytime soon, OK?" she says through clenched teeth.

"You got it." I'm suddenly nervous about the state of the company; what did I miss? I rack my brain, trying to think back on every major decision that could've been made over the last two weeks. Even though I've been remote, I've worked my ass off, keeping up with my regular duties while ensuring that each proposal went according to plan. Though I admittedly didn't need to worry so much about Elliot's project; she hit the job out of the park. I can't wait to arrange for her to get the raise she's so clearly earned with this multimillion-dollar deal. I'm sleeping easier knowing I've got a competent leader on my team, and it makes me sick to think of her current job title and salary.

"Eliza, what's my schedule like today? For some reason I'm locked out of my Outlook this morning."

She pulls up my calendar, something that isn't technically her job, but I know that she never minds. I need to know what exactly I'm walking into today. Will I be in a stuffy conference room in back-to-back meetings, or will I be able to catch up on the paperwork that I'm behind on?

"Let's see here." She clicks into the calendar to find my schedule. "It looks like you've got a ten o'clock with a Chase Knight and a one-on-one with Mr. Powell from noon until the end of the day. That's about it; looks like a pretty easy first day back. I don't mind ordering lunch for the meeting; would you like your usual?"

"Yes, thank you, Eliza, that'd be wonderful. Why don't you grab yourself something as well." I take off toward the elevator before she can thank me, my mind buzzing. What could Chase Knight possibly want?

My mind flashes back to our exchange. It wasn't my best moment, but I'd have defended any of my female employees had they been in the very same position. This is my company after all, and I don't think it's a smart business move partnering with pigheaded men, even if my co-captain is the leader of the fucking pack.

This is Elliot's project; maybe there's something she knows that I don't? I was only there to ensure things were handled and the logistics were all tied up. Where is Elliot anyway? I glance around the modern office space that conceals little between workspaces—another one of Thad's touches—but I don't see her anywhere.

The elevator doors open and I'm face-to-face with Thad, who's wearing a shit-eating grin. "Well, well, well, did you have fun on your little vacation? You look rested. Now you're making me jealous, Benjamin. I'm going to have to schedule a conference near a ski resort very soon. I can't have you walking around glowing and outshining me, can I?"

"No, we wouldn't want that." I push past him, unwilling to back down, and my shoulder collides with his. It's a little more aggressive than I'd normally be, especially on a Monday, but I can't shake the feeling that Thad's been up to no good since I've been gone.

"Mr. Powell, Elliot's waiting for you in the conference room," a young blonde woman who can't be older than twenty-two reminds him. Jesus, there he goes hiring another staff member behind my back.

"Thank you, Lydia. I was just heading there." He straightens his tie while pinning me with an intense glare. "I've got some business to attend to with *my* assistant." He emphasizes the 'my' and I can't help but wonder what exactly he knows. "Benjamin, please excuse me. It seems she and I have a lot to talk about." He turns to leave and it takes everything in me not to yank him backward by his Brooks Brothers tie until his face turns purple.

"I'll sit in on the meeting." It comes out more like an order than a request, and when Thad gives me a surprised smirk, I don't react. Elliot is much too fragile right now; I don't want her to be bombarded with bullshit requests right out of the gate when she's practically worked herself to death over the last several weeks. I don't know what the hell is going on with Chase Knight, but I'll be damned if I let him anywhere near my girl without being present.

"You will? Of course, you will, Benji." He smiles, almost knowingly, but how could he know anything? He punches me in the shoulder, and I don't flinch. He gets the message and removes his hand. "Ah, Benjamin, you dog, I thought you'd learned your lesson by now, but it seems you simply can't help yourself. Your Achilles' heel will always be a damsel in distress."

Red-hot rage blinds my vision and while I'd like nothing more than to punch Thad right in his delicate face, I know better. I grip my knuckles and distance myself from him as fast as I possibly can, for both of our sakes.

*What the fuck is going on?* My mind starts to spin, and all I can think of is Elliot and how I haven't had a chance to explain anything further about Sarah. And now I'm sure that Thad's about to fuck it all up.

---

I see my beautiful, naive Elliot at one end of the table, with her PowerPoint presentation queued up on her laptop and her notepad and pen at the ready. My heart swells with pride at the sight of her, but I can't help the fear that's churning in my gut like I'm waiting for the other shoe to drop.

Thad seems to be behaving himself, keeping conversations strictly professional. He's even chosen a seat where he doesn't have a prime view of her bare legs in the pencil skirt I insisted she wear today just for me. Maybe I'm overreacting. Maybe it's just the grief creeping in, and I'm freaking out for no reason at all.

I relax my shoulders and all but collapse into my seat, exhausted from the adrenaline rush I've experienced over the last ten minutes, then Chase Knight, the king of the douches, prances into the conference room wearing a smug look and a twinkle in his eye.

Thad leaps from his seat to greet him. "Brother, how's it going?" They exchange a token frat handshake and Chase takes a seat right next to Elliot. I think back to the last time I saw this son of a bitch. I believe my last words to him were, 'You can all go fuck yourselves' or something of that nature. Why the hell is he sitting here in the boardroom across from me? We rejected the deal. I told him I'd never do business with someone like him.

Before I can ask any of the questions running through my head, though, Thad laughs. "Chase and I go way back. We were at boarding school together in London, from grade nine to ten. As soon as I heard his gym was a candidate for our sponsor partnership, I reached out to him, letting him know that we were here for him, no matter what he needed. You know he always had a crush on my sister. I always felt like there was something there and one day *he'd* be my brother-in-law."

The room falls silent. I glance over to Elliot whose face has drained completely of all color. I try to pipe in, to reassure her that no matter what seems to be going on, her decision, our decision, was the best thing for the company. But right now, the business is the least of my concerns. I see the look on Thad's face and he's clearly ready to ruin everything he can for me. I just hope I can tell Elliot first.

Thad continues. "You can imagine my surprise when he called me after your meeting saying how rudely he and his staff were treated by *my* company's representatives. At first, I didn't believe it, but then I looked back over the records and I saw that we did indeed cancel our proposal with Mr. Knight because of 'company cultural differences.'" He pauses, letting the last bit of information settle in the air between us. I had to fill out the paperwork after we stormed out of the meeting with Chase, and I chose to say something on the vaguer side; I thought it'd fly under the radar.

Elliot's twirling her long strands of hair, her leg shaking heavily under the table—it's her tell that she's completely and utterly overwhelmed. I've got to do something because there's no way I'm letting Chase—or Thad for that matter—win.

"I just don't understand why I was treated the way I was," Chase interrupts. "Mr. Williams and his... colleague—" he points to Elliot— "showed up to my office unprepared, wearing an extremely inappropriate outfit. Her legs were exposed and her top button was left unbuttoned, causing my coworkers to lose focus on their tasks. I think it was an attempt to seduce me. I gave them thirty more minutes than I intended and then was late for my mother's birthday lunch because of it. Then to have Mr. Williams here so rudely dismiss me from the contract because I told the lady she looked nice."

I try to get a word in, to stop the hideous lie that falls from his lips, but he continues.

"I mean, it's nice to see an organization give young women with absolutely no experience in the field an opportunity, but as your friend, I don't think she was ready. Dare I say, it was embarrassing hearing her stumble over her lines... her *lines*," he emphasizes. "Thad, she tried to memorize an entire speech; the poor thing was shaking with worry, and it took everything in me to take her seriously. I mean, I was going to do *you* a favor by agreeing." He pauses, biting the knuckle of his finger. "Then to be so rudely accused of something I'd never say. You know me, Thaddeus, I'd never belittle a woman; I love women. The whole thing is just sickening."

My vision blurs and rage seethes under the surface of my skin. How can this man come into the company that I've built from the ground up and call me a liar to my face like this? He doesn't know who he's dealing with; he doesn't know the power that I hold, and I'll be damned if I let him barge in here and accuse my girl of something that's completely fabricated.

"Mr. Knight, I'm sorry if that's the impression you got from our encounter—" Elliot starts.

"No. You will not speak unless you're spoken to." Thad growls. "You, young lady, have done enough damage. Do you understand?"

She breathes in sharply and nods.

"Mr. Knight was lucky that he had a friend here on the inside that will not allow POW! to be portrayed in such a way. So here's what I'm going to do. Elliot, you're being assigned to help Mr. Knight find a new sponsorship opportunity; you'll relocate to Nashville for as long as it takes to get the job done. To help him regain any compensation he missed out on with POW!."

"You sleazy bastard!" I jump up from my seat, getting in his face. "You forget that I own fifty percent of this company, and there is no way in hell I'd let that happen." I slap my hand on the conference table with a sharp *thwack*. "Everything he said is a fucking lie and you know it. Your pretty boy, childhood friend can go fuck himself because there's no way any of that is happening. You want to make money like a big boy? Well, you've got to grow the fuck up and accept the consequences of acting like a fucking child."

I can practically feel the steam flowing from my ears, but Thad just smiles.

"Oh, Benjamin, you are so predictable. Elliot." He turns his attention to face her, presenting her with two pieces of paper. "You have a choice to make right here, right now. You can either sign this waiver and go work for Mr. Knight, or you can fill out your termination paperwork. But please know that you'll have a tough time finding another opportunity in this city with such a horrible stain on your record."

She looks at me in astonishment, confused as what to do.

Thad speaks before I can. "Benjamin, look at her trying to decide. You really took a step down from my sister with this one. Sarah owned every room she walked into; she was bred for

249

greatness, and power flowed through her veins. It's insulting that you'd choose this incompetent Jezebel as a replacement."

Elliot looks up at me in confusion. "What's he talking about? Who's Sarah?"

"This just keeps getting better and better!" Thad turns his attention back to Elliot and before I can stop him, he says, "I can't believe he didn't tell you. Sweetheart, Sarah was my sister, whom he was married to just two years ago before he killed her and her daughter driving recklessly. He ruined everything my parents built with one bad decision. And now it seems he's chosen you, of all people, as a replacement."

She looks up at me, confusion in her eyes. "What? No, that can't be true."

The shock of the moment, of the giant secret I've been keeping, feels like a sock in the gut. I look down at my feet, dodging her gaze.

"Benjamin. Tell me right now. Is that true? Did you have a wife? A whole life that you've kept a secret from me? Were you married to his sister?" Her voice strains and tears well in her eyes as she waits for me to answer.

"It's true," is all I can muster. A million words flow through my head, but somehow none of them seem good enough as an explanation. I'm a piece of shit and I've just hurt the woman I love. It may not be a physical death, but any chance we had to be together is gone. Just like Sarah and Maddie. And it's all my fault. Once again.

"What kind of monster are you? How could you keep such a *huge* secret from me this whole time? It's not like you didn't have an opportunity on our cross-country road trip over the last two weeks." She holds up her hand. "I trusted you. After last night and this morning, was that all this was? Was I just a challenging lay?"

Elliot takes in a steady breath and looks me right in the eyes.

"I never want to see you again. Do not follow me. Do not call me. I want to forget I ever met you."

She grabs the transfer paperwork as she chokes on sobs and hurriedly signs. Then she storms out of the conference room, taking the last piece of my heart with her.

"Oh, and Benjamin, your two-year obligation as co-CEO has come to an end," Thad says. "It's your lucky day, you son of a bitch. I can't say that I'm not jealous."

What is left of my broken heart shatters into a million pieces, again. This time, though, I know I'll never be able to put the pieces back together.

# THIRTY-THREE

Elliot

How could Benjamin do this to me? After all we've been through, after what we did this morning? I choke back the sob that burns in my throat, trying to escape. What was I to him? Some kind of game, a challenge to see if he could make me fall for him, get in my pants? Am I just another notch on his headboard? There's no way that he could've led me on like he did and not explained his situation. He was fucking *married?* My mind has been blown so many times in the last hour that I don't even know what's real anymore.

My mind flashes back to last night. I finally built up the courage to stand up for myself, to kick Destiny out of the apartment. I only did that because I thought my job was secure. I am so stupid. Of course, he just saw me for the piece of ass that I was. I can't believe I threw it all away for a freaking guy. Benjamin gave me no choice in the matter; I had to sign Thad's paperwork. The alternative was losing everything that I've worked for over the last six years and move back home to small-town USA with my parents. I can hear my mother now: 'Oh, Elliot, we knew you'd be back. The big city is no place for people like us. You just need to settle down here and let your daddy and me help you. Maybe you could reconnect with Daniel; it's all water under the bridge really. The past is in the past.'

I clench my fist at the thought. "The past is not in the fucking past!" I slam the bathroom stall door open and come face-to-face with Eliza, who looks like she doesn't know whether to hug me or call the police because I seem to have lost my mind.

"Are...are you OK? she asks.

"It's just that everything is falling apart, and my life is over, and now I guess I'm moving to Nashville where I will be working in an office full of horny men who have no sense of boundaries around women, and I'll probably need to shave my head so they'll leave me alone." I turn away from her, feeling a spark of hope. "I bet if I shaved my head they'd be so confused by their attraction to me that they'd probably not say anything... at least in front of the others and I could fly under the radar."

I pull out my phone.

> Change of plans. Benjamin is a pig. Dinner at my place tonight. Gwen, bring pizza and lots of wine. Maggie, bring your clippers.

MAGGIE

> Fingernail clippers? Are we doing a spa night? I just learned a new Reiki technique!

GWEN

> Oh shit, Elly, are you OK?

MAGGIE

> What do you mean is she OK? Elly, you're OK, right?

253

**GWEN**

Mags. She's not talking about fingernail clippers. This is bad.

**MAGGIE**

In that case, I'll bring a sage bundle too.

**GWEN**

OK... but I'm bringing vodka.

---

I'm sitting on the floor in the middle of my bare living room, drinking boxed wine out of a soup can. Destiny wasn't joking when she said she was taking the couch; she took all the glassware too. What has my life come to? I thought I was a smart girl—I certainly had the grades to prove it—yet here I am sitting on flea-ridden carpeting in an apartment that I can barely afford on the bad side of Chicago. The only person to blame here is me.

Gwen introduced me to Thad and he so generously threw me a bone, even if it was for all the wrong reasons. I was doing a great job, I could tell, and then I let myself be swept away by Benjamin Williams, literally the only man in the world that I needed to stay away from. And now I've got to pack my closet of belongings—well, now that I think about it, maybe it's not that much stuff—and move to a new city where I have no one—again, OK, maybe not such a bad idea—and work around a bunch of pigheaded men with no manners—OK, that part really sucks.

Gwen barges through the door, decked out in her super chic workwear, with two large pizzas in her hands and a bottle of vodka shoved under her armpit. Maggie follows closely behind with two bottles of wine, a box of tissues, and a plate of what I can only assume are her signature brownies.

"Elly, we're here," Maggie cries, rushing toward me.

"Jesus." Gwen sets everything on the counter. "It's worse than I thought."

"Just pour me a drink and bring me that box."

---

Thirty minutes later I've spilled the tea, giving them each a play-by-play of the happenings of the last several weeks. I reach for a brownie and try to grab a handful, but Maggie stops me.

"No, no, no, no, no, no.... These are special; you'll just want one this time."

"But, Maggie, I don't think this is a time where we need to body shame anyone..." I give her a suggestive look. "I'm not afraid of a few LBs. Stop trying to push your issues on me."

Maggie looks annoyed and then laughs. "You know what, why don't you have two." She plates my brownies on a paper towel and passes it to me.

I take the brownies from her and quickly shovel them both into my mouth, hoping to numb any pain I'm feeling with Maggie's delicious concoction of fresh cocoa and the hint of salt and pecans. "*Oh my God*, Mags, these are incredible. Oh, they're so good." I take another big bite, talking over the food in my mouth. "You've really outdone yourself this time. Dare I say, this may be your best batch yet." I take another bite and wash it down with a gulp of red wine.

Maggie tenses, turning to Gwen. "She's really going to regret that in about forty-eight minutes."

Gwen places a steady hand on Maggie's shoulder. "Sometimes the best thing to do is let the problem implode, then you rebuild from the ashes."

Maggie nods her head and sits up straighter. "You're right. Elliot's a phoenix, and we're her spirit guides."

"Whaaat...what are you talking about?"

Maggie points to Gwen, who stands there unyielding. "It was Gwen, she told me to do it. She said you needed the master treatment, that it was an emergency!"

"Yes, Magnolia," she spits. "It *is* a fucking emergency!" She snatches the brownies from my grip and shoves one in her mouth. "Elliot needs us, and this is the only way I know that helps this level of heartbreak." She trudges toward me. "So forgive me, Elly. I just want you to relax for the evening, and maybe we can resolve this."

My mouth falls open in shock. "Gwenneth Bennett, did you give me drugs?" I slap my hands over my mouth in horror. "Never in my twenty-eight years has anyone offered me drugs, and now here I am, fed pot via the most devious and, dare I say, moist dessert that's passed my lips?"

Gwen shoves my shoulder. "Eww, Elliot, you know I hate that word."

---

As Maggie predicted, forty-eight minutes later my problems seem a lot less overwhelming. In fact, I think it's all kind of funny—well, except Benjamin losing his wife and child; that part is actually really sad.

"Elly, you were just laughing, so why are you crying?" Maggie crawls toward me, falling into my lap to wipe my tears.

"It's just so sad, you know?" I wail. "I mean, he's so young and handsome and he had it all and life just ripped the rug out from under him." I look around and notice that I don't even own a rug, and I'm not sure if this is a horrible omen or a good thing because I wouldn't miss the rug if it was ripped out from under me.

"OK, sweetheart, that's enough of that. He's a pig,

remember? We need to focus on you, not the piece of shit who used you. You've got to see the big picture here." She pulls me into her side and stretches her hands out like there's a screen. I focus my vision and concentrate, hoping that maybe the answer I'm looking for is literally written in the space between her fingers.

"Jesus, Elliot." Gwen throws her head back and cackles like the evil witch she is for drugging me. "Are you trying to read between my fingers?" She doubles over in a fit of laughter, joined by Maggie. I don't know why we're laughing anymore, but their laughter is infectious.

"OK, OK, why haven't we done this before now?" Maggie wipes the tears from her eyes, her grin spanning her entire face.

"Probably because I'm a good girl, and you've both obviously been holding out on me!"

"Oh, sweetie, we've got to stair-step you into these things. You've only started to hold your liquor just a year ago." Maggie pushes my wild hair out of my eyes and my memory flashes to my massive hangover in the cabin, Benjamin so sweetly taking care of me. A rush of heat floods me and I grab my phone and pull it to my chest. I need to text him and apologize; this is all so silly. I'm clearly in love with the man; I can forgive him. I can almost smell him if I close my eyes hard enough and focus.

Before I can type anything into the keyboard, Gwen's petite frame flies across the carpet and pummels me to the ground, wrestling the phone from my grip.

"Don't you dare even think about it!" she screams. "You are not calling him."

Maggie jumps up to pull Gwen off the top of me but accidentally trips over our purses that lay in a heap on the floor and falls on top of both of us.

She lies there, the cherry on top of our dogpile. "Oh no, Gwenny, Elly, I'm so sorry!"

"Ugh, get off. You're pinching my nipple! It feels like it's stuck under a steamroller! Ouch!" Gwen cries. "Hurry, you're going to stretch it out and my nipples are my best feature! I'm going to have orangutan titties!"

Picturing Gwen with stretched-out hanging nipples makes us all erupt with laughter. I may have had shitty luck in the men department, but my girls are worth their weight in gold. I grab them each in a bear hug. "I love you both so much, even though you gave me drugs and may or may not now have orangutan titties."

"Ugh!" Gwen pushes us off and pulls her shirt back to assess the damage. She breathes a sigh of relief. "They're perfect little nubs just like always."

---

"Seriously, though, sis, you're going to come out of this season of life stronger than ever." Gwen lies on her side facing me; it seems the pot brownies have loosened us up enough to lie down on my carpet.

"I think so, too, and Nashville is so much fun!" Maggie adds.

"Yeah, just think of all the penile opportunities wearing cowboy boots and serenading you with sweet country melodies." Gwen's eyes actually seem to sparkle at the thought, and she takes a long gulp of her water. "When are you leaving anyway?"

"Eliza emailed me with the trip details. I'm on a Greyhound first thing Sunday morning."

Gwen spits her water straight into Maggie's face. "A fucking Greyhound? Elliot, you can't be serious. why wouldn't you just fly?"

"Well...part of it is that Thad's trying to save some money, and this is kind of a punishment, but the other part is because I'm technically still on the No Fly List, remember?"

"Oh shit, I forgot about that!" Gwen laughs and lies back down. "You're such a spaz, and I love you for it!"

"Did you just say what I think you said?" Maggie squeals.

"Yeah, yeah, it only took a magical brownie, but there you have it and I love you too, Mags."

"So here's what you're going to do. Tomorrow we'll wake up and I'll help you create a killer capsule wardrobe; Maggie can sell your shit online. This shithole isn't going anywhere and there's no use in wasting your money. Go to Nashville on Sunday, work hard, and save your money. Have all the revenge sex you want with hot cowboys, and Mags and I will be waiting here to welcome you back!"

# THIRTY-FOUR

Benjamin

Elliot flies out the door and I turn to Thad. "What the fuck was that?"

"Benjamin, what are you talking about? I was simply doing some damage control here, trying to do what I can to improve the company's reputation. I'm sorry your whore got you suspended early."

"Don't fucking call her that!" I charge toward Thad but stop an inch or two away from him, daring him to lay hands on me. I glance up at the security camera and make sure it's on.

Thad shoves me and knocks me in the chest and I stumble back, but I don't touch him. He pushes me again and one more time. Then he clenches his fist and I close my eyes, absorb the blow, and charge.

I grab Thad by his throat, lean him over, and get in a punch to the gut, the force making him groan.

Chase launches himself across the room and I can't wait to get my hands on him; I want nothing more than to expel some of my pent-up anger. He lands on me and we fall to the ground in a heap, knocking over a row of stacked chairs.

A fist flies right into my jaw and my ears ring from the blow. I know it had to have been Chase, the bodybuilder, because there's no way Thad's gotten that much stronger in two years. I duck my head and flip to the side, throwing Chase off me. I stumble to my feet and give everything I have to the right hook planted directly at Thad's nose. I feel the crunch of his bone under my fist, and savor the feeling of causing him a fraction of the pain he's caused me since I've met him.

I spin around and block a swing from Chase. Thad's nose is pouring blood, and he's huddled in the corner, trying to keep the blood off his jacket. "What's wrong, Benji? You didn't like the way I talked to your girl?" Chase swings again and I block him, stopping the punch and getting a jab right into his exposed stomach.

I lunge toward him but he moves to the side. "No, I didn't you, piece of shit."

"Thad told me everything, you know?" He smirks and I take the opportunity and throw a punch, skimming his head but clipping his ear. I know it must hurt like a motherfucker, but he doesn't flinch.

"He told me about how you were the one at fault. How if you wouldn't have been chasing them like a lunatic, Thad's sister and niece would still be alive today. How do you even live with yourself?"

His face crunches under my punch and I know I've probably shattered his cheekbone. I leap over his crumpled frame and make my way to the control room and send a copy of the security video to my email, just in case the bastards try to sue me.

"Did she leave? Have you seen Elliot?" My breathing strains from the nineteen flights of stairs I've just run down. I shake out my stinging knuckles, and a few drops of blood hit Eliza's desk. She stares, her eyes full of worry.

"What the hell happened to you?"

"I got in a fight. When? When did you say she left?"

"She ran out of here twenty minutes ago, crying hysterically. CJ was even worried and made sure to walk her out to her car."

"Dammit!" I slap my hand against the counter, and Eliza jumps back at the sharp echo. "Shit, I'm sorry, Eliza. I didn't mean to scare you. I'm such an asshole. Listen, Thad just terminated my contract. I've already worked out your Christmas bonus with HR, so you'll still get it even if Thad doesn't pay out this year. That's about all I can do for you. Thank you for being such a hard worker." I give her a salute and turn to leave.

"You're not always an asshole, but I've definitely seen you in a better light. Do you need stitches or something? Do you want me to take you to the hospital?"

I grab a wad of Kleenex from her desk and lump them over my bloody knuckles. I probably do need stitches, now that I think of it.

"Benjamin, can I give you some advice?"

"Sure, what is it?"

"You've got to tell her the truth." She pins me with her stare. "*All* of it." She grabs my coat and shoves it toward me. "Do the right thing, Benjamin! And for the love of God, get your hand looked at!"

---

I know Elliot has to be at her apartment. It's taking everything in me not to go straight there right now, but I'm not in the best headspace and I'd be lying if I said I didn't think she should leave me. Hearing the words come out of Thad's mouth made it sound so sleazy, but it wasn't like that. I need to tell her, but I know that's not what she needs right now.

I pull out my phone and send the guys a message:

> Sam, I'm coming over. Get your stitching kit out.

SAM

> You got it, brother.

JACK

> Sam, will you please let me take a turn doing the stitches this time?

> You're not going to be there. I just need my hand fixed and I'm going home.

JACK

> Oh, so you want me to stop and grab scotch?

SAM

> Yeah, it sounds like you probably need to grab scotch.

> This is not a boys' night. I have a fucking black eye and a set of busted knuckles.

> But, yeah, you should probably bring some scotch.

I push the door open, not bothering to knock, and take a seat at Sam's modern dining table. I hold my hand out, and Sam assesses the damage while I hiss at his touch.

"It looks like you could use about three stitches here."

Jack pours us each a glass of scotch and slides the rocks glass

263

toward me. I take a long gulp and slam the glass down in pain as Sam pours a little scotch over my wound.

Sam jabs the needle into my flesh and threads it through before tying it off. "So, explain."

After college, the guys and I had quite an affinity for dangerous activities. After our third trip to the ER from various injuries, thanks to Sam's then-girlfriend, a registered nurse, we decided to learn how to give emergency stitches. They're not beautiful, but it saves us time and money for the inevitable accidents we have on regular occasions. Sam's the best, then me, and—considering he can barely tie his shoes—Jack's only a last resort.

"Everything is shit. Thad just fucked up my world. And now the woman I love is hurt by me and I don't even know if I deserve her forgiveness."

"So, I take it you haven't told her?" Jack flips the scotch bottle up in the air and catches it and hands it over to me. I give myself another hefty four-finger pour, knowing I'm going to regret this tomorrow.

"Of course he hasn't told her," Sam snaps. "Otherwise, he wouldn't be here bitching to me and cut-up from a brawl in the office."

"Dude, I told you, honesty is the best policy. There's nothing to be ashamed of; you know that, don't you?" Jack adds.

"That's not true and you know it. This time I really fucked up." I let Sam wrap my hand in the loose bandage. Once my hand is stitched and bandaged, I take another gulp of my scotch, draining the remainder of the glass.

"Hey, take it easy, will ya? This here is Glenfiddich—she's not some side piece of ass you slam back. You've got to savor this baby. She's wifey material or at least your secret mistress that you put up for life." Jack snatches the bottle from my hand and cradles her gently, giving her the slightest slap on her bottle-ass, and then winks. "Yeah, she likes it a little rough sometimes. She likes me to wear the pants and toss her around."

I push my chair away from the table. "And I see that it's now time for me to go."

Jack stops me as I pull on my coat. "Oh, come on, Benjamin. Sit the hell down and tell us your problems. I've been waiting for this attention from you for the last six weeks. It seems your mind's been 'other places' lately and I can't say that I blame you...but I'd be lying if I said I wasn't a little jealous."

I drop back down into my seat. "Fine. I'll stay, but I'm only going to stay if you cut out the weird shit. No more slapping the bottle's ass or whatever you were doing. Got it?" I poke him sternly in the chest.

"Jeez, I got it." He rubs his pec. "I'd think you'd be happy for me; I've found love that stands the test of time—well, as long I keep an extra bottle around."

Sam slaps his hand on Jack's shoulder, clearly startling him. "Why don't we let Benjamin tell us the whole story, and you and Glenfiddich can pick up where you left off later?"

"Fine," he whines. "But you better not skip out on the sex details because I know you slept with her. You're wearing your red shirt and all three of us know that that can only mean one thing, not to mention you've got this post-coital glow about you. I could recognize Benjamin's after-sex glow anywhere. Spill the tea, sir." He crosses his legs and sits back, silently waiting for all the details.

I spare nothing, pouring my heart out to the two guys who have had my back through the hardest moments of my life. We drink, I cry, and Sam even gives me a warm piece of his fresh sourdough bread, but it does nothing to dull the ache in my chest.

# THIRTY-FIVE

Elliot

It's been six whole weeks since I got on that Greyhound for a very long, very stinky, ten-hour drive to Nashville. I throw open the wobbly-hinged door to my motel room, balancing my Wendy's 4 for $4 bag and Chase's houseplant in my free hand.

I thought working for Thad was a nightmare. Chase and his brothers at Bros Gym are so much worse, and I don't even have Eliza to vent to or CJ to walk me out to my car at night. I'm working tirelessly from sunup to sundown to find him a handful of decent sponsorships that can add up to the original deal we were going to offer him. Since Benjamin's not around anymore, I thought we could just do our original plan, but Thad and Chase both agree that we need to start fresh, and Chase doesn't want to be anyone's second choice. I know this is all a giant power trip. Thad and Chase felt inferior and wanted to throw their power around, but I'll play their game. I'm determined to make the most out of this experience. I'm going to get Chase a deal and Thad will have no choice but to take me back and give me a promotion, then I'll live out the rest of my miserable existence with a broken heart in a big city. At least I'll be able to afford a decent place to grow old in alone.

I fall on my squeaky bed that—weirdly enough—smells like Destiny's body spray, curl on my side, and let out the sob I've been holding in all day. I bury my face in the pillow to mask my cries—it wouldn't be the first time I've been complained about for crying too loudly since I've lived here. I let the tears flow. I let them out because holding them in has taken so much of my strength and I am so tired. I don't know how much longer I can keep this up.

The burning sensation builds in my chest and my arms start to tingle. It looks like I'll be battling another panic attack all alone in this sketchy room. I push myself up and force myself to take a shower. The water comes out brown at first, and I don't even wait for it to run clear before I step into the cold spray. I go through the motions, doing my best to scrub away my fear. I wonder if I could just scrub him off of me, if that would make me feel better. But deep down I know that I'll savor our touches for the rest of my life. I know that the pleasure, the safety I felt around Benjamin was a once-in-a-lifetime thing that I'll never have again.

The panic attack finds me, just as it always does. Fear takes over my body, tightening its grip around me little by little, like a boa constrictor slowly taking my life with each pass over my tense, shaking body. I drag myself from the shower and curl into a naked heap on my bed. I let the panicked thoughts take over, not having the energy to fight them. *I am so pathetic. I've done this to myself. I'm going to die here in this hotel room alone, and no one's even going to know I'm missing. I can't handle the stress of a real job. I should just move back home. It shouldn't have to be this hard.*

Hours that feel like days pass before I finally stop shaking and fall into a restless sleep. I toss and turn before I find Benjamin who's smiling at me. I know this has to be a dream so I still my body and sink into the springy mattress to enjoy the fictional bliss.

———

Last night was rough; the panic attacks are coming more frequently these days. Normally I'd have time before or after work to run a few miles so I can manage them. You'd think I'd have an opportunity during the day, considering that I'm working at a gym, but Chase has me running around doing sporadic bullshit tasks throughout the day. Sometimes I wonder if he knows that exercise is how I cope with my mental illness and is purposefully withholding it from me. I'm beginning to wonder if I need to increase my medication since I can't manage the stress, but I don't know when I'd have time to make a doctor's appointment.

"Elliot, goddammit, would you come here?" Chase yells from his office. I hop to my feet and hurry over to him. He's sitting at his desk surrounded by headshots of himself. "I can't find the right photo. I'm being featured in the 'Nashville Bachelors Under 30' and I want to look sophisticated and rich."

I choke out a cough to mask the laugh that almost escaped. I suppose it's a good thing he already had his headshots made because the swelling in his cheekbone is only just now starting to heal. Dare I say, I actually felt sorry for him after seeing what Benjamin did. I reach for a black and white close-up of him shirtless, wearing only a bowtie. "How about this one? You look youthful and you've even incorporated formal wear." I grab the photo and turn to leave. "I'll just send this off for you."

"Wait. Wait just a minute. Are you mocking me?"

His voice cuts through me like a knife and I stop in my

tracks. "No, I wasn't mocking you, Mr. Knight. I was just trying to help you with your decision-making." I laugh nervously. "You know, I read that we can only make about fifteen decisions a day, and then our mind struggles."

He stands up slowly, making his way over to me. His solid frame towers over mine. "You know, I've been meaning to talk to you about something."

Chase reaches behind me to close his office door and I hear the click of the lock. I stand there frozen in place. A wave of fear comes over me, but I hope I'm just overreacting. I think back to all the times where I freaked out, thinking my life was in danger, only to make matters worse for everyone, including myself. My mental health isn't in the best place, and I don't trust myself to act, to run away like everything in my gut is screaming for me to do. Instead, this time, I square my shoulders and push my worry deep down into my belly. I'll deal with her tonight just like every night since I've been here.

"I know I haven't exactly been easy on you, Elliot, but you have to know what your little mistake could've done to my company." He begins rolling the sleeves of his button-up shirt up to his elbows and takes a seat on the side of his desk, motioning for me to do the same.

I nervously sit across from him on the plush velvet loveseat. He continues. "Thad told me about you and Benjamin, and I'll be damned if I can get the image out of my mind."

I swallow hard and shock hums throughout my body, but I don't trust myself to move.

"You've surprised me, keeping up with the various tasks that I've assigned you. I thought you'd have run for the hills after the first week, but here you are." He removes his watch, and it clinks on the glass dish next to his computer. "That makes me wonder, how bad do you really need this job?"

He crosses his arms over his chest, waiting for me to

respond. I open my mouth, close it, and open it again before I shake the nerves off enough to speak.

"You're right," I say, "I really need this job. I'm willing to do whatever it takes to repay the damage I've caused. Just today, I made contact with a popular soap brand that I think would be a great fit—"

He smirks. "See, that's exactly what I want to hear. I want to know just how sorry you are, and I want to offer you an opportunity to make things better." He slaps his hand against the desk and pushes himself up to stand. Walking toward me, he cocks his head to the side and begins to unbuckle his belt. My palms start to sweat, and my heart begins racing. *Danger. Danger. Danger.* My body screams, and a tear falls from the corner of my eye, but I'm too afraid to move. My exhausted body is so confused, my fight or flight responses seem to have their wires crossed. I'm up all night in the relative safety of my room, fighting for my life, and right here, right now, where there seems to be actual danger, I can't seem to form a coherent thought.

Chase continues walking toward me, slowly unbuttoning his pants. I see the white of his cotton boxer briefs, and my mouth goes dry. Maybe he's just going to get my opinion about a worrisome mole? I don't know why he thinks I'd be an expert; I guess I do have a lot of moles but that doesn't mean I know if they're good or bad ones. I should go to the dermatologist and get them checked out; for all I know I'm a walking case of melanoma waiting to happen.

"I'm going to give you a choice, you can suck me off, right here, right now, and as soon as those pouty lips are licked clean, I'll pick up the phone and tell Thad you did an amazing job. Hell, I'll even demand that he give you a raise." He pauses, letting the realization of his proposal sink in. "Or...." He reaches out and flicks the top button of my shirt open. "You can try to run, and I'll get off on the chase."

His eyes darken like a shark in blood-infested waters, and the blood drains from my face. The intensity of the moment finally registers in my brain, and it's like zombie Elliot is finally waking up from the trance of constant panic from the last month. I make an assessment of my surroundings, noting the locked door with a padlock and the small window on the opposite side of the room. At least the building is only two stories; I could probably make it if I jumped.

I feel Chase's hot, clammy palm slide up my bare leg, pushing underneath my skirt, finding the lace of the top of my thong. He hooks his fingers around and pulls them away. I fall backward from the force and that's when he lunges toward me. He brings my panties up to his face and takes a long drag of my scent.

"You smell so good, like cupcakes."

I try to flip him off of me, but he doesn't budge.

"I knew you were going to be a feisty one," he cackles. I kick with all my strength, but he catches my leg and pins me down. He positions himself on top of me, and the sheer weight of him is enough to overpower me. Fear pulses through my veins, and it seems for once in my life that the panicked feeling finally matches a correct situation. The irony is not lost on me.

Tears flow from my eyes. "Chase, please don't. Don't do this." I squirm beneath his two-hundred-fifty-pound frame, but I can't manage to make him move.

He uses one hand to hold my wrists over my head, and the other one grabs my breast. He squeezes me so hard that I know he has no intention for me to feel an ounce of pleasure; he wants to scare me and it's working. My mind races, playing back every scenario I've ever thought of before. All those times when I thought I needed an escape route, where my mind was racing ninety to nothing making sure I had a way out. That's when I think back to the first time I ever met Chase Knight, and suddenly remember what I ate for lunch just thirty minutes ago.

My heart rate starts to slow as if my body knows I'll need to calm down to pull this off. I stop struggling underneath his grip and allow his hands to roam over my body. I fight back the bile that starts to rise in my throat, pushing down the pain that I'll inevitably deal with later, and do what I have to do to get out of here. "Well, if we're doing this, can I at least use my hands?"

Chase stiffens above me, shocked by my response. He studies my face and I wet my lips, not trusting myself to risk the sexy lip bite in fear that I'd look more like a donkey trying to bite its own lips. He looks smug, as if he knew I'd come around to his irresistible proposition, and lets hold of one of my hands. It's better than nothing, so I go with it. I let my hand roam over his abdomen and bring it to the seam of his pants, sliding my fingertips under his underwear. I wait, and when he inhales sharply, I grab his penis and lunge toward his mouth. I take his tongue in mine, doing my best to spread as much saliva as possible. When my hand takes hold of his tiny dick, suddenly everything makes sense. Mr. Knight here has either seriously harmed himself in the steroid department, or he's just really unlucky. It's little man syndrome at its finest.

Despite having a massive bodybuilder lying on top of me and hardly being able to breathe and having a handful of penis that I never wanted to hold, my anxiety level is surprisingly low. I work my way around Chase's mouth, not caring that my kiss is closer to a dog eating peanut butter, and I wait for my peanut butter and jelly sandwich to take effect, thanking past Elliot for remembering this tiny detail.

I feel his body stiffen and he jumps off me, heading straight toward his desk for, I presume, his emergency EpiPen. As soon as he's off me, I bolt upright, pull my shirt and skirt back down, and run toward his door. A sob escapes my lips as soon as I make it to the stairwell. I can barely get out a breath, but I pull out my phone and dial.

"Hey, Mom, I'm coming home."

# THIRTY-SIX

Benjamin

I've been wallowing in my apartment for weeks. I haven't showered in days, and there are empty beer cans on the floor around me. I've even fallen back into my bad video game habits, channeling my inner eighteen-year-old. It's not a good look, but I can't help myself.

I hear familiar pounding at the door, but it quickly subsides, because Sam and Jack both have keys to my place. I don't even make an effort to get up from my spot on the couch.

"Dude, it smells like a dead body in here!" Jack walks straight to the refrigerator and peeks inside. "What have you been eating?"

Sam grabs a trash bag from under the sink and starts throwing away the assortment of takeout containers, napkins, and empty beer bottles. "Get your worthless ass up and go take a shower. It's been six weeks, Benjamin; you can't keep living like this."

Yeah, it's been six weeks, six very long weeks, and I don't need the reminder. I'm well-aware how much time has passed since Elliot was shuffled off to work for the king of the douches. I've wanted to reach out to her and explain myself, but I want to do what's best for her, and right now I don't know if that's me. I've been worried about her, hoping she's taking care of herself and staying safe. I've caught myself looking at alternative modes of transportation a few times, but I know it wouldn't be fair to spring in on her like that. Elliot made it abundantly clear when she left that she never wanted to speak to me again. I hurt her, and fuck, if that's not something I'm going to have to live with for the rest of my pitiful life.

Jack plops down on the other end of the sofa. "So, I like what you've done with the place. It reminds me of college, only back then you were filled with ambition and life. Now you're just kind of pathetic."

His words sting, but I know he's only trying to help. Jack's never been one to beat around the bush; he tells it like it is. That's one of the reasons our partnership worked when we were building the company. Between the three of us, we ate, slept, and breathed work. We kept each other in check, motivating and inspiring one another to chase our dreams. When Jack and Sam left, Jack to become an adventure guide turned YouTuber and Sam to start his own consulting business, I missed them but was happy to see them in the lives they had always dreamed of.

"What about moving this depression train to a beach in Costa Rica? I could hook you up with a deal." Jack says, and I hear the faint pop of a beer can opening. Sam shoots him a dirty look. "What? Day-drinking isn't a problem if you're not depressed. I can have us on a charter plane in a week. I'll give you the grand tour."

"He can't go to fucking Costa Rica, Jack," Sam spits.

"Why?" Jack and I say in unison.

Sam just rolls his eyes. "Dude, I'm not going to sit back and watch you lose the love of your life, for the second time. I don't know how the fuck you need to apologize, but, Benjamin." He places a gentle hand on my arm. "I've never seen you so happy. If there's anyone who can help you clean up this massive pile of shit you've created, it's us."

Jack sits up a little taller, looking smug as hell. Sam's right. I think back to that time during our senior year of college and Sam, Jack, and I convinced the dean of business to let us study abroad in New Zealand for three months. We called it a cultural experience for our international business classes, and he totally bought it. We spent those three months drunk on beaches, camping under the stars on pool floats, and having the time of our lives. That trip was where we came up with the idea to start Williams Enterprises.

Nostalgia flows through my veins, and I feel a comfort that I haven't felt in weeks. I think of Elliot and my heart hurts. I wish I knew how her day was going. I wish I knew if she was sleeping well at night. I wish I knew if she was taking the time to exercise and take care of herself. I wish I knew how her mental health was. I wish I was there to hold her at night and reassure her of just how badass she is.

"The way I see it is this—" Sam's voice pulls me from my heartache, and I look up to see each of them staring at me in concern. "Dude, you OK?"

"Yeah, yeah. I'm good. What were you saying?" I wipe away the tears that I didn't realize were falling and gesture for him to continue.

"The way I see it is, you can sit here and wallow over losing your girl *and* your business, or you can try to get them back." He shrugs.

"How do you think I could manage that, exactly?" I give Sam an annoyed look.

"Well, I don't know about the girl, per se, but I do know Thaddeus Winston Powell III, and the little prick hasn't changed since middle school. He cuts corners, Benjamin. He's a lazy son of a bitch that's had everything handed to him his whole life. All you've got to do is find out what he did wrong, and we both know what department you need to go to first."

The wheels begin to turn in my head. I know what Sam's saying is true, and if you would've asked me yesterday if I wanted my company back, I don't know what I would've said. But right now, at this moment, I've never been more sure of anything in my life. I spent the two years after Sarah died trying to run away from my life. I did everything I could to distance myself from everything and everyone that I loved. It wasn't until I met Elliot that I realized there's so much life I have to live, and so much I still care about. And the truth is that I fucking care about my company. I care about Eliza and CJ. I care about Janice who cleans the office every night. I don't want those wonderful people's jobs, their livelihood, to be put in the hands of Thad Powell.

I may not be able to win back the love of my life, but getting my company back would be the next best thing.

"Uh-oh, he's got that look in his eye," Jack singsongs.

"So, whatcha going to do, brother?" Sam asks.

"I guess I need to start fighting."

"Yes!" Jack leaps from the sofa. "That's the fucking Benjamin Williams I've been missing."

"So, where do we start?" Sam asks.

I collapse back into the couch cushions. "First I've got to teach Thaddeus and his whole family a lesson, and then I'm going to go win my girl back."

"Please tell me you're going to need my amateur PI skills; I've been dying to put that Skillshare class to use."

"I can't believe I'm saying this, but yes, Jack, I think I may need your help."

"*Really?* Oh, Benji, I promise you I won't let you down!" Jack laughs gleefully and rushes to the door. "I'm going to find the telescopic camera lens for my iPhone!"

"Why don't you clean yourself up and meet us for drinks tonight?"

"Terry's?" I ask.

"Yeah, sure thing. See you tonight."

He pulls the door closed, and I collapse back onto the couch. What am I getting myself into?

---

Four hours later I'm wearing stiff jeans, sitting in a booth at the very bar where I first met Elliot. She was all lips and eyes, and I will never forget the way her red lipstick made me want to bite those pouty lips. The lipstick never washed out of that shirt; I had to throw it away.

I've opted out of drinking tonight, considering I've been holed up drunk every night for the last six weeks. I think I'm going to give my liver a much-needed break. The bar's mostly filled with men, and because of that, Sam and Jack are probably really annoyed that I insisted on taking a trip down memory lane, but they're good sports.

Out of the corner of my eye, I see two beautiful women walk in and march up to the bar. They look vaguely familiar and I hope I haven't hooked up with one on a dating app. You'd think guys would be all over them; you don't see hot women to that caliber—well, other than Elliot—in places like this. They get their drinks, and I'm astonished that no one gets up to talk to them. Sam and Jack seem to think it's odd as well.

The little blonde one perks her head up and squints at me. I see her stand up and swing her purse strap over her shoulder, and suddenly she's darting straight toward us. The leggy redhead follows, trying to hold back her friend, but the woman is feisty. I lean back in my seat, waiting to see which one of the assholes I'm sitting with is going to get his ass handed to him by this pixie, because I would've remembered her.

"Benjamin Mother-fucking Williams!" she screams and I bolt up ramrod-straight and glance behind me.

"Yes, you!" She points right at me, her finger in my face. "Do you have any idea the shitstorm you've caused us?"

The redhead reaches the tiny blonde and tries to apologize.

"No, I'm not fucking sorry." The blonde shrugs her away. "He tore Elliot's heart out and took a shit on it!"

"Sorry, she...uh, she, well, this isn't our first stop tonight." The redhead tries to usher her away.

"Did you say Elliot? Do you know Elliot?" I say with a little too much excitement in my voice.

"Of course we know Elliot." The blonde laughs. "She's our best friend and that makes you our enemy." She points to her eyes with two fingers and then back to me.

"So you're Maggie." I point to the redhead. "And you're Gwen." The girls nod.

Jack jumps up from his seat. "Gwen and Maggie, why don't you two join us. We're having a very important conversation over here." He gestures for them to sit together on one side of the booth and grabs an extra chair to put on the end for himself.

"I think you may find it interesting. Benjamin here was just crying about how much he misses Elliot."

I know Jack's just teasing me, but I don't have the energy to fight it. I sink into my seat. "Yeah, I fucking miss her. I fucked up and now I'm just racking my brain, trying to think of anything I can do to get her to listen."

"Oh my God, that's the sweetest thing I've ever heard," Maggie whispers to Gwen.

Gwen crosses her arms over her chest. "Well, I'm not buying it."

"This one's feisty. I call dibs on Baby Spice," Jack calls to Sam.

Gwen reaches up and grabs his ear and twists until Jack cries out in pain. "Don't you call dibs on me like my body isn't my own to give. I'll rip your ear off right here in this bar." She digs in her sharp, pointy fingernails and he yelps.

"OK, fuck, I'm sorry! Just let me go."

Gwen releases Jack's ear and pins him with a smug smile. It's not every day that Jack Manning gets his balls handed to him, and damn if it's not the funniest thing I've seen in a long time. I like these girls; I can see why Elliot's friends with them.

"Jack, put your tongue back in your mouth for just a minute, OK?" I turn toward Maggie, who seems to be the most reasonable at the moment. "Do you think you could put me in touch with Elliot? I've tried calling her phone, but it says it's disconnected."

Maggie looks down as if she's trying to decide how much information to share. "I can't give you her number."

"Can you tell me if she's OK? Is she happy working for Chase? Does she need anything?" I hold my breath, waiting for any sliver of details about Elliot's life.

"She's going to be just fine. Listen, Benjamin, I don't want to be in the middle of this. I think we should go." Maggie stands to leave, pulling Gwen with her.

"Can you just tell me what hotel chain she's staying at?

"She's not staying at a hotel anymore. She left Nashville this morning."

My leg starts bouncing incessantly. "She left? Is she coming back here? Is she going back to her place?"

"No, Benjamin, she moved back home." Maggie's words cut me with shock. I know how hard Elliot fought to make it in the big city. She would've done anything in her power to stay, so what happened to my girl to make her run?

# THIRTY-SEVEN

Elliot

Moving back home isn't the worst thing in the world. I mean, we do have the second-largest American flag in the country, so that's something. And the town's finally got a Wendy's.

I take in the dilapidated country town in front of me; somehow it's even sadder than I remember. A truck engine revs loudly next to me and I glance over to see John Avery McDonald, who graduated two years ahead of me. He looks almost the same, except the hair from his head seems to have migrated to his unfortunate goatee. I shiver at the sight of him, remembering how my friends and I thought he was the sexiest thing to walk the earth our freshman year.

Maybe John Avery is single. He was nice enough in high school. I even remember that my friend, Jane, went out with him once and said he was a very gentle lover. Maybe that's what I need to heal my heartbreak, a little gentle loving from John Avery. A carnal flashback of Benjamin's face between my legs lit by the warm glow of the afternoon sun slaps the thought from my brain, and I shake it away. I make a mental note to ask my mother about John Avery later.

"You're never gonna believe this, sweetie, Ronald Douglas is coming to Delancey next month to do one of those rallies. The tickets were twenty dollars each, but I went ahead and grabbed us all one. It'll be a fun family outing, just like old times. I even grabbed an extra, so if you want to invite Daniel...it could be just like old times!"

My mother's squeal pierces my ear, and I shudder at the memory of Daniel. Though since it's a small town, I know that word's already spread that I'm back home, it's only a matter of time before he shows up on my parents' doorstep with a sad bouquet of wilting flowers.

"Look at that, home sweet home. Your daddy's going to be so happy to have you back under our roof. You know, your room's exactly the same as you left it. I couldn't bring myself to take down my little girl's things. Deep down I knew you'd be back."

Mom grips my knee and gives it a squeeze as she pulls into the gravel driveway of my childhood home. I take in the sight before me. It's not much, but my mother did her best to fix it up as nicely as she could. In fact, if we'd pick up this simple little white shotgun house with a tin roof and move it to a cool city, all the Karens in the world would fight over the farmhouse style. I decide right then and there that that's how I'm going to choose to look at the circumstances. I'm lucky to have somewhere to fall back on, and at least I'll be eating better than I was in Chicago, or Nashville for that matter.

My stomach grumbles at the thought. It's been a long day and I could really use a home-cooked meal right about now.

"You poor thing," Mom says. "You've lost so much weight living out there on your own. I knew you weren't taking care of yourself. Mama's put on a pot roast before I left to pick you up at the bus stop. Let's go. I bet Daddy can't wait to hug your neck."

My mother's habit of referring to herself in third person only reminds me of how far removed I am from the vibrant city I just left. Maybe I didn't know what I actually needed in life. Maybe I thought I wanted the excitement of a big city, but what I really need is to settle down in the small town where I was born and raised. Maybe my ambition was actually too big for me; maybe I aimed my dreams too high.

"I invited Daniel over for dinner tonight. I hope you don't mind. I ran into him and his mama at the Walmart last night and I was just so excited you were coming home that I couldn't help myself. Ooooh, I hope you'll give him another chance. You two were so sweet together in high school. I just knew you'd end up marrying him."

Her voice becomes stern and she pins me with her glare. "Baby, I know you thought you were going to be some big important business lady in the big city, but your daddy and I always knew you'd fall down and we'd have to pick the pieces back up." She pats me on the shoulder and turns off the car. "But we love it. I'm so happy you failed at your job! Now I get my little girl back and I can teach you to sew and cook. We can go to the women's group at church and enter the gumbo cook-off next fall!"

"Yeah," I agree. A pain stabs me in my chest, as if I've just betrayed myself by conceding to her plans. I gently but not-so-gently remind the universe that I tried. I tried my damndest to make it. I worked my ass off for months, even landed a job at my dream company, but nothing I did was ever good enough. I guess I really don't have what it takes. My parents are right; they've always been right.

A painful memory of Daniel's shaking body hovering over me in the back of his Mustang, parked outside the post office in the next town, flashes through my head. My stomach begins to ache and I'm not sure if it's from the hunger pains or the sad memory.

I force out a smile, though. "What time is dinner?"

My mother grins as if I've just waved a magic wand, making all of her dreams come true. "Dinner will be ready at six, just like always."

---

I walk into my mother's traditional dining room. It's decked out in my great-great-grandmother's china that's been passed down three generations, complete with a gravy boat. Jeez, she's really pulled out all stops with this.

I hear the familiar chime of the doorbell, and my gut sinks for the millionth time today. "Oh, honey, that must be Daniel, could you get the door while I pull the pot roast out of the oven?"

I fight back a grimace. "Of course."

She wraps her arms around me and squeals. "Thank you, sweet girl. I'm just so excited to see this little reunion tonight! I even made Daniel's favorite blueberry pie."

The doorbell chimes again, and I trudge over. I open the door to reveal an older, balder, and heavier version of the boy who destroyed my heart what feels like a lifetime ago. I take in his short, stubby frame that's only about two inches taller than me, his yellow teeth, and greasy skin. *Jesus, what was I thinking?* I cough to cover up the surprised shriek my throat makes when I see how badly Daniel has aged over the last five years. Time certainly did him no favors. It's almost comical, really, compared to Benjamin.

A loud thud startles us both and I see a tall figure disappear into my mother's azaleas. Daniel looks over his shoulder and shrugs the noise away. I guess everyone in the neighborhood really is excited to see me. There's no sense in hiding in the bushes though. I mean, yeah, maybe I moved away and fell flat on my face, but give me a little room to lick my wounds already.

I straighten my shoulders and stand up to my full height, choosing to ignore whoever is in the bushes. "Daniel, what a surprise. You look, well, you look great." The lie stumbles out of my mouth.

"Wow. Your mama said you were different, but goodness gracious, Elly Belly, you really do look so much better than you did when we were together." He pushes past me, plopping down on the sofa. He reaches for the remote and props his feet up on the coffee table, just like old times. "Hey, grab me a Bud Light out of the fridge, would ya?"

I cringe at the old nickname that I haven't heard in so long. "Sure, Daniel, I'd be happy to get that for you."

---

Two hours later, I've stuffed myself with my mother's delicious home-cooked meal. I pick around a piece of blueberry pie that only reminds me that I prefer cherry, which once again reminds me that Benjamin also really loves cherries. A warm blush creeps up my cheeks, and I'm thankful my mother isn't a mind reader because that would be super uncomfortable right about now.

"Dear, would you like some more coffee?" my mother asks in a polite tone that she usually only reserves for my father's coworkers and the ladies at church.

"Yes, ma'am, thank you." It may be seven in the evening but my family drinks coffee after a meal like some people smoke cigarettes. It's one of our little family quirks that I actually like.

I take the warm mug in my hands and allow the heat to soak

into my chilled skin. It reminds me of warming my hands over the fire at the inn. When will the painful memories just stop tormenting me already?

"Daniel, why don't you and Elliot go break in my new porch swing. It's a lovely evening and I'm sure you two are just dying to catch up and reminisce about old times."

I stand up abruptly. "Oh, I don't know about that. You spent so much time cooking this delicious meal, so why don't I do the dishes?" I try to take the platter from her hands, but she doesn't relent.

"Absolutely not. You've just had a long journey, and it's my job as the woman of the house to cook and clean. I am here to serve you." She bops me on the nose. "Tonight, you have my permission to relax."

Daniel leads me to the porch swing. He sits next to me and manspreads so that the side of his leg pushes against mine.

"Alone at last. I've missed seeing you around, Elliot." Daniel's hot breath tickles my ear and I scoot all the way to the edge of the swing until I'm almost hanging over the side. He doesn't get the message, he simply scoots in closer, pinning me in place and draping his heavy arm over my shoulders. "I knew you'd be back, you know. This town is too ingrained into who you are. You can't run from it, Elly; you just need to stop fighting it and embrace it."

I hear a rustling in the bushes on the side of the house, and stand up to get a better look. I stick my head over the porch railing, but I don't see anything.

"Did you hear that?"

"Hear what?" Daniel asks, not bothering to get up to check for potential murderers.

"I swear I saw something hiding in the bushes when you got here, and I just heard it again, just now."

"Some things never change, you know? I have no idea how you managed to make it as long as you did in Chicago; you were always so paranoid." He drapes his arm back over me and I sink into the swing, remembering the familiar twist in my stomach that can only be described as repulsion.

"You know, I think about us a lot. You and me, we just make sense."

I open my mouth to correct him, but he cuts me off. "Just listen. Hear me out, OK? You've just moved back to town; you've had your fun and gotten the whoring around out of your system—"

"Excuse me?" I jerk away from him at the comment, but he grabs my hand, holding me there.

"Oh, don't act like you're some innocent little angel, Elliot. Your mama's had you on the prayer list at Sunday school ever since you left. Everyone knows you've been whoring around, sleeping with your boss."

I open my mouth to argue, but he's right. I was the one who pursued a relationship with my boss. I was the one who caused the deal to fall through with Chase. I was the one who freaked out and got us put on the No Fly List, and it finally dawns on me. This whole time I thought the world was out to get me but now I realize, all this time I've been the problem.

A wave of disgust shoots through my veins at the realization. Every time I thought I was doing the right thing, following my heart, I've just created more trouble for everyone that I love. I can see now that Benjamin, though he hurt me, deserves so much more than I can give him. He doesn't need a broken, anxious woman who's always messing things up; he needs stability, dependability. He needs someone completely opposite of me. This whole time I thought I was my own hero, but it looks like I've been the villain, sabotaging myself every step of the way.

"Elliot, I think I can forgive you. I think we can work through this and I promise to make every attempt to forget your past mistakes. What do you say? Do you want to give this another go?" I feel Daniel's grip on my knee, but it doesn't register anyway. It's almost like I'm watching this moment as an outsider looking in.

I consider my options, replaying every stupid mistake I've made over the last year. All of those decisions were made with my heart, and that stupid bitch has led me astray. Clearly, I can't trust her so now, I'm going to start thinking with my head.

I lean in and press my lips against his. The sheen of sweat on his upper lip presses into my skin and I'm left with a salty aftertaste that makes my stomach turn. I forgot he's a sweater, but I'll get used to it; it'll be just like old times.

A crash tears my attention away and this time I see the source. Lying underneath the roof eave is a large man with a man bun and a scruffy beard. He's wearing all black and has a ninja mask that's fallen off his face, and an expensive-looking camera hangs from a lanyard around his neck.

"Oh my God, were you taking pictures of me?" I scream. "Have you been spying on me all night?" I lunge toward him to snag the camera.

The man panics, scooting back away from me, but he's stunned himself, and his reflexes seem to be lagging. I leap from the porch on top of him and wrestle the camera out of his hands while Daniel sits in shock, frozen as if he's afraid to move.

"Hey! That camera costs five thousand dollars and that's a new lens!" He tries to grab it from my hands, but I'm too quick. I scurry away to a safer distance and pull out my mace that I haven't put down since Chase's attack. I wield my weapon and he backs away, hands lifted in surrender.

"Who do you work for and how did you find me?" I ask.

"I...I...I don't work for anyone. I'm actually self-employed. I'm a YouTuber—"

"What does that have to do with me?"

"Oh, um, right. I was just stalking you for the day; it really wasn't a big deal. You're actually really funny. I enjoyed the karaoke session you performed before dinner; where'd you learn to dance like that?"

"Oh my God, you're insane. I'm calling the police. Daniel! Daniel, hand me your phone!" I call out behind me, but Daniel's nowhere to be found. Did that coward really run off and abandon me with a potential serial killer? Sounds about right.

"No, no, no, don't call the cops!" he cries, holding his hands up even higher. "I was just doing a little recon for my boy, Benjamin. He just wanted to know you were OK."

I gasp. "Benjamin sent you to spy on me?"

"Well, not exactly. He didn't specifically say to spy on you, but he did ask me to help...um, help him with his plan."

"I can't believe this." I drop the camera and the man comes running to retrieve it.

"Oh, baby, it's OK. You look like you're going to be fine. That was a close call though," he says as he polishes the camera lens.

"Why would Benjamin send a lunatic who talks to his camera to spy on me?" I spit.

He extends his hand for me to shake. "Oh, I'm not a lunatic; I'm his best friend. I'm Jack."

I take his hand in mine and squeeze as hard as I can. "Nice to meet you, Jack. Now please leave me alone and tell Benjamin he can go fuck himself."

"I'll, um...I'll give him the message."

# THIRTY-EIGHT

Elliot

I burst through the door, filled with rage. I find Daniel sitting at the table as my mother serves him another piece of blueberry pie.

"Are you fucking kidding me right now?" I look around, hoping someone here will recognize how screwed up this situation is.

"Elliot Elizabeth! You watch your mouth, young lady! I've never in my life."

My mother's rebuttal falls flat as I launch myself toward Daniel, pulling him out of his seat by the collar of his shirt.

"No. No. No. *No!* I've had enough! I will not mind my manners; I will not be your good little girl anymore. And this piece of shit"—I shove him toward the kitchen door—"just left me alone with a strange man who could've been a murderer!"

"Now, Elliot, stop with the theatrics," my father says.

I turn toward him and hurl Daniel's glass plate, pie and all.

It crashes into the wall sending shards of glass and blueberries in every direction.

"There you go, Dad, that's theatrics. My not wanting to rekindle a *horrific* relationship with Daniel, where I gagged at the sign of his penis—fun fact, I thought I was just disgusted by penises in general, but it turns out it was just his—or be murdered because I was left alone with a strange man while the man who just stuck his tongue down my throat was more excited to have another piece of pie!"

"You will not disrespect your mother's pie!" my father yells, sending spittle flying.

"Oh my God," I say more to myself than to anyone else. "I really would be better off on my own in Chicago."

"Don't be ridiculous, Elliot. You've had a long day and you're exhausted." My mother tries to comfort me, but I brush her away.

"Elliot, calm down," Daniel says. "I saw that you had it handled out there. Your mom's pie is just so good; I wanted to get in another piece before I left. Sheesh, I could hear you anyway. I had my cell in my pocket. You know my dad's a volunteer firefighter. I would've called him if I heard you screaming."

My mouth agape, I turn to my parents who seem perfectly complacent with Daniel's explanation.

"Sweetie, why don't you just calm down and have a piece of pie. Your mama will make you a warm glass of milk and clean up this mess. Everything will be fine in the morning." My father's attempt at calming me only backfires as his purposeful misunderstanding of the situation is more like throwing gasoline on an open flame.

"I'm not going to calm down and I don't want to become Barbara! I want my husband to bring *me* pie after a long day and to listen to me and to be there for me, to hold me when I'm having a panic attack, and to protect me when I'm afraid." I have a painful realization of the giant mess that I've made. I was so convinced that I failed, that the damage I caused my career was irreparable, that my relationship was over, that I wasn't any different than my family.

"Well, I wish I was George Clooney. Let's see whose wish will come true first." He chuckles at his joke.

Daniel crosses his arms over his chest. "I hate to break it to you, baby doll, but I'm the man, and I work outside all day, and I ain't bringing you pie. You're bringing me pie."

"OK, that's enough. Everyone just needs to calm down and take a deep breath." My mom bends down to sweep up the mess.

"Daniel, I don't know how to put this any clearer for you. There will be no pie sharing between us." I gesture between us. "You will not bring me pie, and I'll be damned if I bring you pie! I hate to burst all of your bubbles, but I'm not the same girl I was in high school. I've changed. I've grown up and even though I may be a screwup in almost every aspect of life, I still know that I'm smart and I'm good at my job—Well, I was good at my job when I had one."

I push Daniel toward the door. "You need to leave now."

"Will you stop using that foul language in this house. Really, Elliot, what has gotten into you? You come back from the big city and suddenly you think you're better than everyone here? This is who you are, this is where you come from. The sooner you accept that, the sooner you'll be happy with the life you've been given."

My mother's words sting. But not because she's right. I realize that my whole life I've been reduced into the smallest version of myself. I've always been too much for my parents, too much for my teachers. I dreamed too big. I laughed too loud, and I had too much energy; hell, no wonder I developed anxiety.

I've been trying to live my life in a shell that was too small for me. I could listen to my parents, settle down with Daniel, and start having babies like all my classmates. I could rekindle old high school friendships and try to fit in with the women's group at church, but deep down I know that's not who I am. I could fake it for a while, but eventually, it'll catch up to me. I don't want to live my life appeasing everyone else, being the perfect girl who fits into the box they've assigned me to. I want to be free to make my own decisions, free to fail, even if it means I've got to find a new roommate on Craigslist and clean up dried Cool Whip off the countertops every night. I want to chase my dreams, and I'm willing to fall, and I'll keep getting back up until I finally find my calling. I want my friends next to me while I find out who I really am and I want so badly to heal my broken heart, so that maybe one day, I can find love again.

"I'm sorry. I don't think I can be the girl that you all think of me as anymore. I don't want to be held back by your expectations because I'll never be able to fulfill them. Daniel, this thing between us isn't going to work. You had your chance and you blew it. Thank you for showing me exactly what I don't want in a relationship." I turn to my parents. "And you ought to be ashamed of yourselves for pushing him on me like you've done. Do you know that he pressured me into having sex with him because he was the only virgin in his graduating class senior year? In the back of his car parked out in the middle of a field, where I had nowhere to go to escape? And then I found out he wasn't a virgin after all. He lost it to Chastity Dillan his freshman year!"

My mother gasps. "Is that true?"

Daniel bows his head in embarrassment. "Elly, you know I was a different person back then. I just didn't want to lose you, and I thought, well, I thought if I took your virginity that you'd feel like you needed to stay with me."

My heart sinks at his admission. Daniel's pathetic excuse is the exact reason why I stayed with him as long as I did. I thought no man would want me because I was damaged goods, but after meeting Benjamin, I saw myself through a new lens. I saw that I am so much more than my body; my worth isn't determined by anything other than who I am on the inside. This is the exact bullshit I want to get away from. I want to break the cycle of oppression, and I can't do that when I'm surrounded by people who don't believe I can succeed.

"Daniel, here's some pie for the road. I think you need to leave. Please don't come back around here bothering my baby girl anymore." My mom's soft voice surprises me. She hands Daniel the rest of the pie which is covered up in plastic wrap and turns to me. "Elliot, I am so sorry. I shouldn't have meddled. I had no idea about Daniel. I just want what's best for you. You know I don't ever want to see you fail. As your mother, my heart aches for you every time one of your jobs fall through. I just want you to stay here with me and your daddy and be safe from the world. I wish I could wrap you up in Bubble Wrap so no one can hurt you."

My dad places a gentle hand on my shoulder. "I haven't been the most supportive of your career, but like your mama said, it's so hard for us to see you struggle. We just want you to be happy, sweetheart, and I guess I'm just now realizing that all this time, you weren't happy living here." He turns to Daniel who hasn't seemed to have gotten the message. "And you, you get your scrawny pie-hogging ass out of my house and don't come back, you hear me?"

Daniel clutches the pie to his chest and scurries out of the house.

"Christ, Barbara, you had to give him the rest of the pie? I was going to eat that for breakfast tomorrow!"

My heart swells with relief. I'd have never thought kicking

out my ex-boyfriend and slinging my mother's famous pie across this kitchen could be so cathartic. I lean up and kiss both my parents on the cheek. "Good night. I love you both. Thanks for sticking up for me tonight. I'm going to go get some rest. I've got a big day ahead of me tomorrow."

# THIRTY-NINE

Benjamin

"And what does that say about you?" Rashonda, the therapist I've been seeing for the last month, peers over the top of her reading glasses. We've come to the end of another grueling session, and as much as I hate to admit it, it's getting a little bit easier each hour I spend on this sofa.

I hesitate, struggling to form the words that have been tormenting me for so long. "Nothing. It says nothing about me; it was an accident. There's nothing I could have done differently. I went after her because I came home early and found the note. I didn't do anything wrong by chasing after her. I was trying to help." A tear falls down my cheek and I wipe it away, sinking my face into my palms in exhaustion.

"Well done, Benjamin." Rashonda places her pen down on the side table next to her and leans forward. "Now tell me, how much of that do you actually believe?"

I blow out an exasperated sigh. "About twenty percent."

"Well, I'll take twenty percent for now, but, Benjamin,

torturing yourself by not processing this grief isn't going to bring them back. It's not going to honor their memory either. This week I want you to focus on loving yourself. Do something kind for yourself and spend some time with your friends. And if you're feeling froggy, you could reach out to Elliot and explain why you lied to her." She pins me with a stare.

"Rashonda, we've been through this," I say. "Elliot is better off without me. I destroyed her. I'll regret not telling her the truth every damn day for the rest of my miserable life. That I deserve."

"Mm-hmm. It may not sound like it to you, but Benjamin, I think you've just had a breakthrough." Rashonda's smile spans across her face. "I think you're masking your grief of losing Elliot with the grief of losing Sarah and Maddie. And you feel guilty about it."

My jaw drops at this sudden revelation, the hamster wheel in my head spinning like crazy. I open my mouth to argue, but there are no words. I can't refute her theory. "You are allowed to heal from losing your wife and stepdaughter, Benjamin. You shouldn't wear your grief like a badge of honor; it doesn't serve anyone. Sarah would want you to move on with your life, wouldn't she?"

"But I fucked things up so badly with Elliot," is all I can manage.

Rashonda nods. "Yes. You did. That's up to you to fix, but don't you think it would bring you so much peace to at least try to explain yourself? You may not get her forgiveness, but I think you'd be able to move on with your life without this giant weight of suffering you've been carrying on your shoulders for so long. Of course, that's just my professional opinion based on what you've told me."

I stand up abruptly, wiping my sweaty palms on my pant

legs. "Thank you, Rashonda. I've got to go before I can change my mind." I rush to the door and swing it open.

"Benjamin," Rashonda calls just as I take a step outside. "Good luck, and remember to tell the truth."

"Thanks, Rashonda." I run to my car and pull out my phone to text the guys.

> SOS. I need your help. Meet me at my place in an hour.

SAM

> I'll be there

JACK

> Is it weird that I'm currently sitting on your couch now? My Benji-senses were tingling. Plus, you've got that NFL Redzone so...

> Jack, you know breaking and entering is a crime, don't you?

JACK

> It's only entering if you know the passcode.

I drag my tired ass across the threshold of my apartment, exhausted from lack of sleep and today's therapy session. Fuck if Rashonda didn't hit the nail on the head. All this time I thought that I was honoring Sarah's memory by torturing myself and not letting myself move on, but all I've actually done is make myself and everyone around me miserable.

I've been going back and forth trying to figure out what I want to do about the Powells, and I finally have my answer.

"Sam, could you reach out to your buddy at the coroner's office and ask him to do me a favor?"

"I thought you'd never ask." Sam pulls out his phone to text

299

his friend and my gut sinks a little, but I know this is the right move.

"So, Jack, did you see Elliot? Did she look well?" I'm not sure what I want him to say. Yes, he saw her and she was perfectly happy and thriving? Yes, he saw her and she looked utterly miserable?

"Yeah, about that." Jack sets his beer down on the coffee table. "You didn't tell me how feisty she was. She nearly broke Nikolette's new lens when she tackled me."

"I'm going to pretend that I didn't hear that you named your camera." I stop. "I thought I told you to keep your distance, only watch her coming and going? You weren't supposed to get close."

"That's easy for you to say; you weren't there. Benjamin, did you know that Elliot's mother looks like an angel reincarnated into a fifties housewife? Really, dude, she's got curves in all the right places and she was even wearing an apron. Once I got a little closer to the house, the smell of her delicious cooking assaulted my nostrils, and it took everything I had not to knock on the door and fight her dad off so I could have my way with her mother. I think I may be in love."

"Enough about her mom; how was my girl?" My breathing hitches in my chest waiting for his answer.

"She was...well. Benjamin, I hate to say this but I think she's still pretty upset. She told me to tell you, and I quote, 'tell Benjamin he can go fuck himself.'"

I wince, but it's not like I expected anything different. I've got to move forward with my plan and fix my life, then just maybe she'll let me explain. I can only hope.

# FORTY

Elliot

It's been two weeks since I crawled home with my tail between my legs. After my blowup with my parents, things have been completely different, like I'm living in the upside-down version of my actual life.

"Elliot, you know you don't have to leave us so soon." My mother pulls me into her tight embrace. "I was just getting used to having you around the house again. You know you can always stay here as long as you need."

We're at the bus stop, and this time I'm leaving to head back to the city with a plan. With Gwen and Maggie's help, I've managed to get my own branding and marketing business off the ground, and I've already secured three clients on retainer, one of whom is Damian Johnson. When I reached out to him, he answered on the first ring, said he'd been expecting my call for weeks, and asked me what took me so long. I plan to build up a small clientele that I can manage on my own for the first year until I'm unable to do it all on my own, then I'll expand slowly but keep things small with everyone working from their own home offices.

"I know, Mom. Thank you for everything. This is something I've got to do on my own but, don't worry, I won't wait so long until I come back home to visit." I give my parents another quick hug and for the first time in my life, a prick of homesickness stabs me in the gut. "I'll call you as soon as I get to Maggie's place."

This time, I swallowed my pride and agreed to let my friends help me. I'm only staying with Maggie for a couple of months until I can save enough to afford a decent place by myself. A wave of excitement tingles up my spine at the thought of living alone and not having to depend on anyone else to pay half of the rent. I'll no longer have my retinas burned from walking in on scandalous sexcapades in my living room or have to stay up all night scrubbing the floors and countertops clean so we don't get ants.

The Greyhound pulls up to the bus stop with a high-pitched screech. This is it, this is my new beginning. I inhale a deep lungful of pollution and load my luggage into the carrier. My fresh start is just around the corner, only this time I'm ready.

I wave to my parents and weave through the rows of seats. I glance around and find a vacant seat in the back. The doors squeak closed and I exhale a sigh of relief. My new life is only a fourteen hour drive away. I relax into the stiff seat and pull my book from my bag. My eyes find the opening line when I hear a thud.

Thump. Thump. Thump. "Stop the bus!" Thump. Thump. Thump. "Stop the bus!"

My ear prick and my heart begins to race at the familiar voice. The other passengers start looking around, some even standing up, to find the source.

"What the hell?" The bus driver yells, as he slams on the breaks and cranks open the door. "Are you insane? I could've killed you! You can't just run in front of a moving bus!"

I stand in my seat and I know the minute I see his dark brown hair peeking over the top of the crowd in front of me. Benjamin races down the aisle, frantically surveying the rows from left to right. His whiskey brown eyes meet mine, and the world stops. He races toward me and hesitates only a moment before pulling me into his embrace.

I take an unsteady step back, confused about the rush of desire flowing through my veins. I should be furious with him after what he did, but my body betrays me, flooding my mind with flashbacks of us wrapped up together, bodies entwined and sated from the exhaustion of lovemaking.

"Benjamin." His name comes out like a gasp. "What are you doing here? How did you find me?"

He reaches for my hand. "Don't be mad, I had some help from your friends. Please hear me out, Elliot."

I look down at our connection, feeling the sparks shoot through me like electricity, and pull my eyes back up to his. "What do you need to tell me?"

He takes a long breath. "I'm so sorry about what happened. I was a fucking idiot. I should've told you about Sarah and Maddie, and there's no excuse for that." He tugs at his messy hair and I notice the dark circles under his eyes. He doesn't look good, like he's lost weight and hasn't slept in days. A stabbing pain shoots through me. Maybe it's the final piece of my heart breaking.

I snatch my hand away. "Benjamin, I told you I never wanted to see you again. You can't just show up here on a bus and trap me into talking to you. You don't get it, do you? I trusted you and you broke my heart."

I try to push to the side, and scoot around him. "I've got to get off this bus. I can't do this with you again."

He grabs my arm to stop me. "Elliot. Please. Fuck. Can you just hear me out? Give me five minutes, and if what I say doesn't change your mind, then I'll leave. I'll walk off this bus and you'll never hear from me again. Just please give me a chance to explain. I'm begging you."

I see the pain written all over his face, and it kills me. As angry as I am with Benjamin, I never want to see him this upset. I can't imagine what he's been through.

"Fine," I say. "You have five minutes."

I cross my arms over my chest and gesture for him to get it over with. We take our seats and the bus begins moving again.

"Before I say anything else, I want to show you this."

He pulls a folded-up piece of paper from the inside of his jacket pocket and hands it to me. I take the letter and begin reading.

> *My dearest Benjamin,*
>
> *I'm sorry to do this to you, but it was only a matter of time before the secret was out of the bag. I know you had your suspicions about my addiction, and you were right. I'm using again. I relapsed over New Year's. I'm taking Maddie, and we'll be staying with my parents for a while until I figure out what my next move is.*
>
> *I never wanted to hurt you, Benjamin, and I hope you know that. My life is complicated, and you swept in like my knight in shining armor. You took care of me in a way that no one has ever done for me. I'll*

*never deserve you. I only hope that one day you'll meet someone who does.*

*Please don't follow me. We both know you're better off on your own anyway. I'm checking myself into rehab as soon as I get to New York and Maddie will stay with my parents until I figure myself out.*

*Again, I'm so sorry but this was never supposed to get this far. We're cut from a different cloth and I hope you can find someone who can give you the things I can't.*

*Goodbye, Benji.*
*XOXO Sarah*

I finish reading the letter through blurred tears and glance up at Benjamin. Before I can ask, he holds up his hand. "Just listen, all right?"

I nod.

"I found this letter the morning before she left. I had a client emergency. This was the early days of my business, so every client was my bread and butter. She left the letter out and had only just left when I got home and found it." He pauses, looking down at his fidgeting hands. "Of course, I left immediately and went looking for them, even though I'd been up working all night. Sarah and Maddie were my life. I didn't know how I would make it without them. I just wanted her to stop, to listen to me. It was raining so hard, and as soon as I caught sight of her car, I tried to flash my lights to get her to pull over. She freaked out and ran a red light, trying to get away from me. That's when a semi-truck barreled into the side of them. Everything happened so fast. The paramedics said they both died on impact."

A tear falls from his eye and he wipes it away with his shirt sleeve. "I blamed myself for a long time. Hell, until you stormed out of my life, I still believed what happened was my fault. The truth is, fuck, she was high when she left. She was paranoid and she wasn't being herself, so when she saw me in the car behind her, she freaked out."

He pulls my hands between his. "Elliot, I want you to know that I've been doing the work. I've been in therapy and now I realize I can't live my life torturing myself for Sarah's mistakes. I've realized that the accident wasn't my fault. Listen, I should've told you, but I never thought anyone could love me after what I did. I thought you deserved better. Fuck, I still think you do. But from the moment you walked into my life, it was like you had a flashlight of your sunshine and you shined it on all of my darkness. You came into my life and flipped everything I thought I knew about myself upside down. You showed me what it feels like to be accepted for who I am."

He pauses and plants a gentle kiss on my knuckle. "You have captivated me mind, body, and soul, and I know I'll never deserve you, but I hope you'll let me try."

I open my mouth to speak but he stops me.

"Hang on, I'm not finished." He pulls a second piece of paper from his jacket and hands it over. It's the coroner's toxicology report stating that Sarah had amphetamines in her system. "I didn't want her parents to know. I thought I was protecting her image by keeping this a secret. Elliot, Thad and his family tried to blackmail me into saving their business. All I had to do was show this to them and they pulled out. My company is much smaller now; we lost a lot of money due to Thad's spending habits, but I've been able to keep all of my original staff members. I want to offer you a job as a director. I know you're hardworking and smart and you've got what it takes to—"

"Benjamin, I don't need your handout." My voice comes out sharper than I intended, but it feels so good to say it.

"Oh, I didn't mean it like that. I know you can take care of yourself. I just wanted you to know you have a job, you know if you need it."

"Well, I'm proud to decline your generous offer because..." A grin spans across my face and I still can't believe it myself. "It looks like I may be your new competitor."

Benjamin's eyebrows shoot to his hairline.

"You're looking at the new CEO of Clutch Media," I say. "We specialize in representing influencers and helping them to discover their voice while finding the best brands to partner with for their personal brand." My chest swells with pride when I hear myself say it out loud.

"Of course you are." His pulls my hand to his mouth and brushes it with another soft kiss. "I'd expect nothing less. I'm so proud of you, and if anyone is cut out for entrepreneurship, it's you."

I smile at the warmth of his words.

"Elliot," he says, his tone more serious, "I'm in love with you. I think I've been in love with you from the moment you spoke up in that meeting and showed everyone how fucking smart and capable you are. I've done everything to try to push you away, but somehow my heart keeps coming back for more. From the minute I tasted your sweet lips, I knew I was ruined for anyone else. So, here I am, a broken man sitting on a Greyhound bus, begging you to give me another chance. You may not be a princess who needs saving, but it would be the honor of my life to spoil you and to be your equal, to grow old alongside you and laugh with you, to hold you and comfort you when your anxiety is high, and to always remind you of your worth."

My eyes fill with tears and I blink them away. How could I

have known the pain he's been through, the misery of living his life alone while blaming himself for the loss of the people who were the closest to him? In that moment, on a stinky overcrowded Greyhound bus somewhere in the middle of Louisiana, my broken heart is mended and everything we've been through seems like a lifetime ago. All I want is to climb into his strong arms and let him hold me.

But for some reason, instead of telling him any of that, I say the first thing that pops into my head. "Truth or dare?"

A hopeful smile creeps up into his eyes and his smile wrinkles make my heart skip a beat. "Dare."

"I dare you to kiss me," I whisper as warm tears flow down my cheeks.

"That's what I hoped you'd say." Benjamin's lips find mine, and a wave of emotion floods into my chest. His stubble scrapes against my cheeks as his tongue sweeps into my mouth. Before I know it, I'm climbing into his lap in the cramped bus seats, not caring about anyone around us.

"It's about time, honey," says the old lady in the seat across the aisle. "I was hoping you'd jump his bones after that speech. You two are entirely too young and attractive to be at odds with each other. If I were you, I'd be banging it out every chance I got."

"You know what, she's right." Benjamin stands, waving his hands in the air. "Stop the bus. We need to get off."

"Benjamin, we're in the middle of nowhere," I say, pulling him back down into the seat. "What are you doing?"

"Elliot, I've been miserable for the last two months without you, and if you think I'm going to sit back and patiently wait on this crowded, smelly bus until we get back to Chicago to make things up to you, then you're sadly mistaken. I'll take my chances at the Best Western and we'll rent a car in the morning and road-trip ourselves back home."

*Home.* There isn't a better word to describe what Benjamin makes me feel. "OK, Casanova, let's go but there's no need to carry me this time. It's not cold and there's no snow in sight. Come on, I'll show you which direction we need to go. Follow me."

"I'd follow you anywhere," he whispers, and just like that all is right in my world.

# EPILOGUE

Elliot

*Six months later...*

Life's been a whirlwind over the last few months. I moved back to Chicago and stayed with Maggie for a few weeks until Benjamin finally wore me down and begged me to move in with him. I obliged...only because he lets me pay my half of the bills.

After losing so much money cutting Thad loose, Benjamin had to crunch some numbers to keep his old staff on board. We operated as competitors for a while, but eventually he caved and begged me to join forces. I am happy to say that my days of slumming it are long gone. Clutch Media has seen tremendous growth, with Instagram influencers knocking on our doors to represent them from word-of-mouth alone. I guess word spreads fast when you sign one of the fastest-growing beauty influencers of all time. I don't think I'll ever be able to repay Damian enough for all of his, well, influence.

We now have a staff of ten and work from a small building across from Maggie's Yoga loft, a few blocks away from Gwen's apartment. We work from home on Wednesdays and have two-hour lunch breaks. We wanted to create a place for our staff to do valuable work they believe in, without all the corporate hoopla. We still get our work done, but we make sure to enjoy our lives along the way. Even CJ is adjusting nicely to the new work structure, though we still have biweekly fire drills and morning announcements.

As for Thaddeus Powell, well, let's just say payback is a bitch. As soon as Benjamin dropped the bomb about Sarah's toxicology report, the Powell family quickly changed their tune. Apparently, Thad wasn't just making poor business decisions, but he'd been dabbling in a similar circle as his sister. They begged Benjamin not to say anything to ruin their reputations, and shortly after they went bankrupt.

With Benjamin's encouragement, I filed a police report against Chase Knight, shining light on his criminal behavior. Shortly after the news broke, several other women came forward with similar stories. Girls from college, previous employees, and even some of his gym members brought charges against him. I'm happy to say that his trial is next week, and it's not looking good for him. I think Chase Knight will have plenty of time to learn from his actions while sitting in a jail cell for the next several years.

"Elliot, get your ass over here and do a shot with me!" Gwen calls from the bar top as Benjamin and I walk in. Tonight we're celebrating a huge milestone. I've officially held a job longer than I ever have, just barely beating out my time as a perfume sprayer in high school. Six whole months and two days with the same employer. Who'd have thought I'd have to work for myself to obtain that kind of streak?

I look around the modest bar, taking in all the excessive party decorations. I should have known better when Gwen and Maggie suggested grabbing drinks at Terry's to celebrate tonight. They've really outdone themselves this time. There's a three-tiered cake, a ceiling full of confetti-filled balloons, and flutes of champagne lining the bar. CJ and Eliza are here sitting in the corner, and they've even invited a few of my favorite clients.

I make my way to the bar and see the shots are none other than cherry Jell-O shots. I guess I'm never going to live that one down.

"A toast to my quirky, extremely talented friend who could never find the right path because she was dreaming too small," Gwen says. "You are so big, Elliot. I hope you never forget how wildly capable you are!"

"Cheers!" everyone yells, then we take our Jell-O shots in unison.

Benjamin pulls me to the side and lifts my chin so he can look into my eyes. "I'm so proud of you, baby." His eyes crease with my favorite smile wrinkles, and my heart swells with pride for all that we've overcome. "You want to know what I'm thinking?"

"That you want to save some of the Jell-O shots and recreate one of your favorite memories?"

"Well, obviously, but also..." He bends down on one knee. "Elliot James, I'm desperately in love with you and I can't stand the thought of living one day on this planet without you by my side. Will you marry me and make all of my dreams come true?"

He pulls out a stunning diamond ring. I scream in excitement, jumping into his arms before he can even stand up all the way.

"Yes!" I scream. The crowd erupts with cheering and applause, and Benjamin spins me around in a circle.

"I love you so much. I can't wait to grow old with you and fight over who lost the remote. I can't wait to raise children together, and I can't wait to stand by your side while you chase your dreams down and tackle them one-by-one like a linebacker."

"I love you, too, and I promise not to let a day go by without showing you." I kiss him deeply like we're the only ones in the room.

He sets me down on my feet and steadies me from the spinning. "Now I need you to listen very carefully. We're going to need a plastic bag and at least ten of those Jell-O shots. I have big plans for you tonight."

My eyes light up in excitement. "CJ will send out an email and tell everyone tomorrow is a paid holiday?"

I turn to Gwen and Maggie. "I couldn't have done any of this without you two. I am eternally grateful."

"We know, sis. Now go finish celebrating; honestly, I don't know why you're still standing here." Gwen and Maggie pull me into a hug.

Benjamin scoops me up in his favorite caveman carry, and I wave goodbye to my friends. My heart has never felt so full and when I look around me, I know that this is so much more than I was searching for. I never knew things could be this amazing. I guess Gwen was right; I just needed to dream bigger.

# ACKNOWLEGEMENTS

This book wouldn't have been possible without the tribe of people that stood behind me, motivating me to keep going throughout the entire process. Without the support of my amazing husband, Stephen Anthony, I can assure you this book wouldn't exist. Thank you for holding me together during the many times I fell apart. Thank you for picking up the slack around the house and with the kids. Thank you for all the hours you spent driving the children around to hunt Pokémon so I could have a few peaceful hours to write. You are my real-life hero.

I'd also like to thank my friends Natalie Ferrington and Becca Peterson for supporting me, reading the very first chapters I'd send at 5 A.M. and telling me exactly what I needed to hear. I don't know if I can ever repay you for helping to build my confidence. You've been so supportive, I only hope I can someday return the favor.

To my author friend Colleen Young, your mentorship has been invaluable throughout this process and your kindness is like a breath of fresh air. Thank you for your help, encouragement, and support. I hope to pass the kindness along someday and pour into other new writers just the way you've done with me.

Thank you to my children for having the patience with me during all the weekends I spent writing, tucked away at my desk. My hope is that one day you'll look back on this time in our lives and remember your mom had the guts to chase her dreams. I hope you remember the sacrifices I made and know that you are so very capable of chasing down your dreams as long as you put in the work.

Lastly, thank you to all of my readers, especially my early Instagram followers and beta readers, Katie Haley and Kyra Flatow. I promise to keep writing books that you love and to take you all along for the ride.

# AUTHOR'S NOTE

Thank you so much for reading my book! I hope you enjoyed reading it as much as I loved writing it.

Elliot and her friends showed up in my head one day and refused to leave. My first inspiration came on my way to work after eating peanut butter crackers with my freshly manicured almond-shaped nails. I noticed a chunk of peanut butter underneath one nail and thought how crazy it would be if someone near me had a peanut allergy. I sent a Marco Polo to my friend, Becca, and the let my imagination run wild with the whole scene.

You see, much like Elliot, my imagination also has a way of running wild. I can daydream about different scenarios and watch things play out like a movie in my mind. It's a lot of fun, but I'm sure you can imagine, it got me into a lot of trouble growing up... especially in school.

I started thinking of this anxious woman who couldn't seem to find her big break and the things she'd have to overcome to find herself. Reflecting back on my own personal work experiences, I couldn't help but think of all the small acts of sexual harassment that I had to overcome along my professional career and how since they were so small, there wasn't really much that could be done about them. From there the character of Thad Powell was born.

Thad was named by my Instagram followers when I polled them about the douchiest guy name. Ultimately we could all agree that names rhyming with "Chad" were the ultimate douchiest. Since I had a friend in real-life named Brad, I decided to go with Thad... sorry to any Thads out there, I know you're not all bad!

I wanted to open up the conversation of managing anxiety as an adult and what that can sometimes look like in real life. Though many of Elliot's reactions are a bit exaggerated, I can't say I haven't thought the exact same things many times during my life. In fact, the airplane scene is an exact recount of a similar experience I had when flying to Disney World with my whole family. Though I didn't act like Elliot, I would have done it in a moment if the person would have been just a tiny bit more suspicious. I wish I was joking, y'all.

Elliot's friends were everything I wish I had at the time I wrote them. Our family had just moved to a new state and I was completely alone and the thought of a girl squad that had my back no matter what was so enticing. I think women have an extremely powerful thing in female friendships and I hope this book will help you to identify your ride-or-dies in real life because we all need a Gwen and Maggie to our chaotic Elliot.

And if you don't have those friends in real life, I'd love for you to become one of mine. Find me on Instagram and let's stay connected!

# BOOK CLUB QUESTIONS

Book Club Questions

1. What character in the story do you identify with the most and why?
2. If you suffer from anxiety in any form, has it ever gotten in the way of an important opportunity?
3. If you could give Elliot one piece of advice, what would it be?
4. Elliot was repeatedly sexually harassed and even hired based solely on her appearance. This is something that is all too common in the workplace. What are some examples in your own life where you've had to navigate sexual harassment and how did you handle it?
5. How would you describe Elliot's character in the beginning of the story? What was the major change that took place over the course of the story? How would you describe her in the end?

6. How did you feel about Benjamin at the beginning of the story? How did your opinion of him change when you learned about his past?

7. Most of the time Elliot's anxiety was unnecessarily preparing her for a made up event. Have you ever experienced a shift where your anxiety helped you think quickly and get yourself out of a situation?

8. Have you ever felt like people close to you have put you in box that you didn't fit into? What are some of your boxes?

9. Sometimes people close to us, many times our parents, take a snapshot of who we are at a certain age and hold on to it even though we change. How is this true in your life?

10. Strong friendships are a central theme of this book and are what helped Elliot and Benjamin in their journeys. How has friendship helped you overcome hardships?

# WILD FOR YOU - CHAPTER 1

Gwen

"And that's how I know Big Foot's out there, just walking around among us, yet to be discovered. You can mark my words; I'm going to find him if it's the last thing I do."

Why are the pretty ones always the weirdos?

This always happens to me—I meet a hot guy, we flirt back and forth, and things seem promising. But the minute I agree to a date, it's like the switch flips, and they bring out their inner weirdo, which I have to suffer through just to get laid.

I drain my martini and sneak a glance at my phone, conveniently located in my lap underneath the table. I know it's bad date etiquette, but it's not as if Preston's giving me a lot to work with here. Call me crazy, but I'm a bit of a workaholic, so it's going to take more than a Big Foot story to keep my attention ... But if you want to get laid, sometimes you have to pay the price, and tonight, that price is lending an ear to his god-awful story.

I close my email and check the time. Shit, it's only seven-thirty. I've only been listening to Preston's childhood Big Foot encounter for an hour.

We haven't even gotten our food yet, and I'm already bored. He's attractive enough, in a pretty boy, conventional way. Tilting my head, I study his tall frame, letting my eyes roam up his khakis; they've been pressed *properly* with a crease down the middle, heavily starched. I crinkle my nose. Starched pants just don't give me that rugged throw-me-against-the-wall vibe I'm looking for tonight. Letting my gaze wander higher, I see a slight bulge, and I'm pleasantly surprised. Maybe I'll give him a second chance? Who knows, maybe he took his clothes to a new dry cleaner? Though, he's wearing his long-sleeve button-up shirt—with crease—tucked in and with the sleeves fully down to his wrists. I'm disappointed by the lack of forearm action, but maybe he's got a tattoo sleeve and doesn't want to scare me away?

A girl can dream, right?

"What about you, Gwen. Are you superstitious?" Preston's question breaks me from my internal assessment of his clothing until he pulls out a rabbit's foot from his pocket and lays it on the table. "I've carried it with me since I was a kid. This was actually my pet rabbit, Buster. When he died, I was so upset that my grandfather cut off his foot and made it into this token to protect me—it's like he's always with me everywhere I go." He pushes the foot closer to me just as the server brings our food.

"Pet him. See how soft he is."

I close my eyes and take a long, slow inhale, calming myself. *It's not weird to keep your pet rabbit's foot in your pocket and show it to someone on a first date. Nope, that's not weird. Just look at his eyes. They're moody blue, and his eyelashes are long and thick. Plus, he's tall. You know how much you love tall guys. You can do this, Gwen. You need this.*

Okay, so maybe "need" is a bit of an exaggeration, but I could certainly use the distraction of a one-night stand, considering I've worked over sixty hours this week alone. I deserve to have a little fun, and why should I not let Preston here blow my back out? I mean, haven't you ever experienced post-coital clarity? Orgasms offer the best stress relief, plus I need to be on my A-game for tomorrow's meeting if I want to stand any chance at earning that promotion.

I stifle a yawn and sit up a little straighter with a newfound determination. If I can just get past the small talk and move us toward the dirty talk...

"You know, I don't really like animals... especially their detached appendages, so I think I'll pass. To answer your question, I'm not superstitious. I just work hard and trust that good things will follow because I've earned them." I push the foot across the table, making as little contact as possible, and I hate to admit it, but the foot *is* surprisingly soft. "Why don't you tell me about your job. What is it you said you do again?" I force myself to take a bite of my chicken, though my appetite's taken a hit after the foot bit.

"Oh, I own a taxidermy shop outside the city. I specialize in deer and elk heads, but every once in a while, I get to work on a bear for a special project. Bears are my favorite." His eyes widen in excitement, and the chicken forms a lump in my throat as I try to swallow. It's like he knows my vagina is desperate for a suitor to call on her.

Is this a test from the universe? Either way, it's not funny.

I grit my teeth and force out a smile. "And what size shoe do you wear?"

"That's a funny question. Um... a thirteen but sometimes a twelve. It depends on the brand. Why do you ask?"

"No reason." I force down another bite of chicken and order a second martini. It seems like I'm definitely going to need it.

"Wow, you're really strong. Hey, that kind of hurts," Preston whines as my teeth slide down his jaw. We're riding the elevator back up to my apartment, where I plan on finding out if his shoe size is an accurate predictor. Who am I kidding? I'd dry hump a man with a micro-penis at this point. I'm desperate, so desperate that I'm actually going to let a Big Foot-hunting taxidermist into my panties for the night. I'll have to do a whole vagina cleanse tomorrow. Maybe I'll get Maggie to bring over a sage bundle, and we can hit the factory reset or something.

"Shut up and take off my bra," I order once we're inside my apartment. I shove him into my now-closed front door as I set my purse and keys aside. He obliges, though his hands shake as he unclasps my bra and yanks my shirt over my head. Once I'm undressed from the top up, his eyes seem to pop out of his head, and I let him take in my delectable breasts in all their glory. At first, he hesitates, but after a little more encouragement, he lunges toward me in a frenzy. Preston's hands roam my body frantically as if he can't get enough. He grips my ass as I climb up him, wrapping my legs around his waist and moaning into his ear. "Yes, I like it rough," I whisper.

Yes, ok, I may be putting on a bit of a show, but if I can turn myself on enough, then I'll hopefully be able to chase down my big O tonight, which is all I'm after.

"You like it rough, do you?" He carries me through the apartment and kicks open my bedroom door. *Wow, maybe I underestimated Mr. Khaki's after all?*

He drops me onto the bed, and I bounce on the soft mattress. "Do you like it dirty, Gwen? Do you want me to fuck you?"

My heart skips a beat, and a grin spreads across my face. Who could've predicted this? Surprise overwhelms me. "Yes, I want you to fuck me," I say, trying to lose the crazy grin. I don't want him to lose whatever act this is.

Preston unzips his khakis, and I lean back on my elbows for a better view, my heart racing in anticipation. I may be a master vibrator operator, but every once in a while, I need a good dick-down to reset my operating system. The big reveal is my second favorite part of the equation. His khakis fall to the floor in a crumpled mess, and I can't help but think of how noticeable the wrinkles will be when he walks out of here tonight.

I almost miss the sight of his extremely long, extremely thin penis before he pounces on top of me, wearing only his white crew socks. The force knocks the air from my lungs, and I cough several times to regain my breath.

"You want dirty; I'll give you dirty," he growls.

As a final cough leaves my lungs, I hear him hock up something in his throat. Before my mind can register what he's planning, Preston spits a thick wad of phlegm into my open mouth. "Yeah, baby. I like it dirty, too."

Repulsion rips through me, and I launch myself off the bed with the strength of twenty men. I don't care that my tits are on full display or that Preston's pencil dick is out at attention. I run past him straight to the bathroom and proceed to hurl everything back up.

He pokes his head around the corner, "Come back in here, you nasty little bitch. I want to show you just how dirty I can be."

"Stop. Do not come anywhere near me, you fucking lunatic. Get out of my apartment before I cut off your dick and you have to carry it around in your pocket as your new good-luck charm!"

Mouth agape, he blinks several times and covers his penis in a protective stance. "You, um, you said you liked it dirty ... I was just trying to be dirty for you. I've actually never done this before. I just watch a lot of porn, and the women seem to enjoy

"OUT," I scream, pointing to the door.

"Yeah. Ok. Let me just go grab my pants." He waddles away, his head hanging in defeat, as I crawl toward the shower to turn on the scalding stream. There isn't a shower hot enough to wash away the shame I feel, but it's a start.

I hear the door open. "I'll, um, I'll call you, ok?" he calls before closing it behind him.

"Yeah, I wouldn't hold your breath on that one, buddy." I grab the entire tube of toothpaste and my toothbrush and climb into the shower, where I proceed to wash every orifice until the water goes cold.

The things I do in the name of stress relief. I guess it's me and BOB once again tonight.

---

The next morning, I drag myself into my office, not nearly as spry as I hoped to be, and make my way up to the eleventh floor. My office building is sleek and professional, with a strong feminine influence. Mauve and lavender geometric murals cover the white walls, and colorful rugs bring warmth to every conference room. We've got pastel pink leather sofas in the common areas and a full-service coffee bar on each floor. The whole building was designed with the motto, "Make pretty choices," which flows over into our company culture. Éclat is known as the leading PR agency in Chicago. Celebrities, influencers, and brands line up for our services, especially when shit hits the fan, and I don't mean to brag, but I'm the very best at cleaning up shit—metaphorically speaking, anyway.

Monthly meetings are the bane of my existence, especially when we're starting a new quarter. My boss, Sandra, seems to get off on inflicting as much pain and fear onto all of us as she can; I think she gets off on the drama. She's got that whole Miranda Priestly from The Devil Wears Prada vibe.

Starting as an entry-level billing clerk straight out of college, I've worked my way up at her company, and now, I'm one of her top two performing PR specialists. Sandra hasn't made it a secret that she's considering me for the VP role opening up in the near future. In fact, she's all but promised me the role for the last three years after I almost took a job offer from a competitor who sought me out. She's dangled the promotion in front of my face like a carrot, and I just need something big to push me over the edge. Then she'll have to promote me.

My mouth practically waters at the thought of having those infamous two letters following my name on my office door. I can already see it now: Gwen Pierson, VP.

I want to prove to Sandra—but mostly to myself—that I've finally made it all on my own and I'm good enough to sit among the best in the industry. That I earned a leading title on my hard work alone, not because anything was handed to me. This promotion would provide me with a solid, stable income and plenty of clout to go with it.

I've worked my ass off, representing the most difficult clients, spinning their horrifying fuck-ups into solemn apologies that somehow make them more lovable and approachable than they were before. Every one of my clients has left me with a better reputation and because of my track record, I'm known as the crisis-intervention queen around the office. After I've worked my magic, spinning their story to reflect whatever positive outcome I can manage, I hand them off to one of my co-workers to maintain, rinse, wash, and repeat.

I glance over at Pantone Brown, my arch-nemesis. If anyone beats me out of this promotion, it'll be her. Pantone is a couple of years older than me and has the reputation of a snake. She's one of those people you have to keep a close eye on. I wouldn't put anything past her when she's trying to get ahead. She comes from a powerful family with plenty of money and prestige. Every job she's gotten has been handed to her by her daddy—be it her biological or *sugar*. Honestly, even having her as my direct peer is insulting.

We take our seats in the cushy conference room around a large, crisp white table with views overlooking the cityscape of downtown Chicago. Sandra sits at the head of the table facing an oversized TV monitor, showing all our clients' information. Today's meeting is primarily focused on assigning new clients.

"Laura, what do we have on the horizon? Do you have any rocks you're working on this week?" Sandra peers over the top of her delicate designer glasses and scribbles something in her notepad.

Laura, the newest team member fresh from her internship, clears her throat. "Actually, we've just picked up a new client who'll need a little help. His name is Wombat Willy, and he's an adventure tour guide turned YouTuber. He recently had an incident on one of his guided tours where a man lost his hand from a caiman bite. His sponsors have insisted he seek a PR agency to repair his image. Apparently, the accident happened on a live stream."

"How many followers did you say he has again?" I chime in as the wheels in my head start turning.

Laura flips through the deck until she finds what she's looking for. "1.3 million followers. All organic within the last five years–"

"I believe we can all read the slide deck, Laura," Sandra interrupts.

I feel a bubble of excitement in the pit of my stomach, and my fingers itch to pull out my phone and Google him myself, but I resist. There's nothing Sandra hates more than seeing someone on their phone during a meeting. It's a total oxymoron considering that's most of our job, but it's one of her pet peeves.

Laura takes a shaky breath before she continues. "We've also got the Thorstein sisters who've recently decided to split up their shares of their businesses. There will be a lot of handholding for the middle sister. We need to get her out and break away from her shy image. VIP parties, house tours, we need to appeal to a younger audience. Maybe we set her up with a B-level celebrity to get some coverage? Their mother is sick about the dispute and wants to make sure all the girls are on an equal playing field."

I wipe my sweaty palms against my pants and blurt out, "I'll take Willy," before I think better of it and change my mind. It's a risk, something completely out of my comfort zone, but with the limited information I have, I think I can spin this. This could be exactly what I need to show Sandra just how valuable I am here at Éclat.

Sandra's eyes widen, then narrow as she searches my face for something only she can see. "Interesting. That's quite *ambitious* of you, isn't it?"

I swallow the lodged lump in my throat, "I'm up for a challenge. Besides, if his sponsorships reflect his following, this could bring Éclat to the next level." I steady my shoulders and hold eye contact.

"Great. It's decided, then." Sandra slaps her notebook closed. "Gwen will be onsite with Wombat Willy while Pantone takes Pheobe Thorstein.

"Whoa, whoa, whoa." I hold up my hands as if I'm a watch guard directing traffic. "What do you mean when you say *onsite?*"

Sandra scoffs. "Gwen, do I really need to give you a basic vocabulary lesson?" She grabs the clicker and scans through the slides. "It says right here in the agreement that the Public

Relations Representative is needed in-person to help aid Wombat Willy during his next filming session in Costa Rica." She tosses the clicker and stands, brushing non-existent lint off her jacket. "For someone so good at their job, you're really off your game this morning." She pulls her glasses down and peers over the top of them as if she's staring straight into my soul. "I suggest you take this assignment seriously if you even want to be considered for the VP role in the fall. Meeting adjourned. Good luck, ladies!" Then she turns on her heel, leaving me wondering what I've just agreed to.

"Ooh, that doesn't sound fun at all." Pantone's nasally voice pierces my already aching head. "Have fun with your assignment, though. Maybe you'll embrace a whole new lifestyle and finally stop trying to be something you're not." She flicks the rogue coffee stain on my blouse. "I think you and the wild man may have more in common than you think."

I grit my teeth, forcing a smile because VPs generally don't punch their colleagues. *It's just a two-week assignment. I can do anything for two weeks, right?*

# ABOUT THE AUTHOR

Jeré Anthony (pronounced like hooray with a J) writes steamy, swoony, and hilarious romantic comedies with depth.

She is a mental health advocate, a lifelong anxiety warrior, and is ADHD AF. Her quirks bleed out into her stories making for an exciting group of characters. Because of her undiagnosed ADHD, growing up she always felt different from everyone around her. Now she strives to create stories that give readers an escape from reality while also helping them feel seen.

She loves a strong cup of coffee and thinks beer + buffalo wings are a delicacy that is unmatched.

Jeré currently lives in NW Arkansas with her husband, three children, dog, and two cats. When she's not writing, you can find her reading, driving her kids all over for travel soccer games, watching cat videos on her phone, or trying to convince her husband to go on another family adventure somewhere new.

Connect with Jeré:

NEWSLETTER: https://mailchi.mp/87e346b13331/jere-anthonynewsletter
INSTAGRAM: @author_jere_anthony
TIKTOK: @author_jere_anthony
WEBSITE: JereAnthony.com

Sign up for my newsletter to stay up to date with future releases, sales, and freebies